Craobh

COPPER PENNY
PUBLISHING

Titles by Donald D. Allan

The New Druids Series
Duilleog, Volume One
Craobh, Volume Two
Stoc, Volume Three
Freamhaigh, Volume Four
Cill Darae, Volume Five

Gaea, Volume Six (coming in 2020)

Leaf and Branch (The New Druids Vols One & Two)
Stalk and Root (The New Druids Vols Three & Four)
Priestess and Gaea (The New Druids Vols Five and Six – coming 2020)

The New Druids Compendium (Volumes One to Six - coming 2020)

DONALD D. ALLAN

Craobh

**A New Druids Novel
Volume Two**

CRAOBH: A New Druids Novel, Volume Two
Donald D. Allan

All inquiries should be addressed to:

Copper Penny Publishing
E-Mail: donalddallan@gmail.com
Web page: donalddallan.com

National Library of Canada Cataloguing in Publication Data

ISBN-13: 978-0-9947956-9-4

Cover Design—	*JD&J Book Cover Design. http://www.jdandj.com*
Cover Credits—	*Images and art purchased from http://www.123rf.com/profile_designwest, http://www.123rf.com/profile_1enchik, and http://www.123rf.com/profile_epantha. Use of the triskelion within this novel from http://en.wikipedia.org/wiki/File:Triskel_type_Amfreville.svg. The image is licensed under the Creative Commons Attribution 3.0 Unported license and is attributed to the author Cétautomatix (artéfact), Ec.Domnowall. Title page art: Copyright: http://www.123rf.com/profile_olivier26 from http://www.123RF.com. Part Three Title page art: Copyright: http://www.123rf.com/profile_martm*
Map Credit—	*Stephen Chase*

For Mum and Dad
(Senga and Hector)

Thanks for letting me read under the covers until the wee hours of the morning.

I miss you, mum.

Craobh

A New Druids Novel

Volume Two

Map of North Belkin: Munsten and Cala Counties

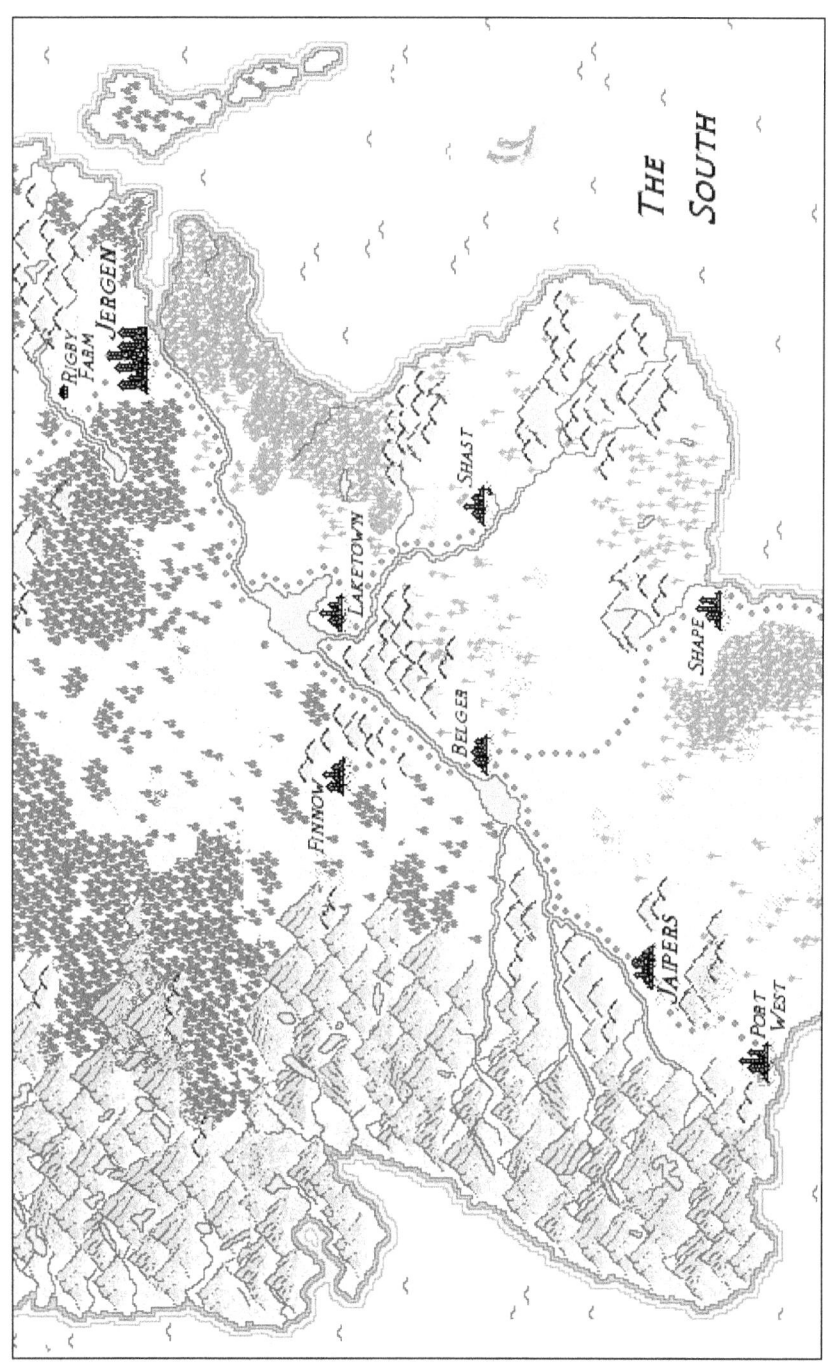

Map of South Belkin: Turgany County

Prologue

Archbishop's Office inside Munsten Castle, 900 A.C.

ARCHBISHOP REGINALD GREIGSEN sat at his desk reading the missive from Seth Farlow. All it said was: "Praise to the Lord". It was enough, and the Archbishop smiled to himself. His plan was in motion and he could see the path it would take. He raised his eyes to the icon of the Lord hanging on the opposite wall of his office and murmured his thanks and prayed for Seth to be successful. The Sect was in motion and would soon descend on Jaipers. The Target would be destroyed, and the Church of the New Order would rise to place the bastard of the dead King on the throne. He smiled and turned in his seat to toss the missive into the roaring fire behind him. The heat from the fire soothed his aching joints.

He grasped the edge of his desk with a trembling hand and steeled himself. With a lurch he forced himself to stand despite the desire to remain still. Agony blossomed like fire through his hips and back and he swore he could feel the bones in his knees grinding against one another. His arthritis was almost unbearable. He couldn't sit still for too long; mere moments being stationary would seize his joints and getting them moving again was proving harder and harder. The only thing that seemed to dull the pain somewhat was wine, but it was no longer an option as it burned his gut with fire. He knew all his pain was a reminder from the Lord that life was fragile and to appreciate each day. He understood the message and tried not to complain. But some days it was so hard not to find anger simmering in his daily thoughts.

He was expecting a visitor soon. A boon from the Lord Protector who seemed oddly pleased with him these days. While the Archbishop moved around his desk to get himself ready to receive the man, he thought back to the strange meeting with Healy two days ago.

* * *

"You'll enjoy this, Greigsen," said Lord Protector Healy as he moved to pour the wine. They were seated in Healy's luxurious outer office in his private quarters at a small dining table.

"I'm afraid I must decline the wine, Lord Protector," said the Archbishop. His stomach was already on fire and the thought of wine on top of the acid was too much.

Healy sat back with a look of disbelief. "Refusing wine? How strange. Pray, tell me what is wrong my good friend? Is it your stomach? I had heard it would not settle."

The Archbishop looked away and declined to answer.

"Come now, Greigsen! You can tell me. I've heard your joints are full of arthritis and you can barely keep food down. Eating oats with milk for most meals. Is it true?"

The Archbishop did not like this line of questioning. His health was his own concern and he would rather not share it with the one man between himself and placing a King on the throne. *How am I to get through this meal without telling him?* he wondered. He thought for a moment and then nodded sharply and waited to hear laughter at his plight. When he looked at Healy, he was surprised to see genuine sympathy.

"Well, now," said Healy. "I feel for you, my friend. Old age is bad enough without the pain that goes with it. You have my sympathy." Healy picked up a small bell and rang it. A server appeared and placed a carafe of milk on the table, bowed and disappeared. "Here. I suspected you had stomach pains. I had this brought in special. Cow's milk. Fresh and whole. Will you take some?"

The Archbishop thought of the cool milk hitting his stomach and soothing the burn and nodded. Healy filled his wine glass with the milk and then lifted his wine and offered a toast. "To health."

He lifted his glass of milk and touched the Lord Protector's glass and took a swallow. The cool milk hit his stomach like water on a fire. He closed his eyes and gave thanks to God.

"Our meal will be out soon. White fish with white sauce. Something that won't upset your stomach. Before that, I want to offer you something."

Greigsen raised his eyebrows. *Since when does Healy offer me anything for free? He seems in a peculiar mood. He's too happy.* He looked around the room and then scowled.

Healy laughed. "Oh, if you could see the expression on your face. Come. Hear what I have to say and if you aren't interested so be it."

"Fine. What is it?"

"Think of it as a peace offering!" boomed the Lord Protector, smiling benevolently behind clasped fingers with his elbows on the table. "You'll feel ten years younger if not more. Trust me in this." Healy rose and circled around the table to clasp the Archbishop with warmth on the shoulder. The Archbishop glanced at the hand in surprise. "I have a man. An expert in pain. I'll have him come round your office in two days. He is out on an errand up in the North region but I expect him back by then. Fair enough?"

The Archbishop's mind whirled, and he tried to reason himself past the overwhelming desire to grasp this unexpected boon. He was certain this was another ploy of the Protector, a way to undermine him. They had sparred so many times in the past, each of them angling to get the better of the other and, now, he expected nothing less. For decades they had played this out. The pain in his joints begged him to at least see this through. *Perhaps this time he is being sincere? It wouldn't hurt to at least meet with his man.*

Greigsen nodded and Healy clapped him on the back and returned to his seat. He rang the bell again and two servers appeared carrying silver trays with a silver lid. They placed the trays in front of them and then simultaneously lifted the lids. Steam billowed, obscuring the plate below. When it cleared, Greigsen could see a perfectly prepared piece of halibut with a béchamel sauce. It smelled heavenly.

"Dig in," ordered Healy. "Don't let it get cold."

* * *

He raised his head at the soft knock at his door. The Archbishop moved over to unlatch the door before he remembered he had already done so. He shouted, "Come in, the door is unlatched."

A moment of silence greeted him before the door swung open a mere inch or two. The Archbishop watched a thin face thrust into the narrow opening to peer inside. "H-hello? Arch b-bishop, sir?"

The voice was meek and high pitched, and the Archbishop took an immediate dislike to the man. "Yes. Come in. Don't dawdle!"

"Y-yes, yes, of c-c-course, s-sir!" stuttered the man and pushed the door open to reveal his short, emaciated body. He looked like a boy aged beyond his years. He had a large prominent nose that drew the eyes and made it hard to see past it to the man. He was dressed in black wool clothes and the Archbishop shuddered when he recognised them. The clothes were the uniform of a chirurgeon. He knew, of course, who to expect after the Lord Protector told him, but seeing one in his office was still hard to accept. Chirurgeons were universally reviled throughout the Realm. They were charlatans preying on the invalid. They administered impossible elixirs and potions and delivered fake promises and false hope. The man entered the office and closed the door behind him. He turned back to the Archbishop carrying a black leather satchel in front of him with both hands. He stared at the Archbishop a moment before bowing his head.

The Archbishop sighed and held out his ring hand and waited. The man merely blinked blankly at him and then stared at the hand for a moment. *He is clearly not gifted with an encouraging intellect*, thought the Archbishop. "You kiss the ring." For emphasis, he shook his hand a little. The man looked from the hand to his face, still not understanding. "You kiss the ring. The ring on this hand. It's respectful to my office as head of the Church of the New Order."

Understanding dawned on the man's features and he rushed forward. He placed his satchel carefully on the floor and grabbed the hand and kissed the ring. "H-how's that, sir?"

"It's not *sir*. It's your *Grace*."

"S-sorry, sir. I m-mean, your G-grace."

"That stutter is something, isn't it?"

"S-sir? I m-mean, your g-Grace? W-what sat-st-stutter?"

The Archbishop raised an eyebrow and looked to see if the man was in jest. He waited, but the man just continued to stare back at him with a confused look. *Chirurgeons*, he sighed. *They are all the same.* "All right, let's be about this. Sit over here. What do you have for me?"

The Archbishop led the man over to the small table by the wall. He motioned to one seat but remained standing himself. *If I sit now, I won't get back up again.* He watched as the man stood next to the table but didn't sit. The man placed his satchel on the table and opened it. The satchel opened like a book, and inside were many silver instruments. *No doubt used for cutting and dissecting failed surgeries*, thought the Archbishop. The instruments were known to him. His Sect had used them on the demons to draw out their secrets and lies. They were amazingly accurate and fine-tuned instruments, equally good for surgery as they were for torture. The Archbishop smiled and felt his cock stir in his robes.

"S-So, ah, your g-Grace. The Lord p-p-p-Protector said t-that ya-you w-were in p-p-pain? C-can I p-p-p-lease see your hands?"

The Archbishop held out his hands, and the man grabbed them and felt the swollen, red knuckles looking from joint to face as he squeezed them. After a moment the Archbishop tore his hands free. "Enough! All the joints are the same. Red, swollen and painful."

"Y-yes. Rheumatism. Very advanced. N-no surprise at your age, n-n-no? T-t-tell me your p-p-parents? They t-t-too, n-n-no?"

The Archbishop was annoyed now and waiting for the stuttering fool to get his words out. He had almost had enough of this idiot. The Lord Protector was having his fun again and likely knew he would raise his hopes and had purposely given him this court fool to deal with.

The man, oblivious to the look of anger on the Archbishop's face, continued talking. "I have t-tears."

"Tears? Tears!" roared the Archbishop. "You offer me tears? You are a fool! Enough of this! The Lord Protector has played me for a fool! Now get out!"

"Your g-Grace! P-p-p-please! The t-t-Tears of the P-p-poppy! The p-p-poppy!"

The Archbishop closed his mouth and gawked at the man. He had heard of this. The demons had spoken of it when pressed but his men had found none and he had forgotten about it. It was one of the demonic conjurations. Devil juice. He sputtered. "That's a product of the Devil!"

The man blinked in surprise. "The d-Devil? No. No, it comes from a p-p-plant. A p-p-poppy p-p-plant. I have some here for you. The Lord p-p-Protector b-bade me come and give you as much as you require. I have here some d-d-dozen vials. I will explain how to t-t-take it and some c-c-caution on its use. This will help with the p-p-pain." The man opened his satchel further and inside were a dozen small glass vials placed in separate leather sleeves. They were exquisite in their craftsmanship. Inside the vials was what looked like brown water. The man drew the vials out and placed them on the table, all in a perfect line. He then placed a small silver spoon next to them. Next, he reached into his clothing and pulled free a small pouch and laid it on the table, too.

The Archbishop struggled to seat himself, his eyes glued to the vials. The torchlight in the room glinted off the glass and mesmerised him in their beauty. It was so tempting. The Devil was tempting him, now in this moment of his greatest weakness. He fought to remain strong and resist the urge. He glanced up to the icon on the wall and gasped in shock. He grabbed at his heart. The chirurgeon followed the Archbishop's eyes and looked curiously at the icon of the Lord and looked back with confusion clear on his face.

The Archbishop was lost in rapture. He looked upon the face of his Lord standing bathed in light before him. He stared at the glory of the Lord and felt His love for him. His pain was too great to fall to his knees, but he knew the Lord knew and felt no anger.

My son. Remain seated and be calm. Take what this man offers you. It will ease your pain. You have suffered enough. Take it. It is not the Devil that presents this to you, but I. Your Lord.

With those words loud in his head, the voice ceased, and the Lord was gone. The Archbishop cried out in the sudden absence. The room felt so empty and plain. His breath came in short gasps. His heart beat irregularly and painfully in his chest. Slowly he calmed and realised what had just happened. The Lord had appeared to him and approved what this man offered. He slowly turned his eyes to the man and could see that he was talking to him and was quite agitated.

"Your Grace? Are you all right? You look in p-p-pain and in d-d-distress? Your heart? Has it stopped?"

The Archbishop laughed at that. Stopped? He thinks my heart stopped and yet I still sit here next to him? Chirurgeons!

"I am fine. Fine. Show me what you have for me."

The man composed himself and looked over the Archbishop once more before turning to the vials. "These are vials of the tears of the poppy. I won't explain the extraction method but suffice it to say it is a laborious and painstakingly slow process. The vials you see here represent but a small sample of my supply. The worth is... well, it is considerable, you understand? Courtesy of the Lord Protector. Let me explain how to take it."

The Archbishop raised an eyebrow at the man. His stutter had disappeared now that he was speaking about his craft. How very strange.

"Each vial contains about fifteen doses. It is best if you smoke it, but that is not in habit here in the Realm. It is a much better method for effect. But no matter. You simply take this small spoon and drink its measure. Each dose will last half a day at least, so each vial will last a week. There is enough here for three months. At first I suggest you take it lying down. It is quite powerful and will overwhelm you until you get used to it. I will help you take the first dose and after that—well, you will be on your own. I will return in three months with more for you so you must make this last until then. Once gone you will crave it.

Not having it will be painful. I suggest you pace your intake. I cannot stress this enough. Your Grace."

The man paused a moment before continuing. "This pouch contains chalk. Nothing more. Mix a spoonful with milk and drink it when your stomach is at its worst. It will help greatly. Take as much as you need. Too much, though, and your bowel movements might prove difficult. Take fibre with breakfast—I suggest prunes—but I suspect a man of your years already knows this."

The Archbishop nodded but heard nothing from the chirurgeon. He was repeating the words of the Lord in his head.

* * *

A short time later, the man excused himself and left the Archbishop's office. He left the Archbishop lying on the small cot in the office corner complaining about the bitter taste but now blissfully free of his pain. As he expected, the Archbishop had succumbed to the opiate, and all but passed out. The man smiled to himself. *This would be a lucrative business. I need to thank the Lord Protector personally for giving me this opening into the Church. Business will soon be booming.*

Craobh

Part One: Flight

Craobh

One

On the road to Laketown, 900 A.C.

THE ROAD OUT of Belger continued to meander alongside the river. At times, the river would fall out of sight, but, soon enough, it would return as a pleasant meandering companion to my journey. Occasionally I would sight a laden barge easing its way downriver through breaks in the trees, and sometimes I would run into travellers heading past me on the road. I wished those encounters were more amicable, but I found they were typically a nervous time for all involved. It was simply the nature of travelling the roads: the risk and fear of bandits or highwaymen were very real threats and those people who did travel the roads were those with wealth, and, by necessity, they travelled with armed escorts of various sizes.

I was now three days out of Belger, and I had returned to my usual routine on the road. Thankfully, no one in Belger had recognised me as Will Arbor. Nonetheless, the feeling of being watched had followed me out of town, but as with all fears that persist for a long period of time, I simply became inured and quickly explained away my fears with a variety of rationalisations. It was a skill Daukyns had taught me over the years. It was merely a way to remove distractions—to force myself to concentrate on the here and now and push through whatever bothered me. Thoughts of my talks with Daukyns reminded me of how much I missed him, and I felt the now-familiar pang of grief.

Memories of Daukyns had me remembering just how much I missed the quiet solitude of Jaipers. I wondered how my friend Dempster was faring and whether he thought to build the herb garden out back of the inn like I had suggested. *Probably not.* With a laugh, I realised the teachings of Daukyns were failing me and all I was thinking about was the past.

"I think I've been walking out in the sun too long," I said to myself. "Soon I'll be talking to myself..." I shook my head to clear my thoughts and found myself thinking of the Church.

The discovery in Belger, that the Church was probably behind the murder of Bill Burstone, sat heavily with me. The two proprietors at the salt store for Finnow Mines in Belger had recognised the black boots I had worn. They had treated me with reverence and given praise to the Church of the New Order. I had realised then the assassination of Bill Burstone in Jaipers, the killing of the assassin by Reeve Comlin, and my discovery of my healing powers were all tied to the Church. The manuscript papers from a tome about magic and herb lore had me heading to Jergen for knowledge. Selfishly, I had left my life in Jaipers behind and my good friend Reeve Comlin in possible peril. Here, I was safe on the road and away from those troubles, but I knew Reeve Comlin was still back there in Jaipers and unaware. I thought ahead to Laketown and tried to think how I could send word back to the Reeve. I had a little coin and I could write. I had no idea how to pay for the delivery of a message between towns. It was not something I had ever had to do. After a few miles of too many thoughts, I simply opted to wait until I was in the town where I could try to get a barge captain to carry a message. A regular barge captain would know him and be glad to help; I was sure of that. Once settled in my mind, I felt my load lighten and the feeling of eyes on me was forgotten. I turned my attention to the road.

"How's that Daukyns?" I asked with a smile to the air. I waited but, with no reply, I shook my head and looked down the long road ahead of me. *The answers are up ahead somewhere. I just know it.*

To further distract me—and honestly, it was more from the sheer joy of being able to use my powers—I *reached* out with my gift to the surrounding countryside. I was becoming adept at using my gifts to sense the nature of the world surrounding me. I felt the birds and animals around me and joined in their joy of flight or in finding food in the woods and hills. I drew in the immense power of the plants, grass and trees. It was all around me and so full of life it stole my breath away. I drew strength from it and knew I belonged. Nature seemed to notice me as well. Small animals would move to intercept me and watch me walk past. Birds would swoop and cry as they danced in the air above me. I was careful to shoo the animals away when strangers came in sight. What I could do was not something I wanted to have known or seen. And so I used my gift, I'm not ashamed to admit, on the people who approached me on the road. It gave me a unique insight into what to expect. Emotionally the people usually felt curiosity toward me, mingled with only slight apprehension. Anyone could see I was merely a young man and on my own and posed no real threat. I had the look of a simple beggar who sold minor things.

I also found my powers let me gauge the truth behind the lies. When watching the colours surrounding people, I now found I had more of a sense about them. People projected one image of themselves and hid another behind words. It was interesting to observe. I figured out quickly it was all merely a self-preservation technique, and I respected that, being guilty of having kept myself hidden for years. My gift eased my worry and the road trip became a pleasant one. I looked forward to meeting these other travellers.

The other aspect of road safety was that the road was open enough that you could see approaching travellers at least a mile away. I could spot the caravans typically from a couple of miles away by the dust of the road rising up from the wheels. The land by the river undulated gently, and the trees were clumped together and often cleared from the road all the way down to the river; stripped over the years, I surmised, for the repair of barges. So, for the most part, the region was wide open and the valleys and hills gave me unobstructed views all around. The benefit was you really couldn't hide unless you were determined and the travellers walking or riding on the road were usually not trying to hide.

The people I passed on the road would almost always stop and converse politely before continuing on to their destinations. Common themes were often about the weather and how the summer heat made any road trips a simple matter of necessity over desire. At first, I was uncomfortable speaking with strangers but, once I recognised the patterns and what was expected, I found I could play the part. Observations were exchanged on what lay up ahead on the road and what to expect in the next town. They were all mundane topics but of value nonetheless. Sometimes we exchanged wares but mostly I would politely refuse. I carried more than I needed and I wanted for nothing. Sometimes the merchants and farmers just wanted an opinion of what they carried. The desire to meet the approval of others seemed to be a dominant emotion from people. At least the gentle folk—for others it was about power. I didn't like those people too much but, thankfully, they were rare.

I had now abandoned trying to remain unobserved by other travellers. My efforts to leave the road and travel in the brush had quickly become tedious. More embarrassingly, I had observed others walking more warily near where I had secretly ducked off the road, and it had become clear I was not unobserved. One group had even called out to my hiding location to wish me well. And so, now, I kept to the road. We would meet openly on the road, talk politely, part, and continue our respective journeys. It was pleasant, and I found myself eager to spot another caravan or group of travellers.

Soon after I left Belger, I had spied a caravan approaching from ahead of me to the East. I used my senses to determine it was a small one made up of only two carts, four hired guards, the owner and his wife. The bond they shared was bright and vibrant to my senses. They slowed the horses as we closed, and, when they stopped the cart, I raised a hand in greeting. The guards studied me closely, but, with me so clearly being a young man, I didn't pose much of a threat. I think they were simply glad to be able to rest for a moment. The couple waved in return and called out to me, gesturing for me to approach. I walked forward, nodding to one of the guards as I passed him. I looked up to the owners on the wagon bench.

"Good day to you, gentle folk," I said in greeting, bowed, and made the sign of the Word, three fingers up and spread, thumb holding the pinkie down and with the palm forward. "The Word is the Path."

"Likewise, young sir," answered the man sitting on the cart bench with the reins loosely held. He wore a tam and loosely woven tunic and pants. Perfect for the heat. He was heavily freckled and his arms were sunburnt and red. He smiled, then, from behind his wire-frame spectacles, surprisingly thick, and bobbed his head, relaxed and looked to the woman seated next to him.

"Greetings," she said with a full smile and lowered her head politely. The brim of her large straw sun hat bobbed up and down with her motion. It was a lovely bright yellow woven straw hat, hand-painted with exquisitely detailed sunflowers. She was a short woman, with strikingly green hazel eyes. The crinkles at the corners of her eyes exposed the mirth and joy that was her constant companion. She made the sign toward me in return. "The Truth will set us free," she replied.

The man pushed the brim of his tam up so he could take a good look at me and I could see he was completely bald. I stole a glance over to the guards who remained within sword reach and I could see they were watching me with only bored curiosity. I was relieved to see their hands remained clear of the pommels of their sheathed swords. I could also see the rearmost guard was not watching us at all but was instead intent on looking to both sides of the road toward the distant tree lines. I returned my gaze to the man and woman and tried to look as non-threatening as I could. My senses felt nothing threatening coming from them. They were middle-aged, cheery, and by the amount of dust on their clothes and carts, they likely had been on the road for some span of days. They were dressed in the loose-fitting clothes typically seen on people from the eastern shore. They seemed good people.

"I'm Will," I said. "Out of Jaipers and travelling to Laketown." My destination was obvious but I felt no need to mention Jergen. "I gather herbs and sell them at the market. Well, met."

"I'm Domhnall Lynn and this is my wife, Maire. We're travelling to the market in Jaipers. We hail from Laketown, young sir."

"Hello," I replied and nodded to both. I was starting to feel foolish.

"Well, young sir," said Maire and her smile grew broader. I sensed she found my discomfort amusing. "Wonderfully clear weather we are having. It has made the road that much faster than we could have hoped."

"True words," I replied. "I would not complain if the temperature were slightly less oven-like," and I mopped my brow and laughed and they joined me. I felt what little tension remained quickly fade. It was these moments I cherished these days: the peaceful and comfortable meeting of new people and the quick sharing of experiences. My days of being alone in the wild were quickly being replaced by a yearning for a better understanding of people in general. My ability to sense how people felt and would likely react was a huge boon for me and probably the only reason I could bear to stand and talk for so long.

"You'll enjoy Jaipers," I volunteered. "The market is rather large and quite diverse. They have commerce through to Port West. But you probably knew already." I felt my face redden.

They nodded together. "Yes," they spoke together and startled, then stopped abruptly and looked at each other and laughed. Domhnall nodded for his wife to continue. "We have a unique sweet to sell there and hope the West market will develop a taste for it." Domhnall nodded at her words. "We have already established a good hold in Laketown and Jergen and have small shops there. We're on a reconnaissance mission of sorts. Our hope is that Jaipers will open the West."

I raised my eyebrows at this. It was not every merchant who managed to establish a shop, let alone two. Certainly only the most prosperous were able to do so. These two must be doing well and I wondered what they sold. The four guards with them were alone worth quite the number of groats to maintain, arm and feed. The mercenary guilds were quite specific on costs and provisions to be provided as a minimum to guard companies. I could see these guards were of the reputable sort. I had met enough guards in Jaipers and here on the road to be able to recognise the order, discipline, and well cared for equipment of these men.

"Quite impressive," I said and meant it. I then spoke about my experiences in the marketplace in Jaipers with my herbs and what worked well and then mentioned the Reeve and the cook at the inn. I felt I could trust these two and knowing they were heading to Jaipers had me considering asking a simple request. "Could you say hello to the Reeve for me? He'll be grateful to hear word of me." They quickly agreed to speak to Reeve Comlin and promised to stay and eat at the inn. I then suggested which stall they should seek to acquire in the market, explaining the sun didn't touch it as much throughout the day and buyers would favour it to escape the heat. "But you will need to be early to capture the corner!" I warned, and they thanked me.

I asked them about their product and, at once, their eyes lit up with the pleasure of the telling. I could see the pride in their eyes as the wife quickly rummaged in a large shoulder bag she had placed beside her on the bench and drew out a few samples and handed them down to me. I stared at the strangely shaped little wooden sticks with clear coloured crystals stuck onto it.

"It is called Rock Cane," they explained excitedly each talking over the other. Their auras lit up with their faces. The guards rolled their eyes and looked away, clearly having heard this many times before. "We invented this lovely sweet by accident one day. A truly fortuitous accident! We found we could form these rock-like crystals out of a new sweet source that has started to attract interest in Jergen and in the capital. We flavour it with extracts of peppermint or spearmint and form the crystals on the small stick you see there."

I looked at the stick in my hand. It was a simple carved piece of wood roughly resembling a plain walking stick and hence the name they gave it. I could see the hard clustered crystals were grown on the wood through this secret process they had discovered. I tentatively took a taste and was rewarded with a strong peppermint flavour and intense sweetness. My intake of breath felt cool and refreshing. The sweetness filled my mouth, and I salivated at the pleasure. They must have seen the pleasure in my eyes for they laughed.

"See?" they exclaimed together. "Wonderful, no?"

I nodded in vigorous agreement and took another taste and then another. *Addictive little things*, I realised, and I was suddenly glad I had been given a few more to take with me.

I gave them some of my herbs and they exclaimed at the bounty and strength of them. They couldn't stop praising my mint, pinching the leaves and inhaling the smell. We talked for a while longer until it was time to resume our journeys. They were a friendly couple, and I was certain they would do well in Jaipers and beyond and I told them so. The leader of the guards politely asked me, during a pause, if there was any trouble on the road ahead and was visibly relieved when I told him I had travelled alone from Jaipers and had seen no sign of bandits or highwaymen anywhere along the route. They asked about the garrison in Jaipers and were pleased to hear Captain Gendred ran a tight group. These were professional mercenaries and took their business seriously. Their guild was very strict about enforcing the laws of the Realm. They had to be to continue to allow their men to be openly armed.

We said our farewells and parted soon after. It had been a pleasant meeting. I sucked greedily at one of the confections as I walked and marvelled at the cool and strongly sweet flavour. *The caravan owners might be on to something*, I thought. It certainly explained them having two shops. The sweet was startlingly energising, and my step seemed lighter for the consumption. I *reached* out with my senses and was surprised to see the energy clustered in the sweet. It was such a concentration of energy, much more so than the honey to which I was accustomed. I was glad I had a few more stuffed in my backpack. They would come in handy on the road.

As much as the sweet cheered me up, it was the news from the mercenary guard that the road was clear all the way to Laketown that was of much happier interest to me. I found myself relaxing and enjoying my journey all the more now I knew bandits were not patrolling the road ahead. I lengthened my stride and walked confidently forward towards Laketown, a smile ghosting across my features. It was a mile later that I realised I should have had the couple bring a note to Reeve Comlin and felt the fool.

Behind Will and out of sight, Peter Custard and Jeremy Lions cursed the delay and waited patiently as they watched the Target finish speaking to the couple in the wagon and finally continue on his way. Peter relaxed his jaw and motioned for Jeremy to remain still. He kept an eye on the couple as the horses took up the traces and the wagon slowly resumed its journey. The couple and their guards would pass near Peter and Jeremy's hiding place, but they were deep in a laughing conversation and oblivious to their surroundings. Not one to take unnecessary risks, Peter hunkered down a little deeper behind the bushes. *Can't be too careful*, he thought.

Jeremy and he were members of the Sect and under orders direct from Seth Farlow, their Sect Leader. They had travelled with Dennis Petard, known simply as the Knife, from Munsten all the way to Jaipers on a simple but important mission—a mission Peter and Dennis had successfully completed many times in the past. But all their plans had fallen apart in an instant and now they were scrambling to set things right. Peter keenly felt the loss of the Knife. He had been the eldest and the leader of their group and now he felt the weight of command. He knew if they didn't recover the Target that Seth would have their balls on a string around his neck. Seth had chosen the Knife, and the Knife had chosen Peter, and Peter had then chosen Jeremy. He owed the younger man, and this was the last chance they had to make a mark in the Sect and gain God's notice.

Seth had accepted them because they had once been garrison men before the Lord called them to a higher purpose. From then it had been an easy matter to obtain the papers needed to gain them access to the garrison in Jaipers. The Knife had lingered outside town while the two had joined the garrison and worked out the daily routine. They had fit right in and no one had questioned them. The garrison Captain in Jaipers had even welcomed them openly, saying he was glad to have more men in his service.

Now, out of habit born of years of experience, Peter looked at himself and Jeremy and could see they continued to look exactly like typical military men. Peter was a couple of decades older than Jeremy and his hair was streaked with grey. He knew he could pass as Jeremy's father if need be. They both had close-cropped hair in the style of most military men; hair impeded vision and made helmets hot and sweaty. They kept their beards neatly trimmed and bathed when they could. The regimen of military life mimicked that of the Sect where cleanliness was next to godliness and they welcomed the routine. The hands they clenched in anticipation were well callused from sword use. They were fit with well-toned muscles that swung a sword with practised ease. But, more importantly, they carried the look and swagger of military men without knowing they did it. Seth had approved of them for these skills and Dennis had tested them on the road to Jaipers and had been pleased. Today they still wore the leathers from the Jaipers garrison and looked every inch the simple military men they pretended to be.

But they weren't military men. They were members of the Sect. They carried secrets that would mean the death of anyone who discovered them.

They carried out God's plan and were blessed by none other than the Archbishop of the Church of the New Order. Their belief gave them strength to do what they must against evil the world should know nothing about.

Peter rose up onto his haunches and then beckoned for Jeremy to follow. The men slowly emerged from their cover as the wagon carrying the young couple and the last of the couple's guards disappeared over a rise in the road. Around the bend and obscured by trees was the Target, still ambling down the road. He was the most sought-after person the Church had ever wanted in their hands—and none other than the offspring of the demon woman who had birthed him. Peter started down the road—keeping to the side—and looked up and down the road. Jeremy fell in behind him about twenty paces. The road was clear.

It had been a trying journey over the past few weeks and it would have been miserable if not for the excitement that had them uniquely focused on their new mission. They should have picked the Target up outside Jaipers as soon as he had left the town but Jeremy had reasoned they needed to be sure it was him. Peter knew Jeremy spoke from youth and a fear of failure. Peter had ignored him and sent a missive off to his Eminence at once. This had angered Jeremy but Peter hadn't cared. He knew to whom he owed his allegiance. And he also understood why this had to be handled carefully and quietly. Too much could go wrong.

They had finally caught up to the Target only to lose him in the small town of Belger. He had simply disappeared in the market and they immediately suspected he was using his evil powers. They clenched their bloodstones to see through his magic and searched the stalls and alleyways. But they failed to locate him and, in desperation, they circled the town before Peter reasoned he must have continued his journey down the road. He was correct and, now they had only just found him again.

Their frustration and their relief had been extreme and, when they had finally found him strolling along the road, they had fallen to their knees in prayer to the Lord, for surely this had been His work. Soon they would act, and fulfil the long-delayed mission of the Sect and find glory with God, the Archbishop, and Seth. Peter knew from experience that God's justice was swift but, for the Target, it would be slow and painful. The thought lightened his step.

Peter knew the traffic along the road would become heavier soon and they would have to act. They couldn't afford to take the chance that a witness might see too much and speak to the wrong people. *Little events lead to bigger ones and, before you know it, it all unravels*, quoted Peter in his head from one of the

Knife's favourite sayings. The simple truth was the Target must be recovered and brought to Seth alive. Failure to do so was unthinkable. To be successful, they must remain covert. This was the Sect way. It had been beaten into them through rigorous training. Peter was the hardened expert at this while Jeremy was a mere novice in experience with the demons. Each night Peter whispered details of past hunts to Jeremy and warned him of the demon tricks. He spoke of their ability to hide from human eyes in broad daylight and to manipulate the earth to do their bidding. Peter could see the fear in Jeremy's eyes but he could see the resolve there as well. He reminded Jeremy of the bloodstones they each carried and their ability to unmask the deception. Nightly they blessed each other, shared communion and prayed for righteous strength to fulfil their mission. There was strength in ritual.

Peter had participated in the demon hunts while Jeremy had only heard of them. Peter remembered and missed those days of fear and excitement. Dealing with the druids had been tricky and dangerous work and he had been uniquely talented at doing it. God had gifted him with the skills he needed., skills he knew his friend Dennis Petard had in ample supply, for he had been the Sect's top enforcer and the favourite of Seth Farlow. The Knife had personally removed from the Realm dozens of the heathens. *Now he was dead and buried in an unmarked grave in that shit-hole town of Jaipers*, thought Peter and seethed at the insult his burial represented. These people should have been grovelling in thanks for the great work Dennis had done for them and for God.

Instead, Dennis had met his death out in the wild and in the hands of the demon, they now followed. Thoughts of Dennis' ridiculous death often drove Peter to see red. His long-term associate, a highly respected and admired member of the Sect, had been taken down by a country Reeve and a fledgling demon. It was unthinkable. *How could God have let this happen? All their plans so easily laid to waste.* They had tracked the coin all the way to Jaipers and had watched for days as that man, Bill, had studied with the town Wordsmith, Daukyns. A quick look inside the home of the man had revealed this "Bill" was none other than the infamous traitor Bill Redgrave. On hearing this, Dennis had had a fit. He had declared God himself must be smiling down on them and led them to his doorstep. Their purpose could not have been clearer. Excited, Dennis had abandoned caution and moved too quickly to recover the coin.

With his caution abandoned, it was no wonder he was so soon discovered. Jeremy and Peter had already infiltrated the local garrison and were being housed in the recruit portion of the barracks. They had been out that night providing eyes for Dennis when the random patrol had caught Dennis exiting the house by the rear. It had been a rookie mistake, and it had led to a sad comedy of errors—one after the other. The traitor at least had been killed, but far too cleanly to repay his crimes. Dennis had escaped over the wall as planned and Peter and Jeremy had been relieved, thinking their companion safe. They were to meet up a few days later but, unbelievably, the Reeve had returned only a few hours later dragging the remains of their companion behind him like a common criminal. At the time, it had been all Peter could do not to run out onto the street and strike down the Reeve. Afterwards, once he could think clearly, he reasoned Dennis had underestimated the man. No man should have been able to follow the Knife that night and, somehow, the Reeve had done so and planted an arrow in his eye. Their grief had been unbearable and prayer hadn't seemed to help.

They had prepared to act to seek vengeance but then they had fallen gravely ill. And, later, after they had miraculously recovered—thanks be to God—they heard the garrison captain bragging to one of the senior rates about the young herb gatherer who had been involved in the death of Dennis. It had been the boy they had seen enter town the day after the murder. Peter had felt something wrong but hadn't put it together with the boy. Young men the age of the Target were never in their power and he hadn't expected to find a demon. He admonished himself now—years of inactivity had dulled his instincts. He had failed the Sect, and he added an extra twenty lashings to his nightly ritual—his self-flagellation was the path to righteousness. With each stroke, he released his sins.

After the funeral for the wordsmith, they had spied on the boy and watched as he caused flowers to spring from the soil. Peter had recognised him for what he was. Jeremy had argued against it, but Peter knew. He could see it in the boy. He had seen the same look, the same far-off stare that sometimes filled their faces; the look they had when they were using their foul magic. *Oh yes, this was the Target.* For over a decade they had searched high and low. Most thought him dead. *Seth never did, and neither had the Knife*, thought Peter with satisfaction. His only concern had been Jeremy. He was talented, but he had never been on the Hunt. He didn't appreciate the danger the demons presented. There was nothing he could do. Peter was alone with Jeremy. The two of them would have to be enough until Seth could join them.

None of this was a coincidence, Peter knew, the Lord had put this all in motion. He turned his attention back to the present and as he turned the corner he spotted the Target disappear over the next rise. He could see the road was too open, and he turned to the tree line and sprinted forward, knowing Jeremy would follow. His black boots muffled all noise as he ran swiftly to the next copse of trees and disappeared behind them. Jeremy waited a moment and followed behind him.

I hadn't bothered to check behind me for days now and, as Laketown drew closer, I felt a strange stirring in my gut to raise my level of caution. It was an odd feeling and not one that I had felt in a long time. My old fears of capture returned and with them the memory of my promise to my mother to always stay safe. I had the feeling someone was watching me and it was getting stronger and closer.

The number of travellers coming out of Laketown had trickled to none, and, when the last caravan passed, I stole a long glance behind me. From where I was I could see some good distance down the road, and, with relief, saw nobody approaching either behind or ahead. But still, the feeling of being followed persisted.

I watched as the caravan dipped below a rise and disappeared, and, in turning back on my way, caught a movement out of the corner of my eye. Being careful not to stare, I probed with my senses and there, hidden behind the trees, I felt the presence of two men. They were crouched down, hiding, and I knew they were focused on me.

An oily feeling came over me, and something about these men seemed familiar. In a flash of recognition, I remembered the two guards from Jaipers and knew, without a doubt, that these were the same men and it was me they hunted.

The Reeve had been right all along.

My heart nearly burst as panic overcame me, and I turned and ran as fast as I could toward Laketown. All I knew was I had to reach the town and find safety inside its walls. My eyes searched the road ahead for any sign of help, but the road was empty. Soon all my senses were focused on the sound of my feet pounding the road and of my breath rasping in my throat. With every bounce of my stride, my backpack straps would dig deep into my shoulders. My clothes were soon soaked through with sweat. The muscles of my legs screamed at me to stop but the fear pushed the pain aside. The heat of the day was at its highest and I knew, with rising horror, there was no way I could reach the town before they caught me. But I had to try. And so I ran down the dusty road stealing feverish glances behind me for any sign of my pursuers. In my mind, they were right behind me reaching out with grasping fingers. With my senses, I felt some surprise from them, then anger, and I could feel them running behind me and I sped up.

The road shimmered in the heat and the sound of grasshoppers was a loud buzz in my ears. My world narrowed to the will required to keep myself running and tracking the two men behind me. On each rise of the road I hoped to see a caravan plodding along toward me, but the road remained empty. I stifled a scream and pushed my legs to obey and move faster. I thought once to drop my backpack but I couldn't do it. It was as much a part of me as anything else and I could not leave it behind. Salvation would come. I just had to keep running.

Craobh

Two

On the Road to Jaipers, 900 A.C.

GENERAL BRENT BAIRSTOW urged his horse to move to the side of the road and allowed the animal its head so it could graze at the grass that grew thick where the road, the stone bridge, and the river all met. He turned his head to watch his men slowly make their way along the road. His own men in the first cart nearest him were laughing at some jest and pointing to an Army regular who plodded along on his horse near them. The poor fellow had suffered miserably over the past week. His arse was a seething mass of blisters after the idiot had wiped himself with poison oak leaves. It had spread all up his hands, arms, and chest. Even from where he sat on his horse, Brent could see it creeping up the man's neck.

What's his bloody name? he thought furiously. *I can't keep these Army types names straight in my head. Oh, right, Private William David, the man with two first names. Or, was it David Williams?*

Brent watched as the man scratched furiously under his tunic and then turned his head to bark something at the men on the cart; which led to them laughing all the harder. The Army sergeant—Henson was his name, Brent remembered, pleased to recall it much more quickly this time—rode up hard beside the cart and, with excellent aim and timing, managed to whip one of the cart riders on the back of the head with his riding crop. Brent winced when the sound of the strike carried to him in the still air.

"Quit yer laughing', ya dunderhead!" barked the sergeant.

By now the poor fellow was visibly cursing and rubbing his head with a hand before peering at it for signs of blood. He held his hand out for the sergeant to see and so, no doubt, the sergeant had drawn blood. Brent clenched his teeth. *That was abusive*, he thought. *I'll have to have words with the sergeant in private.*

"Show yer mother the blood, I dinna care," spat the sergeant as he wheeled his horse back to the road. "One more word from you and its jacks detail for a week."

Brent could see the grimace on the face of the struck man but kept his expression clear. He was sorely disappointed in his Guard. They were too quick to quarrel with the Army men and both sergeants were having a hard time keeping them disciplined and off each other's throats. The past two weeks had been particularly difficult. *Thank God, Frederick made me ride all those times.* And then, thinking of his brother Frederick Bairstow, the Knight General of the Army of the Realm, he once again wished he knew what difficulties he faced in the capital of Munsten and prayed to God he would be all right.

Brent waited and watched as the carts and men on horseback moved past him in line. A few of the men nodded in some semblance of respect to him but it was paltry. The Army major and the Army captain pulled off the road across from him and watched the men, horses, and carts pass with keen eyes. They represented his only officers on this trip. *This task is routine for the Army regulars*, thought Brent. *A mere simple ride down the road for weeks on end—suits them no end. And that would be reason number twenty-three on the list of why I'm glad I volunteered for the Guard.*

"Private David!" barked Captain James Dixon to the startled private. "You will put more of that ointment on you at the next rest break. Clear? You'll scratch yourself into one big blister at this rate!"

The private nodded meekly and stopped himself from scratching mid-scratch. Guardsman Corporal Oliver Waite, riding in a cart, laughed, and the captain snapped his head over to stare at the culprit.

"Any more laughter from you, Waite, and you'll be the one to rub it on his ass, you hear?"

"Yes, sir," was Waite's meek reply. His partner on the cart bench, Army Corporal Peter Reid, smacked his leg and smirked sideways at him. Brent was pleased to see some camaraderie between Army and Guard and a glance at the captain proved he too had noticed and approved. The major was scowling as he was most often wont to do. *There was simply no pleasing that man.* Brent realised he was furrowing his eyebrows and forced his face to relax.

Brent could see his officers wanted a quiet word with him. The captain kept stealing looks at him to see if he had noticed. Brent ignored them both. He was too busy looking at the men's gear and tackle. One of the horses looked a little blown and, when he turned his head to observe it better as it passed him by, he saw the captain noticing his observation and seeming pleased. *Ha!* Thought Brent. *I'm not clueless after all.* With a start, he stopped the thought. *What world have I landed in where the opinion of an Army captain matters to me? But still, I am pleased, I must admit. The Army knows horses better than anyone.*

Captain Dixon was the only man he trusted on this road trip to Jaipers. Brent had been pleased to discover he had replaced their assigned Guard Captain who had fallen down some stairs and struck his head the morning they departed from Munsten. He hadn't regained consciousness but was expected to fully recover. The Guard chirurgeon had informed Brent that morning, all the while wringing his hands in an annoying fashion. The blow hadn't been hard, he said and then looked quite pleased with himself. Brent thought nought about it until, later, Dixon quietly told him Knight General Frederick had assigned him to the detail in person. Dixon told him the Guard Captain had socialised in known circles with the Lord Protector and his cronies and the Knight General had arranged an accident. Brent smiled at the memory of finding out. *My brother is looking after me even this many miles from home. If he trusts this man, then so do I.*

"Corporal Gately!" yelled out Dixon to the guardsman riding the winded horse. "Once past the bridge, switch to one of the spare horses! Tonight you brush that horse till it shines and I want you apologising to her the entire time. You need to learn to read your horse better!"

"Her?" was the startled quick reply from the guardsman.

"Yes, *her*! It's no wonder the ladies want nothing to do with you. You can't tell a mare from a stallion."

Brent bit the inside of his cheek. Even the major seemed to be smiling. *Or the sun was in his eyes. Hard to tell.*

"Sorry, sir," Dixon said to Brent as the last cart passed them. "I should have noticed earlier. That's not a strong horse. Her mum was a weak one as well but the sire was strong. I had hoped for better. I recommend we sell her at the next town or outpost. She won't survive the journey with men in armour. Too big a strain on her heart. She can't take the weight. She'll do well for a farmer or the like."

Brent merely nodded and waited for the tethered spare horses to cross the bridge. The man watching them called for them to halt and Gately, now off his horse, moved over to select another.

Satisfied, Brent turned to his two officers. "Gentlemen, what's up?" Brent couldn't fail to notice the tightening of Gillespie's jaw. *That man has more tells than anyone else I know.* He waited as they crossed the road over to him. Dixon glanced over to where Gately was trying to select a horse. By the look he was giving the horses he still couldn't tell a workhorse from a riding horse.

"Have you given any thought to where we camp tonight?" said Gillespie. Brent waited. After a moment, Gillespie clenched his jaw a little harder before adding "Sir." *He is getting closer to insubordination all the time,* thought Brent. *I doubt I'll finish this trip without having to discipline him.*

"No, I have not. Somewhere along the road, I expect, major. Why?"

"It's just that I know a village a little ways outside what we normally cover in a day with this lot," he paused then added, "Sir." The insult was plain but not enough to take affront.

Brent waited in silence. With Gillespie, he had learned, it was easier to just sit in silence. The major was one of those people that needed to fill silences. The captain, on the other hand, could sit for days saying nothing at all. Brent admired him. *James will be a fine senior officer one day.*

Sure enough, after a few seconds of silence, the major elaborated. "I know the town. It has an inn that will house us and a large community room to house the men. Large enough stable for all the horses and it would be a welcome break. A chance to clean up and take stock. It's been a hard two weeks on the road for the guardsmen, sir."

Brent kept his eye on Dixon for the entire conversation. Dixon thought he was hiding it but Brent could see the surprise on his face. It was not lost on Brent that Gillespie had added a "sir" at the end to suck up to him. *He wants this, but I don't know why.* Brent could understand why Gillespie disliked him so much but not why he so openly displayed it. *He's Army and I'm Guard, but that's not it, is it? He's the Protector's man—probably thinks it covers him. But his attitude is startling considering I'm a general and Gillespie is a little shit Army major. It would be smarter to be nicer.*

Brent put a bored expression on his face before replying. "Just how far beyond our normal distance, major?"

"Only about two hours more, sir. We should still have sunlight on arrival. The road is fairly maintained, and it has good visibility all around. We can travel fast."

"And you, captain? What's your opinion?"

The captain looked thoughtful and pretended to consider the question. Brent kept his face calm. He had no doubt the major had coerced the captain into agreeing with the idea and had planned this coordinated attack. Brent had no interest in the comfort of an inn. They were military men, not barons. He looked at the captain and watched as he exchanged a glance with Gillespie.

"Sir," he began slowly, no doubt making sure he had the prepared words right. "We're only two weeks on the road but the men have been working hard and improving their skills. Plus, honestly, the horses could use a night in the stables. A good cleaning, new shoes, oats. It would make a world of difference to them."

Brent nodded at the logic of what he said and had no doubt Dixon cared more for the welfare of the horses than the men. *Perhaps I can convince myself one night under a roof again will improve morale.* He looked thoughtfully at his officers. The major looked hopeful and maybe even a bit anxious about it, the captain more embarrassed than anything else. No doubt, word of his decision would reach the men faster than the flight of a sparrow.

He nodded and watched Gillespie smile. It was not a normal action for the man and it looked wrong. "Very well, make it so. I want it clear to the men that any problems in town will be dealt with harshly. I will not tolerate drunken or disorderly conduct. Does the town have a wall?"

Gillespie nodded still looking pleased.

"Very well, send our best rider on ahead to warn the garrison of our arrival and to arrange rooms in the inn and community room. Plus make sure the farrier is ready to receive our horses on arrival. I want new shoes on all the horses with no delays come morning."

"Sir, yes sir!" replied Gillespie and started to turn his horse away.

"One more thing," added Brent and Gillespie quickly heeled his horse. "I want that weak horse replaced. Captain, see to that personally. I trust your judgement."

"Sir!" replied Dixon, saluting and turning back to the road. As he and Gillespie rode ahead to catch up to the train, Gately, still working on his new horse, grinned up at Brent and gave him a mock salute.

"Mind your manners, Gately, and get your fucking saddle on that horse. We won't wait for you. You'll want to gossip this latest news, fast, no? Earn an extra cup?"

Gately's eyes went round with the realisation of what this news could mean to him socially and he turned his attention to the saddle and reached under his horse for the dangling girth strap.

"That's not the strap, Gately. That's a stallion."

Brent could hear Dixon laughing up ahead and grinned to himself.

Major Gillespie looked around the stables at his men and waited. Intentionally absent from the gathering were the General, Captain Dixon, Corporal Gately, and Private David. A noise from the stable doors drew his glance, and he watched Corporal Waite look up over the stall to give him a thumbs up before disappearing back outside to join Corporal Reid and stand guard. They would give warning should anyone approach.

"All right, let's make this quick," Gillespie said, and the men nodded. "You've done a great job making the General believe you're all hating each other. Keep it up, but tone it down a bit."

Gillespie looked at Sergeant Henson who looked startled at being singled out.

"Wuhan, suh?"

Gillespie hated the man's accent. He had that Northern twang and stretched out words and had him grasping sometimes to make sense of what he said.

"You hit that bastard with your riding crop. That was excessive. I was surprised that prick Bairstow tolerated it. Stay in line and keep to the Army rules."

The men grumbled a bit.

"Shut it! Guards come from Army, so shut it and remember where you came from and whom you serve." Gillespie glared at the loudest of the men until they looked down to the dirt floor of the stable. "Our mission is clear. Stick to the plan and keep your fucking noses clean."

The men looked at one another and some nodded in agreement.

"Now. Beginning tomorrow I want you to start getting along a bit better. Start tossing out the occasional *sir* to Bairstow and Dixon. Get them relaxed a bit more. Make them think they have your respect. Slowly, though. Slowly, all right? Figure it out with the sergeants. I want a couple of the men starting it. Then spread it to the others over a few days. Slowly like. Let them two officers overhear you talking favourably about them—but mostly Bairstow. Pump his ego till its ready to burst. By the time we reach Belger I want him thinking he's the cow's tits with you lot. Got it?"

The men murmured agreement and looked a little too pleased. Gillespie was annoyed with the men as a whole. They were too cocky and having far too much fun. It was important that they work hard at maintaining the illusion that Bairstow was their leader. The Lord Protector had ordered it done this way. He was quite clear on the matter. *No sense arguing the orders*, he thought. *This is my shot to advance, and quickly. I'll do whatever he wants and how ever he wants it.* There was a certain quality of horror to this approach that even Gillespie admired. He would have just slit his throat and be done with it. *This approach,* he thought, *was a bit more, inventive and cruel?*

Gillespie turned his thoughts from Bairstow to Dixon. Beside Gately and David, he was an unexpected addition to their troupe. Gillespie's picked man had fallen in the castle on his way to the staging point leaving him with only his sergeants to handle matters. Gillespie was no fool. He was sure his man had been taken out so that Dixon could replace him. *I haven't risen to Major in this man's Army without knowing how to make and break the rules and force the process to work in my favour.* He recognised when he was being played. Dixon was well known in the Army and known to Bairstow's brother, the Knight-General. Gillespie knew a plant when he saw one. It warmed his heart to know that he would get to rid the Army of a brown-nosed suck ass such as Dixon. His time would come, and soon. His death would be a tricky one to pull off. That would have to be clearly an accident of some sort. Right now he just didn't know how to pull it off. Gillespie smiled to himself. He was confident he would find a way. It was a confidence won after having all the right connections and an assured rise to the top.

The Lord Protector was a distant cousin of Gillespie; somewhere on their mothers' side. They shared a great-aunt or some such nonsense. But it was enough that Healy had trusted Gillespie to take care of this mission and had for many other missions in the past. This task was critical. It required a special touch and Gillespie knew how the Lord Protector wanted to play it. When he had laid out his plans to the Lord Protector he had been pleased to have the Protector approve it with such enthusiasm. He had even clasped him about the shoulders like brothers.

Their meeting in the Lord Protector's private chambers was memorable to him. He remembered it vividly: the wine, the camaraderie, the feeling of being a part of something truly important.

* * *

"Agreed, major!" exclaimed Healy, the Lord Protector. He clasped the major's shoulder briefly. Gillespie looked startled at the sign of affection and smiled and tried to hide it with a sip of his expensive wine. He sat at the Lord Protector's dining table and meat, fruit and wine were laid out for the two of them but it was enough to feed eight or more. The Lord Protector sat on the table edge right next to him and piled a generous portion of venison on his plate, so rare and tender the blood pooled around it, so much it almost floated. Spit filled his mouth with hunger and he swallowed it to speak.

"The men are shit, sir. 'Cept for my sergeants and my captain. They've all been with me from the start. Share a like mind, if you see. The others, they're all garbage. Can't be trusted to keep this quiet afterwards. Not like me, you see. And my sergeants. And the captain, too, of course."

"Yes, yes, I do understand and I agree with you," murmured Healy with an odd gleam in his eye. "Dispensable. But, tell me. You do trust the men to do this right? To get to Jaipers and back again with all matters attended to? As we discussed?"

"Oh, aye, sir," he said. "You've me word! On our mums' sisters!"

Healy smiled and nodded. "One thing I must stress: I want you to string Bairstow along. Make him feel he's turned the men around. Start it off rough and then warm to him. Get him to trust them. Then take him down. I've words I want you to say to him just before you finish him. I want you to note how he looks. How he reacts. What he says. Precisely. Clear, my dear major?"

"Sir, yes, sir!" Gillespie couldn't hide his smile. Feelings of warmth flooded him. *Glory will be mine! I'm favoured by the Lord Protector!*

"I want the gold returned quietly. Outside of Munsten, you are to drop the gold at the location I told you about. Convince Bairstow to stop there. Once there, you'll finish him. Then your men. Then hide the gold. There will be bodies of highwaymen hidden nearby. Use them as a cover story. You were ambushed in camp. Your men died, including Bairstow. You escaped with the sergeants. It must look like an ambush. The Knight-General will investigate and it must be perfect. We will arrange the timings as you get closer. Use the message routes. You know where they are positioned along the road and in towns. Keep me informed at all times."

Gillespie nodded, pleased and watched Healy return to his seat at the table. This was his plan. He had come up with it. Nothing could go wrong. It was simple and simple always worked. Killing the men would be pleasurable and that was gravy on his meat. And when he returned home, he would be promoted and rise to the position of Knight-General. *It is fortunate the Lord Protector is my cousin, even five or six times removed or whatever the hell it is. Family is family though.*

The thought of all the gold tugged at him. He had already decided almost all the gold crowns would be returned to Healy. Some of it—enough to make him comfortable for the rest of his life—would disappear on the way to the capital. The Lord Protector had let slip the count of the gold had never been done. The chest had been locked up and placed under guard in Jaipers. No one would know if he skimmed a little off the top.

Gillespie turned his attention to his meat and tore into it with gusto, smiling with blood covered teeth.

* * *

The men in the stable glanced at one another as Gillespie stood quietly smiling at some private jest or memory. Gillespie pushed those memories away and looked at the men and thought, instead, about how good it would be when he got rid of them for good. All of them were rotten to the core.

"Right," he said and looked to the sergeants who smiled back at him. Loyal to the cause of the Lord Protector, the sergeants knew the plan and would benefit from the gains. There was enough gold for them all. "Then let's be about it. I want sore heads and black eyes by the morrow. Give Bairstow a discipline issue to solve and he'll think he has the gift when he solves it. Now get out. Sergeants stay."

The men thumped each other on the back and grinned, careful not to make noise and give themselves away. Gillespie approved how they staggered their exit out of the stables and pitched their voices once they were well clear. Once the men were gone, he waited for a spell. He motioned to Sergeant Henson and watched him exit the barn.

A few moments later the sergeant returned. "All clear, suh! Marry a soul aboot."

"Fine. You two. Get the men in line smoother. This has to look natural to Bairstow and that prick Dixon. One whiff of something not right and all this falls apart and the heavy-handed solution will have to be enforced. Speaking of which, you two are being too rough and your words are out of character. Get smarter. Watch yer mouths."

"Sir," responded the sergeants in unison.

"Gately and David. I want them removed in Belger. We'll be there for three days resupplying and meeting with the local authorities on capital matters. Bairstow has a busy schedule there with the Chamber of Commerce and so we have time to do this carefully. I don't care what you do, but figure out how to do it and execute it. No signs, no evidence. I don't want the men starting to figure out what lies in store for them. Afterwards, act surprised. Worried.

Confide in the men and gain their trust again. They will be nervous. Clear?"

The sergeants grinned at one another and nodded. Gillespie could see they were looking forward to killing the two men, and it amused them as much as it amused him. The men didn't matter to him and their deaths certainly didn't, but that didn't mean you couldn't enjoy it and these two seemingly did. The Lord Protector had used the three of them—four with their missing captain—many times in the past for just these types of covert actions. The truth was they excelled at it and they were reliable. He knew without asking that Gately and David would simply disappear in Belger and after a time Bairstow, pressed for time, would assume they fell prey to foul play or deserted. Either lie worked. In truth, they would be dismembered and fed to the sharks off the coast.

The Lord Protector counts on me, thought Gillespie. *Only I can do the dirty work that needs to be done. And it's high time for me to earn a little pay on top of the promotion waiting for me when I return to Munsten.*

"Watch the men tonight. Make sure they keep their fucking mouths tight as traps about our mission. But I want drinking, singing, whoring and fighting. I don't care in which order. Just so long as half of them are sorry asses in the morning requiring the direct attention of Bairstow. Butter him up. Make him think he's swayed us over to his way of thinking. When we take him down in Jaipers, the pleasure will be that much more enjoyable." He eyed the men to make sure the message was understood and saw understanding in their eyes and pleased looks, he nodded. "Dismissed."

The sergeants snapped to attention and saluted and left the stables quickly. Gillespie waited a half hour and then, hearing nothing, went to the back corner of the stables and lifted a flagstone using a hoof jack. He was disappointed to see the small hollow in the dirt under the stone was empty. He reached into his tunic and extracted a small piece of paper and dropped it in the small hollow and dropped the stone back in place and stood to listen once more. The note would be picked up by the Protector's messengers and delivered right to him. The network of drop holes and the like were all over the country.

Hearing nothing of interest, he quietly headed to his room in the inn. He had stayed here many times in the past and, by now, his favourite girl in this shit hole of a village would have warmed his bed. She liked it rough and didn't seem to mind the bruises the next day.

At least she's never complained to me! He laughed loudly with his head thrown back and strode out of the stables and into the warm evening air.

Three

On the Road to Laketown, 900 A.C.

I WOULD LIKE to say I fought them in the end and that, after a valiant effort on my part, they bested me, but sadly, it was not the case. I could not run for long in the heat of summer. After about thirty minutes of running, I slowed, unconsciously, to a shuffling walk. When I would cast out with my *senses*, I would quickly find the two men moving unhurriedly closer and closer to me. Panic would stoke my energy anew and I would burst into speed down the road. I tried to draw strength from the earth, but I could not draw enough to overcome the drain my haste caused. I clawed outwards with my power and *reached* for whatever I could find, but my mind would not settle enough to allow me purchase. I sensed disquiet around me and it only heightened my fears. My thirst grew, and I could no longer swallow with my dried throat and I feared I would choke.

At some point, when I knew for certain Laketown remained out of reach, I turned and ran off the road in desperation to escape into the wilderness. That seemed to open the distance to the men, and I thanked my quick thinking. I soon found a stream and its lure overcame my fear and I dropped to the bank and greedily sucked in as much water as I could. I sensed the men entering the woods and drawing closer to me and soon I could linger no longer, and I leapt up, feeling a little better, to run off again into the woods.

It was soon after they caught up with me. Too late, I realised I had made the job easier for them by leaving the road. I was in a clearing and crawling on my hands and knees. I sensed them behind me and I turned and screamed in terror. They stopped at the edge and stared at me. One had his head cocked and looked at me like he would a piece of furniture. I recognised them from Jaipers. They were the same men from the town. The garrison men who had tried to stop me from leaving.

I scrambled backwards. "Please! Leave me alone! What do you want from me?"

Silence descended on the clearing and only the rough rasping sound of my laboured breath could be heard. The older one drew a short piece of thick wood and rushed me. I screamed and turned to escape and felt him strike the back of my head. My last thought was I had failed my promise to my mother and then I knew nothing.

Peter and Jeremy sat a good distance away from the Target and watched him carefully with trained eyes. Peter had been surprised at the ease of the capture. When they had seen him bolt off down the road, they knew they had been seen. Peter, having seen this before knew the boy had used magic to discover them. He also knew—with no small amount of shock—that his range must be exceptional. Normally the heathens could only sense a few tens of feet at most, but the Target had sensed them at over half a mile. All the while with Peter and Jeremy carrying a ruby clenched in their fists. This was extraordinary. No wonder the Sect feared him so much.

They had trailed the demon for a few days, watching outside the normal detection range. It had been many, many years since he had hunted a demon, but Peter had known soon enough something was not right. They had bided their time out of range to get a feel for him. They were ready to grab him when the Target had sensed them and bolted. Peter had stood and watched him disappear down the road with his backpack slapping back and forth. The image of the demon running blinding down the road was a tale he would gladly tell once back with the Sect. Demons were powerful creatures and almost unstoppable. The red stones the Sect carried helped deflect demon power but nothing could stop their control of plants and animals. And he watched the boy run at full speed in the heat of the day down an open road.

They had glanced at one another and ran after him. Jeremy had laughed and joked that all the tales couldn't be true. Peter had ignored him. He had witnessed too many Sect members killed by the heathen powers. It stole the heat from his body to think of it.

Peter suspected the boy knew little of his magic. He wouldn't have simply run off like he had if he had known what he could do. Watching the boy sprint away, Peter had hesitated, waiting to see him melt into the surrounding hills and disappear. When he continued straight down the dirt road in plain view, he first began to suspect that, perhaps, the Target was not in control of his powers and he bolted after him in pursuit. A few minutes later, Peter watched as the Target veered off the road into the woods and he and Jeremy stumbled on the road, certain they were being led into a trap. Everyone in the Sect knew what powers the demons controlled in the wilds. So they slowed and bided their time a little longer.

Witnessing the aimless crashing of the Target through the woods had made him realise the boy was simply running in full panic and did not possess his true powers. Normally demons drew massive amounts of power from the ground as they moved through the world. The boy should have been able to run for days without stop and yet he had stopped at the stream and drank like any another parched man.

The end of the chase had been strange, to say the least. Peter had expected to have to fight off plants, vines and animals but nothing had happened. It had been like chasing down any normal boy. From the stream, Peter and Jeremy had loped off after the boy, his stride no match for theirs. As they entered a large clearing, they found the boy screaming and scrambling to get away from them. The demon was exhausted, drained and panicked—everything Peter had not expected to find. Overcoming his surprise and caution, Peter reacted quickly. He drew out his cudgel and struck the boy behind the ear and then quickly retreated to watch him for a moment. When the Target didn't stir Peter felt giddy and afraid at the same time. He waited for animals to appear and vines to wrap around his ankles. When nothing happened, he took out the special binding ropes, stripped the boy with help from Jeremy, and tied him up as he had done so many times before to the other demons.

He was pleased to see his skills had not diminished despite the years since the last demon had been hunted down. He smiled at the feel of the rope in his hands. At times it felt like a snake and at other times like the strongest steel. The rope was special and, according to Seth, it had been created by God, and none doubted it. Seth said once a demon was bound with the rope it thwarted their ability to reach the earth with their senses. It never failed. Peter watched it tighten on its own around the Target and felt pleased and safe at last.

He turned to look at Jeremy and was disappointed to see he had a fear in his eyes. "What do you fear, Jeremy? This?" And he pointed to the Target who was expertly tied with his knees drawn up tight against his chest to restrict his breathing. "He won't escape that rope. He's bound and impotent now."

Jeremy nodded and licked his dry lips and looked quickly to Peter and back to stare at the Target. "The ropes. They move like they're alive. That's not natural, that. Not at all."

"Aye, lad," snorted Peter, understanding the fear in the lad now. "The ropes were created by God through Seth they are. You are witnessing God's power, lad. Sure as by God. Right there."

"Truly? Gaya outta that!"

"I wouldn't lie to you. Never to a Sect member. You swore the oaths. You saw the power Seth has. God's own power. Do you now dare to doubt?"

Jeremy squatted and stared at the ropes and reached a hand out before stopping it mid-air and looking at Peter. Peter nodded and Jeremy touched the rope end. The end slithered around Jeremy's wrist and he gasped in shock. The rope continued to caress his hand and a smile slowly grew on Jeremy's face. "That's... that's beautiful Peter! I admit it—before it turned my heart crossways."

"Aye. The rope won't release unless a Sect member orders it. This is God's gift to our cause. Proof of His righteousness and ours on our path. Seth says it is divine providence. Now, enough gawking. We need to hoist him up over that branch of that big tree there. Quickly now before he wakes."

Peter took the free end of the rope, coiled it, and tossed it up and over the large branch that extended horizontally out from the massive trunk of the oak tree that dominated the centre of the clearing. Together Peter and Jeremy hoisted the Target up into the air until he hung parallel to the ground with his face down. Breathing was exceptionally difficult and forced the victim to narrow their focus on just breathing through their nose. The Target's eyes were covered; a gag forced deep into his mouth and softened wax pushed deep into his ears. This was the proven way to deal with the demons until Seth could arrive to deal with the rest.

Now that he was captured he didn't look like much. Certainly, he did not look like the demons who preceded him. Those demons had always had an air about them. A strength borne from their heathen magic. Something to be feared. This boy merely looked like any wild waif you would find begging in the streets. During the capture, his eyes had been wide, round with fear and darting all about looking for a way out. The smell of urine filling his trousers was strong in the clearing and knowing the boy had pissed himself when they had grabbed him caused Peter and Jeremy to glance at each other more than once.

It had been years since Peter had captured one of the demons, but he hadn't forgotten a single aspect of the process. Years of training guided his hands without much thought. Now Jeremy and Peter watched the boy closely. This was important if they wished to remain safe. They had to be sure he was secured before they tried to do anything else with him. They would need to stay and observe him for a couple of days. He would not eat or drink in that time. He needed to be isolated from his powers and forced to focus solely on human needs such as hunger, thirst, breathing and surviving pain.

Capturing demons was always the worst detail in the past. It was much easier to just knife them and be done with it. Jiggle the brain matter was always the preferred way. Demons can't heal when they can no longer think. Peter had seen a demon come back from having her throat cut and bind her captive's feet to the ground before running clear into the night. When they caught her again, the next day they drove an axe into her skull and that was that. Dennis hadn't liked it, had said it was far too graphic for his tastes. He had always been a fan of the knife behind the ear and into the brain. *Quick, painless and efficient*, he always said. Seth had preferred the crossbow and a bolt in the eye. Hard to say which was the best, they had both killed dozens. Seth had even killed the head bitch with a bolt in the eye. The same bitch that had spawned this boy. The only demon to ever escape Seth. Peter again allowed a small sense of pride to fill him when he recognised he had done what Seth could not. It was sinful but so exquisite and he allowed himself a small sip from the fountain that led to Hell. A smile ghosted across his features before he smothered it internally. He would repent this sin later. He focused once more on the Target.

Seth was on his way, Peter knew with certainty. The missive he had sent would have reached His Holiness and Seth would now know he and Jeremy would soon capture the Target. Seth was probably making all haste to their location. Peter would send Jeremy to mark a trail from the road so Seth could find them here. Once Seth arrived, they would be able to relax their vigil. Then he hoped Seth would bless them and allow them to return to the Sanctuary and be allowed to watch as he tortured the last demon. Peter shuddered with pleasure at the thought.

The next few hours saw no change in the Target, but Peter knew it was too soon. It took many more days to weaken a demon. He lay unmoving, hanging from the tree limb two feet from the ground. He hung with a rope centred on his back, face down, with his knees drawn up so tight into his chest that his breathing was severely restricted. The blindfold, the waxed ears, and the gag continued to isolate the demon from the earth and their power. Peter looked at the fingers and toes for signs of blue skin that would indicate lost circulation and, seeing the bright red hue, relaxed and knew the Target was still intact. He knew from personal experience the bindings cut off just enough circulation to make the limbs feel numb. He could not risk harming him beyond what Seth would want to see: a whole and hale demon. Seth would understand the black eye, a result of discovering Dennis' black boots hidden in the heathen's belongings. Peter sucked the air in between his teeth remembering the discovery. Finding them smugly in the Target's backpack had spun Peter into a violent rage he probably would not have escaped if not for Jeremy who had held him back. The boots had explained much of why they had such a difficult time tracking and locating the boy. When they failed to find a trail outside Jaipers, they had assumed demon powers were at work and they had hurried straight to the next town to wait him out. It was in Belger they heard from the Finnow Mines shop of the boy stopping in.

When they had stripped the demon, Peter had been stunned and excited to find the pouch around the neck of the Target containing the coin and obsidian sickle. The coins were well known by the Church and they knew they were used to first open up a demon's power. For whatever reason, demon powers needed to be started, much like a fire is started with a spark. The coin was the spark and, once lit, the demon powers would grow quickly. The Church had all the coins accounted for except for one. There had always been one missing coin. Long lost during the Purge and suspected to have been taken by the bitch. Seth had never found it and had feared the boy had it and feared, most of all, what that portended for the future. It was good to recover it. It could have been the seed to grow a whole new legion of demons.

But what had excited him the most was discovering the sickle. When Peter had watched Jeremy spill the contents into his hand, he had almost cried out in elation. The small sickle was one of the most revered icons of the heathens and was carried by none other than the Cill Darae. The Sect had discovered the Target's heathen mother had been the Cill Darae of the Tree and her powers had been considerable, the strongest the Order had ever seen. The Tree had considered the sickle as a symbol of life and renewal, but Peter knew it symbolised nothing more than death and pain.

As if in response to this thought, he watched as the sickle sliced cleanly through one of Jeremy's fingers and the sound of the finger hitting the ground seemed excessively loud until the wail from Jeremy replaced it. A fountain of blood jetted from the hand where the finger had once been. It had been an incredibly beautiful sight to see. The blood jetting with such strength had stirred something deep within Peter and he watched fascinated as Jeremy struggled to contain the blood loss. He clamped a hand over the wound and blood leaked between the fingers to drip heavily to the ground. Those crimson drops looked so beautiful to him and he watched transfixed. Only at the crying pleas from Jeremy had Peter finally stirred himself and he spent the next hour cauterising and wrapping the wound. Jeremy now rested on the ground with his back propped up against the tree and with his head lolling about on his chest. He had lost a surprising amount of blood in a short period and he was weak and delirious. The cut had been so clean it was as if his body hadn't even noticed the loss and had continued senselessly sending spurt after spurt of heart blood out from the opened veins. *He's an idiot*, thought Peter and laughed to himself. *It had been fun to watch.*

With Jeremy now resting, Peter had decided to thoroughly search the Target's backpack. The backpack itself was a wonder of design and construction and Jeremy had claimed it for himself when he saw the quality. But Peter knew Seth would take it for the Church—everything went to the Church first. The backpack would be sold, and the coins transferred to the Sect to maintain operations. Inside the backpack, Peter found much he had not expected to find. The unguents, a fortune in Life Salts, and the herbs were only expected to be found on senior demons—the Stocs, as they called themselves. Through the lore learned through the Purge, Peter knew that only Stocs had the skills required to work the plants and make the salves. And yet the boy possessed rather potent ones. He used some on Jeremy and was not lost on the irony.

Peter reasoned this boy couldn't be anything more than a Duilleog, one of the apprentice demons. He was barely a man—still a child in many ways important to the demons. He had been separated from his mother, the Cill Darae when he was barely eight summers old when Seth had put a crossbow bolt through her eye. Finding the unguents and potent herbs had Peter concerned. He suspected the sickle leant its powers to the boy. How else could it have made the potions? But, if he were a powerful demon, he should have easily evaded them. He could have just snared them in the woods. Instead, he had gone down, drained of strength and gasping for water in the heat. A demon would never have used his own body strength. Instead, he would have pulled power from the surrounding land. *No*, he thought to himself. *He has no real power; he's a Duilleog at best.*

The ranks of the Tree members were from the old tongue, now long forgotten. The ranks went Duilleog, Craobh, Stoc and Freamhaigh, with the Cill Darae, also known as the Priest or Elevated Druid, holding a unique and specialised position reporting only to the sole Freamhaigh, the head of the Tree. Of course, the tree huggers had tree names for the same ranks: Duilleog was the Leaf, Craobh was the Branch, Stoc was the Trunk and the Freamhaigh was the Root. The idiot demons had it all in reverse; everyone knew the tree itself was the important part and not the roots.

Peter was cautious but professionally confused. His experience was telling him one thing but the evidence another. The coin and sickle were in the possession of the Target. The boy had detected them at over a half mile distance—an impossible skill. The herbs, potions, and salves were harvested and made with the potency only a fully trained demon could manage. The Target was an enigma. And yet, here he was, trussed in the Sect bindings—deaf, blind and mute—and suspended from the ground and cut off from his powers. For the hundredth time, he prayed to God for Seth to hurry up and arrive. He knew it would be another couple of weeks before Seth could arrive. The journey from Munsten was a long one. He grimaced. He needed Seth. Only Seth, imbued and blessed with God's Holy power, could counter a demon's powers. As always, good triumphed over evil. *God must surely be watching out for me*, hoped Peter, reverently.

Peter opened the bag of Life Salts and removed a pinch. He held it up to a nostril and inhaled it deeply. A feeling of euphoria and well-being filled him and he closed his eyes. Many of the Sect members were addicted to Life Salts. They claimed it brought them closer to God—Peter was one of them. He took another pinch and tucked it inside his cheek beside the gums. The salty taste filled his mouth, and he felt the tips of his fingers tingle. Peter resumed his vigil of the Target and lost himself in the feeling of wellness that consumed him. He mouthed the Sect prayer:

Dear Lord, save us from the deceit of demons.
Lord Have Mercy.
Open our eyes to the lies of demons.
Lord, don't let demons divide your Church.
Help us to reject lies presented to us as the truth.

Lord, give us Strength.
Lord, give us Hope.
Lord, flood our souls with the Holy Spirit.
Amen.

Jeremy moaned softly and held his wounded hand to his chest. Peter glanced over to where he lay propped up against a tree. Peter cursed under his breath and considered ending the idiot's life now to shut him up. He regretted bringing him along. The vigil would be hard with only himself to give watch. *I can't trust Jeremy any longer*, he realised. *Seth will end him when he arrives.* The Sect never tolerates failure. From themselves or those who work for them. Such as the Finnow Mines salt proprietors in Belger.

Peter recalled with pleasure the joy he had experienced in killing the two store owners for their lapse in judgement. How they could have confused this whelp with a member of the Sect was beyond him. They hadn't deserved to remain alive. *The night could have been a pleasurable one*, he thought sadly, *but with time against me I instead had to limit my pleasure to the quick death I gave them. Much too quick*, he thought with regret. One of them, the short older one, he had punished years before and he remembered the savage glee he felt when he saw his own marks on the man's back. The Knife had approved the *signing* of his work on the skin of his charges. When he saw his own mark, he had been elated. It had been one of his first tests so many years ago. It had felt good to complete God's good work.

They had been delayed by having to get the shop cleaned up and new proprietors arranged to take over. Finnow Mines didn't question the need. As always, they complied. They all did. God's work was the only authority needed. Soon after they had raced after the target and found him strutting down the road like he owned it. Peter shook his head in remembrance at sighting the boy. It was only demons that could evoke fear in his heart. The sight of the demon in the open walking down the road in plain sight had almost weakened Jeremy's bladder and Peter knew it shamed him. He was right to fear them. Their unholy powers were terrifying to see. They controlled the very ground they walked on. Plants moved and animals ran to their calling. It was horrific. *They die like normal men and women though*, he thought with satisfaction. *And they bleed, shit and piss just like anyone else.* Seth taught him that. It strengthened him at times.

Now he had to merely hand over the boy to Seth once he arrived. The mark on the road had been laid out, clearly visible to members of the Sect. Further marks on the trail would lead them directly here. He would go back later once they were in control and leave the second mark. That was important. It told those who followed it was safe. It could be a little while, but Peter knew how to proceed carefully. Plants and grass were dug up and removed around where the boy hung. The rope provided the only contact to the tree, but the rope would not allow the heathen to reach out to nature. All was in accordance with Seth's instructions, the instructions that had protected the Sect members for all these years. Peter followed them religiously.

More than twenty-four hours had passed, and Peter was starting to feel more relaxed but warned himself to remain vigilant. It was the first day that always proved the most difficult. If they had missed something, it was the first day when the druid would use whatever powers they retained to escape. Peter smiled to himself; time was his enemy and his friend. The longer a druid was bound, the harder it was for them to escape. The lack of food and water and the pain from the reduced circulation always clouded their minds. And by now, Peter knew, the boy's limbs must feel on fire and, judging by the muffled whimpers, he was sure he was correct.

Peter watched the midges coming and going on the exposed skin of the Target and grinned. Mentally he urged them to suck and eat their fill. The boy's body was covered with them now. They added to the distraction required to keep the demon off balance. Peter watched them carefully despite the glee he felt. He looked for patterns—anything to indicate the demon was using them somehow. You could not be too careful with demons. Their evil powers could do much with nature. Peter and Jeremy had carefully laid tripwires on all the trails leading to the clearing. They needed as much advance warning as they could get to alert them to approaching animals—animals called by the demon for help. Peter had lost count of how many Sect members had lost their lives to that heinous trick.

In two days they would feed him a little. Each day he would get a measure of water—the total amount based on the weight of the demon. It was necessary to maintain the fine balance between life and death. And Peter was one of the best at maintaining the fine line. The Knife had taught him well. He knew how to prolong a man's life just at the edge of death. The Church had required those particular skills and had honed him well under the apprenticeship of the Knife and, finally, under Seth himself. There wasn't a day that went by when Peter didn't thank God for providing him with the skills to honour Him. He basked in the righteousness of his task. God's work was so humbling and satisfying.

Four

Somewhere between Belger and Laketown, 900 A.C.

W HEN I WOKE I found myself deaf, blind, gagged and hooded. I could feel myself swaying and realised I was suspended in mid-air. I tried to reach out with my senses but felt nothing. Whatever the source of my power was, it was simply gone. It was like losing your sight and I reeled internally at the loss. I tried everything I could to try to grasp my power. At some point, I rationalised they had suspended me for some reason and that was probably to sever my connection to the earth. I had no idea how high above the ground I was, but I imagined it must be very high. I was completely isolated. The ropes that bound me were doing more than simply binding me. At first, I could feel them tightening on their own with every exhalation, making it harder to breathe with each breath. It was almost like they were alive. It was the only sensation I was aware of and I felt every squeeze. It frightened me very much. And so I hung in the air, knowing only pain and fear. Panic beat my senses continuously and I fought it off as best I could, knowing I was losing the fight.

I had never experienced such pain in my life. At first, it had merely hurt to be tied up so tight and I couldn't imagine it being worse. Then my own weight put a tremendous strain on my joints and spine and after moments, my muscles cramped into unbearable knots of pain. My eyes were covered, my mouth gagged, and something had been pushed painfully into my ears where it had set solid blocking all sound. I screamed against the gag but heard nothing. Soon I felt my arms and legs go numb and the loss of the pain was such a relief. When the ropes didn't loosen I remembered that limbs cut off from circulation too long can quickly go bad and would need to be cut off from the body lest they infect the person. This fear of losing my limbs consumed me completely and the fear I was holding back overwhelmed my remaining senses.

The ropes that bound me frightened me. That is a strange thing to say, but I felt such hatred from them and I knew they were not of this earth. They moved over my body like a sentient thing. They undulated and squeezed me when the pain seemed to lessen, always working to heighten their strength and my pain. I felt they drained me and left me helpless. I reached out again and again with my powers and felt nothing. I was in a void.

Unexpectedly I felt the ropes loosen ever so slightly and I felt a surge of hope. It was only a small movement but, when nothing further happened, I was dismayed and wondered at what it was. Then I felt the first tingling in my limbs and I sobbed in gratitude despite the gag and blindfold. The tingling became a feeling of my limbs on fire and I writhed against the bindings and strained to escape. The pain grew and grew, and I soon lost myself in it. There was no escaping the pain. It went on and on and remained constant in strength. At first, I was able to fight it mentally and push the pain and insanity away. Then it took hold of me and I was lost. Tumbling and twisting in the fear and pain I screamed into my gag, unable to move a finger. I focused on drawing breath through my nose into what little room remained in my compressed lungs. It was torture. My pain was causing snot to flow like water and I blew air hard through my nose over and over again to keep it clear. For once I was glad to be hanging with my face to the ground. With any other position, I would have drowned. With no warning, I felt the ropes tighten again and with relief, my limbs soon went numb and I lost consciousness for a time.

I woke, and the cycle repeated. This happened again and again, and I lost all sense of time. My sanity was almost gone. I lived for those moments when the ropes tightened, and my limbs went numb again. It was my only respite. That, and the loss of consciousness.

I have no idea how long I remained in the cycle before they gave me water. They removed the hood and opened my gag and placed a pan under my mouth. They shoved it into my face and, when I realised what it was, I tried to suck in as much water as I could and ended up with some in my lungs. I spasmed with coughs and they returned the gag. The hood was drawn over my head and the opening tied close to my neck. Between coughing and trying to draw air in through my nose I was sure I was going to suffocate. Their timing was perfect. I was unable to speak but could only focus on the water, clearing my lungs through my nose and breathing. My despair was almost complete. I could determine no scenario that saw me escape the bindings. I lost all hope. I lost myself to the pain, thirst and hunger. The isolation was complete, and I started to long for a quick end. My death would be welcomed if offered.

Despite my anguish, I was thankful I could at least breathe through my nose. Without a clear nose, I would have suffocated by now. And I could smell despite the hood over my head. It started small at first. I could smell a fire nearby but distant. Then more smells became noticeable. What little piss I had passed was strong to my nose and so was the smell of my own shit. What surprised me was after a time I could smell the men that had captured me, each of their smells sharp and distinctive. My sense of smell became alive to me and my world opened up.

I tried to smell everything I could around me. Hours and maybe days later passed without reckoning. I could start to form images of the world around me. I was still in the clearing. I was only a few feet from the ground. The two men were still alone and no one else had joined them. One was hurt and the other still strong. They were never together. There was a pattern to my world.

I remembered my life amongst the wolves and came to fully understand the world they lived in. It was a world of smells and it was wonderful. Hope blossomed inside me and my sanity snapped back into focus. The rope binding me tightened in response and I forced myself to relax as much as I could.

I imagined I could smell the rope. It was so very faint at first. It didn't smell like a normal rope should smell. It was rope but then something was alive within it. Something held captive by the rope. Metallic, like copper. The rope was vile, corrupted by something not natural and I shuddered in horror. I recoiled from it at first but, with little else to do, I found myself returning to it again and again. It blocked me. I found I could follow the rope up a ways until the thing bound to the rope stopped me with a feeling of cold hatred. It was like walking up to a cliff with no way up and over. It was frustrating. Its presence was always there. Vile, oily, and malevolent. I felt dirty just sensing it.

And then I felt the fool. All along I had been smelling campfires and the two men. I could sense everything through my sense of smell. The rope looked like it was the way to salvation and I had focused my effort and remaining energy on trying to get past it. It was a finger puzzle. The harder I fought the rope the stronger it resisted me. But that was all illusion. I had not placed myself in a finger puzzle. The rope was nothing.

All at once I smelled the tree I hung from. The entire world opened up to me and I saw my predicament. My nose became my eyes and the image of the clearing opened up to me. I hung from an old oak tree. The rope was wrapped around a thick branch and I could see where the bark had split and sap bled from the wound the rope made. The rope then travelled down to the roots of the tree where it was tied off. It was the root system that was the true tree. Everything above the ground is nothing more than the support system for the roots. The leaves breathe in the air and transfer strength from branch to trunk to root. I could sense the roots and the tree and, for hours, I pushed my awareness to the tree and pleaded for help and, finally, I felt the tree stir in awareness. My joy at this small tendril of awareness knew no bounds. My hope leapt into my heart and I cried in relief despite the gag and blindfold. Then, to my horror, I felt the tree dismiss me and turn away to other matters. The silence was so profound and so deep it almost shattered me completely. The withdrawal of the tree was such a traitorous act to me. I screamed in defiance at it and promised to hew it down when I escaped. I fell within myself and focused on keeping my nose clear. I was again completely alone.

Sometime later I was fed broth. My mouth and throat could barely swallow. I choked a couple of times and received no assistance from my captors. I choked and coughed. Drawing what little air I could into my lungs and trying to force the broth out with sharp coughs. I blacked out twice only to wake still fighting the liquid in my lungs. I wished for death at one point and stopped fighting it. I woke from the blackness to find myself still suspended and still in agony. The liquid had cleared my lungs and a few coughs later I could once again breathe much clearer. My lungs had betrayed me and let me live. The burning in my limbs was now commonplace, and I ignored the pain completely. It meant nothing to me.

At some point, I entered a trance-like state where all I did was count my breaths to pass the time. I stopped counting when the number lost all meaning to me and I would start again. I hung and waited. And waited. I watched the small world around me through my sense of smell and time lost all meaning. I was weak and not much remained to me that I cared about. I thought of my mother then and her face appeared to my memory so fresh and so remarkably beautiful that I cried against my bonds for hours holding the image central to my inner sight.

I miss you, mom. I'm sorry I didn't keep my promise. I let them find me. I didn't stay hidden. I miss you so much.

I sobbed again but fell asleep with her face still clear in my mind.

I woke from a nightmare of watching the world fold itself over until nothing was left but barren earth and stone. The foreign feeling of the weight of something on my back had woken me. I had just begun to figure out what was happening when the rope snapped, and I fell screaming for what felt like an eternity to land face first in the dirt. Trussed up as I was I rolled helplessly for a bit before coming to a stop on my side against something soft. I smelled wolf and dog and blood. The smells were very strong. I felt the pressing snout of an animal—a wolf? —trying to grasp something on my back and then I felt its front teeth start to work on the ropes that bound me. The rope writhed and squeezed harder against me and I felt its fear. The fear I felt from the rope fed my elation. I mentally urged the animal to hurry and, after an eternity, my arms were freed but I could not move them despite my best efforts. The teeth continued to work on the ropes and I felt something snap within the rope and its despair. I soon felt my knees slacken and, as the pressure of my knees against my chest was released, I drew my first deep breath in my lungs and marvelled at just how much air I could suck in. For a time, I revelled in the simple joy of breathing. My sense opened up, and I felt nature rejoice and lend me its strength. My head felt light and then the circulation hit my arms and legs and a blinding pain knocked me unconscious in an instant.

When I woke later, I found I could move my arms and hands but had no strong feeling other than a dull throbbing pain and I hadn't recovered any fine movement skills. Several fumbling attempts finally let me remove the hood and blindfold and the first thing I saw was the sightless eyes of one of the Jaipers guards staring back at me. A strange expression that I could not read was on his face. Horribly, I could see his throat had been savagely torn out. It was ghastly and only mere inches from my face. I could feel I was lying in blood. I tore my eyes away only to lock them on a large timber wolf sitting calmly near me, panting in the summer heat. Blood covered its maw. I saw him look from me to something behind me and I felt a head poke my back a little and, a second later, the head of a dog came into my view. It was a beautiful dog as dogs go. He was large and reminded me of the ones I typically saw working with sheep and the herders. He was grey and white—there being more grey than white. He looked pretty rough with thick matted fur and I could see he needed some attention and grooming. He licked my face enthusiastically and for some strange reason, I started to cry. The dog whimpered a little and licked my tears until I managed to get a hand up and stop him.

I struggled to get myself into a sitting position. After my energy ran out, I gave up but I had managed to roll myself away from the dead man beside me. I was grateful for that one blessing and I lay there exhausted. My limbs were throbbing and still not responding to my thoughts with any accuracy. I was very thirsty and hungry but knew I could wait a little longer if I had to. I could move my head though and, with an effort, managed to take in my whereabouts from my new vantage point.

I could see I was under a rather large oak tree in a clearing. This was the tree that had ignored me rather pointedly. A little way away from me was the corpse of the other guard, now with one hand wrapped in a thick bandage. From what little I could see I was certain his throat had been torn out, too. I looked over to the timber wolf and queried him and got a negative reply back. So then, not this wolf. Then I spied the other wolf lying dead on the ground just past the dead guard. A knife was buried in its head and I shuddered to think of the force of the blow required to pierce its skull. This wolf had died saving me from these two men and I had trouble coming to terms with it. It did not sit well with me that a life had given itself for mine.

I realised this wonderful wolf and the other one had probably saved my life. I had no idea where the dog came into this. I wished I could recover faster and then berated myself when I remembered my powers and I reached out to the earth and pulled energy in and started to heal myself. After a long period, I restored my arms and legs and stood at last on shaking legs and took stock of the area. The silence was intense and then I remembered the plugs in my ears and dug at the lumps and worked the first one free. The sounds of nature filled the air, and I smiled at the beauty of hearing once again. I removed the second lump and tossed them angrily into the bushes surrounding the clearing.

I looked at the men and then recognised them once I imagined their faces animated with life. Dead they were unrecognisable to me. These were the two guards who had stopped me at the gate in Jaipers. They had followed me this entire time. I felt a chill. It seemed I couldn't escape the fates. The assassin, the guards, the salt shop and now this capture. I was a wanted man for some reason. Not knowing why was consuming me and the need to find the manuscript Daukyns had hinted at became more important to me.

I looked at the dog who was sniffing the crotch of the dead man lying on the ground. "There will be more. I have to assume that. I'll never be safe until I can figure out what is going on."

The dog ignored me and moved over to bite at the rope on the ground. Now free of it I could sense it better. It was the opposite of life. It was imbued with rot and sickness. I reached out to the earth and drew strength and tried to wipe the rope clear, but my effort washed over the rope like it didn't exist. I frowned.

"That is not normal," I said to the dog. "I have to do something about this." I thought for a moment and realised I was in a sorry state. "Maybe later... when I'm stronger."

I took stock of myself: I was naked and covered everywhere with insect bites. The midges had drunk their fill from me over and over again until it seemed every inch of my skin was covered with angry, itching welts and scabs. The rope had left deeply infected grooves on my skin and I fingered them feeling the imprint of the rope. I was covered in my own filth, but I was now more or less used to the stench. Cleaning myself up was not one of my immediate priorities. What bothered me the most was the ache that had settled deep down within my bones, and I couldn't be more miserable. I knew I could attempt to heal myself more thoroughly later but only once I figured out just how safe I was.

The dog was moving from spot to spot in the clearing sniffing everything he could. Now and then he would return to my side and brush up against me to remind me he was there. Annoyingly he would continually try to sniff my ass and crotch. *My stink must be extreme*, I thought.

The whole time the wolf remained where he was watching me, or so I thought at first. Then I noticed he was watching the dog the entire time with only an occasional glance at me. I had been with wolves for many years and I was not afraid; however, this behaviour was not normal. Every time the dog would pass by the wolf, the wolf would dip his head. The dog was more alpha than the wolf. This was not the normal way of things but I had no desire to figure it out at the moment.

I looked over at the dead wolf and my guilt flooded over me. I felt terrible that a life had been given to provide me with mine. I was honoured by the death of the wolf to save me but knew his death in his pack would be regarded as simply a loss. It was merely a death which came about from the wolf's lack of ability to survive. He would be mourned by his pack, but he would soon be forgotten. It was the way with wolves. Only the living were honoured. The dead were soon forgotten. I would not forget though. I gave his death meaning, and I held on to that.

I turned to the wolf and reached out to let him know I was impressed by his strength, prowess and ability to fight the bad humans and thanked him for his help rescuing me. The wolf held my gaze for a moment and then quietly stood, turned, and trotted quickly into the trees and disappeared. I sighed. Wolves led a simple life but without all the hang-ups and restrictions humans apply to their society. Why he helped me, I would probably never know, but I was certain the dog had something to do with it.

I remembered communicating briefly to the tree what seemed like days ago. I looked over at it and reached out but only sensed its life force and its tie to nature all around it. Its roots dug deep and wide in the forest all around and the tree filled the balance here. It was staggering, the influence the tree held in this quiet glade. It touched all aspects of the area. There was no awareness of me from the tree. I remembered the tree turning away from me when I needed help the most. I put an image of an axe in my head and me striking the tree and that woke it up. The dog turned and growled at me. Fear washed over me in waves and I felt ashamed at what I had done. I reached out and tried to soothe the tree and after a while I was successful. It was not one of my proudest moments. I sent an apology to the tree, but it had again moved away from its awareness.

"Sorry," I said meekly to the dog, and I found it hard to speak with my dry mouth. I needed water and food.

The dog tilted his head at me and then went back to sniffing all around the clearing. I watched him for a while admiring his lines. I did not know the breed but I could see through his matted fur he was a strong and agile dog.

I remained standing in the clearing drawing strength into me. I looked quickly at the two men and finally noticed their identical black boots. With a sinking feeling, I recognised them. This was all some strange conspiracy, and I knew not what my part in it was, only that I was in the middle of it. What linked the coin, Bill Burstone, the assassin, my powers and the druids? It all had to be related. And I hadn't a clue as to why or what. I stood in the clearing shaking, looking in disbelief at the slain men who would have done me such great harm and I finally collapsed onto the ground and wept in frustration and fear. I was not a very strong person. I wanted nothing more than to simply escape into obscurity and put all this nonsense behind me. I looked over at the dog and wished I could trade places. The simple life of a dog for all this trouble. I would welcome the chance.

Sensing my watching, the dog stopped and looked excitedly at me, barking softly and then, with a leap, disappeared through an opening in the bushes. I watched the opening for a moment and then laughed as the dog poked his head back through and, again, barked softly at me, turned, and disappeared once more. The meaning was clear. I groaned and stumbled after him on my weak legs. I felt as if I was walking on someone else's legs. I would tell my leg to move forward and, after a delay, it would obey. I must have looked a sight as I followed after the dog through the thick bushes.

In a short time, he led me to another clearing where the two men had camped. A small fire was central to the clearing with a couple of logs for seats placed nearby. After a quick search, I found my backpack empty of its contents lying at the end of one of the log benches next to my bedroll. The contents were gone, and I looked around for my stuff. I saw pieces of my equipment lying in piles. They had taken my food and combined it with their own and I hastened over and started cramming whatever food I could find into my mouth and I sucked water out of my water skins. I was so hungry and so thirsty. After a time I managed to stop myself before I was sick.

I lay back and looked around the site. It was a mess. It looked to be mostly my own gear. My herbs were damaged and torn apart and they were wilted and no longer potent and so, with regret, I threw them into the bushes. Everything else was missing. My pots, my tin cup and kettle were used but blackened with soot and greasy with the remains of what looked like a poorly skinned rabbit. My flour and oats had been poured out onto the ground for some reason and ruined. My teas were thankfully intact, and I gathered them up. Nothing I had owned had mattered to these men except I was certain I would find the journal, my money, potions, sickle and coin somewhere nearby. My clothes lay in a pile nearby and I remembered my nakedness. I quickly dressed wincing at the feel of the rough cloth against my wounds. I had to find my other gear, and I looked around.

These men had travelled light, and I reasoned they must have hidden their gear. After a small search, I found two small waist packs hidden under a fallen tree and I happily rummaged through their meagre possessions. In one of the packs I found my sickle and coin and with a sense of relief, I returned the small pouch around my neck. I also found my Life Salt and Daukyns' journal. I flipped open the journal and found the notes he had left me still intact and I wondered if they could even read. The rest of the contents were just some hard road rations, water in a small skin, and some minor equipment such as a flint, a wire saw and my own healing ointments and potions. Seeing my own ointments and potions placed in their packs made me pause but I took them all the same. No sense wasting them and I doubt they tampered with them. The potions were worth a lot of coins.

Lying next to the waist packs I found my own black boots and claimed them back but I stuffed them in my backpack. Lastly, lying next to each pack I was surprised to find two leather whips. They were small, too small to whip anything in practice and I didn't understand their purpose. They each had a leather handle attached to several small whip strands only about a foot long each. Each strand was leather and ended with stone beads. Something about them disgusted me and I discarded them. I wanted nothing to do with their equipment.

I stood up with my hands on my hips. Nothing in the packs hinted at where the men had come from or why they had followed and captured me and then tried to harm me. It was frustrating not knowing what was going on. I felt like I was lost in a whirlwind of events. These men wore the same boots as the assassin in Jaipers and the reaction of the Belger salt shop owners hinted to me they were somehow tied to the Church. It was all I knew.

I used my senses to locate a likely source of water and I found water plants nearby and small minnows. The dog joined me and soon we found a cool, clear stream and I eagerly cleaned myself up. I stripped down and washed my clothes with my soap and laid them out to dry. The dog busied himself with biting at the water and growling at imagined threats and his antics kept me amused. He would stop now and then and make sure I was watching him. He was like a small child and my heart warmed to him. Eventually, I ended up sitting in the middle of the stream and scrubbed the filth off my body with the sand off the bottom. I could sense the minnows swimming all around and enjoyed the serenity and took my time.

Once I was cleaned up my head felt clearer. I studied the dog and, using my powers, cleared the fleas and lice away with will alone and watched with some disbelief at the sheer numbers of insects that leapt and fell away to hide in the long grass. The dog growled at a few he spotted but then sat and cocked his head at me. He looked like he couldn't believe what had happened.

"Yes," I replied to his questioning look. "All gone, now hold still for a bit, dog."

I reached out with my senses and found all the bite marks and healed them. I found a couple of ticks and urged them away and they fell clear. The dog whimpered with relief and I smiled. I could easily make out the hundreds of nits in the fur and was tempted to crush them with my power but even the thought of it resulted in a feeling of nausea and I stopped the thought immediately. I needed to clear them away the hard way.

It took the better part of half the day, but I used my knife and powers to groom the dog and clear up all the matted hair. The dog, at my urging, remained still and patiently waited out the treatment but he would steal a lick at my face if I put it too close to his snout. I then crushed all the remaining nits by hand, using my power to locate them and then using the old tried-and-true method of crushing them between finger and nail. It wasn't an abuse of my powers but it did take a long time to clear them all away. Satisfied, I leaned back and admired the dog. He glowed with health now and he seemed to hold his head higher.

"There," I said smugly. "All done. Now, what do I call you, hmm?"

The dog just looked at me and cocked his head again. I think at that point I realised I had bonded with this dog. I looked back at the dog and reminded myself dogs and wolves don't need names. When I was with the wolves, they used smell to identify others. Smells were names. But not so for people— people need names for their dogs. So, whatever name I came up with, it would only matter to me. And, I realised, I didn't need to decide now. It could wait.

* * *

I returned to the guard's campsite dressed in my dried clothes and made a small fire and found comfort in returning to a pattern of normal activity. I gave the dog some of the meagre meat I had recovered and then made myself some lentil soup and tea. Soon the food in my belly drew my eyelids down, and I collapsed on my hastily laid out bedroll and slept the sleep of the dead.

When I woke it was morning. I felt the unfamiliar form of the dog curled up tight against me and I smiled. I relished the feeling of security of having a dog by my side and I remained still so as not to disturb him. It reminded me of my days with the wolves. I would be by myself most of the time and sleep where I felt safe. I would wake with one or two wolves pressed up against me like the dog was now.

As I lay there, I took stock of my condition with my powers. I explored my numerous bites and pushed the liquid that was causing the itch out through the bite marks. I knitted the bites closed and calmed the swollen areas and then basked in the absence of itching. Now with the itching gone, I could tell just how bad it had been. I don't know why I hadn't fixed myself earlier. The infections from the rope burns were actually a simpler matter and in time my skin was unmarked and back to normal. I was getting better at using my powers. They took far less thought and more of just a focused will. Intuitively I knew what needed to be done within my body. I also did not feel as drained as I used to. I was now able to use my powers and simultaneously draw from the earth. I was pleased with my progress and I sensed the earth was pleased, too.

I could almost no longer ignore the need to pee, but I opted to remain there for a little while longer. The events of the past few days were still foremost in my thoughts and would remain so for a long time. It was not long ago that I had survived the attack by the assassin. I had to be sure I was whole in mind and body and so I methodically went through the events and assigned blame where it belonged. I would not be the victim this time. One thing was certain, I had to focus on understanding my powers and how they worked. I couldn't be the victim again and Jergen and Munsten offered the greatest hope I had of finding the truths I needed. Since the night outside Jaipers at my camp when the assassin had nearly killed me I had been out of control. I knew it wasn't my fault, but I could tell I was suffering from the results. I was reminded of a phrase Daukyns would say sometimes. He said: "There are in nature neither rewards nor punishments, there are consequences". I never understood that until now.

I found determination easier to arrive at than I expected and, feeling smug, I nudged the dog. Dog raised his head, startled, and looked around with confusion plain on his face. It was such a human expression that I laughed and the dog immediately focused on me, darted his head forward, and licked furiously at my face. I pushed him away, sputtering, and sat up. Already I could see dogs were much different from wolves. They cared more for one thing. Especially about people. I looked at this strange dog and wondered again what he could be doing out here with the wolves. Dogs and wolves did not mix. He was a puzzle.

"Right you, dog," I said sternly. "Let's break our fast and get cleaned up for the road, shall we?"

The dog, now sitting up, lolled a long tongue out of his mouth and snorted, his tail thumping on the ground.

"I'll take that as a yes," I laughed and rubbed his head as he chased my hand with his tongue.

Five

On the Road to Jergen, 900 A.C.

I HAD BUILT up a small fire, boiled tea, and made oatmeal from what I could salvage from the ground. It was a lovely meal, and I found myself relaxing. Returning to old habits gave me comfort. While I was finishing my tea, the dog came whining into the clearing with the rope in its mouth. He dragged it to the edge of the fire and dropped it out of his mouth. The dog started tearing up tufts of grass and I realised he was trying to clear the taste from his mouth.

I tried to sense the rope again and recoiled at the horrible feeling it gave off. I looked at the fire and stoked it with more wood and then quickly gathered the rope and tossed it on the fire. The rope emitted a deafening high pitched keening sound, and I collapsed to the ground holding my hands clamped to my ears. It was an ethereal scream, and it seemed to reach into the core of my being. The dog was on the ground pawing at its ears and after what seemed an eternity the rope burst into flame and the sound cut off.

I lay on my back panting and the dog did much the same. I sat up and stared at the remains of the rope. Black oily smoke drifted up into the air and the smell was horrible: not unlike what I imagined a burning rotten corpse would smell like. I decided then I needed to take the time to try to do something with the two dead men and the dead wolf. It was the right thing to do and Reeve Comlin in Jaipers would approve. I also knew this was going to be easier said than done.

I took my time clearing up the site and washing my pots. I packed my backpack and looked around the small campsite before returning down the path to the clearing. When I arrived at the edge of the clearing, I stood there for a long time staring at the bodies. They looked so fragile there. They were people who no longer breathed, and the lack of chest movement gave them a sense of not being right. They were too still. Flies were now buzzing thickly in the air but, thankfully, I couldn't smell the sickly-sweet smell of rot from the bodies—it was too soon, but it wouldn't be long with the summer heat. These men had hunted me and strung me up like a pig to be drained. I had done nothing to them. Or, to anyone. I was a young man trying to earn a living in a quiet corner of the world. They were to blame. Not me.

I stood there and did a bit of soul-searching as I looked down on them. I went from rage to anger to sadness. As much as I hated them somewhere they must have mothers who loved them and would never know how they died. They deserved some measure of respect despite their treatment of me. I settled on feeling pity.

It took me a bit of time to get the nerve to finally approach the men and even longer to touch them. I had never touched a dead person before. At least not intentionally, I thought. Having the assassin fall on me that time didn't count. This was me touching them on purpose and it repelled me and filled me with trepidation. They stared sightlessly and unblinkingly, and I found their open eyes frightened me more than anything else.

I slowly became aware of the sense of confusion from the earth about my fears. I frowned, finding it strange the earth should be sensing me so keenly. I think I knew at some level the earth was watching me all the time now. Its confusion was interesting, and I realised the earth was trying to teach me something. I suppose death means little to nature. We all die and return to the earth, don't we? I grimaced and tried to accept that but couldn't. Death represented to me only the tragic loss of life. I sighed. The truth was I wanted to be a healer and being a healer meant death would always be part of my life and work. I sensed acceptance from the earth and I moved to each man and closed his eyes. They were oddly cold to the touch. At least they wouldn't be staring at me now, I admitted to myself, and I did feel better.

I made a quick search of their pockets and found they each carried a red gemstone. They were exactly like what the assassin in Jaipers had carried. I pulled my small pouch from around my neck and added them to the sickle and coin. I was keeping them until I understood what they represented.

Remembering how the Reeve had dealt with the assassin I grudgingly stripped off their clothes and put their black boots into my backpack. I was startled to see multiple scars across their backs. Lines and lines of angry red scar tissue stood out in stark contrast to the rest of their skin. I could see a few lines were recent and immediately thought of the two small whips I had found with their possessions. Why would they whip themselves, or each other? It made no sense. I had to bury these men, and the wolf, and I had no digging tool. I could build a cairn, but it would take days to gather the rocks needed.

I stood with my hands on my hips looking down at the men and imagined two large holes for them. I shot an inquiry to the tree on a whim and was startled when I felt joyous acceptance. The earth suddenly boiled around the men and I saw roots writhing and loosening the soil around the bodies. Slowly the men were pulled into the earth and they disappeared from sight leaving only the disturbed earth to mark where they had been.

Dog ran over and sniffed quickly all over the new graves and then, grinning up at me, raised a leg and let loose a stream of urine to land expertly on both graves of the men.

"Dog! Stop that! Have some respect," I said, but my laugh gave me away.

I couldn't help myself and let myself laugh in earnest. The stress of the past few days seemed to melt away from me and I welcomed the tears of laughter as they escaped me. I knelt and pulled Dog into my embrace and murmured thanks into his ear. I felt the laughter in Dog in return and stood feeling whole. Dog and I stayed that way for a time before I saw the corpse of the wolf nearby and I stiffened.

"That wolf died saving me, Dog. It sacrificed its life for mine."

Dog whined.

"I spent a long time with wolves, did you know? I know a lot about them. I know, for example, they would not understand my feelings on this. The wolf they knew was gone. They probably already mourned him and moved on. That's their way. The wolf they knew is gone, and what remains is a part of nature and is returned to the earth."

I patted the head of the wolf and thanked him silently. After a moment, I rose and hoisted my backpack on my shoulders and squared it.

"Alright, Dog," I said turning to my new companion. "Let's hit the road. We have a long way to go to get to Jergen." I sensed Dog's agreement, and he moved a few feet in one direction before stopping and looking back at me.

I looked over at Dog, smiled, and pointed in the other direction. "That way, Dog."

Craobh

Dog lowered his head and walked past me in the direction I pointed and disappeared into the brush.

"Oh, and you're called Dog now, did you know that?" I yelled at where he had disappeared. A soft woof was the reply, and I felt the acceptance of the name. I walked over and placed a hand on the tree and gave thanks. The tree ignored me.

* * *

Dog and I walked at an easy pace for the rest of the day and stayed well clear of the road, keeping to the trees and hills. Eventually, the trees became sparse and ahead of us, I could see grasslands and flowers growing from horizon to horizon. I could see the river a good distance away at times and contented myself with making my way farther and farther away from the graves of the men. Admittedly, I enjoyed being amongst the trees and fields more so than on the road. The solitude was welcome and knowing I would not run into caravans or brigands this far from the road relaxed me. I watched as Dog loped ahead of me and gave chase to rabbits. He would return to me for praise before bounding off once again. He never barked, and I was thankful.

Once during the day, I sensed the wolf who had saved me keeping pace nearby for a spell. I sent it thanks and felt a sense of bemused acceptance. Later in the day, I spied the wolf squirming on his back in front of Dog, belly exposed, looking excited and happy. Something passed between them and I felt a small mixture of sorrow from Dog. Whatever their association, it was clear the wolf and dog had been companions of a sort. Perhaps, like me, Dog had been adopted by the wolves. I would have to ask him later about it. Whatever his history was, I owed him some respect if the wolf recognised his position in the pack as being Alpha.

I soon discovered having a travelling companion made all the difference in the world. Dog would range ahead and report back to me when the way was clear, and this allowed me to relax my vigilance. Some part of me knew the men I needed to fear were now gone, and the way was clear for me all the way to Jergen. I thought more and more about what I would discover there in the book I sought. My powers had been growing, and I had become much more comfortable with them.

I seemed to be in constant communion with the earth now and felt the female nature of her. She nurtured and protected, but I knew there was much more to her. I was only seeing a part.

"Dog, is she uncaring?"

As soon as I asked I knew I was not correct. She cared, just not in a way I understood yet.

"Maybe we don't have words for how she works? What do you think?" Dog just stared at me. "She cares nothing for one person's life. She cares only about the whole. But. But! Of all that she does care about, she also cares for the one, but almost accidentally. Right? Always the whole and the whole is her." I looked to Dog, but he was watching a flight of birds wing by.

This was proving difficult for me to put into words. To people, each life mattered. I don't think the earth cared either way. The earth knew a person lived but would die, needed to die, and cared not when.

"With exceptions in only the most specific cases," I said to Dog, and he turned to look at me. "Such as me. She cared that I lived, needed me to live, but it was for purely selfish reasons and nothing personal at all. She sent the wolves and you to free me." I felt a sense of humour from the earth at this thought and again I was perplexed. It seemed I would never figure her out. But I was close to the truth of it. I felt it.

Just then, the earth focused on me. I felt small and yet part of a larger whole. *How odd*, I thought and felt the hairs stand up on the back of my neck. My life was never going to be simple ever again. I wasn't sure if I should be happy or sad about that. After a time, her attention moved away, and I released the breath I had been unknowingly holding.

* * *

I opted to avoid Laketown altogether. I came to the decision through a bizarre conversation with myself, Dog and the earth. Recent events had me trusting people less and less and the thought of entering a busy town had me on edge and worried. I was only a few days out of my capture area and Dog and I were having a lovely dinner of rabbit and mixed greens. Dog had caught the rabbit. He had been totally surprised when he had clamped the poor thing in his jaws. He had killed it clean and dropped it at his feet and stared at it looking a little pleased with himself, to be honest. I sensed it and came over and praised him for his hunting prowess. He ran around the camp for a bit in excitement and would dart in to snap at the carcass as I cleaned and trussed the rabbit. After multiple interruptions, I managed to roast it for our evening dinner. It was a big fat juicy one and the smell of the roasting rabbit had Dog drooling a puddle by the fire where he sat and watched it cook.

Dog had the first taste, for it had been his kill. I had enough to satiate me and gave Dog the rest. He crunched the whole thing up in no time and then fell asleep and dreamed of catching more if I could judge by the movement of his paws. It had been a glorious day.

The next morning, I packed up the camp and started talking to Dog. At some point in the past few days, Dog had become my companion, and we talked all the time now. Only a few weeks ago I would have thought myself insane to accept it so simply. But today I had powers the earth gave me and I could heal people in miraculous ways. I think my mother would be proud of me.

"So maybe we should avoid Laketown," I started saying as I tightly rolled my bedroll.

"I mean, what's in Laketown that I truly need?" I said a second later. "I have all the food I need. Except for flour and oats and stuff, but I am okay. You can hunt rabbits and I can forage for greens and berries no problem. I just have to sense them, you know?" I glanced over to Dog for agreement and I was surprised to see him sitting there listening to me.

I waited but Dog said nothing and so I continued.

"Who knows who is lying in wait for me there? More of these black boots, probably."

Dog continued to say nothing, but he did seem to lean back and settle on his haunches. I took that as a positive sign.

"Don't get me wrong, Dog," I said while securing the bedroll to the bottom of my backpack. "I'm not trying to talk myself into not going. It just seems prudent."

Dog snorted, and I looked at him in surprise and narrowed my eyes. "What?" I asked. "You don't think so? What would happen if I ran into more of those thugs? Huh? I was lucky the last time. I could easily have died if not for you and the wolves."

Dog lolled his huge tongue out of his mouth and panted at me with what I was sure was a glint of humour in his eye. The earth seemed to focus in on the conversation as well.

"What? You didn't think that was luck?" I asked and reached out with my senses to Dog. I sensed his agreement. Not luck then.

"What then if not luck?" I asked out loud as I adjusted the straps of my backpack.

I sensed from Dog a calling. He was called by something. The earth seemed amused.

"Oh great, so the earth just called you and you came, is that it?"

An image of the wolves came to me then and I could see them running across some plains with the moon high in the night sky. They had run for a couple of days nonstop. I could almost feel the fatigue in their stride as they ran to where I was tied up and their wild sense of urgency. It was a pretty specific image, and I felt the Earth more closely now. Her focus always seemed so vague and distant, but not now. For whatever reason, she felt it important to make sure I understood what had happened. I looked to Dog to see him scratching some itch on his cheek.

"What's so important about me that the earth would send help?"

Dog looked at me and said nothing.

"If I was so important why didn't she stop me from being captured in the first place? Hmm? How about that?"

Dog barked and ran off after a noise in the grass.

* * *

Dog and I made great speed across the land. Dog seemed to be able to find the easiest paths for me to take and, more than once, he had come running out of the bushes or trees to conduct mock attacks on me. Invariably they were diversions to have me move down a preferred path. Once I recognised this, I spoke at length to him about it and he had strolled patiently alongside me until I was done before bolting off into the distance. I had no idea where he was finding the energy but he was making me tired just watching him.

Dog and I were now a team. I was not sure when or how it had happened but we had become inseparable. I found myself conversing with him as I would any other companion and the truly strange part was I was certain Dog understood me completely. I was scared to put it to the test and merely accepted it as I had all the other changes in my life these past few weeks. I spoke, and he listened. His previous owner must have taught him well.

Jergen was only a week away and the closer I came, the more apprehensive I was becoming. It's not that I feared the town. The simple matter was I stood out in towns. And, after the attack by the two men, I feared exposure. But the lure of the manuscript drew me ever closer. And so it was with a weird conflict in my heart that I closed the distance to the city.

Dog kept ranging far ahead and then waiting patiently for me to catch up before loping off again. I would spy him leaping over a small dun after a rabbit or some such scared and witless animal. I resisted an urge to extend my senses and merely watched as Dog chased his prey. It was entertaining and oddly therapeutic.

Jergen would be a challenge for me. I had never been in a city. I was not comfortable around people and I worried about standing out and drawing attention surrounded by so many people and buildings. I thought through possible scenarios and came up with tales to explain my travel. Always I came back to what I was comfortable with: a simple man who sold and traded herbs and made potions. *Perhaps that is what I should just remain*, I thought. *Perhaps I should gather some herbs to sell.* I only had a few bunches on me and I felt I could spend time gathering more.

I spent the afternoon gathering dill, thyme and oregano, and some other herbs. This time, using the sickle, I found I sensed the plants more intimately. I asked for parts of them and explained why I needed them. In response, the leaves and stems would part from the plant and into my waiting hands. Soon I found I had no need for the sickle and I put it back into the small pouch that hung from my neck. With my senses, I found I could locate any plant near me. My range kept growing, and I had to rein myself in to keep my senses from being flooded. Soon I could think of a specific plant, locate it, approach, make my request, and pick the donated stems and leaves up from beside the plant. It excited me but I felt that I missed the old way. It had been more personal. In only an hour, I had managed to resupply most of my lost herbs. I admired the quality, it exceeded what I had been able to do in Jaipers. I made my way back to Dog, and I started telling him of the herbs I had gathered when we pushed through some bushes and unexpectedly burst clear to stand blinking in the bright sunshine next to the main road leading to Jergen.

I heard a shout of alarm near me and turned to see a couple standing protectively together. The man had placed himself between the woman and I and had his head turned toward me. Dog stood beside me and wagged his tail and gave a polite bark of welcome.

"My apologies," I said by way of introduction. "I'm sorry I startled you. I was just gathering some herbs nearby." I held up a bunch of dill for emphasis. "I'm quite safe, I assure you. My name is Will."

The woman glanced at the man before her and then nodded. He moved beside her and I could see she carried an infant slung across her chest. "Hello, young man. Pleased to meet you. You did give us a scare jumping out of the woods like that! We're with the caravan, don't you know. Well, we follow the caravan I should say. Are you heading to Jergen?"

"Aye, ma'am. I am."

"Ma'am? How old dyed think I am, ya wee scamp?" She laughed, and it sounded like bells. "Come we us, ya hear? We're just around the bend of the road. Ya looks like ya could use some company."

Over the next few days, I joined and stayed with many fellow travellers to Jergen. They had naturally just come together for mutual safety and, as we met up with others, they joined the group. The threat of highwaymen was always on everyone's mind and there was safety in numbers. We were an odd bunch of people. Just up ahead of me was a small caravan made up of two carts. They were slow moving with the weight of their cargo—iron ore, according to the owner—and allowed those of us who walked to easily keep pace with it. The owner was a proud man, sure of his business, a braggart with an overly loud voice. And yet we could all see he could only afford two mercenaries to guard his cargo and by the looks of them, they had come cheaply. The man rubbed me wrong—his avarice was almost visible for all to see and when I examined his thick yellow aura, it made me feel oily and dirty. I couldn't fail to notice how Dog kept his distance from the caravan. Most of us did. I felt I should probably do the same.

Anyone could see the two guards he had hired were sallow and filthy. They had taken a long measure of me until it became almost uncomfortable. A tension filled the air, and I was at a loss to explain what was happening. Dog made a commotion, and the guards turned their gaze to what Dog had chosen to chase down with excessive noise. I scurried away from the men, my memory of my capture giving strength to my speed of departure. I sensed a bit of mirth from Dog and, when I looked his way, he was staring at me, tongue lolling in an unmistakably cheeky laugh. He was pleased with himself.

Since then I had remained a goodly distance behind their cart and out of sight as much as possible. I chose instead to spend my time walking with the young mother who had met me when I had emerged onto the road. She and her husband were named Rebecca and Kennit, and their newborn child was Euan. The mother had their son slung across her chest in the way of south Turgany. I enjoyed their company. They were happy and eager to the life which awaited them in Jergen. Dog liked them too, and that was enough for me. Dog also seemed to want to constantly smell and lick the child which delighted the young mother and wee Euan for some reason. We had spent the last few nights sharing a campfire. Dog had hovered close to the child the entire time, and the parents had trusted Dog unconditionally and without hesitation. He had an immediate positive effect on people. He was a large dog and was not afraid to get into everyone's business, smelling this and that with abandon and sneaking in a nose lick if you weren't careful. He was an expert at getting food out of people. I had no idea how he managed to eat so much.

I, on the other hand, had found another way to gain acceptance. I had provided the mother with a tonic to settle their child's stomach the first night. They had warned me the child would cry at night and the others were in constant complaint. I knew what I needed and with my senses had found both plants nearby. The ginger root and peppermint plants had appeared as bright lights to my vision and led me to them. I mashed the leaves and roots together and boiled the mash in water. I ran it through a cloth, added what little honey I had left, and the mother spoon-fed the liquid to the wee bairn. The poor wee thing was awful colicky and my tonic had eased the pain. I showed the parents how I made it and gave them supplies of their own. In the end, my tonic had given the couple their first quiet, uninterrupted sleep in a long time. Afterwards, they had proclaimed me a healer and everyone befriended me.

"Yer a druid, you are," she told me quietly the second night.

"A what?" I asked.

"A druid, sure as you are," She gave me a knowing wink. "My gran was a druid. She could heal all sorts of people. As soon as you made that wee tonic for my wee bairn I knew it. You've the gift, lad. Druid could commune with nature. Heal people. Tend the plants and the like. Same as you."

I sat in silence and thought of the book and what I knew so far. A druid may be what I was. Something resonated in that with me. The image of my mum smiling at me when I was a child came unbidden, and I blinked. Whatever I was, I could heal people, and that was all that mattered to me.

"Yer secrets are safe with us, Will," she said and patted my knee. "Kennit knows as well. He grew up next door to my gran and me mum. By the Word, the whole village knew, I think. But nowadays—probably wise to keep it tae yourself, eh?"

I nodded. To be honest, I wasn't sure I believed her. I only had a few pages torn from a manuscript that hinted at something larger. Draoi or druids, either way, it lay before me. I heeded Rebecca's word of caution and pretended to be what I truly longed to be: a healer. I then spent most of my time gathering herbs and such and showing people how to mix remedies and how to care for a wound by first cleaning it and then wrapping it in clean cloths. Simple things that most seemed not to know.

By good fortune, I found out Kennit was a cook by trade and he was hoping for work in Jergen. Over the course of the nights and days, he and I shared our recipes and talked about herbs and spices at length. He was amazed at my knowledge and he gained much from our talks. He and I shared the chore of cooking for everyone and it was a constant point of discussion for our group as we strolled toward Jergen. Meals at night became a special event for everyone.

Soon our little group was joined by more road travellers until we numbered about two dozen in all. We talked, and shared tales, and laughed at some jest or another. It was a relaxing time, and I enjoyed the company. I grew more comfortable talking to people and joined in the laughter when I could understand the jape. I tended to people's hurts and scrapes and used my powers in subtle ways, usually mixing it with my unguents. I learned to simply smile when they brought up just how young I was to be able to heal so well.

Everyone marvelled at Dog and how well trained he seemed to be. He quickly found out how to entice treats from the travellers and was shameless in his efforts. He was also fond of catching rabbits and game hens and he managed to bring in enough meat for all of us to enjoy. He certainly earned his stay and the treats. The guards were impressed with Dog and offered me coin for him. It took several firm no's before they finally stopped asking.

Despite keeping a social distance, the caravan crew provided a large cooking cauldron and Kennit and I filled it each night with shares of food from everyone willing to contribute. It soon became a communal meal each evening. Last evening, after we had trussed and skinned Dog's brace of rabbits, Rebecca and Kennit had trusted me with their child and they had walked off hand in hand to spend some quiet time together outside the light of the campfires. The older couples with us made some pointed comments and had everyone laughing at the couple's combined blush. It took me a little while to understand and then it had been my turn to blush. The laughter didn't stop their hurried pace to move down closer to the river's edge and out of sight.

I soon found myself with their son held awkwardly in my arms and staring down into his eyes with his rapt attention on my own. I held his gaze and felt an odd sense of kinship with the child. Dog poked his head and gave the boy a solid tongue slobbering before I could push his snout away. The baby squealed in laughter and tried to grab Dog's fur. We stayed staring at each other for some time: the child in my arms, quiet and not fussing, and Dog sitting pressed up tight against me, tongue lolling out his mouth. It was a peaceful hour. I found myself singing a quiet song that came to mind and a few of the people around the fire pushed each other and tilted their chins in our direction. They didn't think I had noticed, but I had. Little happened around me now that I was not aware of. I was connected to the world around me and could extend that sense out quite a distance if I put my mind to it. I politely ignored the others and simply contented myself with keeping this perfect moment alive as long as I possibly could. I raised my voice a little and sang the song.

Wee child of life,
Let troubles fade from sight,

Beneath the starry night
Sleep safe from any strife.

From leaf to branch,
And branch to stem,
And stem to root,
Harmony, balance, life.

Wipe worries from your sight,
Safe in my arms tonight.
Bundled up warm and tight,
Until the bright of the morrow light.

From leaf to branch,
And branch to stem,
And stem to root,
Harmony, balance, life.

In the end, we were interrupted when Dog started sneezing repeatedly and I soon discovered the baby had soiled himself rather spectacularly. People came by to slap my back and compliment me on the song. None had heard it before and I was not sure from whence it came. They pointed out the obvious to me: the child had soiled himself. Not knowing what to do in the slightest I suffered the stink until the parents returned, red-cheeked and smiling. They merely laughed at my expression of horror and cleaned him up with a speed I could never hope to match, and soon we were enjoying a light meal I prepared with Dempster's special touch. Everyone pitched in an ingredient or two and were eager for their share and a taste.

During the preparation, many argued emotionally with me about using tomatoes, for most thought them poison. Kennet and I laughed and took bites from the beautiful red fruit to prove them wrong. Some still watched us for signs of sickness. It was funny how some people simply refused to believe something even when it was thrust in front of them. Most caved quickly and the rabbit and tomato stew was emptied in no time at all. The flatbread I made was wiped across every surface until the pot hardly needed a cleaning.

I made tea and an elderly couple waited close by with their cups held ready. Each night I made a special tea for them that eased the ache in their joints and now they eagerly awaited it. I had examined them when they had asked me a few days ago. The people we travelled with thought of me as a healer and I was glad to help when they asked. It made me feel useful and needed. My powers showed me what I knew already, their joints were worn with age and there was nothing I could do for them but ease their pain. I had given them a small mixture of tea leaves and spoken to them quietly about how to duplicate it. I doubted they would manage to find herbs of the same potency as mine and warned them they would likely need to drink it most of the time and in larger quantities.

With the mercenary guards near us and watching for highwaymen, most of us quickly went to sleep and passed an uneventful night of welcomed rest. And so it had been over the past few days. We got to know each other fairly well for strangers. I managed to distract their own questions about who I was and why I was headed to Jergen. They gave up trying after a few attempts. I think they understood the need for privacy and they respected mine. Everyone had secrets. All that mattered to them was if I could provide healing and wonderful meals. In truth, it was all that mattered to me as well.

Before I knew it, we could smell the smoke from Jergen. While the trees along the road still hid the town from our sight, the unmistakable smell of wood smoke, cooking, and human waste could not be hidden. Dog had smelled it first and had lain down and rubbed at his nose. I couldn't understand what had been bothering him until a short hour later I too felt like rubbing the acrid smell from my nose. Jaipers was a very small town, and it had its smells. Jergen, on the other hand, was a city and had all the waste and the stink of thousands upon thousands of human beings. The city was so large. I couldn't imagine all those people living inside its walls. Hundreds of thousands of people lived here. It was more than my imagination could handle and I took a step backwards. The others laughed at my discomfort. Dog and I shared a long look, and I shook my head. Civilisation was dirty, I decided then.

We approached the gate, and I was shocked to find it unguarded. I had worried myself over the entrance to Jergen for I had thought I would have to face an interrogation from guards. We merely passed through and then I said farewell to my travelling companions as we separated down different roads. Rebecca and Kennit gave me a quick hug and held their son, Euan, up to me to say goodbye.

I found myself staring at those eyes again and then something passed between us. Or I should say something passed from me to him. A measure of my magic touched the child and his eyes gleamed for an instance like a flash of bright sunshine. I immediately felt a strong sense of approval from Dog. The couple glanced at one another and I thought perhaps they too felt something. But then the moment passed, and they waved farewell and disappeared into the throng of people bustling through the dirt streets. I smiled to myself. Soon they would find the bag of Life Salt from Belger tucked inside the child's swaddling wraps.

I soon stood in the street with Dog pressed up against my leg, watching people split around us as if we were stones in a river. We stood in the shadow of the towering buildings lining the street and I shivered. Despite having my feet firmly on the earth, I felt Jergen was removed from reality. Perhaps a separation from nature was unavoidable with large gatherings of people. I felt out of my element and I reached out and placed my hand on Dog's warm head and the feeling diminished a little.

I knew nothing about this city except what Reeve Comlin had told me. He had shown me where to stay and, with my memory of the map he had shown me forefront in my mind, I cautiously started to walk the streets to find the Purple Rose Inn. Dog walked beside me and I kept my hand firmly on him the entire way. The city was overwhelming and Dog didn't leave my side. He seemed okay with all the noise and bustle.

Jergen was huge, larger than any town or city had any right to be. The buildings dwarfed those from Jaipers and they crowded one upon another with barely the width of a man's shoulders between them. I shuddered to think what lay in those dark alleys—the smell alone kept me clear. The smell of sweat, smoke and who knew what else soon had my eyes watering and nose running. I hated Jergen and wanted to do nothing more than walk out and not come back. The only thing keeping my feet moving deeper into the city was the prospect of getting my hands on the manuscript.

The people here looked much the same as the people in Jaipers. Just a little better dressed, and all wore shoes. Even the children who darted from building to building and betwixt the horses and throngs of people wore shoes. Missing was the shared friendly banter of the people of Jaipers. I realised everyone here was a stranger to one another, and I felt saddened. Very quickly I recognised a pattern to walking the streets and kept as far right as I could to allow horses past while I walked the streets.

Soon we reached what must have been the centre of the city. The road circled a small grassy park, with a few trees along the edges, and with a large stone statue of someone on a horse erected in the middle. I could see a few roads all met in this location. The break from the buildings meant the entire area was bathed in sunlight and it cheered me up. Benches ringed the statue and people of all sorts sat and talked. A couple of vendors sold cooked sausages and sweet bread from small carts. Dog and I paused here to get our bearings, and I bought two sausages for two tuppences. We devoured them in no time. Dog breathed his in and then tried to snatch mine from my hand.

As we stood in the park I had soon discovered having a map in your memory and actually walking the streets were two different matters. I was already sure I was lost. Dog didn't seem to care. He had obviously grown more accustomed to the stink, and he constantly smelled the air for who knew what. He kept looking at the sausage vendors and licking his chops. I laughed and closed my eyes and reached to embrace the small slice of nature existing within this bustling chaos of a city.

I sensed eyes on me and, turning quickly, I opened my eyes to find the pigeons on the statue staring rather pointedly at me. I looked around quickly and was thankful that no one seemed to notice. I mentally bid them to fly away and startled myself when they all did. The birds drew the eyes of all the people nearby and they turned to watch the whole flock of pigeons circle the park and then fly out over the rooftops to disappear. Everyone started talking and laughing about what they had just witnessed and I hustled to clear the area.

The breeze blew in from the direction the birds had flown and I caught the smell of the ocean. I smiled, remembering the Reeve of Jaipers telling me the inn lay down by the port. I had my bearings and soon was back on the road circling the park.

Cries rang out, and I turned, alarmed to see soldiers on horseback and some carts emerge from a road to enter the area. Dog ran up and pressed himself against my legs. The soldiers up front cried out and ordered the people on the road to move clear under the order of the Lord Protector. I put a hand on Dog to calm him and to keep him close. My eyes were drawn to the officer up front. He sat straight-backed and solid in the saddle, gleaming with gold and reds, his cloak billowing out behind him. His uniform looked almost exactly like the one I saw in Bill Burstone's house back in Jaipers. His eyes found mine and I could see they were bright and intelligent and I sensed a great mirth behind them.

The officer and I shared a long glance at one another. This was a man I could trust, and I smiled. I felt an acceptance from Dog. The officer nodded his head at me and smiled briefly back at me before turning his attention back to his progress through the city. *That was strange.* Then I watched another officer ride past him and felt his glare on me. That one, I thought with dread, he was someone I couldn't trust. Dog growled low and feral and the man glowered at me. I felt sorry for the first officer and hoped he outranked the other. The first officer talked to another and then looked at me once more. He looked a little sad and then he moved on.

The carts rumbled past, heavy with their load, and the people of Jergen closed in behind them and, shortly, they were gone. I shook my head and waited for a gap in the road and crossed and headed down the road following the path the pigeons had shown me. The smell of the ocean led the way.

* * *

Along the way to where I hoped I would find the Purple Rose Inn, I was marking in my mind those shops appearing to be worth exploring later. I spied an apothecary on a corner. At first, I noticed the shop had taken the time to plant flowers and bushes in the soil in front of the building where the sun would shine the longest during its passage across the sky. Then I read the sign and I felt compelled to enter.

As I pushed the door open to enter, a small bell overhead gave a tiny peal and Dog woofed gently at the sound. It rang again as the door closed behind me and I made my way past shelves lined with small clay pots and glass jars. They were labelled with tiny meticulous writing and I quickly read they contained medicines with descriptions of their use. Most I had never heard of and I felt a stirring of excitement. *Here was knowledge I could use. Perhaps this place could share with me?*

As I approached the counter, I heard a stirring on the other side of the open doorway. Someone called out "one minute" and I waited quietly, feeling a bit out of place. I looked down at Dog and he just sat there and began enthusiastically scratching an ear with a hind-leg.

"Stop it!" I whispered loudly to him. Dog stopped mid-scratch, with his paw still in the air, and stared at me for a moment before going right back at it. "Dog!"

At that moment, a large, tall man dressed in a white cotton robe with an apron tied tightly to his massive girth shambled through the opening and stood at the counter peering down at me and Dog. A frown creased his forehead. I immediately took a dislike to him and, by the scowl on his face, I suspected he felt the same way.

"What do you want?" he demanded. "Why are you in my apothecary? Get that mangy mutt out of here!"

"I-I-I just wanted to see your wares, sir," I stammered, shamed at how quickly he made me feel so small.

"Get that dog out of my shop!" he shouted, his face flushed red. "He'll ruin my wares! OUT!"

"Sir, he's very well behaved, I assure you."

"I don't care, get him out of my shop!"

I turned to Dog and looked at him. Dog lolled his tongue and then turned and started toward the door. As he passed the last of the shelves, his tail whipped across and disturbed some glass jars. He looked back at me and then nosed the door open and disappeared out onto the street. I sensed his amusement and tried to keep the smile off my face as I turned back to the proprietor.

"My apologies, sir."

The man was looking a bit shocked, and he looked away from the door to me and back again.

"Yes," he finally replied. "Yes, well good. What do you want?"

"I was hoping you could tell me a bit about your salves and such. I've never seen so much! And all the descriptions, please, I must know. What goes into them? How do you create some of these?"

The man blinked at me for a long moment. I watched as redness crept up his neck. "What? You want me to tell you how I make my salves? Do you take me for an idiot? Don't insult me! Whatever should I do that for?"

"So I could make them, too."

"So you could make them, too?"

"Yes, sir."

"You can fuck right off and get the fuck out of my store," he said and his checks blossomed red and his face was screwed up tight in anger.

I was startled. I hadn't expected such vehemence. And I had never been sworn at. At least not that way.

"But sir, I make these as well! Just not so much. And some I've never heard of."

"Bullshit. Who sent you?" he said.

"Sent me?"

"Yes, by God, who sent you? Rasguard? Did he? That thieving bastard."

"Rasguard?"

"Yes, Rasguard! No, it couldn't be him, even he's not smart enough to send a boy to do his dirty work. It was her, wasn't it?"

"Her?"

"The deighty old woman! It is, isn't it? Her with the plants, always coming here trying to peddle her wilted things."

"She sells herbs? Who?" I asked interested at once about hearing about someone else who gathered herbs. "Where is this woman?"

"Where is she? You'd know wouldn't you?"

"What? No! I have no idea who you are talking about! I've only just arrived here. Truly! Wait, look at this…" and I lowered my backpack to the floor and opened the top. I reached in and pulled a bunch of dill from the top.

I laid the dill on the counter in front of the man. I had picked them a few days ago and they would stay fresh for another week or so. Fresh enough to hopefully make a positive impression on this man. He reached out and picked it up and brought it to his nose. He took a sniff and his eyes opened a little wider. He rubbed some between his fingers and smelled them.

The man pulled free a rag tucked into his waistband and dabbed at the sweat on his brow while looking me over.

"Humph," he finally said. "Where'd you get this?"

"I picked them… today… just outside of town. Still fresh as you can see and high quality, sir. That's what I do, I gather herbs and sell them at the market."

He handed the dill back to me and looked at me for a moment as if deciding something. I just stood there waiting, trying to look exactly like who I was: a simple young man who gathered herbs. It must've worked for he relaxed and then spoke.

"Take Highborn Street down to the water. Ask around there. Someone will point you the right way. Everyone knows her."

I paused then, wanting to ask more questions, but knew I should just vacate the shop. I started toward the door and then turned with a question I knew was important.

"What's her name?"

"Nadine, the Herbalist. Crazy Nadine is what everyone else calls her. She has a house far out along the cliffs. Ask around. Someone will point her out to you."

Six

Jergen, 900 A.C.

"**M**AJOR GILLESPIE, I don't care. You will gather the men immediately for inspection."

There was a momentary pause, long enough that Brent noticed the insubordination and raised his eyebrow at the major. "Suh, yes, suh," said Major Gillespie quietly and with little emotion. He turned and strode off, shoulders hunched towards the main camp and the cook fires. Brent could see his uniform was crumpled and dirty from the previous day.

Brent glanced up at the lightening sky and then nodded to Captain Dixon, who stood nearby, to approach. He came to attention and saluted sharply.

"At ease, captain."

Captain Dixon stood at ease and then relaxed and strode a step closer. "General, sir. Please excuse me. You should have spoken to me about the inspection this morning. The task falls to me. The major won't take the slight well and I'll pay for it, sir."

Brent looked at the young Captain standing before him. He saw himself in the man. *Myself during the long journey to Bill Redgrave's house and the slaughter. I was poorly treated on that trip. Everyone was against me, much like this young man. Hopefully, this ends better for him.*

"I see you don't yet understand this, Captain."

"Sir, beg your pardon. Understand what exactly? Is it the men? Have they offended you somehow? They seem sincere. I think we've made a difference with them. Morale has improved. They get along with one another now. This only pisses them off. Sir."

Brent snorted. "There's a reason I'm a general, captain. I know I don't look like a wise senior officer but trust me in this."

Captain Dixon started to speak and then shut his mouth and thought for a moment.

That's a good sign, thought Brent with approval. *Think first, then speak.*

"Sir, I know they aren't to be trusted. But they seemed to be listening. Following orders. Getting along with each other. What more could I ask?"

"You seem to forget the way things were only two weeks ago. Do you really think the Guard and Army could be getting along so well so quickly? Watch them, James. They hide smirks and jest. But not about each other. They jest about something other than themselves. It's you and me, James. They are playing us."

"I see, sir. I'll watch closer, just as you ordered me."

"It wasn't an order, captain. It was a suggestion. You are the only man on this team I can trust. I won't tell you why that is important—just do as I suggest. Watch your back. Keep your ears and eyes open. Never turn your back to them. Understood?"

The captain nodded. "Yes, sir. Understood. But, this makes the third inspection in as many mornings. Can I ask why?"

Brent looked the captain over for a moment. His gear was immaculate. He had prepared himself. He had assumed another inspection was coming and had prepared just in case. Brent was tempted to simply tell him but recognised that it wouldn't help him. *Best he figures it out himself*, Brent thought. "No."

The captain pursed his lips. Brent suppressed a desire to smirk. *He's piqued by my curtness.* Brent waited a moment, and the captain nodded once. "No matter. Let me know when you figure it out. For now, we are almost at Jaipers, James. First to Jergen to resupply and take some rest and then we push hard to the West. Hard. I want to be back in Munsten by Yule. Buy new horses in Jergen. Strong ones. I trust you alone in that task." Brent waited a moment to let it sink in. "Anything else, Captain?"

"No, General," he replied, then sensing he was dismissed he came to attention, saluted, turned and strode off.

He's walking away mad at me for a different reason than the major, sighed Brent to himself. *He'll learn. I have no doubt about that. I just need to keep him alive until he figures it out.* Brent saw the signs. The men were most definitely playing the two of them. Brent had not made the rank of General by being a fool. *The hilarious thing*, thought Brent, *is the major actually believes he is fooling me.* There was a reason the major was still a major. He was abusive, crass, uncaring and exhibited the most alarming un-officer like qualities. Even Brent, head of the Lord Protector's Guard, had heard of Major Gillespie from the Army. It had taken him awhile to remember the officer but once he started putting one and one together he most certainly came up with two. Major Gillespie, the proud sixth cousin of the Lord Protector. Abuser of women, abuser of men under his command, and an abuser of his rank and privilege.

Brent watched as the captain joined with the major. They spoke quickly, the captain at attention, and the major visibly talking the captain down. *He's pointing his finger and everything*, thought Brent. *Wow. He really is an ass.*

The major would blame the captain for this third, unexpected inspection. It was the captain's job to schedule them and arrange them, with advance warning and approval from the major. *No doubt the captain is explaining that he didn't know.* With that thought the major turned to look at the Brent, then back to the captain, before striding off in anger. Brent didn't care just so long as the inspection started within a candle mark. Automatically, Brent looked over his own uniform and flicked a horse hair off his sleeve. He sidestepped the offending hair as it drifted down to the ground.

Brent remained outside his tent and kept an eye on the movements of the major and the men. Theirs was a small camp, only a half dozen tents, an area for the horses and carts, and a common area for meals and the like. Four men were on guard duty and watched the approaches from the road to the north and south. Their camp was placed about two hundred yards from the main road with the road between the camp and the ocean side. The coastline here was sandy, and the surf roared and crashed incessantly. The cries of seabirds were only just now starting with the rising sun and a gentle breeze blew onshore carrying with it the smell of the sea.

Brent looked south where he could see the far-off city of Jergen where it nestled on the coast around a deep bay. The city was built around the cliffs rising up from the sea and wrapping around the bay. It was a naturally defended bay, one the Admiral of the Fleet often bragged about. Brent could see numerous ships ploughing the approaches and spotted two Navy schooners conducting manoeuvres. Their scarlet sails were unmistakable. The winds over the past few days were enough to raise the seas, and the schooners pounded the waters hard with visible spray. *Reason number twenty-four of why*

I'm glad I joined the Guard.

Road traffic in both directions was much busier. A train of caravans was positioned about a quarter mile north of them and followed them to Jergen for safety. Captain Dixon had gone off to speak with the caravan owners and had reported that they checked out okay and were glad for the military escort. Brent had been impressed with the initiative. The road between Munsten and Jergen was a solid one. It was well maintained and fast. Nonetheless, travellers on the road often stopped them for news and gossip. It was a rarity these days to see such a fortified band of the military. The Guard and Army mix were what gained the most attention and Brent was getting tired of meeting it with the same vague responses. The road between Jergen and Jaipers would be sparsely travelled and Brent meant to push hard.

Jergen was the hustling and bustling city on the south-east coast. It was the second largest city on this side of Belkin and trade was focused here for distribution elsewhere in Turgany. There was a large underground market here, and it was a den for highwaymen who hung like vultures along the roads to the north and west. It had a very large garrison of over three hundred men and Brent knew the colonel in charge. He was in the Lord Protector's pocket and one of the men on the list Frederick now possessed. For this reason, Brent was worried. *If something is to happen, it is in Jergen.*

Brent wondered how his brother was faring with the list. It was important, he gather evidence against the Lord Protector. He prayed his brother remained quiet about it. The last man to follow the trail of corruption was now dead and buried in Jaipers. Brent worried about Frederick but recognised when there was little he could do. Brent pushed the emotions aside and focused on the surrounding city.

The one thing Brent was looking forward to was visiting the Cathedral of Jergen. When the Revolution happened the churches in Munsten had been demolished. The Cathedral in Jergen was protected by the garrison so it had withstood the mob. It was arguably the centre of the Church of the New Order. Brent was eager to visit and pray in solitude. *It saddens me my faith must be kept in such secrecy. I would like nothing more than to profess my belief in God to all who could hear. It shames me I must stay quiet and hidden.*

Faith within the military was one of the few things he and his brother had disagreed on. Brent felt the fear of God provided a moral compass for men in uniform. Frederick thought that was his job. They had discussed it once. Brent recalled the conversation with ease.

"More people are killed in the name of their god than for any other reason,

Brent," his brother had exclaimed that day when Brent had raised the topic. "Usually those men are in uniform and just carrying out orders."

"So much good happens because of faith!"

"Bullshit. Men do good because it is the right thing to do. I don't need some god to tell me what is right and wrong to know killing someone is wrong. Ludicrous to think otherwise."

Brent still disagreed with that sentiment. He knew within his heart the way to righteousness was through the word of God.

Now, Brent turned to watch the men emerge from their tents, blinking away the sleep of the night. They looked around blearily and Brent heard raised voices of discontent. Captain Dixon moved through the men explaining what was up and giving quiet orders. A few complained and Dixon turned on them. Brent caught the oddly yelled word from where he stood. Dixon left the men to head towards him and Brent noticed the dark looks the men threw at his back. *There,* thought Brent. *More evidence they are playing us.*

For the last week, ever since the night in the small hamlet where they had stayed overnight, the men were behaving better. Army and Guard started to get along and the men started saluting him and showing proper respect. *Respect that never meets their eyes,* thought Brent. *Frederick always said 'Watch their eyes'.*

Brent was almost fooled. He almost led himself to believe the men had turned a stone and found a new purpose. However, the looks, the tone of voice, the dullness in their eyes, all gave proof to the lie. Gillespie was playing a game here. *One that did not bode well for myself and Captain Dixon.* Today would be the third inspection in as many days. Everything unannounced and unplanned. *Petty and spiteful on my part but I have to admit to a certain level of satisfaction. Sucks to be them*, thought Brent and smiled broadly.

Brent and the men approached the main gate of Jergen. He watched as three men on horseback emerged from the gate and trotted toward them. The two on the outside carried flags raised high. One was the flag of Belkin and the other the city flag of Jergen. Central to the three was Colonel John Masters. He was resplendent in his finest armour and rode like the expert he was renowned for across the Realm. He had won the horse riding championship at the Realm Tournament two months ago and with it a purse of a hundred crowns. More importantly, he won bragging rights. *And he often did*, thought Brent. *Thank God I outrank him.*

He glanced back at his men and was pleased to see they rode with their backs straight and looking professional. He had stressed at the inspection this morning he wanted the men to shine. They were representatives from the capital and they would look the part. Dixon had finally caught on and had smiled and nodded at Brent. *Yes, the inspections were in preparation for this moment. It takes days to get men of this low quality to look half decent. Half of being military was the pomp. It didn't matter if you could swing a sword better than anyone—or ride a horse better for that matter—it was how you looked.* Brent chuckled to himself and watched as the colonel rode up and stopped his horse without command or the use of reins. *The horse looks frightened*, thought Brent watching the horse flare its nostrils with eyes a little wide. *Poor thing probably gets beaten if it doesn't perform well.*

The colonel saluted and then raised a gauntlet in greeting. "General Bairstow, sir. Colonel John Masters. It is my honour to welcome you to Jergen. Your men have been given accommodations in the barracks and my sergeant will see to their comfort. Your officers have been given rooms in the bachelor officer quarters. You, sir, would be most welcomed to stay with my wife and I and our three children in our home."

Brent winced internally. He had been afraid he would be pulled into county and city affairs. He was hoping he could stay in the bachelor officer quarters with his officers. He thought briefly of saying he would stay with his men but no doubt the colonel was under orders to keep an eye on him from the Lord Protector himself. "Those arrangements will be admirable, Colonel. My thanks."

"Your comfort is my prime concern, sir. It is not often the General of the Lord Protector's Guard is travelling the Realm. You will want for nothing while here, sir. Just ask and it will be arranged. Your quest is too important to let trifling matters such as comfort be ignored."

Brent looked thoughtfully at the colonel. *He knows my mission, how is that possible?* "That would be fine. I appreciate your generosity and I graciously accept. I will accompany my men to the barracks and see to their comfort and join you at your home later, would that be acceptable?"

"Yes, sir. By your leave, I will have my second escort you to the barracks and to my home. The Mayor of Jergen humbly requests you join him this evening for supper. You and your officers of course. Supper is served at eight in the evening. It will be a formal affair."

"It seems news of my mission has preceded me, Colonel. Please inform the mayor that my officers and I would be honoured."

"Of course. The Lord Protector asked me to see to your comfort. No one knows, except myself, of your mission to Jaipers."

And the two men on horseback beside you. Brent kept his face immobile. *I should have expected this. I knew there would be pomp and ceremony but my mission should be secret, by God. I have to return to Munsten with a wealth of gold on me and now every highwayman between Munsten and Jaipers will be waiting for me.*

"Lead on then, Colonel. My men will follow you."

* * *

A short time later, Brent was inside Jergen and moving through the streets with his men. Garrison men had cleared the way for them and they moved quickly. The city was made of an odd mix of stone and woodwork. Munsten was almost all made of stone. Stone didn't burn and buildings didn't collapse. Munsten also had a septic system in place, buried beneath the buildings and roads. Jergen still used the streets and Brent's eyes watered at the burning acrid smell of human waste filling the ditches beside the roads. The sea breeze was not enough to clear the air.

Up ahead was an open courtyard and Brent could see trees planted in a circular grove with a large statue of some forgotten hero central to it. *Lord Jergen, no doubt,* thought Brent. *The man who put the old King on the throne. A pious man, who—oddly enough—had killed more people in the name of religion, and the throne, than most men cared to remember.* With that thought, Brent passed through the stone arch and into the bright sun of the courtyard.

He looked around, admiring the view, and noticed a young man with a dog standing nearby. The man still had the look of a boy about him and he was burdened with an overly large backpack with all sorts of items tied to it. His blond hair and blue eyes stood out amongst the dark-haired people of south Belkin. Just as he was noticing the man, they locked eyes and Brent felt a jolt. The startling blue eyes drew him in and, for an instant, Brent felt he should know this man. The man seemed to recognise him by the widened eyes and the smile now on his face. Brent found himself smiling back.

Just then Major Gillespie pushed past him and Brent watched the man shift his eyes to follow him, his eyebrows lowered in a glare. His dog seemed to growl. *They seem to be good judges of character,* thought Brent. Captain Dixon rode up beside him and Brent turned his attention to him.

"Almost there, sir. Just to the left and down a block. Just past a terrific pub called the Dark Horse."

"Seems you know this city, Dixon."

"Yes, sir. This is my hometown."

"Your hometown? Why'd you not tell me that earlier?"

"Beg your pardon, sir. I wouldn't presume to tell you my personal affairs."

Brent glanced over at the grinning captain. "Ha! Fine. You are correct. I should know my officers better than this. But you are Army, how the hell should I know your background? Or care?"

"Good that you don't, sir! Jergonians are known for their laid-back ways and religious zealotry! You wouldn't trust me if you'd have known. You'd think me a God fearing man!"

"Hmm. God fearing. I suppose men must fear something, eh captain?"

"Sir, yes. Lessen they become old and soft."

"Ha! Speaking of God. Where is the cathedral then?"

"Sir?"

"The Cathedral of Jergen. Famous place."

"Sir," said Captain Dixon and jutted a chin over Brent's shoulder.

Brent turned in his saddle and looked. There, towering over the buildings, was the white stone of a massive cathedral. *You couldn't miss it if you tried,* thought Brent. *And yet I did. I feel the fool.* He turned back to see Dixon's eyes twinkling with mirth.

"Don't ever mention this, Captain."

"No, sir, never!" and Dixon rode ahead laughing out loud.

Brent chuckled to himself and then found himself looking for the young man with his dog. He was still standing there with his dog staring at him and looking more than a little lost. *I wonder who he is?*

Brent clucked to his horse, and they moved off down the road to the barracks. He glanced at the position of the sun and grimaced. *At least three hours before I can soak in a tub. That Colonel Masters better have a large tub.*

Hours later Major Gillespie read the short missive he'd found in the drop location in the officer quarters. It simply warned him of a church interest in Jaipers. *That was unexpected,* thought Gillespie and touched the paper to the candle in his room. It flared and Gillespie dropped it into the ash bucket by the cold fireplace.

Gillespie sat and thought for a while before he heard a soft rap on his door. "Who is it?" he asked the back of his door.

"Sir, Captain Dixon. As you requested."

"One moment, Captain."

Gillespie rose and strapped his sword to his waist. He looked at his reflection in the full mirror and admired his ceremonial uniform. He had bitched about having to take it with him but now he was pleased he did. He was resplendent in rich golds and reds. A thick gold band ran down the outsides of his dark blue pant legs. He tugged his tunic down and turned his shoulders a little to better see his rank. A small golden crown stood proudly on raised red velvet epaulettes. *Soon to be joined by the pip of a Lieutenant-Colonel*, he thought and he smiled at his reflection. *I should have shaved,* he thought and stroked his whiskers.

Everything was set for Jergen. Gately and David would be dealt with and disappear into the belly of fish. Then it would just be Dixon they would need to deal with and Jergen was not the city to do it in. He would be too closely watched. Timing was everything and Gillespie had decided to deal with Dixon at the same time as Bairstow. *Two birds with one stone.* He looked forward to dealing with the young upstart of an Army captain. He turned to the door and swung it open to find the startled officer standing there blinking. *He's smartly dressed and looks better in uniform than I do*, he thought. *And he is freshly shaved. I hate this man.*

"Let's be about this," he said through clenched teeth and a forced smile. "Dinner with the mayor awaits."

Craobh

Seven

Jergen Waterfront, 900 A.C.

I FOUND A street sign informing me I was on Highborn Street and after a few dozen yards I found the street plunged down a steep incline. As I made my way down the road, I was surprised by just how steep the road was. *Who would design such a road? Carts and horses would have to avoid it.* Despite how difficult it was, the view was spectacular, and it provided a direct path to the harbour district. Down ahead I could see the street ended at a crossroad with the road beyond it reaching down to the docks, the massive cliff-enclosed bay, and an expanse of sea beyond gleaming in the afternoon sun. Seagulls soared and circled with their constant cry filling the air. I could make out ships of all shapes and sizes tied alongside the piers. As I watched, a ship was on a broad reach and fighting the onshore wind to make it out of the harbour. On board, the men scurried across the deck and hauled on ropes on the masts. Sails snapped taut and spray washed across the decks. It was a glorious sight.

I was glad I was going downhill, and I pitied the people struggling to climb the hill to my right on the weathered wooden steps laid down to help them. It was a steep climb despite the stairs. When I reached the bottom, on what the street sign called Shoreline Road, I looked right and then left, not sure which way to go. With a bark Dog ran off to the left and, with the direction decided, I stepped out after him, relishing the flat road.

The buildings grew farther and farther apart and less solid and cared for as I made my way down the road. The wood was bleached white with the sun and salt. Sand and stringy long grass were everywhere. Just a few dozen feet from the road was a cliff edge hidden by the shoreline, but beyond was the sea. *The ground must really drop off,* I thought. The smell of the ocean was stronger this close, and I drew in deep breaths. The sea smelled of life and I loved it after the stench of the city proper.

As I made my way along the narrow road, I would watch Dog bound into view from around a house and then just as quickly disappear again behind another. He was excited about something, his nose barely clearing the sand as he tried to smell everything he could. I wondered what would excite a dog so much and thought of cats and rats and shrugged. Dog was a strange animal.

The dirt road bent sharply to avoid a large outcropping of rocks. I nodded to the few people who pulled handcarts along or walked with some purpose in mind. Few returned the gesture and most kept their eyes on their feet. Jergen was not a pleasant town, but at least the cliffs offered a wonderful view. I looked around at what grew here. It all looked so rugged and barren. Thin trees struggled to grow here and there on the thin soil and most of the area was filled with a scurvy grass and strange bulbous flowers I didn't recognise. With my senses, I could tell they struggled to maintain a grip on the loose soil topping the cliffs. They drew what nutrients they could despite the deluge of salt spray. Life always found a way, it seemed. Only tough plants could survive here. The people of Jergen were probably much the same way. I could hear the surf pounding a dozen or so yards down below with deep muffled thuds that I could feel through the soles of my feet. I would feel a light spray against my cheek soon afterwards and found it refreshing in the heat of the day.

Soon the buildings and people all but disappeared, and I spotted a lone house off to my right, standing bright in the sunlight. The house beckoned to me and I felt a pull toward it. Here was the sole bright spot in Jergen. It was one story with white-washed walls and a high roof covered with red clay tiles. The yard was surrounded by a fence made from long pieces of driftwood attached to driftwood poles buried at even intervals. The soil around the yard was thick and bountiful and full of nutrients. Fruit trees were precisely placed in four neat rows and helped obscure the house from the approach. The trees were heavy with fruit, early for this time of year, and the branches struggled to hold up the ripe apples, peaches, lemons, and oranges. All around the trees I could see neat rows of well-tended vegetable gardens bursting with vibrant colours. Flower gardens grew here and there and all-in-all the house was breathtakingly beautiful. Dog had already surged ahead and leapt across the fence to run from tree to tree, nose firm to the ground, and he looked up at me, mouth open and tongue panting in a clear laugh. I felt the same excitement he felt now.

I sensed joy the closer I approached the house and my heart lifted. Since I had entered Jergen I had felt disconnected, but here—here at this wonderful house—I sensed only peace and quiet. Dog was at the door pawing at the wood and barking up a storm. He leapt in the air and turned and twisted and snapped at his tail. I was still a good distance away when the door opened and I saw the hunched over figure of a woman standing in the light, one hand on the doorknob and the other on the doorframe. She stood a bit straighter and stared at Dog. She had grey hair and wore a shawl despite the heat of the day. Her clothes were well tended, but loose fitting and I could see the slender build underneath. The skin of her face was as weathered as the driftwood. This was a woman who had lived a very long and tough life.

As I strolled up, she raised her eyes toward me and beamed a smile reaching from ear to ear and lighting up her eyes. It changed her entire face and I smiled in return. I had no idea who she was but somehow I knew she and I were kin, I just didn't know how I knew. Tears started to stream down her face and I felt the same wet tracks from my own eyes. Dog barked and ran from her to me as I walked up hands outstretched. She let go of the door frame and grasped mine. The shock of the connection went through me like a thunderbolt. We stood there staring at one another for a long, long time.

"Come," she said and patted my hands. "Come inside. I never thought I would live to see the day."

* * *

I entered her home and felt it welcome me. The floor was earth; moss grew in the corners and lichens covered the walls. Everywhere on the rafters herbs were hung, expertly bundled up and drying. The air was thick with their smell, sweet and fragrant, and I breathed in deeply, memories of working in Daukyns small room returning. I looked around to get my bearings as she pulled me to the centre of the house. Her home was simple and all on one level and open from corner to corner. Four thick support beams held up the roof and from every conceivable surface, and from all the rafters, hung drying fruit rings and herbs. Crafted art pieces, such as needlepoint and crocheted things, hung from the walls.

I spied her bed in the far corner—a simple mattress stuffed with straw and placed on a wooden frame. Beside the bed stood a tall pedestal with a washbasin and ewer. It was positioned beneath a large round window looking out over the sea. The kitchen area boasted a potbelly stove with wood stacked neatly beside it. To the right of the stove were two raised cupboards and a long counter covered with vegetables, fresh from her garden. Near the stove was a workstation made from a thick slab of oak, stained deep with green and browns, and worn smooth from years of herb work. A woven basket was perched to one side filled with apples and oranges. A high eating table with two tall chairs was placed nearby and covered with a linen tablecloth. A small vase with a solitary flower sat at its centre. This was a home I could love. I felt the earth through the dirt floor and drank the peace and serenity like water to a man dying of thirst. My vision swam with my own tears and I struggled to remain standing.

I could not remember ever experiencing this wonderful feeling of being home. But here I was: at home. After all those years in the wild living on my own with the often-unbearable closeness of Jaipers and the constant need to escape to the woods. Not so here. Here, I was where I belonged. I stood in the middle of the house and slowly turned and smiled so hard my face felt close to tearing in two. Dog was darting around the house sniffing everything and running back to me for approval before bounding away again to smell out something new. I turned to the old woman, and she was staring at me with a smile mirroring my own. She crossed to her kitchen counter and filled two wooden cups with water from a well-water reservoir placed next to the counter. When I saw she meant to bring me one I rushed over to help her. I could sense her joints pained her greatly.

As I took one cup from her she turned and raised her cup to me, which I touched with my own.

"Cheers, young man," she said. "To Health and Harmony."

The toast rang a bell of remembrance in my mind and I knew there was a reply—but I could not remember it. I strained to remember, but it eluded my grasp.

She looked a little disappointed, but she smiled and sipped her water. I did likewise.

"You are supposed to reply 'And to Gaea, our Earth Mother.'"

I nodded and spoke the words softly and the memory returned. My mother used to tease me when I failed to get it right. For a moment, I saw her face again, and I tried to hold the image but it faded just as quick as it had appeared and, already, I couldn't remember how she had looked. I hated those moments. It teased me and taunted me. I hadn't heard the name Gaea in a long time and for the first time, I wondered if the earth presence I had been feeling was Gaea.

"So, tell me," she said. "Are there any more draoi besides you?"

"Pardon?"

"How many more of you are there? The Draoi. The Druids."

"The Draoi?" I said not meaning to make it sound like a question. "I wouldn't know. I'm not a draoi. Someone else mistook me for that on the way into Jergen. I'm just a simple man with a gift for herbs and the like."

"Young man. You are most definitely a draoi. A duilleog or maybe a craobh."

"A dew log or crab?"

She surprised me by smacking me on the arm. "No, a dew-lee-ogg or a cray-oh'b." She replied enunciating each syllable.

"I'm sorry," I admitted shaking my head and rubbing my arm. "I have no idea what you are talking about. Except for the name you used earlier—Gaea. I've heard of her."

Nadine looked at me a little strangely and then she leaned quickly forward, and her eyes went a little wild and wide. *Almost as if she remembers me*, I thought.

"Who are you? Tell me. Your name."

She reached out to me with both hands. They were shaking. I wet my lips and said my name. "Will."

"Will? No!" she shook her head and clasped my arm with both hands. "Will? It cannot be. Your last name, quick, what is it?"

"Arbor. I'm Will Arbor."

She fainted. I didn't even have a chance to catch her, and she hit the ground with a thump. Dog gave a little whine and looked up at me.

* * *

I lifted and carried her over to her bed and laid her down. She couldn't weigh more than ninety pounds. She was such a slim and frail woman. I found a cloth and soaked it in the washbasin and laid it on her brow. I sat on the ground next to her and held her hand. I had a sense of knowing this woman. Something about her seemed familiar to me. Her face was aged and heavily wrinkled but beyond the lines, I could see she was once beautiful and perhaps a face I once knew.

I could sense she was not unwell, just a sudden loss of blood to her head had left her light-headed. I *reached* out to her and examined her health. It was such an easy task for me now. Something had frightened her and constricted her blood flow. I could see that flow returning to normal and looked elsewhere in her body for harm. Immediately I could see she suffered what any woman of her advanced age would suffer. Her heart was weak, straining to continue to pump, worn after so many years. There was little I could do for her except administer some herbs to thin her blood a little and make the task easier. Her joints were swollen, and I could see the wear and tear of her years. I *shifted* back and held her hand for a moment. Dog came over beside me and laid his head on her stomach and looked up at her face. After a bit, she slowly regained her senses and blinked her eyes open and looked around in a moment of confusion. She locked eyes with mine and then opened them wide and raised a hand to cover her mouth.

"Will Arbor?"

"Yes, ma'am. You must be Nadine."

"Yes, I'm Nadine, but, you *can't* be Will Arbor. You and your mother were killed ten years ago."

My heart skipped a beat. *This woman knew my mother?* I froze in place. I felt Dog push up against me and lick my neck. I could only stare at this old woman. I was suddenly afraid.

"You were both killed escaping Munsten after your father found a way out for you. We felt her passing!"

I had no response, but the mention of my father had my anger returning.

"My father abandoned us. Left us to die."

The woman flinched at my tone, but she shook her head.

"No, no," she said. "That's not true. He would never. He didn't."

I could see that she meant to say more, but we grew silent, both lost in our thoughts. I rose to make tea to distract me from the returning dark memories of the night my father left my mother and me. I retrieved my backpack where it lay by the door and placed it on her worktable. I carefully took out some bundles of my herbs in order to reach the tin that contained my dried tea leaves. I found a large water container in the corner and filled the kettle perched on her stove. I blew life back into the stove embers and placed a few pieces of kindling inside, enough to heat the water up without overheating the house. I sensed the woman rise off her bed and make her way over to my backpack. I heard her rustling through it and wondered at her audacity to rummage through another man's belongings. I had nothing to hide from her and, oddly enough, it amused me.

At her gasp, I turned to see what the matter was. She was holding one of my bundles of herbs in her hand and looking at it to me.

"What?" I asked.

"Do you process these?"

"Yes, ma'am."

With a growl, she swatted a hand at me through the air. "Stop calling me ma'am. It's Nadine. You couldn't have done this. You're eighteen. A young man."

I blinked in surprise. "Eighteen? No, I'm sixteen. I was six when my mother died."

Nadine looked at me like I was daft. "No, you are eighteen. You were born on Ostara Day, Marta nineteen, 882 A.C. I was there, I should know. It was a very auspicious day when a future draoi is born on Ostara Day."

"I thought I was sixteen. I lost mum when I was six."

"You were eight. A precocious eight. Smarter than you had any right to be."

"Why'd I think I was six?"

"How should I know? You had a friend in the castle. A boy of one of your father's friends. He was six. Must be you mixed it up."

"How can you be sure? I don't feel older."

"I told you! I helped raise you in Munsten. Wait till you're my age before you start complaining about feeling old…"

I believed her. Suddenly I did feel older. My whole life was changing too fast for me to keep up. Suddenly I didn't want to talk about my childhood. I pointed at the herbs in her hand. "So, yes, I harvested those. I'm pretty sure of that, at least."

Nadine blinked at the change in subject and then looked at the herbs and shook them. "No one ever trained you? No other draoi, correct?"

"Trained me in what? Herbs? No. I kind of picked it up on my own. But my friend in Jaipers, Daukyns, a Wordsmith," I swallowed the lump forming in my throat. "Daukyns taught me somewhat. He knew a lot about herbs. We made unguents for the people there."

"Daukyns taught you how to draw the herbs from the plants?"

"What? No, of course not. I taught myself. Daukyns only taught me some uses…" I stopped when I saw her clutching the bundle in her hands to her chest with one hand while grabbing the table for support. I worried she would collapse again, and I moved closer.

"What, Nadine? What's the matter?"

"You can't have taught yourself to this level. That's impossible!"

Dog barked at this and the woman glanced at him.

"Will, this quality of herbs. The quality of them. That takes a senior draoi! Not a Duilleog! Oh, dear Gaea!"

"What's a Duilleog?"

"What's a Duilleog?" she repeated with her eyebrows raised. She staggered to a chair at her eating table. I joined her and sat down across from her.

"Where to begin? Oh dear, I'm too old for this. Hush, let me think."

I waited in silence, but she seemed lost in thought. I rose at the whistle from the kettle and removed it from the heat and placed it on the table. I brought over my tin of tea and added a generous amount. I searched her cupboards and found a couple of aged porcelain mugs and placed them on the table next to the kettle. Nadine had opened my tea tin and was smelling the contents. She raised a questioning eyebrow at me and I furrowed mine in response. *She was awful snoopy.*

"You harvested the leaves and stems?" she asked.

"Aye, last fall. I dried quite a lot. The cook in Jaipers, my friend Dempster, he keeps it safe for me and I refill the tin when I pass through."

She nodded and slowly closed her eyes and leaned back.

I poured the tea and waited, poised at the edge of my seat. All these years I had a gift. Now it appeared I was one of these draoi and I had to know more.

The smell of the tea opened her eyes and with a shaking hand, she grabbed her cup and then, realising she still held the bundle of my herbs in her lap, she placed them on the table and stared at them.

"Alright. The draoi. You were too young when it all fell apart and so you don't remember. No one could expect you to. How could they? Where to begin, hmm? How to start? By the Word, I was never a teacher. I never had to do any of this. I'm too old, too old! Gaea help me!"

The name seemed familiar to me and I asked. "Gaea? Who's that?"

Nadine put her hand over her heart. "Oh, dear Gaea, give me strength. Who's Gaea? Young man, Gaea is the earth. Some call her Mother Earth. She is the life of our world. The draoi toil for her. We pledged aeons ago to help her maintain the balance of nature which man disrupted. That is our task. Oh dear, oh dear. Why now at my age?"

I listened to this revelation in silence. Whatever was going on with her, I could see she had to work it through. I looked over at Dog and could see him staring at Nadine with amusement. I rose and pulled out a bone I had purchased as I passed through town and tossed it over to him. He caught it mid-air and lay down and worried it with his back teeth, drool flowing freely onto the floor.

Pig, I thought.

Dog snorted.

"Okay, okay. I'll start simple," announced Nadine, and I turned my attention to her.

"Alright. The draoi. I'll start there. Gaea created the draoi. To maintain the balance, you know. But that's not important. At least not right now. The draoi have rank. Rank we take from the parts of the tree. Leaf, branch, trunk and root. Root being the most important."

I nodded. All plants and trees were the roots. The stuff above ground was just what it sent up to feed on the sun. Plants were one with the earth. They drank from it and pulled sustenance from it and when they died, they returned their strength back to the earth. It was perfect and beautiful, and I always knew it as Truth. Dog snorted, and I gave him a look.

"You do see it don't you, Will?" she said with enough wonder in her voice to draw my eyes back to her. "For young draoi, even older ones, they don't accept the concept. Gaea knows it took me a long, long time. Anyway, all draoi start as a duilleog. It means leaf. Then once you master being an apprentice, you are promoted to craobh. It means branch. You are a journeyman and you are paired with a full draoi, or a Stoc. Stoc means trunk. All fully trained draoi are stocs."

She grabbed the bundle of my herbs off the table and held it up between us and shook it for emphasis.

"Only a Stoc can produce something of this quality. Tell me," she demanded. "When did you harvest this?"

I scratched my head and thought back.

"Six maybe seven weeks ago," I said. "Maybe a bit longer. I think it was before I was injured. It was the only bundle to survive my journey." I wasn't ready to talk about my capture.

"Six or seven weeks ago!" she cried and grabbed her chest with her free hand. "That's not possible! Oh dear, oh dear! Gaea, help me!"

Dog burped rather loudly and licked his lips. I was starting to get annoyed. I didn't think Gaea would help her with this and I just wished she would get it out and tell me.

"Will, that's not possible. When I was in Munsten, I was paired with a Stoc of some exceptional ability in herb craft. It was why I was with her. My craft... my craft was not very good, you see. The Freamhaigh hoped my assigned Stoc could improve my skill. She tried, Gaea knows she tried! But that doesn't matter. What matters is she was the best of us. Well, next to your mother that is!"

At the mention of my mother, I leaned in, eager to hear about her. Nadine noticed and patted my hand.

"We will talk about her, Will, I promise. But right now, these herbs! You can't have gathered them as they are. You are untrained. A Duilleog at best. Maybe a Craobh. Explain to me how you collect your herbs. Tell me in detail."

I hesitated, but only for a moment. I'd never been able to tell anyone how I harvested my herbs. It had always been my secret and finding myself with someone who I could open up to and have them understand me was a dream come true. I reached into my tunic and pulled out my pouch. I held it over the table and gently shook out the contents. The coin fell first and then the sickle tumbled out and landed with a soft click on to the coin.

"Is that... is that..." she cried out in what sounded like anguish and hope combined in one. She reached out with a shaking hand toward the pile, but she stopped short of touching the sickle. I looked at her face. Tears streamed from her eyes and her shoulders were shaking violently. A sob burst from her and I rushed forward and held her gently. She cried into my shoulder, her sobs loud in the quiet of her small home. She cried for a long time. I could sense a tremendous release coming from her.

"Oh, Will! Will! Such joy it gives me to see the symbol of the Cill Dara! Gaea be praised!"

Joy? I thought she was upset. Why is she crying then?

"With the death of so many. So many! How could I hope that it survived? I was certain it was lost with your mother. Seeing it again, it brings me hope and such joy. You won't understand. It is of significant importance to the draoi."

"Cill Dara?"

She pushed herself off my shoulder and I returned to my chair. She wiped her face with the heels of her palms and dried her tears.

"The Cill Dara, or the Cill Darae. The High Priest or High Priestess of The Tree. They alone commune directly with Gaea. And they advise the head of the draoi, the Freamhaigh, or the Root. If the Freamhaigh is male, the Cill Darae is a woman, and vice versa."

She paused.

"Your mother was the Cill Darae, Will. She was the best of us. Her passing was a dire blow to the few of us who remained."

I shook my head unable to speak. This was all so new to me. I drank in each word and tried to imagine this was truly my mother she spoke of. But without memories to associate with the words they passed through me. I could not grasp what she was telling me.

"Seeing the sickle, it killed whatever slim hope I still had that she escaped. I had hoped she had hidden somehow. Faked her death. I made myself believe what I knew to be impossible," She thought for a moment. "It explains much about your herb craft, but even with this, the quality is remarkable. I saw what your mother was capable of; I studied under her for a time when my Stoc was called away. The stoc I trained with, at her best, she would have been hard-pressed to achieve this quality. Your mother, though, she could—with little effort. You take after her, Will. You should be very proud. Gaea does not call on all people—only those she chooses. And she gifts them with her power. Her magic. She must have gifted you so very long ago. This is remarkable."

"What do you mean, *she calls on people?* How? With words?"

"Yes, of course. How else would she do it?"

"I don't know. How could I know? Is she like the god of the Church?"

"By the Word, no! God is the imaginary being they created. A cursed, narcissistic deity. Demands devotion and threatens people with eternal damnation. Have you not heard the Great Debate?"

"Um, a little, I suppose. The wordsmith in Jaipers, Daukyns, he was my good friend. He died. He was old," I stole a glance at her to see if she was offended but she merely stared back at me. "Well, he tried to explain it to me once. But I didn't really care to know, and I didn't really listen to him." I thought back to the day, sitting in a small boat on the river, my stomach roiling in agony. Daukyns, ambivalent to my distress on the water, had droned on and on about the Great Debate. All I could remember was it had caused the Revolution to start in earnest. Before then it had been a mild rebellious sort of thing. The Church had conceded to the Word—the King went insane, everyone knew the tale—and it caused rioting. And a civil war of sorts. The Church lost in the end and was reduced to almost nothing. What saved them was the Lord Protector, and the Archbishop had managed to stop the riots. Still, Daukyns used to thank the Word the Church remains so small and had so little effect on people. He said he couldn't imagine a world where the Church continued to rule the hearts of people through fear and punishment. A vision of the two dead guards and the assassin came to mind, and I concluded I knew nothing.

"Well, you should have listened to him," she said. "History is important, young man!" She reached out to finally grasp the sickle and then stopped short again and looked at me. I nodded permission, and she picked it up. She held it with reverence and tested the edge with a thumb. "This too is a part of history. This was given to the first Cill Darae hundreds of years ago by Gaea herself. It has been passed from one Cill Dara to the next over all these years. Gaea imbued the stone with her power. It is a thing of wonder."

"Stone? I thought it glass."

"It is both. It is glass created from the heat of the earth like a stone. But it is magic, too. Filled with her magic and it has never waned. It is still as strong today as it was on the first day, I am sure." I wasn't so sure. Whenever I had used it I had always felt it had become a part of me.

She placed the sickle down gently on the table and snatched up the coin.

"By the Word! A triskelion!"

"A what?"

"A triskelion! Each Stoc carries one. It is a symbol of our order. We all belong to The Tree. The coin is used to allow a person to discover Gaea. It's a little complicated, but it is enough to understand all the living on earth *are* Gaea. It is not us and then her. We are all her. And how can we not be? We are born from the earth and it is to the earth we return on our death. But you are no more aware of a hair on your head than Gaea is that you exist. The coin changes that. Opens you up to her notice."

"I rubbed it and I could see through walls. And people glowed."

Nadine reached out and grasped my arm. "What? You *shifted?*"

"Yes, ma'am."

Nadine let go of my arm and then slapped it. "Will, you surprise me again. That should not be possible. Not without guidance, and a firm and helping hand from your stoc. Finding the means to do that all by yourself is extraordinary. During my days that was unheard of."

I grew quiet thinking about how I had shifted the first time in Jaipers and then healed the town. I now no longer needed the coin to *shift.* I could just do it. And it was as easy as breathing to me now. I didn't know exactly how to tell her. So much had happened to me. And, to be honest with myself, I was starting to think she didn't know as much about the draoi as she thought. It was not something I could ask without being rude. I thought for a moment. "Nadine, how can you be sure?"

She stared at me for a moment and I could see she was embarrassed about something and a little agitated. Dog stood up and sauntered over and placed his wet nose into her hand. It distracted her a moment, and she looked down and let Dog put his head in her lap. She laid her hands on his head and scratched behind his ears. It seemed to console her. She kept her face down and away from me.

"I was never made a stoc," she said so quietly I strained to hear her. "That is my shame. I was promoted to craobh and never made it to full draoi. Gaea never saw fit to award me with the power to do what a full draoi required to perform their duties. I fled here and bought this home and tend the garden and sell my fruit and vegetables and herbs. It is a simple life. One I have come to enjoy and cherish."

I knew not what to say to this. Not knowing anything about the druids, I could only sense she felt she had failed somehow. I looked around her workplace and looked up at her drying herbs. I reached out with my power to examine the plants and I could see they were no different from the herbs I would see for sale in the marketplaces. Perhaps a little stronger in potency but normal herbs all the same. I *shifted* and gave her another examination and confirmed her heart was still pumping hard. I *shifted* back and was startled to see her staring gloomily at me.

"That's quite rude, you know," she said. "Draoi aren't supposed to look into other draoi without their permission first. It's only polite to ask first."

I gawked at her. I had never considered—never thought. I felt my face warm with my embarrassment. When she saw this a grin split her face, and she smacked me again. Dog chuffed on her lap.

"Ha! I don't mind, young man. True words, though, always ask permission from another draoi. But, more importantly, I've seen what you've done. You lit up like a Yule bush! All blue and bright! You need to control the power. Hide it. One of the first rules of the draoi is to never expose your power to non-draoi. It is not debatable and the way you wield the power anyone could see what you can do. Maybe not understand it, but you will certainly stand out!"

I was horrified. When I had used my powers in Jaipers the Reeve there had told me I glowed blue but I never thought to try to control it. I never knew I could. This woman would need to teach me. I needed her help.

"Aye, you need my help, Will. Any fool can see that look in your face and understand what you're thinking. Perhaps that was Gaea's plan. Put me here for you to stumble upon. I always thought she was a conniving woman."

Dog sneezed and trotted over to his bone and growled at it and resumed his gnawing. I nodded and looked at Nadine. She was still smiling.

"It'll do me good," she paused for a long time looking at me appraisingly. "So?"

"So?"

"What did you see?"

"Um, what?"

"When you looked into me, what did you see?"

"Not much," I said. "Except, except, well, your heart is worn. It strains to beat. I think I can make a tea for you that will help. And to help your joint pain."

"Birch tea?"

"Um, yes, exactly that. But with green tea leaves."

"Good. Good. I've been making my own. It's over there on the counter."

I walked over and found her birch bark and green tea supply. I *shifted* and looked at it. The bark and leaves weren't very potent, and I knew I could harvest better quality bark to add to my own green tea. "Where did you harvest this bark?"

She snorted. "Nearby. Come I'll show you. I saw you look at my supplies. Poor quality and not worthy of a draoi, are they? Bah, no matter, I know the answer and I've lived this long with disappointment. Best we sort out my heart before we continue this. I'll need my strength." She rose and came over to me and stopped in front of me looking up at my face. Without warning she wrapped me in a strong embrace and held me, her cheek pressed into my chest. "I knew your mum, Will. She was always very kind to me. Sympathetic to my limits. But, seeing her son returned alive and hale is a boon to me. You've no idea how alone I've been these last ten years." She released me but clasped my upper arms and stared into my eyes. "Or perhaps you do. Perhaps you do." She patted an arm and turned to the door. "Come. Let's get this done."

Eight

Nadine's House, Jergen Waterfront, 900 A.C.

W E RETURNED A little while later with the birch bark. While I made tea from the bark and my green tea leaves, she kept up an endless dialogue of praise of my abilities. I was the first draoi, she said, who could harvest herbs of such quality without formal training. She seemed pleased. When I had least expected it a flashback of working with my mother in the garden somewhere had come to me. In the memory, I was sitting by her side and watching her harvest herbs and spices. When I asked Nadine about the memory, she seemed pleased and confirmed I had often been at my mother's side helping her.

Then she glared at me and added: "At such a young age, it is doubtful you learned much. Certainly not to this level."

Except Daukyns had taught me a great deal about herb lore. Probably all I knew came from him, building on my childhood knowledge with my mother. My added touch simply insured the potency was stronger. And all it took was an ability to communicate with the plant. *Communicate* was the word Nadine had used.

"You need to communicate with the plant," she said as I placed her tea before her. She took a sip and nodded in approval.

"Communicate?" I asked.

"Yes, talk to the plant." At my smirk, she smacked my arm again. "Not with words. With your emotions. You need to project your need."

I nodded at this. It sounded right, for it was what I had been doing all along. I had just never put words to it and I told her as much.

"Yes, that's it. You were doing it right. It comes naturally to you." She grew silent and then I saw her reach a decision. "That's what was wrong with me, they said. I couldn't speak to the plants. Well, not loud enough, they said. It's what saved me during the Purge."

"Purge?" I asked and reminded myself to ask her more about her lack of skill later. It clearly pained her, and I doubted she would be open about it at the moment.

"Yes, the Purge. You would have been caught in the first strike. It started in Munsten. It all started there. Your mother was the Cill Darae in the castle. When it all fell apart, and the city went up in flames, she escaped with you. We all felt it when she died. We were certain you were killed with her. It destroyed what we had left. The draoi fell apart and scattered to the winds. Gaea abandoned us, confirmed by the death of her Cill Darae. It was too much for the draoi. It was horrible, just horrible."

A great many questions came to mind, but I focused instead on the location. "Munsten? I was in Munsten?"

"Of course!" and she smacked me again. "Where else would the Cill Darae be? She was there with the Freamhaigh and your dad."

I felt a burning in my gut at the mention of my father and with it the image of him turning his back on us and walking into the burning city returned. Nadine mentioning the city in flames brought the image to mind, and I turned my back to her to hide my face and anger. I could still see my father walking away from us back lit by the flames of the city. I gritted my teeth. Being in the presence of someone who knew my father made it seem all the worse and all the more real to me. "My father betrayed my mother. I remember clearly."

"No, not true," she stated and struggled to sit up. I helped her until she settled. "You were merely a boy then. I should know. I helped raise you! You were only eight summers old. Talking up a storm, questioning everything, and running around all over the castle. No. Your father loved your mother and you like no other father and husband has loved his wife and child."

I shook my head, disagreeing with her.

"Will," she said and reached out to grasp both my hands. "Here, feel the Truth of my words."

I looked down at her green-stained hands, surprised by the strength of them. She was frail but working her plants gave her such vitality. The intensity in her eyes drew me into their depths. She was intent on showing me something and I felt a connection form between us.

"Will, your father loved you and your mother. He could not have abandoned you."

With her words, the connection between us sounded a single pure tone. My teeth rattled in my mouth and I felt and knew the sincerity of her words. It was Truth. She was not lying. *But her truth*, I thought. I freed my hands from hers and sat back, opening the distance between us. Dog whined once and placed his head on my lap.

"It's been so long since I did that. I'm surprised I had the strength. I was taught how to do that so many years ago. One way, I'm afraid, for me at least. You could lie to me all you want and I'd never know. Did you see the Truth?" she said.

"Yes. I felt it. But Nadine, I watched him. I watched as he turned and walked away. We were safe with him. Almost clear of the flames. My da walked away and left me—left us. I remember my mother's anguish. I felt her anguish. I still do."

"No, you felt her loss. She watched her husband leave her—and you, too—to provide a cover for your escape. He sacrificed himself for his family." She grew silent for a spell and I sat numb trying to digest her words. Could it be true? All these years I had lived with the belief my father had betrayed us by abandoning us. And yet I felt the Truth from this woman and knew what I had believed was perhaps not the entire truth. I was torn, not knowing what to believe anymore. *It is not a simple matter to abandon a belief you have lived your entire life learning to accept.*

"He betrayed us," I said trying for conviction in my voice. "My mother died because he was not there to protect us."

At the silence, I turned my head to look at Nadine and was shocked by the look on her face. I couldn't tell if she was horrified or disgusted. I opened my mouth to speak, but she leaned forward to reach out and grasp my forearm with a bony hand and she squeezed me painfully tight. She pulled me closer to her.

"Betrayed you? How can you believe that? Your father sacrificed himself for you! He found a way out for both of you. He was a captain in the Protector's Guard! A noble and honourable man! Dear boy! You have no idea! When the Church found out what he had done, they took him away!" She let go of my arm and covered her mouth. Her eyes were wet, and she blinked them to clear them.

It took me awhile but eventually, I found my voice. "He did... what? No. He abandoned us. I can still see him turning away and walking away from us with the city in flames! My mother, she was so upset, she..." I fell silent, the horror taking my voice.

Nadine took a moment and then spoke very softly to me as if I was a child. "That was likely the hardest thing he ever had to do—leaving his wife and a young son. The only consolation was knowing you left the city to what he thought was your safety. You were barely out of toddler clothes, Will. He led you out of the city during a massive search for you both when he had been ordered to turn you both in. Imagine that! Your own father ordered to turn in his wife and child! But he turned against his oaths and did what was right for his family. His actions let you escape, but, unfortunately, the Sect found him, soon after. He... he was never seen again. They killed him, I'm sure of that."

I stayed silent. Everything I thought I knew had been changed in a heartbeat. *My father did that for us? All my memories are questionable right now. I don't know what to believe.* It took a moment but her last words sunk in and I grasped at them to try to better understand. "The Sect?"

"Mmm, hmm. The Sect. A terrible thing. The Sect is a branch of the Church of the New Order, and very secretive. Few know of them and if they do know they keep their mouths shut for fear of their lives. The Sect, they do all the dirty work—God's work they call it, or some such nonsense. It was them that found us all—all the draoi. They searched us out. Tortured us and destroyed us. We couldn't hide from them. They called it the Purge. Called us demons. The spawns of Hell. They feared us and slaughtered us. The Sect was based right here in Jergen. Right here in Jergen of all places! In the cathedral. And they still have a hold here on the people. Everyone here knows to stay out of their way. The Church rules the people here, and they fear them.

"They are spreading throughout Belkin. The Archbishop has always sought to regain the control he lost after the Revolution. His Sect is many. They move throughout the counties and move against the Lord Protector and gain trust with the people. They are assassins first. Torturers second. All believe that they do God's work. They wear black shoes. I've observed them coming and going here in Jergen all the time. I hate them and fear them. They were the ones that hunted down the draoi." Nadine shuddered, a full body shudder, and she clasped her middle and held on to herself.

They sounded exactly like the men who had tried to kill me. I didn't know what to make of that and I thought about it for a little. Nadine seemed content and deep in her own memories and didn't notice how quiet I had become. I thought of the black shoes in my backpack. I had three pairs, and I wondered how many more pairs were out there. How many more men did evil in their god's name?

"How do you know what happened to my father?" I asked to fill the silence. Now that I knew he hadn't abandoned us, a part of me hoped he had survived somehow.

Nadine looked at me for a moment and her eyes still seemed wet. Whatever she had been remembering had woken a deep sadness in her. I didn't need my powers to see the pain in her eyes. The mention of my father seemed to make it worse for her and she wiped her eyes dry with hasty swipes of her hands. She reached out a trembling hand and scrabbled to grab mine and hold it tight. She placed her other hand on top and pulled me in a little closer. "You don't want to know, Will. You really don't so please don't ask me. You should know the Sect, they… they tortured people. After the coup attempt against the Lord Protector, your mother was the top of their list of people they wanted. All you need to know is your father died protecting where she took you that night. At least for a time."

"Why didn't he come with us?"

Nadine shook her head. "Your father was an officer in the Protector's Guard. He had an oath and a duty to fulfil. It came before his family. Still, he made sure his family was safe and then returned to his post. Your mother was likely livid with him. But that was the man she married. He had changed over the years. Became more military, more focused on his duty. Promotion. Recognition. All the typical nonsense."

"I don't remember much from that night. Flames. A cellar. My mother's face. And then nothing."

Nadine looked at me closely and then sighed. "Will, you were eight years old. Likely your mom used her power to calm you. It can muddle the memories sometimes, especially when used on someone so young—you were only a wee lad. Ack, it was pandemonium those nights. An attempt had been made to assassinate the Protector only a few days before. The Guard and the Church combined to ferret out the sympathisers. Martial law was declared, and it still hasn't been revoked, for Gaea's sake, even after all these years. Your mother was involved, but not the way you might imagine. She was drawn into something bigger. Something the Church had started." She let go of my hand and struggled to rise, her tea now finished. "But right now I'm tired. Let me sleep some and when I wake I'll explain what happened as best as I can. I wasn't part of it. I was safe here in Jergen. Your mother had moved me here. I was so angry at the time! I felt she had given up on me. Now I know. Now I know." She grew silent, and a tear rolled down her cheek. "It was much later, when the druids fled, that I found out what had happened. Some came here. And it was here the last of us fell. She saved me from the Purge."

I led her to her bed and helped her settle. I reached to examine her again. I could see how the birch bark and green tea was helping. Her blood was thinning, and it was easier on her heart. Her face had a little more colour. She moved a little less painfully. Instinctively I gave her heart a boost. The knowledge of how to help her heart muscle came from within and before I could even begin to question how the work was done, her heart gained a new strength and I knew it had come from me. I could see the tension around her eyes lessen and this seemed to tip her over the edge of sleep and she was soon snoring surprisingly loudly.

I looked over at Dog and he licked his chops and cocked his head.

"She's louder than Daukyns," I said and Dog cocked his head the other way. "Come on. Let's tend to her garden. She needs all the help she can get."

Dog stood and walked over to the back door and stopped looking back at me with what appeared to be a '*what are you waiting for?*' look.

"Coming."

When Nadine rose a few hours later I could see her health had improved. Colour flushed her cheeks, and she moved much easier and with more energy. She met me in the garden and hugged me from behind. I turned and held her and she cried against my shoulder for a long while. I felt my bond with her grow then and, being far from embarrassed, I found myself comforting this poor woman. She had led a life isolated from the druids and had lacked the skills to make a difference. It was overwhelming for her and she cried and shook in my arms and all the while I held her firmly and whispered encouraging words to her. It was probably a strange scene for anyone who could have wandered by and seen us together. It is not every day you see a young man holding an elderly woman so lovingly. And I did feel love for her. A bond had formed between us over the few short hours we had known each other. I added this to the list of questions I had mounting in my head. All I truly knew at the moment was I held in my arms probably the only person who could hope to answer the questions of my past. They hammered at me and it was all I could do to bite my tongue and wait. Her distress—or relief, for I truly knew not which—held my tongue. Truthfully, though, at that moment I felt I could wait years.

Dog pushed up between us with his wet, cold nose, looking for attention and Nadine laughed and broke her embrace and grabbed fistfuls of Dogs fur and bent down and hugged him briefly. "This dog is a wonder, Will. Look at the intelligence in his eyes!"

I glared at Dog and could see the mischief in his eyes. He was loving the attention.

"Where did you find this beautiful creature?" asked Nadine.

"Actually, he found me," I replied and then, sensing the time was right, I quickly told her of my capture and rescue.

Nadine stood quietly for a moment looking from Dog to me. She crouched down, and I was surprised to see she could move so much more freely now. I *reached* and examined her and I could see her joints were less swollen, her musculature strengthened. I was surprised and knew neither my tea nor my repairs to her heart could account for the improvements. The change in her was dramatic, to say the least.

"Hmm, a familiar, perhaps?" she asked to herself. "Perhaps. Do you feel a bond with the animal?" I shook my head. "Do you communicate?"

I shook my head at first then stopped and thought a bit. "Well, not exactly. Dog seems to understand me though. Right, Dog?"

Dog sneezed in response and looked up at me, tongue lolling and spit dripping. *What an animal*, I thought.

Nadine laughed. "Dog? You call him Dog? How unimaginative. But what he does is not normal. Dogs can't understand human speech. Some words they recognise and perhaps associate with actions and rewards. Hmm. Ask him to do something specific."

I thought for a moment. "Dog, please go get me that rag over there," and I pointed at a rag hanging over the edge of a wooden gardening tools crate. Dog looked at the rag and then back at me and then lay down on the dirt.

Nadine laughed. "Well, maybe not! Maybe Dog is just contrary."

"Ornery, too."

Dog growled and Nadine started laughing in earnest then.

"Well," she said. "Gaea sent him, that's for sure. Him and the wolves you spoke of. No doubt of that. You were fortunate, Will, very fortunate."

"Fortunate, how?"

"The Sect knows well how to capture a draoi. They mastered it over the years. They had knowledge of us no one should have known but they did and used it. They hung you from the tree with a rope that repels Gaea. They separated you from the Earth and from the Earth Mother and that separates you from your powers and your ability to ask Gaea for aid. But they underestimated you. For sure they did! They thought you nothing more than a Duilleog. But you are much more than that, Will. I would venture that you are almost a full stoc in your abilities. A craobh certainly. We'll test that soon."

"If you say so. I know nothing of this. Except, hold on, I'll be right back." I left Nadine outside and went back inside and rummaged through my pack and retrieved some items. I grabbed Daukyns' journal and the pages from the manuscript, the black boots, and the two red gems. I brought them back outside to find Nadine whispering to Dog. She stood when I came back outside and I stopped for a moment to look back and forth between them. Nadine looked like she had been caught doing something and Dog just stared back at me and I could sense laughter coming from him. I shook my head and moved over to her and handed her the items. "Don't encourage him!" I said. Nadine pouted and laughed.

"He and I were just having a word with one another. What are these?" and she turned them over in her hands.

"Dear Gaea!" she gasped as she stared at the black boots and the gems. "These are the boots from the Sect! You kept them?"

I nodded.

"These are not natural. Do you sense that?" When I shook my head, she continued. "No, perhaps you don't. I certainly don't but I had always assumed a draoi would. These boots are never found outside the Sect. During the Purge, we only managed to get our hands on one pair and here you have three pairs. Amazing, Will. You are amazing."

I had no response to that. I watched as she held up one of the gems in the palm of her hand.

"This is new," she said and held it up to the light. "Did you sense anything about it?"

"That? No."

"Did you try?"

"Try how?"

"With your *sight*. The same power you used to examine me. Try it on the gem." She held the gem out.

I opened my *senses* to it and a pain struck my head. I cried out and released my sight. "Ow! That hurt!"

"Hmm. What happened? Tell me."

"It—I dunno, I can't explain it."

"Try."

I thought a moment and when I didn't answer right away, she asked me to do it again but with less force.

"What do you mean less force?" I asked.

"Don't try so hard. Like pouring water out of a pitcher, but slowly instead of all at once. I think that's what you are doing wrong."

I tried what she suggested. I opened my *sight* in a way I thought of as being *less* and turned it to the gem. I felt a pressure against my head and I lightened my senses a little more. "Hold on, it's working." I lessened it even more until I was barely using the power. This was a new use for me and I reminded myself to work with this later. I *looked* at the gem until I could get a sense of what was happening. After a time, I could finally see my power was being reflected off the stone right back at me. The gem was like a mirror for my power. With my senses, it seemed more liquid than solid. I told Nadine, and she nodded.

"I see. It is like a lodestone but for draoi powers. This is how they found us. How they protected themselves from us. No wonder we failed at staying hidden and staying safe. Oh, dear. So much lost."

I looked at Dog and he looked sad. I could see this revelation was not good news for Nadine. "The Reeve in Jaipers has another one of these stones. He found it on the assassin that killed Bill Burstone."

Nadine nodded. "I suspect they all carry one. Well, most of them, since you only found one on that pair in the woods." Nadine tossed the boots on the ground and held on to the gem. "Gaea's power comes from life. This is one of the first things about her power you need to understand. People call her Mother Earth sometimes, but she is not the mother of the earth we walk on. She is the mother of the life that walks and grows on the earth. A gem, or a rock, has no life. It is not of her. This gem is not of Gaea. Can you ken that?"

I didn't, not really, but I nodded. She squinted her eyes at me and looked at Dog for a moment. "He doesn't does he, Dog?"

Dog pounced on a beetle, crunched it once, and swallowed it whole.

Nadine sighed and placed the gem next to the other one beside the boots. "Never mind. Later. We'll talk more about this later. Just accept what I say as truth, for now, Will, and trust me."

"I will," I said. *She didn't need to ask.* Dog made a strange noise.

"So what's this book? A journal?"

I nodded and took the journal from her and opened it to Daukyns' notes and handed it back to her. "My friend, Daukyns, the wordsmith in Jaipers, this was his journal. When he died, it came to me. Read here in the back. He wrote something to me." I pointed out the passages and let her read them.

Nadine read a page and then looked up at me and nodded. "The wordsmiths work for the Word and, without knowing it, helped spread the message of the draoi. The Word seeks harmony with nature. It is the word of Gaea that the draoi spread. Daukyns would have known a little of the draoi. He would have seen our work over the years. He had a sense of it, it seems, with you. Recognised what you might have been. He seemed a good man. And a good friend, Will. I'm sorry he passed."

"Thank you, Nadine. You and he would have gotten along famously, I think," I took the book from her and opened it to the back and pulled out the manuscript pages and handed them to her. Nadine gasped when she saw what was written on the pages.

"Impossible!" she said and, after a moment, she looked up to me. "These should not be! These are copied from the Draoi Manuscript! The sacred book of the Draoi! The Aretha Tacuinum Sanitatis! The books are hidden. Only the senior draoi know where they lie!"

"The Aretha tacinum?"

"Tacuinum Sanitatis! The Tree! Oh, for Gaea's sake. I can see you have so much to learn. Perhaps it is Gaea's will you are here at this point in time. You have so much to learn! That was my one strength, you know."

"Strength?"

"The lore. Because I lacked the gift from Gaea, I poured myself into the knowledge. It was how I helped. I had a small amount of power. Enough to barely tend the plants. It was your mother," Nadine looked at me with joy in her eyes. "She recognised that I had a gift for understanding the manuscript and teaching others. I taught the young duilleogs and even helped the craobhs. I know the book better than anyone." She shook the pages in her hand and held them up for me to see. "These pages are fakes. Well, copies, more accurately. Someone copied these. But not perfectly. See?" She pointed at a letter written on the page. "This is not precise. There should be a swirl at the end of this line here. See?"

I saw where she pointed and just nodded and smiled. "If you say so."

"Oh, you!" she said and swatted me with the pages. "Trust me. It's wrong but close. Very close. All the words are correct but the accuracy is off. Copies. I would know! But this shouldn't be."

"Why not?"

"Because the books were closely held and protected by the owners. All were accounted for! For one to be copied so painstakingly means that one was borrowed or stolen for a long period. For months if it is just these pages. Years for the entire book!" She shuffled through the pages and held them up close to her eyes. She strained to read the pages. I *reached* and corrected her vision without a thought and shared her startled look when we both realised what I had just done.

Nadine's legs collapsed under her and she sat there blinking up at me.

"Dear Gaea! What are you?"

I just shook my head and sat beside her and took one of her hands in mine.

* * *

A little while later we sat comfortably inside her home. I stood at one of her windows and watched as the sun rapidly disappearing behind the city skyline to the West turned the ocean to the east dark and brooding. I shuddered and closed my eyes for a moment. I was feeling a bit tossed like jetsam on the ocean. *Or was it flotsam?* I sighed as the sound of the waves crashing on the cliff below soothed my dark thoughts and I turned back to Nadine to enjoy one of my tea mixtures that I found soothed the soul. I had prepared a small meal for us and Nadine was pressed up against her table on a raised stool smacking her lips in satisfaction. Apparently, I was a very good cook. Nadine had insisted on telling me so after almost every bite. Dog had devoured the last of the dried meats I had and was busy trying to make me understand he was soon to perish from hunger. I was thus far successfully ignoring the plaintive look he kept focused on my face. It was almost comical.

Nadine had been reading the journal and the pages throughout our meal and seemed to be enjoying her improved vision. She kept looking around and holding the pages at varying lengths from her eyes and chortling. I was starting to find it a little unsettling and, when she noticed my discomfort, she berated me and told me to wait until I was old as her.

We talked for an hour about the draoi manuscript. She explained it contained all the lore the druids knew about their powers and strengths. "It would also expose our weaknesses. I wonder..." she said and drew quiet for a time. She seemed pleased when I first used the word *our* to express the draoi. She said it meant I had accepted who and what I was. It also earned me another blow to the upper arm.

She was confident I was a craobh. But, she added, I would remain one until I knew the lore the manuscript contained. I told her she could teach me and she cried for a little while. At first, I thought I had upset her and when I expressed my sorrow she smacked me again in anger. Apparently, she also cried when she was happy and my words were quick to remove her happiness. Or so she said with so many words.

With our meal finished we leaned back in our seats and savoured our teas in comfortable silence. She looked more vibrant than before. Her eyes lit up like stars when she laughed. I studied her for a moment and was tempted to *reach* out to her again and see how my tea was helping her pain but I resisted the urge.

"Your mother once told me Gaea had told her I wasn't ready to have draoi powers, you know," she said after pushing aside her empty plate. When she saw me looking out at the sunset, she slapped my hand. "Pay attention! She said I had another calling. The lore, she said to me, was mine to pass along. I thought she meant my teaching of the young ones at the time. I think instead, she meant this. Gaea protected me from the Purge so I could be here for you. I'm certain of that. Well, mostly certain..."

I didn't know how to respond. *Was she upset? Disappointed?* I was afraid to speak and she must have sensed it.

"Silly boy! Stop looking like everything is your fault! This is a good thing! All my life I spoke to Gaea. Pleaded with her to give me her powers so I could make a difference. I felt certain I had disappointed her somehow. I tried everything I could to seek her favour. Mostly I felt so unworthy. Eventually, I just tended my garden. Gathered what herbs I could and sold them where I could, always knowing a duilleog could produce better herbs than I without trying. It hurt my pride. I've grown a little wiser now and I can see it for what it was. Today pride matters little to me when it hurts to simply close my hand."

She grew silent again and sipped her tea. She flexed a hand and raised an eyebrow. She absently grabbed a scone and tossed it to Dog who snatched it expertly out of the air without breaking his attempt to lock eyes on me and swallowed it whole. When I refused to look at him he huffed and turned his attention to Nadine. She reached out and rustled the fur on his head. He bore it without complaint.

"So here I am. With the last of the draoi in my home—and enjoying the best food I have ever had in my life—and I have in front of me a few copied pages of the very lore I was exceptionally good at teaching to young draoi. Brought to me by the same last draoi, who turns out to be the son I helped raise for the woman who once led the draoi. What should I make of that, hmm?"

I knew, this time, I owed her an answer by the way she was looking at me but, to be honest, I had no idea what was going on. The druids were foreign to me. If that was what we were then it was she who understood them and certainly not me. "I admit there is a certain coincidence at play here."

"Coincidence? Bah! There is no such thing as coincidence with Gaea. She is a manipulative bitch when she wants to be, mark my words!"

Dog growled and Nadine tossed him another scone, which shut him up. I looked at him and he winked at me. *Dogs don't wink, do they?* I glared at Dog but he just looked away from me back to Nadine.

"No, this is meant to be," she declared, and the conversation seemed to end.

The darkness outside was getting complete and so I rose and started to light more candles in her room from a small brand I drew from her hearth. The soft candlelight glowed off the walls of her house and the feeling of being home returned. The strength of realisation overcame me for a moment and a small cry escaped me. I stopped where I was with the feeling of a great weight coming off me. Nadine startled me by hugging me from behind. She moved so quietly. How she knew what I was feeling was a testament to her powers of observation. She held me for a time and we returned to the table. I looked at her brown eyes and saw the affection returned.

This was home and always would be. I smiled at her and her smile grew wider. I could see the young woman she used to be inside those eyes and with it a sense of wonder and joy. Her aura glowed so brightly and blue: a deeper and richer blue than that of the Reeve. Then I saw the bond between us. A thick ribbon of blue joined us from heart to heart. I felt along the ribbon and could sense her presence. I closed my eyes and knew wherever she was I would be able to sense her. I opened my eyes and told her what I had seen.

"You can see it? The ribbon?" she asked. I nodded. "That is the bond that joins all draoi."

"What does it do?"

"It allows the draoi to always know where the others are and how they fare," her smile faltered. "And feel it when they pass. I was spared that during the Purge. My bond was never strong. I merely felt a little loss. A moment of sadness. Usually, I had to be told," She bowed her head. "Except when your mother died. We all felt her pass. We all saw what happened. The image of the head of the Sect standing before your mother and leering as her lifeblood spilt to the ground was for all to see. Then the image was gone, and the pain struck. The bond of the Cill Darae is to Gaea herself and when she died a little of Gaea died with her. Gaea bonds the draoi to the Tree. When her bond to your mother was severed, the draoi fell apart in a panic. Normally a new bond is formed immediately but not this time. It was as if Gaea had abandoned us. I hated her then and I still do in many ways. I wonder all the time how she could have let all this happen." She looked at the ceiling for a moment and rubbed the fatigue in her eyes.

The silence deepened and Nadine scowled and slapped the table, startling Dog and I. "Enough. You need to work on your display of power. You light up like a blue flamed candle when you use your power. You need to learn to use less. To be more subtle. Try it now and let me see."

I practised for an hour or so. It wasn't hard to learn. It just required someone to watch and provide comment. After the hour, I made more tea, and I spent some time following the rats outside as they looked for food in the darkness. I worried about Nadine's garden and, with a little thought, marked the area as off limits and felt pride when the rats seemed to stay clear of Nadine's yard. I had so much to learn. I couldn't wait to have Nadine's help on that and hoped to learn where more of the manuscripts lay. After a time, we sat in silent thought.

The silence and darkness grew, and we finished our tea deep in our own thoughts. The candles struggled to keep the night away. Dog lay still on the floor, head on his paws, and asleep. I heard Nadine speak of the death of my mother but felt nothing new. I saw no new memories. I tried to imagine the death of my mother but could not. I had no memory, and the words stirred nothing in me other than my continued grief for the loss of my mother. I knew nothing of Gaea but wondered how, if she could have stopped it, she let my mother die. I sighed and sought solace in the Word. Daukyns had taught me years ago to not worry about things I had no control over and I found a way to break myself out of my stupor. I rose and set to cleaning up the dishes at her sink while I could still see them. I filled her sink with the reservoir drawn from her well. I shaved soap from her bar into the cold water and stirred it with a hand to mix it.

I was feeling angry at something but knew not what it was. I needed to know more about what befell my mother and I the night we fled Munsten. The image of the city in flames returned to me and I grabbed a plate and thrust it into the water.

"Tell me about the coup," I said as I washed the first plate, my voice seemed overly loud in the quiet and I lowered my voice. "My mentor in Jaipers told me the history of it. I would like to hear it from the draoi point of view and how it affected my mother and me."

I paused, and I stopped washing, my hands still in the water. I heard a soft sigh from Nadine before she responded. "Alright."

Nine

Munsten Castle, 890 A.C.

"OH, NO YOU don't, young man!" cried the smiling Belle Arbor, chasing her son across the chamber. Will Arbor squealed with excitement, evading his mother's grasp by mere inches, and flew across the room looking behind him at his approaching mother. Grasped firmly in his hand was his mother's coin he had just stolen from her. Laughing at his mischievousness, he misstepped and tripped heavily. He sprawled on the stone floor landing hard on his chin and the coin bounced free of his hand to disappear under the large bed his mother and father shared. His laughter cut off abruptly and there was a moment of stunned silence before the pain hit the little boy. His eight years of age betrayed him, and a wail exploded out of him.

Belle scooped up her son and grasped his head to take a look at the damage. Will was screaming in terror now and crying for Nadine. The cries hurt her ears with their intensity in their small chambers in the castle in Munsten. She could see his chin was split wide open, and a tooth had pierced his lower lip. Blood ran freely mixing with the tears streaming like rivers from her son's eyes. Her eyes lost focus for a moment and the cuts closed until nothing but the blood and tears remained.

"Hush, shh," she soothed rubbing his hair and reaching in her blouse pocket for a handkerchief. She drew it out quickly and wetted it with her tongue before rubbing the blood and tears away. "Shh, William. Calm down. Shh! It's over. The pain's gone. Settle down. Nadine's not here any longer, my wee bairn. She's left with the young ones, remember?"

In a moment, Will ceased crying with a yelp and opened his eyes wide to stare at his mum. She smiled lovingly down at him and she could see her reflection in his eyes. Her long blond hair was messed up from chasing her son around the room in fun. Her cheeks were bright red and contrasted with her deep blue eyes. Her son was the spitting image of her husband, Captain William Arbor. *It is right that he's named after him*, she thought. Her son had her husband's beautiful brownish-red hair and her blue eyes. But the set of the nose and mouth and the square chin were those of William. She sighed and wiped away the last of the tears. "There, there. All better, my wee bairn."

Will nodded but bit his lower lip. He was always ready to expect the cuts to return, and this time was no different. Belle laughed to herself and reached out to Gaea.

It's a wonder he's survived this long, she sent.

Don't worry Belle. I watch over this one. Trust me in this, replied Gaea.

Oh, I do. You know that. Still, I sense something is wrong. Will you share it with me?

No, my daughter. I cannot.

Belle shuddered without knowing why. She was the Cill Darae and her bond to Gaea was unique. She could tell no one what the bond was like. Gaea had forbidden it. In many ways, she was no different from a true mother, but in so many other ways she was too large to understand or to grasp. *It was like holding a mountain in your hands. No one could and yet if you tried it would be like holding Gaea before you. An impossible task.*

Belle used her sense to observe all the draoi ties spreading from her out to all the other draoi in the Realm. She loved this aspect of the power granted by Gaea. She could sense down each thread and know how each draoi fared. How they loved, laughed and cried. It was a beautiful gift. Sometimes sad when a draoi passed back to the Earth Mother, but almost always a comfort to feel the vibrancy of each thread.

Belle found herself reaching out through those threads more and more these days. *Lately*, mused Belle, *Gaea has been seeming more distant. Saddened.* Belle was worried. She had told her husband, but he had merely shrugged and gone on duty. He never truly understood her ties to Gaea and found it harder to believe she was the second highest ranked draoi in the Realm. *It would be hard to convince anyone of that when only you heard the voice. It's a wonder he doesn't just think I am crazy and be done with me!* Theirs was a marriage sparked by love, strengthened by the arrival of Will, but weakened over time by duty. Now they argued and fought all the time. They tried to keep it quiet in their chamber but many times now Will had stumbled in from his adjoining room crying at the shouting. Tears stung her eyes, and she held Will tighter.

She missed Nadine. Nadine was such a good person and so kind to the young ones she taught. Will loved her dearly. Often it was Nadine who soothed the tears. Unfortunately, Gaea had told her she had plans for Nadine and it meant she had to keep her powers from her. Belle had pressed for more details, but Gaea had simply ignored her and told her to send her away to Jergen. As Cill Darae, she obeyed without question. *Well, not too many questions. Always I know when there is nothing more to learn from the Earth Mother.* Gaea would not and could not help unless it was part of her plans. She was sympathetic but ultimately the minor inconveniences of human affairs meant little to her. The draoi would be stunned to know each draoi meant so little to her. They were tools and nothing more. Gaea was everything and everyone. One small piece of her, like Belle herself, was a speck of dust glinting in the sunlight through a window.

I am a little different though, thought Belle, knowing she was trying to convince herself. *Gaea has told me so and I almost believe her. And she loves my son. Calls him her favourite, but that, I suspect, is merely to boost my ego. But something is coming. Gaea has put something in motion and we will all suffer for it.*

A soft knock on her door drew her out of her thoughts and she released Will. She tousled his hair and took his hand and led him out of her bedroom.

"One minute!" she called out to whoever was bothering her this late at night. She turned to Will. "Run to your room now! Be quick! Into your bed clothes and under the covers. No listening in, you hear?"

Will slipped his hand from hers, laughed, and ran down the hallway to his room.

"I'll be in soon to tuck you in and tell you a story. But only if you stay in bed!" Belle smiled at the giggles coming from Will's room. "Such a cheeky wee lad," she said to herself and walked to the front door.

The chambers provided to her family were large. Part of being the second advisor under Freamhaigh Dalton were these rooms. Everyone in the castle told her how fortunate she was. Married to such a handsome man and a Captain in the Guard. Second to the Advisor to the Lord Protector. Living large in the Realm's capital of Munsten. She sighed and shook her head. *And I'm completely cut off from the earth. It's so lonely and desolate here inside the stone of the castle. And trying to keep my husband happy seems impossible.*

She stopped at the door and turned to the wall mirror. She tucked a strand of hair behind her ear, nodded to herself, and then opened the door. Freamhaigh John Dalton, known by everyone else as the Advisor to the Lord Protector, stood there looking uncomfortable. *As he always does*, thought Belle as she forced a smile to her face.

"Come in, Advisor Dalton." Belle stepped aside and let her Freamhaigh enter her chambers. She looked out into the hallway and, content that it was empty, closed and locked the door and followed Dalton into the living area. "Wine?"

"Please." Dalton perched on the edge of the seat of the sofa and looked around the chambers. "Your place always seems so much more alive than mine."

Belle answered from the pantry as she searched for a bottle of wine the Freamhaigh favoured. "That's only because it is a family that lives here, John. Time you changed that. Found someone to settle down with. It's never too late!" *Except who could love a man as dour as John?*

That wasn't nice.

Hush, Gaea. You know it's true.

Perhaps. Will is listening in. Using his powers. John will sense it.

Belle rushed over to Will's room and poked her head in. "Stop it. Right this second!" she whispered at the form under the covers of Will's bed. Will poked his head up over the sheets and grinned at her. "I mean it! No story if you keep this up." Will's eyes grew round, and he nodded his head before flopping down on his bed.

Belle blew hair out of her face and rushed back to John to find him uncorking one of the bottles of wine he liked. 'Ah, good, you've found it. Cups. One second."

"It is too late, Belle. No one would have me. If Gaea meant for me to produce children she would have made it happen. I'm past middle age. Past my prime."

"Nonsense! She doesn't work that way! And you're not."

"Humph. Well, she does. And yes, I am."

"John! I'm shocked. You shouldn't speak of her that way."

"Why? Is she listening in now? Plotting something?"

Belle returned with two wooden cups and set them down on the low table next to the couch. John poured wine into the cups, took one and finally sat back on the sofa and took a sip.

"Ah," he said smiling for the first time. "Perfect. Now will you tell me where you found this wine?"

"Nope. It will remain a secret, I'm afraid." Gaea had guided her to a room, deep within the castle. Inside she found the belongings of Bishop Arnold Bengold, the man who had arguably caused the Revolution and the downfall of the Church. He had travelled to Munsten with a massive amount of goods and the longer the Great Debate had gone on the more he had brought in from his Northern county. Half of the contents of the storage room was wine from the vineyard near where he had grown up. It was a spectacular wine, and it had kept in the cold room despite the years. Gaea had told her John would like it and sure enough, the first night she had offered it, he had fallen in love with it. Now he returned again and again for more.

They sat in silence enjoying the wine. Their relationship was unique, and she was glad her husband understood. John was the head of the Tree. The Freamhaigh. Chosen by the draoi and his words were law and all draoi obeyed. Belle was the Cill Darae, chosen by Gaea. He represented the draoi, and she represented Gaea. He was the mind and she the heart.

When she had been chosen by Gaea, no one could have been more surprised than her. She was only a young draoi, only recently having achieved stoc status. She knew she was gifted, but hearing Gaea speaking directly to her had been amazing. Since then she had followed Gaea faithfully. She trusted her with her life and that of her son.

She and John discussed matters of the draoi. Gaea expressed concerns about human affairs and impact on the world and John made changes to better provide balance. If Gaea wanted her to give wine to the Freamhaigh and keep him busy, then so be it. She refilled John's cup and sat back once more. The silence between them had grown, and she knew something troubled him. She knew being patient and simply waiting drew the details out the fastest. After a moment, John cleared his throat and Belle suppressed a smile.

"So, Belle," he began. "I was hoping you could speak to Gaea for me. It is a trifling matter, but I have waited on it for too long already. Doubtless she knows already but well, sometimes it is best to clear the air. I'm sure you understand."

"Yes, John."

"Well, the Church of the New Order. They've grown stronger in the past couple of years. I am hearing rumours of their actions. Draoi have gone missing. Some claim they are being watched. They see eyes everywhere if all is to be believed."

"And?" Belle didn't mean to be abrupt. She had heard the same rumours and had asked Gaea about it already. Gaea had not chosen to answer. This was the very thing that had Belle worried and now the Freamhaigh was questioning what was happening. *This does not bode well*, she thought.

"The Tree, the senior stoc, they are starting to press me much harder. They cannot hide from the Church what they must do on a daily basis to maintain the balance. They are watched and followed, and their work suffers. They are starting to fear for their lives. The senior stoc believe the vast majority of the draoi have been identified by these Church members. They are frightened and frightened people do stupid things."

"What would you have me do?"

"Do? Belle, you are the Cill Darae. You have Gaea's ears. Surely you can plead with her to take action or to allow the draoi to do what they must."

"John! Surely you can't be serious. Gaea would never allow her powers to cause harm."

"No, no," he said raising his voice a little. "Of course not. What I mean is they need to be able to defend themselves. Hide from this threat or something similar. They have been exposed. They feel hunted. They want an escape from the threat. Permission to use their powers in the preservation of life."

Belle pressed her forehead into her hand and leaned forward. She was torn. She was a stoc and the Cill Darae. As a stoc, she understood the exasperation the draoi must be feeling. Exposed and unable to do anything other than run. It was tiring being the fearful rabbit all the time, surrounded by circling hawks. The rumours were more than rumours. Gaea had more or less confirmed the draoi were exposed, but she openly admitted she chose not to do anything about it.

Belle recalled Gaea's words: *Keep the Freamhaigh happy. Feed him the wine. Soothe his mind with words and platitudes. It is not his role to resolve this. You, as my Cill Darae, do this for me. It must happen. It is the sacrifice that enables so much more.*

And so Belle lied to this poor man. Time and again. She hated it. It ate at her. Afterwards, Gaea would speak with her and tell her what she did was for the greater good and she believed in those words. Part of her wondered if Gaea was lying to her just as she lied to John.

Belle patted John's knee. "It's okay, John. I've told you. Gaea is aware and not concerned and neither should you be. All is as it should be. That's enough for me. Calm the draoi. Let them see your presence and determination. Your lack of fear and they will be strengthened."

John sighed and finished his wine. "Did you ever read the book written by Benjamin Erwin, Belle?"

Belle blinked. *What an unexpected question.* She had heard of the book but never read it. Gaea told her not to bother with it and she hadn't. "No, I haven't, why?"

"Benjamin, as you know well, was the Freamhaigh when the Great Debate occurred. He was the one who argued against the Church and Bishop Bengold. They were very good friends, I bet you didn't know that. After the Revolution, Benjamin wrote a book. In it, he wrote the two of them had agreed to let the Church win the debate. They both foresaw great tragedy if the Word won the debate. The fires of revolution were ready to be lit, and that debate proved to be the spark. Benjamin wrote Gaea had directly intervened at the end and forced Bengold to say the words he said that day in the capital. Those famous words. So many died as a result. Civil war across the Realm and today we are still reeling from that. The balance has never been worse. The draoi are weary beyond belief. They use their powers without fear of being caught because they no longer care. And they have been observed. By a Sect doing great evil, hidden within the Church.

"I tell you this because I believe that Gaea is setting us up for a great fall. I fear the draoi will be no more. And I don't say this lightly. I say this to you, Belle. You who are the eyes and ears of Gaea herself. I tell you but really I am talking to Gaea." John took a deep breath and looked Belle directly in the eyes. The look was pleading and anguished. "Do not do this. Do not. I beg you, please."

Belle held her hand over her beating heart trying to calm it. She held her breath as well and waited to hear from Gaea. The plea from the Freamhaigh could not go unanswered. *Surely not? Earth Mother? Did you not hear?*

Belle felt a tear break free from her right eye and track down past her nose and she shook her head in sorrow at the Freamhaigh. Gaea was silent.

John's chin trembled, and he lowered his head and Belle watched, shocked, as his shoulders shook with the effort of crying.

Later in the evening, just before midnight, Captain William Arbor finished his climb up the back stairs of the Lord Protector's keep. He was soon to be on duty standing guard outside the main chambers. He would track all who came and went according to the schedule ledger on the small dais outside the chambers. Behind him stood four guards. Their uniforms shone and their weapons gleamed. Their duty was simple: protect the Lord Protector while he slept. All officers from the Protectors of the Realm hated this task. It was long and tedious and was rewarded with a morning of sword drill in the yard. It was an endless feeling watch: first the excruciating boredom from midnight to sunrise and then a thorough pounding from the head man-of-arms of the Lord Protector's guard. Only after the drill were they allowed to break their fast and retire to their bunks. As an officer, William was required to head to the offices to complete paperwork and only then would he be allowed to seek rest. Once a week they suffered this rotation. William longed for his promotion to Major when he could, at last, be excused from this particular duty.

His wife didn't understand. Belle couldn't understand why he worked so hard so he could be promoted. He knew only then would he have enough free time to spend with his wife and child. He worked hard for them and she seemed to resent it. *I need you now*, she would scream. *Not later!* And he would try to calm her and fail every time. *It was unfair*, he thought. *She has a god watching over her and I have nothing to offer her but my love and duty.*

William emerged from the back hallway hidden behind the main wall of the Keep and knocked on the small wood plaque nailed to the stone wall he faced. His knock was a pattern, and it repeated back to him before the section of wall swung soundlessly open on well-oiled hinges. He entered the small chamber and nodded once to the corporal who stood to hold the secret access door open.

"Evenin', suh!" spoke the young man. William nodded to him and moved past and removed a cloak from a row of them hanging on pegs. They were ceremonial, heavy and hot and William loathed them.

"Evening, Corporal Carrigan. Coming on?" he asked even though he knew he was. William knew the watch rotation of the Guard by heart. He had drafted it. It was one of his many secondary duties.

"Suh, yes, suh."

"Very well. The others are not here yet?"

"No, suh, they're here. You are the last. We all came on a bit early tonight, suh."

William frowned. That was not normal. *I'm a good twenty minutes early. I always am. Strange the men were here before me. That never happens.* As if sensing something wrong the corporal continued speaking.

"Bit of a favour, suh. They follow us next cycle and promised to give us extra time off."

This time, William turned to look at the corporal. He knew the rotation and knew this was not possible. He felt he needed to warn the corporal they had been duped. Just as he was about to open his mouth the officer he was to relieve looked into the room and saw William standing there with his cloak fastened around his shoulders.

"Ah, William! You're here early too! Good! Perfect night for it! I've got a date lined up and now I can stop by the larder and pick out some cheeses beforehand! Thanks mate!"

William smiled and stepped up to Captain Brent Bairstow and clasped his forearm. "Brent, well met. How was the watch and what are you doing abandoning your post to look in on me?"

"Easy my friend! The men are doubled out there while they turn over. Rest at ease! The Lord Protector is safe from harm!"

William laughed and wondered how this officer got away with everything. *I work hard and this man seems to hardly need to work to get ahead!* William shook his head in mock dismay. "The ladies will rise up one day, Brent, and drag you down with them!"

"A day I look forward to, my friend!" Brent seemed to notice the corporal listening in on them and turned with mock alarm. "Corporal! You have me at my worst! Pray ignore this tarnished officer's impropriety!"

The corporal's eyes widened, and he held up his hands in surrender. "Suh, I know nothing of any pro-pretty! Wouldn't know it to see it!"

"Good man, good!" laughed Brent and clasped the man on the upper arm. "Good for you," Brent swirled and beckoned William out to the dais for their turnover. "William for the last hour I have been waiting for you to say the magic words! Come! Let's turn this sorry excuse for a duty over. I need to hear you say you have the watch!"

William laughed and followed him out to the dais standing beside the double doors leading into the Lord Protector's private sanctum.

Craobh

Ten

Munsten Castle, 890 A.C.

BELLE ARBOR NODDED politely to Archbishop Greigsen when he gestured with a wide brush of his arm for her to proceed ahead of him up the stairs leading up to the outer chamber of the Lord Protector's inner sanctum. Internally she shuddered. *He is not of this earth*, she thought. *Gaea, please tell me what this man is?* She waited for an answer from Gaea as she always did and, hearing nothing, started up the wide, steep stairs. She heard the Archbishop behind her grunt in pain with each of his steps. She could see he suffered from joint pain but could not help him. Her gift would not let her examine him as she could with everyone else. *Plus, he refuses the teas I provide him. Seriously, I can't do anything more. And I don't think I want to—let me be honest with myself. He is an abomination to nature I simply cannot understand.*

Four months ago, along with the Freamhaigh Dalton, she had tried to convince the Lord Protector John Healy all was not well with the Archbishop. Healy had merely laughed at them. *I have the Archbishop exactly where I need him, my dear*, he had said. And then he had patted her bottom.

It was one of the few times she felt the need to use her powers against someone. The offence shook her to her core. *No one touches me except my husband*, she thought furiously. She looked to Freamhaigh Dalton for help and he looked away. She could still remember the shock of seeing him turn away. The highest ranking draoi in the Realm had chosen to do nothing. It only reinforced her loneliness and helplessness. She could see so much that had to change, and she was powerless to interfere.

She had run from the room then, with Healy laughing at her retreat thinking he had power over her. *Little did he know I was close to causing him significant harm. He was lucky I left when I did.* She could hear the lie she told herself. Gaea forbade the exposure of draoi power. Later, after she had calmed, she cornered the Freamhaigh and laid into him. His response was to try to convince her to simply forget about it. She had screamed at him then and said some very unladylike things. *William was proud of me when I told him,* she thought smugly. *Proud I used the words he taught me over the years.*

As she neared the top of the stairs, she calmed her emotions and prepared herself to enter the outer chamber. *My husband will still be on duty and I need to present him with a calm wife and not a vengeful polecat.* She reached the top stair and strode purposefully into the room distancing herself from the Archbishop who continued to struggle behind her. She ignored the two guards on either side of the entranceway and looked over at her husband behind the dais. She could see the look of surprise that appeared briefly on his face. *No one other than me would have seen it,* she thought. *But it was there for me to see and enjoy. Petty, I know, but if he insists on this duty before family business then I get to have my little rewards.*

"Captain Arbor, sir," she said when she stopped at the red line crossing the middle of the room. No one was allowed to cross the line unless the Captain of the Outer Chamber—who just happened to be her husband at the moment—allowed it. In order to be allowed to cross the line meant your name had to be written in the large ledger gracing the dais. It was maintained and updated by the Lord Protector's Privy Council, twice daily. These rooms were once the only rooms permitting a private audience to the King. The access and control had not changed with the Revolution. *What worked, worked,* she thought and shrugged mentally. She forced her shoulders back and stood as straight as she could before announcing to her husband: "Belle Arbor, Assistant Word Advisor to the Lord Protector, reporting at his summons to his chambers."

Her husband stared at her for a moment before remembering his duty. He blinked and then looked down at the ledger and she could see his eyes searching for her name. He wouldn't find it, she knew. The Archbishop was expected, but not her. The Lord Protector had sent one of his pages to fetch her and tell her to join the Archbishop. Healy wanted her rather than the

Freamhaigh at the meeting. She clenched her teeth while her husband turned the page in the book. Healy disgusted her. She could barely maintain her composure around him any longer and she was worried this latest audience would send her over the edge.

She hated last minute meetings. Especially up here in his chambers. The touch on her bottom had been followed with leers and other attempts since then. Healy was a pig. Infuriatingly, her own husband didn't seem to understand just how belittling it was to have her treated as a sex object rather than the intelligent woman she was. It was one of their latest fights.

* * *

"William! For Gaea's sake, the man is a pig! He touched me again this morning. In view of everyone. He didn't care. This has to stop!"

"Belle, honey, I understand. It's frustrating. He does it for who knows what reason. It makes me angry but what can I do about it? I'm just a captain in the Guard! If I say something they'll put me out!"

"Put you out? That's what you're worried about? Your job? Are you serious right now?" Belle screamed the last words.

"Belle, Belle!"

"Don't you Belle me, William! I can't take it anymore. I can't abide being near him. He *touches* me, William. He is touching your *wife*, for Gaea's sake."

"I know! I hate knowing! I don't know what to do. What can I do to make it right?"

"Tell the General!"

"The General won't care. You know how he is. What about Dalton?"

"Dalton doesn't care either, he..." Belle's words cut off when young Will pushed their door open and slowly walked in rubbing his eyes. "Wee William, what are you doing up at this hour?"

"I couldn't sleep, mum," he said. "Why are you and dad yelling and fighting?"

"We're fighting..." started her husband.

Belle interrupted him and gave him a stern look to keep his mouth shut. "We're not fighting, sweetie. We're arguing a bit. It's nothing important. Adult stuff. Come, off to bed with you." Belle scooped up her son and ushered him to bed, glad to be interrupted before she said something she would later regret.

* * *

Her husband looked up as the Archbishop shuffled to stand next to her in front of the red line. "Captain Arbor," began the Archbishop. "Your wife and I are expected. You will not find her name on the list. She was only just summoned by one of the pages. It was supposed to be Dalton on the access list this morning. Not your lovely wife. My apologies."

Her husband glared at the Archbishop and Belle bit her cheek to stop from smiling. Most people had an immediate dislike of the man and her husband was no exception. *Perhaps it is the lack of any aura that annoys people*, thought Belle. *Amongst other things.* Things had been strained last night with Dalton. His sorrow was so deep she feared he would do something drastic. She felt the same sorrow now. There was a feeling in the air. *A bad feeling.* Dalton had left her chambers last night with two bottles of wine, one in each hand. *It's no wonder he wasn't here this morning.*

"Of course, your Grace," said her husband biting off each word. "One moment while I announce you." William turned to one of the two corporals standing near him and nodded. Belle watched, as she had many times before, as the young man saluted and marched past the dais to knock once on the double doors before opening it enough to allow him to pass inside. The door shut automatically behind him.

Belle waited and looked around at the other guardsmen. There were always eight of them on watch. Two behind her at the top of the stairs, one on the right and left walls just behind the red line, two behind the dais next to her husband, and two, she knew and only because her husband had told her, hidden in the small chamber carefully positioned behind the tapestries lining the walls. There was a noise behind her and she turned her head to watch eight more guards emerge from the stairs. *That's odd*, she thought and when she turned to look at her husband, she could see he was surprised, too.

Just then the corporal emerged from behind the double doors and approached William. She heard him whisper they were expected, and the Protector bade them enter. William nodded but frowned at the additional guardsmen entering the room and the noise they were making and then turned to her and the Archbishop.

"Your Lady and your Grace, please enter."

Belle nodded and walked past her husband. The corporal moved over to one of the double doors and opened it for her. She smiled graciously and slipped into the inner sanctum. She could hear the Archbishop enter behind her. She looked around the inner chamber and was not surprised to see the private dining table empty. The dark woods and gold leaf decorations gave the place a rich look and the large windows showed a beautiful sunrise happening outside. *Such a waste to allow such a boorish man to make use of it*, she thought. As the door swung shut to the room, she could hear her husband starting to raise his voice to the guardsmen, and she smiled. *They were in for it.* She recognised the tone of voice.

The Archbishop looked around the room searching for a Lord Protector. *Who clearly*, she huffed to herself, *was not present in the room.* Belle smiled and gestured to the door to the chamber leading to the large adjoining office. The Archbishop grimaced and limped over to the door and knocked. Hearing no reply, he cracked the door open a little and looked inside. He looked over to Belle and shook his head.

Belle turned to the other door—the one leading to the bedchamber—and grimaced. She took a breath and marched over and rapped on the wood door frame. She waited and heard a muffled "Enter".

"Your Grace," she said over to the Archbishop. "He's in here." The Archbishop nodded and started over to her. Belle grabbed the doorknob and turned it and slowly pushed open the door. The first thing she saw was the unmade massive bed sitting central to the room. It had a soaring canopy cover and was dressed with silk tassels. *Such a large bed for such a small man. My husband and I could make good use of it*, she thought and bit her inner cheek to stop from smiling. She looked left and spied Lord Protector John Healy where he was seated at a small table next to the large bay window. He was eating his breakfast and watching the sunrise outside. The clouds on the horizon were on fire with oranges and reds. It was a breath-taking view, but she was surprised to see the Lord Protector taking the time to enjoy it. *Or being able to appreciate it.*

"Lord Protector, you summoned us?" asked Belle Arbor and stepped to the side to allow the Archbishop to enter first.

Healy rose, placed his napkin on the table, and looked over at the two of them. "Yes, thank you. However, it was actually the Archbishop who called for this meeting. He asked for the Word Advisor but I preferred you over that sour man for obvious reasons."

Belle snapped her head over to the Archbishop and she could see the anger in his eyes and that surprised her. He never showed anger. *Why now?* The Archbishop was a mystery to her. She watched him as Healy strode across the room to welcome them. Healy raised his hand to shake hands with the Archbishop and Belle could see the jaw tighten on the head of the Church. The Protector saw it now. She could see his eyes widen a little. *Such hatred, cold and hard, there for all to see here in this private chamber. This is unexpected. These two go back all the way to the Revolution. Greigsen helped calm a nation and hand the Realm over to Healy. Why the hatred? Why now? Unless it didn't matter now, but why?*

Healy left Greigsen, but gave him one more look, before coming to stand in front of Belle. Belle watched his smarmy smile fill his repugnant face. She curtseyed and lowered her head to hide her disgust. When she rose, expression cleared from her face, he grasped her offered hand and bent low over it to press his dry lips against it. He held it for an unacceptably long amount of time and Belle pulled it free with a tug. Healy rose and smiled knowingly at her. He had the audacity to wink before turning back to Greigsen. Belle felt the heat on her cheeks and turned to see if the Archbishop had noticed. *But,* she saw, *he's not even looking at us or out the window. He's looking over to the fireplace behind Healy.*

She focused on the fireplace and, at first, wasn't sure what she was seeing. Then she saw a figure emerge from a secret door that had opened beside the fireplace. *It was Seth Farlow,* she recognised. *The weasel of the castle.* She gasped. She could sense he had no aura. *He wasn't of the earth! Like the Archbishop.* She saw he carried a small crossbow and was raising it toward the Lord Protector who still had his back to the threat, unaware. Time seemed to slow. Outside the room, she heard a sudden commotion, and she froze confused by what she was hearing and seeing.

ACT NOW! STOP THE ASSASSIN!

The loud voice of Gaea in her head had her reacting automatically. She was the Cill Darae of the Draoi, the Head Priestess of Gaea herself, her power was Gaea's and she felt the strength Gaea gave her now. Belle had trained many draoi in the past on how to defend themselves, how to use their powers against others, and how to heal. She was the best healer of them all. With her knowledge of healing came an intimate knowledge of how to harm a human body. She started to reach out to use her power to stop Seth when she found to her shock he was untouchable by her abilities. A shout sounded outside in the outer chamber accompanied with the clash of steel on steel. She had little time, the crossbow was almost level now and Belle saw many things at once. She saw the gleam in the Archbishop's eyes, she saw Healy start to turn his head toward the sounds in his outer chamber, and she saw there was little she could do against a man like Seth who was beyond her powers.

Belle reacted. She used her new strength to push her body into a motion beyond what normal people could manage. She manipulated her body internally without thought. She was unable to harm another with her power, but she could use the power on herself. She moved in front of the crossbow just as the bolt was released. She reached up with a hand and snatched it out of the air and felt a burn on her palm. She reversed the arrow and threw it back at the strange man who stood before her. His eyes were wide with fright as he tried to track her movements. She watched the arrow pierce the man in the right breast and saw the pain lighting up his features mix with a look of pleasure. *What the...?* She whirled toward Healy and saw first the horror on the face of the Archbishop. He raised a hand toward her and pointed. Belle looked back to Seth and was stunned to see him moving at speed out of the room and back through the secret opening. *He had Gaea's powers, but how?*

"Demon!" cried the Archbishop. "She's a demon!"

Healy looked at her in confusion and then back to the sounds of fighting and cries for help coming from outside.

"She's here to kill you, Lord Protector!"

Healy glanced at her a second time and frowned. Belle heard her husband cry out.

GO TO HIM. SAVE HIM.

Belle pushed her body to move as quickly as possible and rushed out of the room and back into the outer chamber. She arrived in time to see her husband and the guards on watch fighting off the new arrivals. Three of his guards were down and bleeding. Belle knew two could be saved if she had time. She grabbed a sword from one of the fallen men and moved toward where her husband was fighting off two of the attackers. She had never fought with a sword before. The grip felt strange in her hands and the sword heavy. She strengthened her fingers, arm, and shoulders and swung the sword up in an arc to intercept a blow that would have landed on her husband's open side.

The strength of her swing drove the attacker's sword back and into his other arm, the edge biting deep, through the bone, and severing it completely from his body. The sound of the strike was unbelievably loud in the chamber and drew the instant stares of the other men, including her husband. Belle felt vomit rise in her throat. She had never done harm with a weapon before. What she had just done was particularly nasty. Heart blood sprayed from the stump and the man went down trying to staunch the amputation. The need to heal him fought with her need to vanquish the attackers. She was conflicted. *This is not what a Cill Darae was supposed to do. I'm not a fighter.*

FIGHT!

All doubt ended with the order from Gaea. "Fight!" screeched Belle echoing Gaea, and she pushed toward another of the attackers while strengthening her legs to better brace her swings. She swung her sword and moved it mid-swing to avoid the parry and struck the next attacker in the chest. The man flew back in a crimson mist to strike the back wall.

The cry of "Demon!" was heard from the doorway behind her and she recognised the Archbishop's voice. All the guards looked from behind her to where she was standing panting in the middle of the room. The guard against the wall groaned once and Belle felt him pass on. She had killed him. She turned toward the guards and growled. *No one else will die here*, she thought. *Not if I can help it.*

She watched as all the guards united against a common threat turned toward her and raised their weapons. She looked at William, and she saw horror there. *Horror toward me?* She looked at herself. Her sword dripped blood to the carpet floor. She was covered in a fine spray of blood and she felt spots drying on her face and arms. She had used her powers in front of people. *On Gaea's orders*, she thought, *but that doesn't change the fact these guards have all just seen a woman moving at unnatural speeds and with superhuman strength.* She glanced back toward the Archbishop and could see the horror plainly written on his face. Healy was just behind him and staring with equal disgust and fear. *They fear me and think me something I am not. Dear Gaea, what have you had me do?*

Cries could be heard in the castle interior now. The sword in her hand suddenly grew heavy and so she let it go and it thumped to the carpet. She looked at her husband and mouthed *I'm sorry* to him. A touch of a smile touched the corner of his mouth and Belle felt relieved. *He doesn't fear me, thank Gaea.*

Run now, Belle. Take your boy. Leave Munsten. Your husband will help you if you ask. Trust me in this.

A sob broke out of Belle. The fear she had been holding all these months broke free. It was now. Whatever Gaea had planned it was now in motion and she and her child were caught in the middle of it. *Gaea, why? Why now?*

Belle waited for an answer and the silence felt like a fist punched into her stomach and she bent over and retched. She raised her eyes to her husband. "Our spot," she said, and he looked grim but nodded once. Belle forced herself to stand and, using the strength of Gaea, sped out of the room. The cries of alarm fading behind her.

Belle waited in a bastion on the seaward side of the outer wall and kept Will pressed up with his back to her front. The bastion was sheltered from the wind but the smell of fire and smoke was thick in the air and Belle coughed. The city was burning. She had no idea who was burning the buildings or why. The cries from the city folk were getting higher pitched and more panicked. She had watched a couple of families being pulled out of their homes and then questioned on the street. The troubling part was it wasn't guards or constables doing the door-to-door searching. It was members of the Church of the New Order. They were armed and telling everyone they were looking for demons and under the authority of the Lord Protector and the Archbishop. When she heard them asking specifically about her she had become more frightened and started using her powers to stay hidden. Gaea was not answering her pleas, but she continued to pour her power into her. *That was something, at least.*

She was troubled by how quickly the Church ruffians were finding her people and separating them from the masses. She had no idea how but she felt their fear and pain through her links with them when they were discovered. A few had been killed and the shock of their deaths was taking its toll on her. She was shaking now with an effort to keep the pain she was feeling at bay. She wished she could warn them all, and she had pleaded with Gaea to do so but Gaea was no longer speaking to her. Belle was devastated and felt betrayed and abandoned. The sounds of violence in the streets of Munsten were getting louder and closer. Houses had been lit on fire when occupants refused to open up and allow the Church access to search. The smoke from the fires had obscured the sun for most of the day but now night had fallen. The smell of smoke and burnt flesh was thick in the air.

On the way to her current hiding spot in the bastion Belle had watched one of the draoi, a new craobh named Anne, use her powers openly against one of the Church ruffians. The power had washed over the man like nothing more than the wind. He had laughed and held up a red gem for the poor woman to see. The despair in Anne's face had nearly broken Belle. The man had pushed Anne to the cobblestones and then stomped on her throat with a black boot. Belle felt Anne pass instantly with a crushed neck. The violence of the act and the expression of pleasure on the man horrified her. The world had descended into chaos and at the centre stood the Church and the Lord Protector. This was different from the Revolution. This time, her people were being targeted. Systemically and methodically. Hunted.

Belle felt safe with William in the bastion for now. It was one of the few quiet spots in Munsten where no one travelled. It was too high up on the wall. Belle was confident she and Will could remain hidden for a long time if need be. It was here where she and her husband had spent many romantic evenings before they had wed. They had watched many sunrises here lost in each other's embrace and kiss. Belle was starting to get worried about her husband. She had expected him hours ago, and she hoped he hadn't decided to place his duty above his wife and child or been implicated somehow. *Never,* she thought. *He is not that kind of man.*

"William, where are you?" she said out loud causing Will to stir in her arms. She kissed the top of his head and held him tight. She used her power to make him calm and sleep.

After fleeing the Lord Protector's chambers Belle had run directly to their quarters and scooped Will out of his bed. She put them both in plain street clothes, grabbed some important items and food, and then fled and didn't look back. It had been a troubling trip here. The worst point had been when they hid in a root cellar. She had hidden there when a patrol hit the street up ahead from her. One of the guards saw her duck into the cellar and pulled the doors open with a loud bang. She drew so much power to keep the searching guard from seeing her sitting with Will right before him. The guard left confused and called the other guards to search the other cellars all around them. She had lain there for an hour, with the cellar door open, staring out into a street full of chaos.

When it grew dark, she had run directly here carrying Will in her arms. Cloaking their movements from prying eyes was hard work, and she had been drawing on Gaea's strength for a while now but she had yet to feel any fatigue. The power from Gaea had been extraordinary. She wielded it like a Duilleog might and worried she had overused it on wee William. She kept him calm and quiet. He was only eight and apt to cry out. Even now Will was fussing and didn't understand what was going on. She was gentle with her power caress but knew it would dull his memories of the night. Much like how alcohol can make memories vague and confused.

Drawing power in the city should be next to impossible without tapping your own inner strength. Munsten was built on solid stone and stone was not part of Gaea. Belle had no idea how Gaea was lending her strength but she was thankful. Belle sobbed when her emotions again threatened to break her hold of them. It was too much.

She was worried about William. He should be here. For the thousandth time, she considered just leaving with Will and abandoning her husband. She felt the unmistakable push from Gaea to just run. Belle scowled and pushed back, determined to remain here for her husband. *He would wait for me if our roles were reversed. The only sense I have from you is the one to run. To abandon all that I love. It's not fair. Now either help me or leave me alone!*

Without warning, Belle felt the thread to Freamhaigh Dalton sever. She cried out and collapsed, pulling Will down with her into her lap. Will started to cry and looked about confused. Belle grasped at the other threads for strength. Everywhere there was pain and suffering. Losing the Freamhaigh touched all draoi. His death, thankfully quick and painless, resonated throughout all of them. As Cill Darae, it was more than pain. It came with a profound sense of loss. *The man was a misogynist, but he was a good man and a better draoi. So much loss! Why, Gaea? Why?* Belle sobbed until sleep overtook her. She slept until a hand landed on her shoulder. She cried out in fear and started to fight before she realised she was hearing her name.

"Belle, Belle? Love, it's me, William! I'm here."

Belle looked up into the face of her husband. He was covered in soot and reeked of smoke. He had been beaten, his face bruised and swollen. His bright blue eyes were full of worry for her. Her heart almost burst with her love for William and she threw her arms around him, crushing Will between them and she released all her fears and cried into her husband's shoulder. The anguish and grief poured out of her like pus from a wound. She held close to hysterics and struggled to calm herself.

"Lass, lass, calm down. You need to flee. They are tearing this city apart looking for you. They know! They know about Gaea but they call her—and you, too!—a demon. A demon! How could they ever think someone as caring as you could be a demon? You've healed so many of these people. Men, women and children all healed by you would now strike you down in a heartbeat, love. You must flee with Will! Do you hear me?"

Belle tried to get control of her emotions. She lost control of them all the time. It ran in her family and she saw it in Will. Gaea said it was because she was more empathetic to emotions. It was what set her apart from most people. She didn't know if that was true but didn't doubt it. *It's difficult when a deity speaks in your head*, she thought and then laughed out loud at her own jest.

She turned her tear-streaked face to her husband's. "I've shown them Gaea's powers, William. She told me to, and I obeyed without hesitation. Now they all know and they fear it. The Church is hunting down my fellow draoi. I feel their threads breaking, William! It rips my heart out every time. The Freamhaigh... Dalton..." and she stopped with her voice catching.

"Yes, I know, love," replied her husband quietly. He leaned back and released Will from between them, rubbing his long blond hair. "It was me, love. I was forced to kill him. I'm sorry."

Belle reached out and grabbed William by the front of his tunic and pulled him closer. "W-what? You? Why, William?"

William didn't fight her. He looked grimly down at her and spoke calmly.

"He told me to. Said Gaea had said I must do it with witnesses. That the act alone would free me to do what I must do."

Belle felt Gaea for a moment and knew her husband spoke the truth. She dropped her hands from the tunic to Will. "What must you do?"

"Get you and Will out of Munsten. All the ways are blocked. I wasn't trusted, you see. I am the man who married a demon. I've been questioned all day. Beaten really. Over and over again. Killing Dalton was a test. They carried him in and bade me kill him to prove my faith. I refused. They beat me until I agreed. They handed me a knife and watched. I-I don't know how he did it but I heard Dalton in my head. He told me to kill him. I watched his eyes and it was him speaking to me, Belle. He said to get you and Will out as soon as possible." William pulled Belle in tight to his chest and Belle could feel him shaking. "He said Will was meant for great things. Our boy, hon. I did as he wanted. Quick. He felt little. I'm sorry. It felt like murder. I watched the life fade from his eyes. At my hands."

"Shh, hon. I understand. Gaea made this happen. The fault rests on her. Not you. Never you!"

William held her tighter and then pulled back and spoke quietly. "The Church let me go then. I walked out of there with calls of 'demon-lover' following me. I'm not stupid, though. They only let me go so that I could lead them to you. They tried to follow me but I lost them in the chaos. They forgot I was born and raised in the streets of Munsten." William bowed his head and his shoulders shook.

Belle wrapped her arms around her husband and cried with him for a spell. Will stirred and complained about being hungry and they broke apart and gazed at each other. Clear streaks of skin were washed by his tears and marked his face. Belle had never seen him cry before. At that moment, she felt a stirring of hatred for Gaea that startled her.

"I've only ever wanted what is best for our boy, Belle," he whispered. "All those years working extra shifts. It was so I could be promoted. As a major, I would no longer do shift work. No more duty watches. You, Will and I could have had all the time in the world together. Now…"

"I see that now, love. I should never have doubted you."

"You are my life and soul. Without you I am nothing. I cannot live in a world where you and Will are no longer a part of it. I couldn't survive the loss. I couldn't. I'm not strong enough."

Belle nodded and kissed him. She soaked in his love and gave it back. This man would do anything for her and their son. She had never loved him more than right now. She forgave him for killing Dalton. The blood was on Gaea. She told him so.

"Never mind killing Dalton. It was a loss, but he was correct. We need to flee. Gaea is pushing me hard to move, William. Even now. I swear I can feel her hands on my shoulders shoving me."

William tried to smile but failed. "Good thing I have my secrets, then, huh? And even better that I grew up in the streets of Munsten. No one knows their way around this city like I do. There is a hidden way out. Used by criminals. Come. Let's be off. It's far from here."

"Dad, where are we going?" asked a frightened Will and William looked down at his son and Belle watched his chin tremble.

"Away for a wee while, Will. An adventure like in the tales. You and your mum, okay?"

"Okay, dad. That'd be grand. Grand! But, why are you so dirty, da? You need a bath, dad. Mum will be cross with you if you come home like that."

"Aye, son. I do. That I do." William looked up to Belle, and she raised a hand to cup his cheek. William leaned his head into the hand for a moment before lifting Will up in his arms. "Come, love. We need to be quick."

Craobh

Eleven

Nadine's House, Jergen Waterfront, 900 A.C.

N ADINE WAS ASLEEP in her bed with Dog lying on the floor next to her. She was worn out and because she didn't have too much reserve in her, she had fallen asleep soon after telling me what had befallen my mom and dad that night. The past hours had taken too much out of her physically and emotionally and she had gone to bed as soon as she finished the tale. It was a tale of conjecture and some things she said she had pieced together over the years. It was the truth as far as she knew. I checked on her and covered her better with a blanket. I looked around her house for a moment and went outside.

I sat on a wooden, double-seated, swing seat she had placed to look out over the bay entrance and the ocean. Jergen rose dark and shadowed to my right. Street lamps were not present this far off the main roads but the skies were clear of cloud and the stars filled the night sky. The moon was high over the city behind me and I sat in quiet contemplation with enough light to see everything around me. I was neither warm nor cold. The only sound was the waves against the cliffs below. The gulls had gone to bed for the night. I should be enjoying myself, but I wasn't.

My father was not the man I thought I remembered. I had spent the last ten years of my life hating the man. Now I knew he had loved me and my mom so very much he had sacrificed his own life, so we could escape. I couldn't begin to understand having to make that decision. Daukyns had warned me years ago that my memories were likely not perfect, to give my father the benefit of the doubt.

"Will, you were six years old. Seven? Just a boy. You've admitted as much that you only remember a couple of things," said Daukyns after a long sip of wine. I recalled we were seated in front of the common house in Jaipers last summer.

"Yes, but one of those memories was watching my dad's back as he walked away from mom and me. My mom was crying, and he just walked away. That seems pretty clear to me."

"I agree, that doesn't sound very promising. Still, I'm a little bit older than you. Trust me in this: no father or husband would abandon their wife and child. Not willingly. Think about it. Leave a spot in your heart for another truth."

I thought about it now and the Truth Nadine had shown me. I wasn't finding it easy to look back at a lifetime of hating someone only to find out I should be loving them instead. I felt so much guilt. It hammered at me nonstop and so I sought solace in the night. My brain knew I wasn't to blame. I just had to get my heart to understand. I had to find out if I was capable of loving someone who deserved it but for whom I had no memories to tie a love to.

After an hour, I gave up. I hadn't saved a spot in my heart. *I'm sorry, dad*, I said to the stars. *I know I should love you, but I can't.*

The silence grew deeper and my eyes closed. The waves on the cliff were a pleasant repetitive sound and in a short time, they lulled me to sleep.

* * *

I jolted awake when Nadine settled next to me on the double-swing and set it swaying. I blinked my blurry eyes and rubbed the grit from my lashes. I struggled to sit up properly against the swing motion. A sweet, smoke smell wafted over me and I saw Nadine was smoking a weed pipe. I stared at her for a moment before looking out at the ocean. It was halfway through the morning by the brightness of the day. She patted my leg for a moment and took another puff from her pipe. I liked the smell of the smoke.

"Did you sleep well, Will?" she asked.

"Aye. I can't believe I slept this long. Sorry."

"You needed it. You've been running for so long you were tired up here." Nadine poked my head sharply with the stem of her pipe.

"Ow!" I said and rubbed my head and looked around for Dog.

"He's off finding breakfast. He loves to hunt rabbits, did you know?"

"Hmm. Yes. He caught one by accident on the way here. He was very proud of himself."

"Good," she said.

I looked out over the morning sea. It was calm with the lack of wind and the blue of the water sparkled. I watched a cargo ship fight for wind as it left the harbour approaches. Sails fluttered, and I could make out the men climbing the rigging. Two seagulls bobbed and spun behind the ship, their cries lost in the distance.

My sleep had let my mind settle what had bothered me. Daukyn's words about leaving room in my heart for another truth seemed to let what Nadine was telling me seep in. I looked over at her. "Thank you," I said.

Nadine raised an eyebrow and looked at me. "For what, now?"

"For telling me what happened to my mom and dad."

Nadine puffed out smoke. "You're welcome. It's what I was able to put together over the years. Most of it is accurate. Your mom was killed soon afterwards. Hunted down by the top assassin of the Sect. The man named Seth Farlow. An evil man. Cut off from Gaea herself."

"What does that mean, *cut off*? Is that even possible?"

"You wouldn't think so, but it happened to Seth and the Archbishop. Your mom talked about the Archbishop all the time. Seth was one of those strange fellows that flitted about the castle in Munsten. Always spying and sneaking. He reported to the Archbishop. Everyone knew that. The Archbishop thought he was so smart and secretive, but the draoi knew of him. We followed him closely ever since the Revolution. Well, your mom and the Freamhaigh knew. They told the draoi."

"Yes, but cut off from Gaea. Shouldn't you be dead or something?"

"I don't know. I don't understand it either." Nadine took a final puff from her pipe and then looked into the bowl. She blew out smoke and then leaned forward to tap the bowl out on a flat rock laying in front of the swing. I could see the remains of ashes scattered around the rock.

"This is your spot. Out here, I mean, on this swing."

"Yes, I've spent many, many evenings out here. Never a morning though. And I never slept out here either. How was it?"

"Nice, actually."

"Ah, the resilience of youth," Nadine slapped my knee, squeezed it, and stood up. It was such a smooth movement I was a bit shocked at seeing it. Nadine looked down at me and I could see she was shocked as well. "Well, I seem to be moving a bit better today."

"I'd say," I said and reached out with my senses to examine her. The swelling around her joints was gone and I could see her mobility was better. I didn't understand how so much had happened so quickly and didn't know what to say to her. I didn't think my tea was the cause.

"Did you just examine me again?" she asked. "You're always doing that you young rascal. People will talk. Sure as they will." She waggled her eyebrows at me. I saw her then in a different light. I could see the younger woman she probably was and still is inside. She was what Daukyns used to call *spunky and interesting*. I laughed out loud and Nadine smacked me again. "Mind your manners!" and I laughed even harder. "It's not funny to laugh at an old woman!"

"Sorry, Nadine! My fault!"

"Come on inside, you cheeky young thing. I've boiled water for tea and made oats. It's time you broke your fast. Dog will be back soon, and we need to talk about those pages of yours."

We soon settled inside at the table with steaming mugs of tea and a bowl of porridge with honey and dried apples and peaches in it for me. It was wonderful. Nadine had placed the manuscript pages on the table next to us and she was reading them.

"Your friend Daukyns was a very smart man. A wordsmith, you said?"

I nodded, my mouth full of porridge.

"He translated this well. Very well, indeed. I'm impressed. It was written in a language long forgotten. I taught it in the years at the castle in Munsten followed by years longer working with the young Duilleogs at one of our locations. Rarely did I find anyone who was truly interested in the written word. Especially in a dead language. Daukyns seemed like a special find. I'm sorry I didn't get to meet him."

I swallowed. "He would have liked you, I think. He had an eye for beautiful women. Told me all the time."

Nadine looked at me funny and then continued to read. She moved a page closer to me and pointed to one of the drawings. "See here, this is basil. But not just any basil. This one comes from the Northern counties and has a stronger tie to the mint family. You can taste it. Makes this a wonderful component for medicinal purposes."

"It would. Good for the stomach and the blood."

"Yes," said Nadine pursing her lips and nodding appreciatively at me. "Exactly right. What is important though is the drawing is not correct. It is close to the original but whoever copied it got lazy. The colouring is incorrect and not all the leaves are here on this stem in the background. See?"

I saw where she was pointing but had no clue what differences she was talking about. "Not really, Nadine. I've never seen the original—or the plant for that matter."

"I'm just proving it's a copy. Pay attention. What's important here is the colour selection. The colour used here is more commonly found in copies of the book of the Church of the New Order. The use of that colour is predominant in the panes drawn at the end of the first book of John or some other fellow."

"And you know this how?"

Nadine smacked me again. "Don't be insolent. I've seen the book many, many times here in Jergen. Dyes are unique, Will. That green colour is unique. Whoever copied the draoi manuscript used the same dye used to create their book. Therefore, this copy of the draoi manuscript had to have been made at the same place where the church prints their books. Here at the Cathedral of Jergen. Imagine that." Nadine looked radiant and proud.

I could see the lines around her face were less prominent, and I was starting to see a glimmer of the young woman she once was, her eyes were such a bright green, they shone. I could now see a hint of red in the roots of her white hair.

I blinked and focused on what she had just said. "Daukyns had mentioned the library in Jergen, not the Cathedral."

"They are the same, Will. But I'm not surprised he didn't mention that. The Library of Jergen is attached to the Cathedral. Most people from outside of Jergen think them separate but they are not. The Church owns the Library. Hard to miss actually, they are made from the same white stone."

"So you think this copy of the Draoi Manuscript will be found inside the library?"

"Perhaps. Perhaps not. I really don't know. But I think it important that we look. Really there shouldn't be a copy. Gaea shouldn't have allowed it but if it exists, then obviously she must have made an exception. Peculiar, no? Coincidence? We must find it and remove it. It may be the only copy we have now."

"What do you mean the only copy? I thought there were many originals?"

"There are, somewhere. But not many. Only four. Their location died with the owners, I'm afraid. The Purge did more than just kill draoi. It killed our lore, too. We have nothing left of our order. It was ripped from the earth. You are the last, Will. And I the last of the knowledge. Without Gaea guiding us we are stumbling along."

"If you know the lore so well can you not just rewrite the manuscript?"

Nadine laughed. "No, Will. The manuscript contained so much more than the knowledge I had. I taught the young ones about the simple truths about draoi. Lifecycles. How to care for plants and animals. Our history and what it meant to be draoi. Nothing more, I'm afraid. I have no knowledge of the depth of the magic draoi wield. And without powers of my own, I cannot teach any new draoi. You see?"

I did but remained silent. I had come to Jergen to find answers and thought they were in a book. It turned out Nadine alone was providing the answers I was truly after. I now knew where I had come from and why I had been on my own for all those years. Like last night watching the stars and looking for a way past the anger I still felt toward my father, I now struggled to find direction in my life. I thought of the wonder I felt when I had healed the poor woman and her son in Jaipers. I hadn't told Nadine anything of that. But when I had healed her, her son and the others, I felt I was doing something important and I wanted to do more. I wanted to heal the world if I could.

The sound of paws digging into the dirt announced the arrival of Dog. He bounded into the room with a quail clenched in his jaws. He dropped the bird when he crossed the threshold and bounded straight to me and jumped up to place his front paws on my knees. Before I could stop him he was slathering my face with his tongue. Nadine laughed and tried to shoo Dog away, but he was too enthusiastic for anyone to control. He calmed down but remained leaning against me with his head in my lap, still staring directly at me.

I tore my eyes away from Dog and saw Nadine looking at me in a strange way again. "Okay, so we find the copy. Once we have it, we can figure out what happens next. How do we get in the library?"

"Oh, that part's easy. The head librarian relies on my ointment to relieve a problem he has. He'll let me in no problem at all! The hard part will be in taking the book out of there."

The next morning, we left Dog at home and Nadine and I made our way to the Cathedral. It wasn't a long walk, but we had to climb the steep Highborn Street back to the central park. Nadine didn't complain once and she seemed much stronger today. It was mid-morning and Nadine felt the library would be at its quietest. It felt strange walking the street without my backpack—I felt so light. I also never had a friend to walk alongside me. I enjoyed Jergen a bit more now, and I was starting to see its charm. It was large and hugged the cliffs. Trade flowed in and out. People all seemed to be in a hurry to be somewhere else.

Few people said hello or wished you a good day.

"How can so many people be so alone?" I muttered.

"Huh?" asked Nadine then I saw her looking at the people we passed.

I shook my head, and we kept walking. The day was profusely hot already and Nadine carried a small parasol to shade her. We looked like a strange couple. But perhaps most people would assume we were a mother and son walking the streets. Either way, I didn't care. I was comfortable with Nadine and we talked about simple things en route. I think we were trying to avoid talking about what to expect in the library.

"I think I look a wee bit daft with this parasol," she declared once we reached the top of the steep street and breathed heavily. Nadine had managed the hill with no bother at all.

I looked her over pretending to think about it. "Might be you are correct, ma'am."

Nadine closed the parasol and then hit me with it. "Such cheek!"

"Hey! Why are you always hitting me?"

"You need it. Keeps you honest."

"Honest? Who said I wasn't honest."

"Don't need anyone telling me that, I can tell. Your eyes are too close together."

"W-what? What do my eyes have to do with honesty?"

"Everything. Trust me. I'm old and know things."

"Like how to hit people..." I murmured under my breath.

"I heard that!" she declared and then stopped walking. I took a step past her and turned to look at her. "I heard that, Will. Say something else—quiet like."

"You mean in a whisper?"

"Of course, I meant in a whisper!" she shouted and swatted at me. This time, I moved out of the way and she missed. She glared at me.

I lowered my voice and whispered to her. "You are an evil old woman..."

"Dear Gaea! I heard that! I heard that Will! My hearing is coming back. Dear Gaea, what is happening to me?"

I smiled and shook my head. "I've no idea. It appears Gaea is taking some of your years back."

Nadine looked at me with wet eyes. "Do you really think so?"

"I do. I can see the changes in you. You're walking much better. Your back is almost straight again. Your joints don't hurt nearly so much do they?"

Nadine nodded and wiped away a tear. "Why? Why would she do this?

How?"

I just shook my head and smiled. "I have no idea. Except..." I looked around and pulled Nadine off the street and away from ears.

Nadine understood and looked around. "Except what?" she asked under her breath.

"Well, I can see the changes in you. And I can see how I could do some of that. It would take time though and I would have to concentrate. It would take days I think. But..."

"But what?"

"Any changes wouldn't be permanent. I'm not sure I can explain it. I can see how your body works. Ageing is deeper than just wearing out. Age is part of a process and I have no idea how to reverse it. I can only remove the damage of the wear and tear of age. I can't actually stop ageing. So whatever I did it would be temporary and take so much time I doubt there would be any benefit."

Nadine looked into my eyes as if searching for something. I could only look back. After a moment, she lowered her eyes and nodded. "Fair enough. Come. We've still a way to go."

* * *

We reached the Library of Jergen in half an hour. It was a monumentally tall and beautiful white stone building with the Cathedral looming over it. I couldn't believe people were capable of creating something so lovely. The stonework was carved in ornate swirls and all around the roof edge, carved gargoyles and angels danced and flew. They looked so lifelike and real. The centre of the roof was a domed stained-glass structure bigger than most of the homes in Jaipers. I stood with my head tilted back admiring it for a few minutes and Nadine gave me the time.

"It's beautiful isn't it?" she asked after a moment.

"Yes. Yes, it is."

"Too bad it represents the death of so many of our people. And countless others all around the Realm. Enough gawking. Let's go in, young man."

"As you command, old woman."

Nadine laughed and led the way up the two dozen or so steps stretching across the entire front of the building. We walked past two enormous stone pillars marking the entrance and up through the large, red-stained, double oak doors standing open in the summer heat. The steps and entrance were vacant. The library was not a place often visited at midday on hot summer days. It seemed Nadine was right.

Inside the shade of the entrance, the temperature was a bit cooler but still stifling. We stood for a moment to let our eyes adjust to the dim interior of the building. I could smell the dusty old books and I felt an excitement build within me. When my eyes adjusted, I could see deep into the library and saw bookcases from floor to ceiling as far as my eyes could see. The inside was almost one great big room, with the centre of the library lit by the stained-glass dome. It cast beautiful hues of all colours throughout the room. I saw all this without trying but my eyes were locked on the books. *There are hundreds and thousands of tomes of knowledge*, I thought looking to the left and right at all the shelves and stacked books. *Enough to last me a lifetime and I probably wouldn't even dent it.* I wondered what herb lore I could find within and felt tempted to just find books on the subject and lose myself in here for days.

A smack on my arm from Nadine had me following behind her and we stopped at the large square counter area that dominated the front of the room. It held an ornate black desk and an overweight, bald, robed man sat behind it doing something with a book containing loose-leaf pages. The desk was positioned right under the domed stained-glass ceiling. Nadine touched a small bell at the counter and the soft peal had the man looking up. He wore round and thick, wire-rimmed spectacles making his eyes big and round. He squinted at us and then struggled to rise from the desk without toppling the piles of books balanced precariously beside him. He wore a shirt and collar I assumed marked him as a priest of the Church of the New Order. I had never met one before and I was intrigued. He wore a dark brown, almost black, wool robe despite the heat.

"Coming! One second, please, if God grants it," he said in a high and feminine voice that made me blink.

"Take your time, Father Peter. Take your time. It's just me, Nadine, with a young friend from out of town."

Peter glanced up as he rounded the desk and caught the corner on his upper thigh. He let out an *oof* and grasped the sore spot. "Dammit!" he cursed and then looked around in fright at his blasphemy. I laughed despite the need to stay serious here and Nadine elbowed me. Peter fumbled at his spectacles and pulled them off his ears and nose. He blinked furiously for a moment and then focused on us. "Sorry, my reading glasses make it impossible to move about! You'd think I would have learned by now."

Peter came over to the counter in front of us and reached across to grasp Nadine's hands warmly. "Good to see you again, Nadine. How are you keeping?"

"Fine, Peter. Just fine. How is your problem?"

Peter blushed a bright red and looked away. "Oh, well. Oh, dear. Well, fine I suppose. Thanks to you." He looked tentatively at me and then locked eyes with me and smiled. "And who is this gorgeous young man you bring me?"

"Peter! Behave yourself! This is my friend, Will. I'm sorry Father but I have little time. I have a favour to ask if I may?"

"Of course, of course! For you anything! What is it?" He glanced quickly at Nadine and then looked me up and down. He pursed his lips.

"I need to see a special section of the library today, I'm afraid."

"Special? Which section would that be?" Peter was openly checking me over and I felt a little uncomfortable

"The Occult."

Peter tore his gaze from me and frowned at Nadine. "The occult! What would you need to see *that* section for?"

"For my herb lore, Peter. My friend here is visiting and told me the wordsmith from another town mentioned an old book that possibly lay in there that had recipes for some special potions. Ones that speed up healing. Others that stimulate blood flow."

Peter's mouth formed an 'O'. "Blood flow?" he asked.

"Yes, you know. Gets blood moving and into places it can't seem to find anymore."

"Ah." Peter grew quiet for a moment and it appeared his cheeks grew a little redder. "I see. Well. Let me think."

"Take your time, dear."

Peter looked about the empty library. He seemed a bit agitated to me. He leaned in and whispered. "This is most unorthodox! I am not allowed to let anyone in the occult section other than the high priesthood and above. There are books in there that are priceless! You ask a lot of me!"

Nadine patted Peter's hand gently. "It will be okay. We only need a couple of hours. Undisturbed hours, Peter. I have never asked you for anything, have I? Give me this, please."

Peter looked down and thought before nodding. "Okay, Nadine. Only because no one else is here. The building is empty at the moment." He paused and looked pleadingly at Nadine. "Promise me you won't disturb anything?"

"Of course, you have my word, my dear."

"Alright. One second."

Peter hurried over to the side of the counter and lifted the wood countertop and walked through the opening. He crossed over to a door I hadn't noticed before and opened it with a key hanging around his neck. He entered the door and disappeared. I looked over at Nadine and saw she was smiling.

"Easier than I expected," she declared. "He won't be long. He needs to draw the key for the section we want. The occult section is locked tight behind a thick door."

"Why's he giving us access?"

"Let's just say not all members of the clergy are chaste and not all of their members work right. Peter's peter peters."

"What?"

"Nothing. Now shush. This is a library, be quiet."

After a long wait, Peter emerged back through the door. He looked around the library as he approached the counter and he quickly lifted the counter top and passed back inside to his workspace. He came over to us and continued to look around.

"Did anyone come in while I was away?" he asked in a hushed tone.

"No, Peter. Still just us," answered Nadine.

"Okay," he said and slid a key over the counter to us. Nadine reached out and snatched it up quickly.

"Give us two hours, Peter. That's all we'll need. Thank you."

"Just hurry."

"We will."

Nadine grabbed my arm and pulled us past the counter. She led me to a set of stairs that disappeared into a side structure of the library. Nadine led me up several stairs to the back of the library. The place was huge, and it took us a good ten minutes to navigate to the special area of the library. As we walked past all the bookshelves, I could only gawk at the sheer volume of books. So much knowledge right here for anyone to take and read and learn. I felt a little giddy. As we neared the rear of the library on the upper floor, a thought occurred to me.

"Nadine, why the occult section? Why do you think the book is there of all the places it could be?" I asked.

Nadine snorted. "It's a book about the draoi, our magic and our lore. For the Church that would be in the occult section."

We reached the section Nadine wanted. It was cordoned off with a thick red velvet rope hung off brass stanchions. Beyond the rope, I could see four large heavy-set doors. Nadine ducked under the ropes and approached the door labelled *Occult*. She inserted the key into the lock and turned it to the left. A soft metallic click was heard, and Nadine pulled out the key and pulled open the door. It swung quietly on its hinges and beyond we could see it was pitch black.

"Grab a light," she said and held the door open.

I grabbed a reading candle off a nearby shelf and lit it from one of the wall torches. I handed it to Nadine, and she led the way inside. I closed the door behind us and turned to examine the room. It was smaller than I expected. It was only about thirty feet square but rose some thirty feet high. The walls were floor to ceiling covered bookshelves and the shelves were full. Long ladders ran on metal tracks and I could see they could be moved to reach the books on the upper shelves. A long wooden table was centred in the room with two plush leather seats placed before it. In the middle of the table sat a large book. Nadine moved over to the table and lit the other reading lamps. The soft glow of the lamps warmed the room and the rich reds and browns gave the room a very studious but comfortable look. *One day, I want a library that looks just like this,* I thought as I admired the view. *There sure were a lot of books.*

"I think it will take us more than a couple of hours to sort through all this," I said. Nadine looked at me and I could see she was trying to see if I was joking or not. "What?"

"There's a card catalogue, Will. Over there," and she pointed at a tall desk filled with rows of tiny drawers. I walked over to it and I could see each drawer was labelled and the drawers were ordered alphabetically and numerically. I pulled open one of the drawers and saw with amazement they were filled with cards with writing on them. Tabs separated the cards further.

"Um, what do I do with this?" I pulled out a card and scanned it.

"First, we find what we are looking for in the listing book, and then we look it up in the card catalogue. The cards will tell us where on the shelves the book is placed."

"Really?" I could see the card in my hand had an alphabetic group written at the top and, under the group listing, was a book title and, under the title, was information about the author where the book had come from, and the location on the shelves. *Huh, smart.*

"Really, really."

"That's pretty smart."

"Uh, huh. Pretty smart. Now come over here and help me with the listing. It's heavy." I put the card back in the drawer where I found it and joined her at the table, watching as she opened the large book. The pages were loose leaf and held by rings inside the bookbinding. "This is the inventory listing. We will need to figure out what they would have called our book then find it in here. Then we can look it up in the card catalogue which will tell us where to find it on the shelves."

"Okay. So, let's start with *Draoi Manuscript*." Nadine shot me a look with a smirk on it but located a tabbed page for the 'D' section and started turning pages. She ran her fingers down the listings until she completed all the entries.

"Nope," she declared. "Not listed."

"*Druid Manuscript*, then?"

Nadine scanned again. "Nope."

"Well, I'm out of ideas. Let's go."

Nadine smacked me but laughed. I was liking making her laugh. Her whole face lit up. My arm was getting a bit sore. It was strange being so close to her. The bond we had—the draoi bond—was strong. The blue ribbon twisted and pulsed and white tinged the edges of it. I had been practising minimising my use of the power. Nadine said I no longer glowed blue. I closed my eyes and used the bond and could see which way she was facing. I could almost feel her movements and I think with just a little effort I could probably feel what she felt too. I opened my eyes to see her staring right at me. She reached out a hand and patted my cheek and sighed. "Focus on finding the book, Will." I nodded.

We spent the next hour picking titles and searching with no luck. Eventually, we began at page one and started reading each entry. After about ten minutes and little to show for it, we stopped and sat back in the seats to stare at the books all around us.

"How many books do you think there are in this room, Nadine?"

"Too many. And maybe it's not even here."

I nodded and felt crestfallen. I leaned forward and turned pages randomly and looked for anything to jump out. "I wish I knew what it looked like, at least," I murmured.

"Well, I do. But the copy is probably different."

"Why would they make it look different?"

"I don't know I just assumed…"

"So, what does it look like? The original, I mean."

"It's burgundy. Leather all around. The spine is covered in a green leather. No writing on the spine. The front cover is embossed with a Tree, which is the symbol of the draoi, and there's a triskelion."

"Like on the coin?"

"Yes, exactly, except large and more ornate."

"So, a green spine." I looked around at the books on the shelves and spotted green books everywhere I looked. Probably about a third of the books were green. "We know how big it is, too. Based on the pages we have, it's a rectangular book and maybe one foot tall and two feet long."

"Hmm, yes. That's the size of the originals. The drawings require large oversize pages, but they are folded in."

I stood up and started to walk around the room from the left looking for a green book that was one foot tall and two feet long. It would stick out from the other books with its length. "How thick?" I asked.

Nadine stood up sensing what I was doing, and she started scanning the books from the right side of the room. "It was thick. About three inches thick. Maybe a bit less."

I dismissed book after book. The shelves were not deep, and a long, thick book would stand out. I reached the far-right corner at the same time as Nadine and we both looked up and saw a thick, long and green book on the top shelf, right in the corner. I looked at Nadine and grinned. I walked over to the nearest ladder and pulled it over and climbed up until the book was right in front of me. I pulled it out and turned it over to look at the front and saw a large tree painted or stained on the cover with the triskelion symbol underneath. "This is it!" I declared and heard Nadine's cry of joy below me.

I hurried down the ladder and brought the book over to the table and laid it down. Nadine reached out and caressed the cover. "Humph. It's not embossed. It's a copy," she said and opened the cover and started flipping through the pages. "Yes, yes. It's all here exactly as I remember them. This is an exact copy, Will." She flipped through more pages and then stopped and pressed the book open to expose the inner spine. I could see the remains of a few pages that had been neatly torn out.

Nadine looked up at me and I nodded. "The same book. My pages came from this book here."

"Yes, and hopefully that means this is the only copy," she said. I hadn't thought about there being more than one copy. "I think we should try to figure out who had access to this." Nadine turned to the back inside cover. A small pocket was glued to the book with a piece of paper tucked inside. Nadine pulled it out, and I read it out loud.

"The Demonic Bible, copy," I read, and we shared a look at that. "Author unknown. Source unknown. Age unknown. Signed out by Bishop Arnold Bengold, Nollaig 877 A.C., Seth Farlow, Nollaig 877 A.C., Seth Farlow, Feabhra, 878 A.C. And then just more of this Seth fellow over and over for years."

Nadine shook her head. "Seth Farlow is the one I told you about. The weasel that worked for the Archbishop. It appears he's had access and knowledge of this book for decades. He knew everything about us. No wonder they found us so easily! Oh, Will!"

Nadine collapsed against me sobbing. I held her easily and found myself rubbing her back and telling her everything would be all right. Through our bond, I couldn't help but feel her pain and anguish. The loss was mine too, and I cried silent tears that splashed on her head and were lost to my hand stroking her hair. I felt a presence then. The earth was watching us. I looked up at the ceiling as if she were there.

"Hello, Gaea," I said, and Nadine sucked in a breath and looked up from my chest where her face had been buried.

"Gaea is here?" she whispered.

"Yes, she's watching us right now." As soon as I spoke the words she was gone between one heartbeat and the next. "And now she's gone."

"Did she say anything?"

"Say anything? She can speak?"

Nadine leaned back, still in my embrace and smacked me on the chest. "Yes, stupid. Of course. Though, rarely. The Cill Darae, your mother, for example, spoke to her all the time. Your mother once told me it was like having a friend who never left your side. Ever. She was annoyed most of the time, I think."

I realised then we were standing embraced in the room and had been for a long time and I let Nadine go feeling awkward. Nadine raised an eyebrow at me. "Sorry," I mumbled.

"Will, don't apologise. Draoi bonds are often hard to deal with for duilleogs and even craobhs. I admit our bond is a bit strong, but we are the only ones left. It's just our ribbon that we have."

I looked and the one between us was thicker now than before and it rippled with unseen winds. The brilliant blue was just as brilliant as before, but now I could see there was more of a white sheen added to it—an iridescence. But I was more interested in the two smaller ribbons leaving me and disappearing through the bookshelves. Intrigued, I followed the thicker of the two and was happy to find it led to Dog, who, I could feel through the link, was about to finish the chase of a rabbit. My sudden presence on his mind startled him and he stumbled and bowled ass over head in the grass. I pulled back and laughed.

"No, Nadine, I see two more beside ours. Although they are much smaller than ours and different in intensity. I just followed one and startled Dog out of chasing a rabbit."

"Dog? Did you say one went to Dog?"

"Yes, it was Dog."

"That's not possible."

"What? Why?"

"Dogs aren't human. The draoi bond is between draoi. Humans are draoi, not dogs."

"Someone should tell that to Dog," I looked at the bond to Dog. It was the same brilliant blue as the one between Nadine and me. The only difference was the lack of white iridescence. "Looks pretty much the same," I said to her. "Except without the pearly white."

Nadine grasped my arm and squeezed it painfully hard. "Pearly white? Whose is pearly white?"

"Nadine, ouch, let go," I said and tried to pry her hand off me. "Ours, between you and me."

"Describe it!" she demanded.

"Well, it's a brilliant blue, about a foot wide, it moves as if in a wind or on water. It now has a white sheen to it. It's beautiful."

"Dear Gaea," said Nadine, and she collapsed in her seat. "That's not possible."

"Nadine, you aren't making any sense to me."

"I will," she whispered. "I will. Not now. Later. We need to get this book out of here."

I hesitated. Something obviously bothered her, and I didn't understand it. I looked at our bond and it was as strong as ever. Through it, I could sense her distress but not the why. I reached out to Dog and felt amusement there. I looked at the other thread. It was thin as an actual thread and I followed it to discover the baby Euan that I had met on the road into Jergen. I was only a little surprised at that. I had felt something from him when we parted. This was what it must have been. He was content, fed and with his mother. I withdrew and found Nadine still slumped in the chair.

I wanted to tell Nadine what I had seen, but I sensed at the moment it was more important to get out of the library with our manuscript. Our two hours were up, and I had no idea how we could smuggle a book weighing close to ten pounds and the size of a small table out past the priest at the front desk of the Library.

Leaving the library turned out to be easier than I thought. As we made our way back to the front desk, I asked Nadine what we should do, and she just hushed me. Frustrated, I followed behind her. When we arrived near the desk, she pointed at the front door and made walking motions with her fingers. As I started moving, she called out to Peter and strode over to the counter. Once she had him engaged in conversation she returned the key, thanking him for allowing us access, and I walked past and out the front door to the steps. Peter saw nothing and heard what he needed to hear: Nadine would mix him the new potion as soon as possible. I stood on the steps blinking at the afternoon sun and clutching the book tight to my chest. My heart was racing, and I expected Peter to come running out crying *Thief!* at any moment. Instead, Nadine stepped out and took my arm. I could sense her without thinking about it. *I know where she is at all times now, and that makes me happy. Dog, too. I'm never alone now.* I smiled down at her.

She raised an eyebrow at me. "All is well. Relax. Let's head home," she said.

I nodded and started down the steps with Nadine holding on to me. We merged with the people moving in our direction on the sidewalk. Horses and riders were moving in both directions and it seemed like organised chaos to me. Fortunately, everyone was out shopping and running errands and we blended in like anyone else. Only after we turned the corner away from the library did I relax. *We made it*, I thought. *We have the book.*

The past two months all came flooding back. From the night the assassin lifted me off the ground in my camp outside Jaipers to walking into Jergen, I had been on the path to retrieving this book. A wild sense of elation flooded me, and I smiled and laughed.

"What are you laughing at?"

"I have the book. I have the answers I was looking for. I just can't believe it."

"Celebrate when we get home."

"I will. I'll make you a wonderful dinner. Dog has a rabbit and a grouse waiting."

Nadine looked at me. "So it's true. Can you sense Dog? Do you have a draoi connection to him?"

"Yes," I said, watching the surrounding people. We were speaking quietly, and no one could hear us, No one seemed to be paying us any attention. We were an old woman and a young man—a mother and son perhaps, out for a stroll. "A blue ribbon. I have three of them. You do, too, the same ones."

"Who is the last one?"

"A baby boy named Euan I met on the road to Jergen. I think I know when the bond formed. I felt a moment with him when we parted. I thought nothing of it until now."

"You found one of the future draoi, Will. You will know them when you meet them. That is common. It is how we—you—find each other."

"I see. Does a draoi have to meet the person?"

"Well, no. The lore tells us that you can reach out with your senses and Gaea's power will mark them. It hasn't been done for a long time. It takes a great deal of power—a power that has to come first from Gaea."

I grew silent for a time and we walked, each lost in our own thoughts. Something still troubled Nadine, and I wished she would tell me. Daukyns would urge patience and so I decided to wait until she was ready. "Does the book explain all this?"

"The manuscript, yes. It's not a book, Will. A book is... oh, never mind. To answer your question, yes, it does. It explains much of what we do and can't do. It contains our lore. The original manuscripts were given to the draoi by Gaea herself, it is said. Over a thousand years ago."

"A thousand?" I tried to imagine so many years and failed. "Gaea can take form? I thought she was just a voice."

Nadine laughed softly. "It is so easy for me to forget you know nothing. I'm sorry, I will need to explain things better. Gaea can take whatever form she wants. She doesn't manifest—she borrows. We are all Gaea, you see. You. Me. That woman walking ahead of us. All Gaea. When she wants to, she becomes more conscious in that person. It's frightening sometimes. She could become me. Or you. In an instant. And when she leaves, you remember nothing or very little—like trying to remember a dream."

"I don't think I understand. Truly. It seems so... *strange*... I hear your words, but I can't seem to put it all together in my head."

"You will in time. I've only seen it once. When you were born. Gaea came to the birth. She emerged in one of the midwives. She thanked your mom and left. Just like that. *Hello. It's me Gaea. Well done. Cheerio.* She works in mysterious ways. Anyway. All this..." and Nadine waved her free arm aimlessly to take in the city street. "All life is her."

"Okay. Fine. Well, Dog is part of her then. So what's the problem with me having a blue line to him?"

"Because he's a dog. The bond you see is between draoi. Dogs can't be draoi."

"You keep saying that. Why not?"

Nadine shut her mouth in a tight line and went silent. I thought she wasn't going to answer, and she surprised me when she did. "Because."

"Well, if Gaea is all life, and Dog is part of that life. I think that if Gaea wants to give powers to a dog she can," I reasoned.

Nadine clucked her tongue but stayed silent.

I continued to fill the silence. "You mentioned familiars to me. I have heard tales of witches with familiars. Was that draoi with their familiars? Is it what I think it is?"

"Not exactly. You are correct, most witches were simple draoi. It never went well for those caught. It is one of the many reasons why we keep our powers hidden. But a familiar that is different from a draoi bond. The draoi builds a trust with an animal and then asks it to do certain tasks. There is no ribbon between the draoi and the animal but the draoi uses their power to form a bond. It allows a means to communicate a little better that is all. For the animal to understand what the draoi wants. The animal can either ignore the request or do as it is asked. It becomes a trust issue. Animals love just as any human and if an animal loves the draoi there is nothing they won't do when they are asked. We have many tales of familiars sacrificing themselves for the draoi. Anyhow, the manuscript explains it in greater detail. You should know it is a one-way communication path. You sense no communication from the animal and you are limited to what the animal can do. A cat or similar small animal can't carry something large or heavy, for example. A horse could but the horse couldn't go someplace small and cramped. Do you follow?"

"Yes, so any animal then?"

"Well, yes. Any animal capable of forming a relationship with the draoi."

"So, not an insect then."

Nadine glanced up at me and scowled and looked away. "Daft," she muttered and kept walking.

We walked the rest of the way in silence. When we reached her home Dog came bounding up to us, tail wagging. I knelt down and scratched his ears.

"Hey, Dog. Missed you. Where'd you put the rabbit and the grouse?"

Dog bounded away, and I followed him to where the carcasses lay by the back door. I picked them up and Dog grinned up at me with his tongue lolling long and wet from his mouth. Nadine came up behind us and stared at Dog.

"Good job, Dog!" I said. "Can you not sense him, Nadine? Through the bond?"

Nadine shook her head and turned and walked away. I felt her distress at my words and watched, confused, as she quickly moved to go into her house. She told me to stay outside, and she stood fumbling with the latch on the door. I moved behind her and held her upper arm and gently swung her around. She tried to hide her face, but I saw the tears and I felt terrible knowing somehow I had caused them.

"What did I say? Nadine? I'm sorry?" I said in a rush. Nadine grabbed me and pressed her face to my chest and I held her. "What, please tell me? What's wrong?"

Her reply was muffled in my shirt.

"What? I can't understand you."

She leaned back her head and wiped her nose. "I said, I can't see or feel the bonds, Will. I have no power. The only draoi I felt was when your mother passed during the Purge." She laid her head against my chest again. "I can't see or feel the draoi bonds. I never have."

"But you have them. I can see them."

"Yes, I am draoi. But my powers from Gaea are so slight that it is only with extraordinary effort that I can affect anything. You've seen my garden. It's beautiful, but it has taken me years to reach that level of bounty. No, no powers for me. No ability to see or sense the bonds between the draoi. I was one of them and yet separate. Your mother was the only one to show me any true sympathy or love."

With a sudden realisation, I understood the full import of what it had done to her. For her whole life, she had never truly been a part of the draoi world. She had been isolated her entire life and surrounded by wonders she could only dream of being able to do. During the Purge, she had felt nothing of the losses through her bonds and probably sat in her house and waited for the Church to come to her door. She had lived a life alone and afraid. I held her close. *This poor woman.*

"Nadine, I can sense and see the bonds and the one between you and me is beautiful. I wish you could see it. It is wide and blue with a little white swirling through it. I can sense everything about you. I can close my eyes and almost see you through it."

Nadine nodded her head against my chest and cried harder. I felt mixed emotions from her and I couldn't separate them. She was beyond distraught.

Twelve

Nadine's House, Jergen Waterfront, 900 A.C.

NADINE AND I settled into a routine over the next few weeks. Mostly she kept away from me and rarely spoke. I would catch her looking out of the corners of her eyes at me. I did my best to give her room, but the house was small, and we had to interact. When we did, she was furtive. Through our bond, I felt a conflict within her. Something bothered her deeply. She cared for me, that much I knew for sure for a strong sense of it could not be hidden through our bond, but I had nothing to compare it to. And so, I, too, was confused.

"There may be errors in the copy," she said on the first day back from the Library. When I went to question her, she disappeared outside and didn't return until dusk. She ate her prepared supper and went to her bed.

I practised using my power until Nadine confirmed I kept the tell-tale blue glow clear from eyes. Days passed in quiet contemplation. I watched Nadine with the manuscript and waited patiently for her to tell me what she had found. She had replaced the torn pages in the book and it sat on the kitchen table most of the time. I spent my time in her garden and coaxed her plants to greater strength and potential. Dog followed me around when he wasn't off chasing rabbits and seagulls. He was my only confidant for the first week back from the library and I felt almost like I was alone on the road again.

"I don't know what I did to anger her," I said to Dog one day.

Dog looked at me and wagged his tail.

"Seriously. What did I do?" I asked.

Dog inched forward and licked my nose in response. That was the best I was to get out of him other than a sense of amusement. Whatever was going on, Dog was amused. *Good to know*, I thought and went back to tending the herbs.

I made our meals every evening, and we ate in silence except for small talk about plants and my tales of life outside Jaipers. The most we had interacted was once we washed each other's hair. I had started on my own one evening and she had taken over without a word. Her hands strong and sure on my scalp. It was relaxing, and I felt happy for a while as we connected. Then it was her turn. She told me quietly what to do, and I followed her instructions. Her white hair was fading fast, and the red was coming through bright. I told her, and she smiled. She closed her eyes, and I massaged her scalp and cleaned her hair. I dried it and tied some rosemary through a braid and she kissed my cheek. She left me alone after that and barely looked at me over meals.

After another week, Nadine joined me on the swing outside and reported the manuscript was an almost perfect copy.

"I knew at once it was a copy," she had said when I asked if she was sure. "But I spent the last couple of weeks cataloguing the differences. I looked for marks or additions. I wanted to figure out how the copy was made and by whom." She turned pages and pointed out various places which, she assured me, were different from the originals.

I mulled it over and nodded when she pointed out another discrepancy. "Perhaps it isn't a copy at all," I said. We were sitting on the swing outside and Dog lay asleep at our feet. *On my feet, actually.*

Nadine scowled at me. "What do you mean?"

"Well, the first manuscripts, they were written by hand. A hand with Gaea in control. Correct?"

"Yes, Gaea possessed dozens of people at once, according to the legends. They each wrote sections of the manuscript. Others crafted the leather bindings and embossed the covers. All four manuscripts were created at once and all were exactly the same. It was a marvel."

"So, what stopped her from creating this one, too? Or, if she knew about it being copied, to either stop it or assist somehow?"

Nadine moved to speak and then shut her mouth. After a moment, she grimaced and smacked me. Hard on the same spot as always on my upper arm.

"Ass."

"Ass? What for?"

"For being such a wiseass. I never thought of that. I suppose whether it was people who created the copy, she knew, and either helped or didn't care. I suppose it doesn't matter though. It is an accurate copy. But it is a unique version."

"How so?"

"Well, you would have to have seen or held the originals. I was one of the few allowed to do so. I had access to your mother's, in case you were wondering. She would leave it out for me in her chambers. Told me to study it all I wanted. She would smile and leave me alone with it. I spent hours with it. Hours and hours. I loved the manuscript. I knew it inside and out. I was particularly drawn to the drawings of the plants. The vibrancy of the colours. They were so beautiful." Nadine shook her head slowly with a ghost of a smile, clearing the cobwebs. "Sorry. What I mean to say... to get to. Never mind the plant drawings, I'll get to that. It is enough to know that the covers of the original manuscripts were embossed. This copy isn't. It's flat, feel here." Nadine held out the book, and I rubbed the triskelion on the cover. It was smooth to the touch. "This is significant. It was how I knew it was a copy at once."

"Does that matter? That it's a copy?"

"No, I don't think so. I mean, my memories could be wrong after so long, but I am fairly certain that this is an exact copy. The details are all there. Only the plants are drawn a little different. That's all. The words. They seem the same to me. No way to tell for sure. Not until we get our hands on an original to directly compare it to. Still, I am pretty sure my memory of the original is pretty accurate. The manuscript was my life for so many years."

"So, what now?"

Nadine looked at me for a moment and then patted the top of my hand and then held it.

"For starters, I study the book more. Then I find a way to help you. Without a Stoc to guide you, I fear you might hurt yourself. Gaea's powers are not minor. For some draoi, it takes years of practice to gain control. I have no power, but I have the lore. It will have to be enough."

"Hmm. Probably won't be. I'm sure to die. I can feel it."

"Probably."

I smacked her on the upper arm and she squealed and jumped up in shock off the swing. She turned and gaped at me. "You! You!" she shouted, her face red.

"Ha! It serves you right! You are always smacking me! Turnabout is fair!"

Nadine glared at me. Her face twisted from anger to something else and then back again. She leaned forward as if to join me and then stomped off into the house.

I looked at Dog and Dog looked at me. "She looks beautiful when she is angry," I said.

I smiled after her and realised something. She wasn't moving like an old woman anymore. She was more like someone middle-aged, or younger. I sensed her through the bond. Her heart was hammering, and she was confused. Happy and afraid at the same time. I didn't understand her emotions or what her problem was. *It had to be the reminder of the draoi and powers she lacked*, I thought. Our bond was still blue, but the white swirled and stormed. I examined her and looked at Dog as if to seek answers, but Dog just lowered his head to his paws and went back to sleep.

I examined Nadine through the bond and could see she didn't just look younger. She was younger. Her arthritis was gone, for one. Her spine was straight, for another. I could see her heart was one of a much younger woman. Her muscles had gained strength and mass. Her hair was growing in red and thick at the roots and would soon replace the grey. Her wrinkles remained, but it seemed like a false wrapping now. Gaea was making her younger on the inside and hiding it behind the mask of an old woman. *Whatever for?* I wondered and sat back and stared at Dog for a little while, thinking furiously.

A couple of weeks later, Nadine woke me up from my bedroll. To give her more privacy and distance from me, I had placed it as far from her as possible across the house. It wasn't only out of respect for her privacy. It was also because she snored worse than Daukyns and Dog combined. I blinked up at her and could see she was on her knees beside me holding a steaming cup of tea in her hands. She smiled down at me and held it out. She was back-lit by the morning sun and her hair caught the rays and gleamed, framing her face in reddish light. She never looked more beautiful. Her wrinkles looked out of place with eyes shining bright with youth and health. Her eyes were a lovely bright green, and I held her gaze for a moment. *This is how I want to wake up every morning*, I thought. She blushed at my attention and put the mug down beside me and hurried away.

"Get up," she said as she retreated. "Time for school, young man."

"Yes, old woman," I said and laughed at her growl. *She knows now*, I felt through the bond. *She wasn't sure before but now she is. She is getting younger. But something is still bothering her. Perhaps it is the return of her youth? Would that upset someone? It shouldn't. She should be overjoyed. How many people get a second life?*

I rose and sipped my tea before heading outside to the jacks to relieve myself. Dog was already up, and hunting and I could sense his joy as he chased down seagulls flocking by the nearby pond. As I finished my business, I recalled what Nadine had just said. *School? What does that mean?* I thought. Daukyns had given me a kind of schooling. Hopefully, she meant the same thing. Thoughts of Daukyns reminded me of Reeve Comlin and I thought of my need to warn him of the Church.

A week ago I had managed to find a barge captain down by the river who promised me he would get a letter delivered to Reeve Comlin. His barge only went as far as Lakeside, but he said he knew another captain there he could trust. Their schedules ensured he would be able to hand the letter over. I used my power to determine he was trustworthy, and we agreed on four groats to deliver the message He seemed pleased with the amount. Two were for him and two for the next captain who would deliver it to Jaipers. I sat on the dock and, after several attempts, I managed to write out a message to Reeve Comlin. In it, I warned him of the threat the Church presented and let him know the garrison likely had spies. I said nothing else and chose not to tell him of the attack or the draoi. I concluded by telling him I was safe, would stop by the farm, and hoped he was well. It would have to be enough. I handed it to the captain, and he sealed the letter with his own seal. He then took my money, shook hands and left. It would be weeks before the letter would arrive. I felt better knowing the Reeve would be warned.

I left the jacks and entered the home to find Nadine over at her worktable. She had cleared it and had a few objects and the manuscript on it. I sipped my cooling tea and walked over. She was reading from the book and making notes beside it. I tried to read what she was writing before she covered it and scowled at me. "No! This is for me. You sit there and wait." She pointed at the kitchen chair she had moved up to sit opposite her at the worktable.

I sat down and finished my tea while she completed her notes. I had no idea what to expect. I could sense Nadine was excited. I watched Dog through the bond and could sense he seemed bored now. The seagulls had fled, and he was standing beside the pond and wondering what to do next. I sent him an image of rabbits falling to his massive jaws and he leapt in the direction of the rabbit burrows by the woods. I felt a sense of thanks and I opened my mouth in surprise. *That was interesting.*

"Nadine, I..."

"Shush," She commanded, interrupting me. I shot her a withering look, which she ignored. I was bored, so I watched Dog for a while and sent him different images such as meat on the stove, milk in a bowl, and the like. All in an attempt to get something out of him. What I got was a sense of him getting angry at me and I stopped. *Sorry*, I sent. Nothing came back. I finished my tea and looked around the home, which now felt so safe and warm to me. Above, the rafters groaned with the weight of all the herbs I had harvested over the month.

Recently, Nadine had gone to a woman friend of hers. After a brief discussion, she agreed to sell the herbs in the market for a small but fair cut of the profit. Nadine loved all the coin she was collecting. I was stunned at the amount she earned. The market here in Jergen was much more profitable than in Jaipers.

Despite the work in the garden and in the home, I was bored. The lessons with Nadine were fun but, without magic of her own, they were limited. I was about to rise to make more tea when she cleared her throat. I turned my full attention to her.

"Alright," said Nadine a moment later. "This will seem silly to you at first, but you have to bear with me. You know nothing and yet can do more than you should be able to. That we know. Normally a Stoc would guide a craobh and a craobh would guide a Duilleog. But, young man, it appears you have reached craobh all by yourself and now I have to try to fix that. I need to teach you Duilleog magic and guess what? I have no powers to use to help that process. Normally the bond is used to teach the new draoi. So words will have to do. Understand?"

"Fix it? What do you mean?"

"Well, there are ways of using the power. You have picked up bad habits working the power by yourself. I need to correct those bad habits."

"Bad habits? Like what?"

"Well, the way you used to blast your power and let your aura glow out into visible light. Or, when you were chased by those guards. There was a lot you could have done. The surrounding nature can be asked to help. They can slow down the approach of others. You can ask animals to come to the attack in your defence. You did none of that. You simply ran."

I glared at her. *What she was describing were not my bad habits, it was my fear.*

"Will, I am not criticising you! Gaea, forbid! I am trying to educate you. You will need to learn to accept criticism." I grinned at her in response and she smacked me. "You! Be serious!"

"Sorry, Nadine. I know, I'm ready to learn. Teach me, master."

"Better. Okay. We start with basics. There are three powers a draoi can use. One is *Vision*. The second is *Sense*. The last is *Influence*. They are pretty straightforward but how you use each can be complicated and there are many different strengths and uses of each. In simple terms, *Vision* is what you did in Jaipers that first time. It is the first power that draoi manifest once they are opened to Gaea's powers. When you use *Vision,* you are seeing the world in a different way. Some draoi think they are seeing through things. That is not possible, the Word teaches that truth, the human eye cannot see through solid objects unless they are transparent. So, when you use *Vision* you are seeing in different spectrums. People see the colours that make up visible light but that is not the limit to what can be seen with magic. We know from the ancient teachings that light as we know it is a broad spectrum and the colours we see are but a minuscule amount of what is out there. Vision lets you see those other spectrums. Understand?"

I nodded once. I was starting to feel like I was back with Daukyns in Jaipers. I steeled myself for a long lecture. *At least this one is interesting.*

"*Sense*," she continued. "Is almost the same as *Vision* and many young Duilleogs confuse the two. I heard the draoi teachers often explain *Sense* in this way: '*Sense* is seeing with your emotions. You see how another person feels, or an animal, or a plant. You sense all that is Gaea and it is because you and all life *are* Gaea. You are sensing a distant part of yourself.' Does that make any sense to you, Will?"

I laughed at her unintentional pun. She frowned at me. I stopped laughing and nodded. She flashed me a quick smile, and I laughed again. *She was getting to be fun.* Our bond flashed in my sight blue and white and pulsing.

"The last is *Influence*. This is the power that few draoi can use to its fullest potential. With influence, you affect all life around you. You manipulate matter. You can change it. What you can never do is harm other life through influence. It reflects back on you and you harm yourself. It is a defence mechanism of Gaea herself. You can no more rip off your own finger, do you see?"

"No. That one I don't. I might not be able to rip my own finger off, but you could. That is the same thing if everything is Gaea."

Nadine smiled. "Well, yes. Except that, it is a matter of your consciousness. You cannot harm yourself because you know you are harming yourself. Your desire for self-preservation stops that. One of Gaea's gifts is that all life is separate and distinct from one another. And that this life can self-replicate but can also destroy. But the life is bound within itself and can be seen as distinct and individual. When draoi use influence they cross that boundary."

"What if someone had no self-preservation? What would happen then?"

Nadine looked at me like I had two heads. "What a silly notion. Everyone has self-preservation."

"What if you chose to sacrifice yourself for a greater belief, or someone else?"

Nadine pursed her lips. "I don't think Gaea would allow that, Will. You harm life and as a draoi, you are harming yourself. Do you see?"

I thought I did. I had a bad experience before and decided now was the right time to tell her. "Um, yes. I do, I suppose. I haven't told you something. What I did in Jaipers."

"What happened?"

"The day after I rubbed the coin and woke my powers, you remember me telling you that?" Nadine nodded and I continued. "The Reeve in Jaipers took me to see a sick woman. I was using *vision* at the time, but I didn't know it by name. I looked *into* her and found she was infested with a tiny organism. They were everywhere in her. Then I saw that this thing had spread throughout most of the town. I tracked it to the well in town. Infected rats had contaminated the water supply, and it had quickly spread throughout the town. Myself included. I—well, I grew so angry—I *reached* out and killed every mote in the town. I crushed them. Then I felt like my head exploded in agony and I nearly died. Reeve Comlin was surprised I woke. After that, it took me the better part of a week in the inn to recover. It was horrible."

Nadine had her mouth covered with a hand and she stared at me in what could only be described as horror. I felt my cheeks redden in shame. "Dear Gaea, what are you? One draoi cannot heal an entire town. The range! It's too large." Nadine shook her head. "You are the last of the draoi. Well, almost the last it seems. Perhaps Gaea has seen fit to grant you more power than she ever had in a draoi before. She must trust you, Will."

Nadine grew quiet and thought for a moment before she continued. "The pain in your head was the reflection of the harm you caused. You were fortunate that the combined mass of the motes was not much more than a few grains of sand. Scale is everything for Gaea. One life is not worth more than another. The mass of one life, if greater, is worth more than a smaller life mass. Many draoi fought that particular aspect of Gaea. And they could have provided you with many arguments to prove the concept flawed. But it didn't matter in the end, did it? All that mattered was Gaea's opinion, and she was pretty clear about it. And they are all gone. None of the draoi lives mattered, and they were the holders of the balance."

I sat in silence and thought of her words. I didn't think them correct. One life, no matter how small, could not mean less just because of size. We treat children reverently and they are smaller than adults. It had to be something more. Something else. I felt I could almost grasp it, but it eluded me. I focused on what Nadine was saying.

"What do you mean by balance?" I remembered Daukyns spoke often of balance. I knew the answer from Daukyns, but I wanted to hear Nadine's version from the draoi perspective.

"Balance. The Word teaches this concept. And it should. The Word was started by the draoi. The first Freamhaigh introduced it to the world, and the concept stuck. It was easy for the draoi back then. They had proof God didn't exist. They had Gaea, a living deity. But that's not important. The reason the draoi existed was Gaea created them—well, us. She selected people and gave them powers and told them to restore and maintain the balance. Our lore teaches us that long-ago humans were too powerful. They were destroying Gaea herself. Poisoning her. But she stopped it, thousands of years ago. She almost wiped the world of all people. But then she changed her mind. People and Gaea, they were the same thing, you see? People just hold more conscious thought than other life on earth. We are more Gaea than a dog for example."

I looked at Dog who was lying under the table. He was asleep and content. I immediately disagreed with Nadine. All life is equal. From the smallest insect to the largest animal. There could be no balance if life is measured by mass. It made no sense to me. I could see Nadine believed it. She had to. It was all she had ever known. It was her lore and her words. But with no power, she couldn't see the truth. All life has meaning. This couldn't be about balance. It was the wrong word. Balance was unachievable with nature. Wolves ate rabbits. If it was about balance, then a rabbit would eat a wolf. But it didn't work that way. Rabbits found ways to hide from the wolf. They bred at an incredible rate, ensuring they survived as a species.

It must have everything to do with the harmony of life. Co-existing on the earth together, I thought. *Not balance, but harmony.*

A loud and pure tone filled the air and Dog leapt up and barked. Nadine looked startled and held her hands to her ears. I felt a presence fill the room and turned to see Gaea standing before me. She was dressed in a long flowing gown made of vines and leaves. Flowers sprouted all over her and painted the gown in a beautiful shimmering mosaic of colours. The smell of freshly dug earth and flowers filled the air and I breathed deep and smiled. Nadine gasped and lowered her hands from her ears. A feeling of peace filled my heart and I could feel pulses of earth power through the soles of my feet. I felt I knew her better than I did myself. I knew she was me and I was her. I felt small but not afraid.

Gaea smiled at us and took us all in with a slow turn of her head. Her hair was rough and tangled and dirt fell from her to the floor. Her eyes had no whites—just a deep brown colour. Her skin was rough, like bark, but she was beautiful all the same. "Well done, William Arbor." She spoke quietly with no more power or volume than the woman she appeared to be. Her voice awoke a pain in my heart and I struggled to understand the source. "You understand that which eluded the draoi before you, Will. Harmony for all." Nadine turned to look at me with a wonder on her face. "Humans destroyed harmony in the past and I will not suffer that pain again. It woke me and I have not slept since. I am still recovering from the damage and parts of me may never fully heal. In time, with the help of humans, I may but for now, you will help me restore this Realm."

"Restore the Realm?" The question came out of me before I could think. As soon as I voiced it I knew that I had to get answers. I had only just begun to try to rationalise that there was an entity that was nature. Here she stood before me, and the first thing in my mind was understanding how she could have allowed the Purge. Gaea turned to me with a face that seemed to bear no emotion.

"Yes, restore the Realm. Here will be the test that will decide what happens next."

"How could you let them all die?" I said. I heard Nadine suck in her breath, but I didn't care. This woman in front of me had allowed my mother to die. If I understood everything, she had required it to happen.

Gaea's face softened, and she nodded ever so slightly. "It's true. I allowed the draoi to be cleansed from the land."

"Cleansed?" I spat. The word was foul. It implied that my mother was somehow dirty. A felt a tightness in my chest and I clenched my hands to still them. I stared in disbelief at this apparition who stood before me and told me she had allowed my mother to be cleansed. It was just a euphemism for *killed*. She had been struck down when she most needed Gaea. "You let her die. She was killed doing your work. I was eight years old. Abandoned and alone in the world."

"She returned to me. As did all the others. In time, you will understand. My time here is limited. I have much for you to do. First, you will gather the draoi and teach them," she said.

I blinked. Had she just dismissed my entire concern for the lives of the draoi and my mother? *How cold was this* thing *in front of me?* I opened my senses to her and cried out. My vision flooded with light and power blinding me. I turned off my senses and blinked. My vision cleared, and I found Gaea looking back at me with that same lack of emotion.

"It has been some time since a draoi opted to examine me with my own power," she said. "Nadine you had best start teaching him soon. Will, we will talk more about choice at a later time, I promise you. Not now. You must teach the new draoi."

I glared at her. I was far from wanting to give up this discussion. I didn't know how to take this entity in front of me. I felt so drawn to her. I could feel the connection to her and I trusted her. My thoughts fought with my heart. I lowered my head and tried to find peace. I had no idea how to do that. I thought back to a conversation with Daukyns.

"How heavy is this wineskin?" he asked me when I told him I had been particularly overwhelmed with dealing with the loss of my mother. It would happen to me now and then. It would hit me and not leave me for days. I asked him what to do, and he answered my question with his own. I looked at Daukyns and the wineskin held straight out from his body. Not understanding I shook my head.

"It's a trick question, Will. The answer is: It doesn't matter how heavy it is, it depends on how long you try to hold it. I can hold this easily for a minute or two. Maybe for half an hour. But in a day of holding this skin, my arm will start to tire. In two days? I would be forced to drop it. Do you understand?"

I shook my head. With Daukyns, it was hard sometimes to suss out his meaning. And somehow it always seemed to involve wine in some capacity.

"The longer you try to carry a burden, the harder it is to carry it. Sometimes you have to set it down for a little while. When you're ready, you pick it up again."

"What?"

Daukyns sighed and drank some wine out of the skin. He wiped his mouth with his sleeve. "Will set the burden aside for now. Pick it up and look at it now and then but stop trying to carry it around all the time."

I returned to the present and sighed. I missed Daukyns and his words. He always found a way to centre me. I struggled but found a way to set aside the anger I felt about the loss of my mother. I focused instead on the bond between Gaea and I and how I felt I knew I could trust her. *Another time*, I thought. *We will finish this conversation.* "Teach them?" I asked at last. I looked around the kitchen and swung my hands out. "How? This place is a bit small. How many draoi are we talking about here?" As soon as I said the words, a thought glimmered in my mind.

"Will!" admonished Nadine, under her breath. Gaea laughed, and I looked back at Nadine and mouthed 'What?' Gaea smiled at Nadine.

"He speaks the truth, Nadine. I see in him now that he knows where to start. I tell you this: William, you are correct—head to the farm Reeve Comlin told you about. You remember where it is but to guide you and make you move swiftly across the land I give you another bond. She is young. Your age but not as mature. You are an old soul, William, she can learn much from you. The bond will guide you there. She will be the first Duilleog. Your first student and the first challenge. Her name is Katherine."

I looked at my bonds and saw a new one form and snake out to the northwest. It was blue and bright. I sensed wonder down the line and the image of a girl, my age, with her face alight with joy, came to my mind.

"Really?" I shook my head. This was too much and too fast. Gaea was standing there in front of me and giving me orders. *Students? I'm only eighteen. Who would respect that?* "How will I find them? I only found out I was a draoi a month ago." I could sense Nadine glaring at me and I didn't look her way.

"Fear not. They will find you. Already they are in motion. They will arrive soon. It is why you must hurry."

"Um, okay?" I had no other response.

Gaea smirked at me. *Did she really just do that?* Then she bent down and scratched the belly of Dog. He had been squirming on his back in front of her since Gaea had arrived. "Dog, my friend. You have done well. Do you wish to continue?"

Dog barked and stood up, came over to me, and leaned against me. Gaea smiled.

"Excellent. A good choice of name, William. Dog suits him. So be it." Gaea smiled down at Dog and then turned to Nadine and smiled at her with an expression mixed with sorrow. "Nadine. Your task was a difficult one and not one of your choosing. However, you have within you the lore that will teach new generations. Listen to William. He understands the application of that lore better than you will accept. He will guide you as you teach him."

"I will, as you command it."

Gaea shook her head. "No, I do not command it, child. I ask it of you. Perhaps this will help—a boon for you, my daughter. I withheld this from you so you would survive the Purge. I now grant you those powers as I would have before. You and William will make a new world possible. Use it wisely."

The tone sounded again, and I felt an energy in the air. My hair floated up on my head and I looked to Nadine and saw her hair standing on end. She patted at it and then her eyes went wide as Gaea's power joined with her. Through our bond, I felt her explosion of joy and watched as tears sprung from her eyes. With *vision,* I saw her aura burst blindingly with colour and then settle into a most beautiful bright blue. She gasped and held her hands up to her face. Her skin shifted and the remaining years of her body melted away and before me stood a young woman, my age, if not a little older. With trembling hands, she felt her face and then looked at the back of her hands and felt the smooth, vibrant and young skin that covered her. She looked up to Gaea and tears slipped down her cheeks.

"Nadine, I name you my Cill Darae. Henceforth you represent me here in the Realm. I can think of no one better and, in truth, I always meant this for you."

Nadine cried out and collapsed to her knees and clasped her hands to her breast. "I-I don't understand? How can I... what? Cill Darae? But I have no power. Oh..." Her eyes lost focus and I could tell she was using the *sight* for the first time. She looked around the room and then down at the bond between us and raised a trembling hand to her mouth.

"You are wise, Nadine, and you have a strength within you that few possess. You will be the Cill Darae as I always meant the position to be. A position of power. Not second to the Freamhaigh. Equal. Use your strength and teach a new generation. Your powers are equal to Will's. I caution you to not lose yourself in your newfound youth. Move past the age you think you are and embrace the age you now are. Enjoy your second chance at youth."

"I will, Earth Mother. Thank you. Thank you so much." I could sense Nadine examining the bond between us and she continued to stare at me with something that seemed close to fear. I was confused.

Gaea laughed. "Nadine, my Cill Darae. You must be truthful to yourself starting now. You fight it again. This time freely admit your love and follow your heart. It beats true."

"L-love? No." asked a crying Nadine shaking her head.

"Yes. Nadine. You fight it but you love him. You felt it the moment you met, did you not? I admit I did not foresee this, but I am truly pleased. Calm yourself, my daughter. I love you and William loves you. That is enough for anyone. Your lives are too short for missed opportunities. You are equals in this. I made it this way. And you both have much to learn."

My eyes widened, and I stared at Nadine. She was still shaking her head in denial. *Did Gaea just say I love Nadine? Did I?* And then I knew. I had known for a while now but hadn't truly understood it. Now that the words were out I could see the truth of it. I now had a word to associate with the feeling I had when I thought of her. I looked at our bond and also finally understood the white line. A colour that Nadine had understood and had been bothered by. White was love, pure and true. Nadine looked up at me through her tears and my love surged even watching the snot running freely from her nose. Her transformation was startling. I knew her when she was grey and wrinkled, and now I saw her young with snot flowing down her face, and both faces were beautiful. She was a young woman again but with the wisdom of a lifetime. I could feel my heart was bound to her. *True love, without a doubt,* I thought.

"Yes, William. It is a rare thing," said Gaea, and I looked at her in surprise. I had almost forgotten she was here. "It is not often that two parts of me make for such a pair. I enjoy it when it happens especially when it can result in offspring. Enough. You will have time to talk about this. For now, make haste. Leave for the farm. Do not doubt your abilities. Trust your instincts. Hurry."

"Wait!" I said, sensing she was about to leave. "You keep calling me William. Everyone calls me Will. Only my mother called me William. And it sounds...it sounds..." I trailed off, afraid to say the words.

Gaea stepped toward me and startled me by embracing me in a strong clasp. "That is because I am your mother, William. She was Belle and I am Belle. All life on Earth is me. You are starting to understand this. I gave birth to you and watched over you since that day."

My strength left my body and I collapsed into her arms and she held me tight and supported me. She smelt like my mother and seemed shorter than before. "My mother died!" I sobbed.

"Yes, she did. I was with her when she passed and with her when she re-joined with me. We are together. All that pass return to me. Trust me in this: I am your mother, William. I love you. I have never left your side. I was the wolves that watched over you. I was the birds that soared overhead. Never were you out of my sight or out of my heart. Now wipe your tears and embrace what you know is true. All life on Earth is one. Death is only a transition and births another."

We stood like that for long minutes. My emotions were twisted with random thoughts. My mother was dead. But this was my mother. I knew both to be true. It hurt and made me happy at the same time. I pulled back and my mother looked back at me.

"Belle!" gasped Nadine covering her mouth in shock. My mother let go of me and grasped Nadine's hands briefly before stepping back. I stood in shock staring hard at my mother and straining to remember every movement and every gesture. I didn't want to forget again.

"Yes. Nadine, I was always Belle. She was perhaps the closest to me of anyone. This is the face you try so hard to remember, William. You are my son and I miss you. I'm sorry I couldn't be there for you, but certain events had to occur. Before Belle joined me, she understood that you would be cared for. She made you promise to stay hidden and stay safe. Your promise to me, as your mother, is over. No longer must you keep hidden. Embrace the world. Embrace your power. The world will soon learn of the draoi. You and Nadine will make that happen. Now, I must leave. I have focused too long on the here and now."

Gaea vanished. We stood there for a long series of heartbeats. Then, with a cry, Nadine ran into my arms and clung to me and sobbed with joy. Dog barked and bounded about the room. *What to do now?* I thought and held Nadine tighter.

Craobh

Part Two: Fight

Craobh

Thirteen

Outside Lakeside, 900 A.C.

SETH FARLOW SPOTTED the marker beside the road and glanced back down the road he had just travelled, then, after a moment, he turned to look ahead toward Lakeside. The road was deserted. Seth steered his horse off the road and dismounted. With the reins in his hand, he led the horse into the woods until it was out of sight of the road. He reached into his saddlebag and removed a hobble and fastened it to the rear cannons of the animal. It wasn't necessary for him to hobble the horse. He had long ago overwhelmed the small brain of the animal. It wouldn't run. Not now. Not unless he willed it.

But old habits are good habits, he thought. *It is good that God's creatures obey me so thoroughly. It is His will.*

Seth stepped quietly deeper into the woods. His black boots left almost no mark on the soil and grass. In his left hand, he held a red bloodstone. He drew a black dagger from his waist sheath into his right hand. He took several steps and spotted the next mark about four feet above eye level on a tree—high enough to avoid being seen. *No one looks up*, he thought. He stopped and closed his eyes and focused on what he was hearing. It was quiet. Seth scowled and reached out with God's Gift. The silence deepened around him. Ever since he had been blessed, he found God's creatures all drew quiet in respect for his divine powers. Normally he enjoyed the respect of the silence. What he was not enjoying was that by now he should be picking up the sounds of his men. Peter he didn't expect to hear, but his idiot prodigy, Jeremy, he would be making enough noise to wake the dead.

The absolute silence meant something was wrong. Seth crouched down and strained to reach out with his powers to the woods surrounding him. The silence grew deeper. Seth could hear the rapid heartbeats of the creatures around him now. They held their breath in awe of his presence. Seth gritted his teeth and then released his power. He felt a wetness on his upper lip and wiped away the drops of blood from his nose. He would pay later for his use of God's power with a powerful headache. It was all part of the price to him. He hadn't needed to use his whip in weeks.

Seth was concerned. Peter should have left secondary signs on the approach trail, but they were absent. The single signs meant they had managed to capture the demon spawn and then trussed him correctly. The second mark meant they were in full control and that the demon was drained and in their power. With the second mark missing Seth could only assume something had gone wrong. Seth began to seethe inside followed by a sharp and hot acidic burn. A rustle broke in the foliage near him and a rabbit bolted, screaming in fear. With a thought, Seth stilled the rabbit and twisted the brain matter. Seth felt the life-force of the rabbit dwindle and he grabbed it with his powers and fed it to his own. Goosebumps ran up his spine and over his scalp and he shuddered in ecstasy. He loved this part of God's Power. It was his sole reward in this life.

His anger continued to consume him and he struggled to control his breathing. He had trusted Peter to handle this correctly. For Seth, this was his chance at redemption. Peter knew that. Seth had to recover the Target and complete his mission. This had been his chance to atone for his failure ten years ago. He could not return to the Archbishop empty-handed. The promise of bringing the Archbishop back into the Chamber was all he thought about. He wanted—no, he needed—him to see the work he did. It had been too many years since he had stepped in and participated. The past weeks on the road had been filled with his imaginings of how the Archbishop would respond.

How could an untrained eighteen-year-old demon spawn escape from Peter? Peter was one of the best. He had hunted down and captured dozens of them. He was unequalled. Something must have happened. Something unexpected.

Seth followed the trail and came to a large clearing with a small cooking fire in the middle. *This is where Peter and Jeremy camped.* It would be a set measured distance outside the known range of the demon's power. At a second site, called the containment area, the demon would be trussed and lifted from the ground. With only two hunters, one would stay with the demon and the other would stay in the camp. It was a method that had never failed. Seth could see the trail that likely led to the second area. But his eyes were focused on the opened waist packs of the two men. The exposed packs confirmed the men were lost. They would never abandon them or leave them in the open. Now it was only a matter of determining what had happened.

Seth reached out with his powers and sensed where the grass had been trampled. He scented blood and followed it to the base of a tree. His powers told him it was Jeremy's blood. The man had rested there, injured. There was something else. Another scent was in the air. Seth strained with his powers. And then it came to him: wolves. Wolves had come. Jeremy had run down the trail to the containment area. The scents and tracks confirmed it. Seth sniffed the air and smelled dog. Wolves with a dog. Demon powers. *The Target must've broken his bonds. Peter fucked up.*

Seth moved first to the waist packs and confirmed the bloodstones were not there. Seth frowned. The stones had cost him so much pain and anguish to make. They were worth it for they had saved so much Sect members from death and reduced the time it took to conduct the demon hunts. His men thought them to be actual rubies. Seth knew better for they were made from his blood. He had formed each of them over months. Each bloodstone was made from an equal amount of the blood he carried in his body. The bloodstones were the only way to give his men the protection they needed against the demon powers. The boots were the same. Leather soaked in his own blood until it was saturated. Seth was proud of those accomplishments. They came from his own brilliance. He had learned much reading the Demon Manuscript in Jergen over the years. He turned their evil into his gain. *Through blood and pain came salvation.* The scriptures spoke often of it. *Sacrifice yields rewards.*

Seth composed himself and made his way down the trail. He expected to find the worst. Peter had been a friend of sorts. More importantly, he had been one of God's best soldiers. His loss would not be insignificant. He sensed nothing in the area now. Whenever this had happened, it had been weeks ago. He measured out the distance and stepped out into another clearing. Peter had measured the distance correctly. The high, afternoon sun lit up the entire clearing.

The first thing Seth focused on was the picked over remains of a lone wolf. Fur, blood, and bones had been dragged in all directions from the remains. The wildlife had feasted on the animal. The grass was trampled everywhere. Seth could see nothing else. The clearing was empty. There were no bodies, but dried blood was everywhere. Seth looked up at the massive oak tree towering over the area. It had a broad branch extending out over the clearing. Perfect for hoisting up a demon and Peter had obviously thought so as well. Under the branch, the grass had been cut away until only bare soil remained. Seth walked over and looked up and found the signs of the rope they used. The bark was rotted away and exposed the blackened wood underneath. *Another one of my works. A rope infused with my life force and a block to demon powers.*

Seth searched the ground under the branch and found blood, faeces and urine. He used his senses and recoiled at the scent of demon. The Target had been here. Two wolves and one dog had arrived and taken out his men. One wolf fell. The dog released the demon, and he escaped. Once a demon was hoisted off the ground he had lost. Never during any of the Hunts had a demon escaped once it was strung up. This time it had failed. With the one demon he wanted dead more than any other. Seth growled. Despite Peter having done everything right he had failed him. He had failed God.

Seth threw back his head and screamed in frustration. From all around he sensed and heard animals hidden in the bushes bolt in fright. With a vengeance, he reached out and killed them all and laughed at the pleasure surging through his body in reward.

"Lord God! I thank you for this gift!" he yelled into the air.

Seth snapped his head to stare at the large oak. He felt from it a hatred that reminded him of the demons. Was it possible? Could a tree be a demon? Seth reached out with his power and touched the tree. The hatred burst from the tree in waves. Seth reacted without thought. He sensed the entirety of the tree: from the leaves to the roots deep underground. The roots were everywhere drinking up nutrients and water from the soil. They spread out for hundreds of yards in all directions. And there, Seth realised with horror, right under the tree and pierced through with roots were the bodies of Peter and Jeremy. The tree was pulling sustenance from their corpses. Anger boiled his vision red and Seth reached out to the tree and ripped its life force from the sap running under the bark. Seth revelled in the shock and horror of the tree as it ended its long life in such a sudden and helpless way.

Seth wasn't ready for the pleasure that would come from such a long and aged life force. It hit him all at once and it felt like being slammed into the ground if you fell from a great height. He landed flat on his back looking up at the big branch of the tree. He kept his pull on the life force as it raced through his body lighting every nerve in pleasurable fire. A screech heard only in his head started low and rose in pitch as he pulled the energy into himself. It was so immense; it filled him to bursting. Seth had no idea where it was going but the waves of pleasure rocked through him again and again. The power kept flooding into his body. It soon became painful and Seth joined the screech in his head. The two sounds were discordant and rose in pitch and intensity until the tree was simply gone. Seth panted into the absence of sound. Tears poured down the sides of his face and a sob escaped him. Seth lay with his arms and legs akimbo and spasming uncontrollably. He thrust his groin into the air and a dark wet spot stained the front of his breeches. His lips were pulled back in a rictus of a grin.

He lay there for an hour recovering. Before long he imagined he heard a soft whisper. He struggled to rise up on his elbows. Every nerve was on fire and the pain was exquisite. He looked around the clearing. He was giddy and not thinking right. *I should be more alert.* He fought to clear his head and then he saw her. A woman was hiding behind the tree he had just killed. He blinked to clear his vision, and he saw her clearly. There was a look of horror on her face that frightened him deep to his core. Seth tried to sense her, but she wasn't there. She was an apparition. A ghost. She wore vines for clothes and dirt fell from her hair. Like a corpse walking from the grave. He tried again to sense her with his powers, but he felt nothing from her. His eyes told him one thing and his senses another. Seth felt the hairs on the back of his neck stand up.

"What are you?" whispered the woman and then she was gone. One blink and she was gone. Vanished. Without a sound.

Seth scrambled backwards and ended up amid the remains of the wolf. A sharp pain lanced through his hand and he looked down to see a shattered rib bone piercing his left hand. Seth ripped it free, picked himself up, and ran from the clearing down the trail. He ran through the next clearing and out to his horse. He ripped off the hobble and threw himself on the horses back.

"Ride! Ride!" he screamed at the horse and it bolted for the road. The horse felt the panic and ran hard. The chest expanded and collapsed with its effort to draw breath to feed the powerful legs. Seth felt the horse resist, and he *pushed* until something snapped inside the brain of the horse. Seth sensed the horse now ran oblivious to its own death and it would die as soon as he released his hold. Seth shuddered as pain washed over him and he looked left and right.

He spied the woman not more than twenty feet from him beside the road to the right, her arm around a tree glaring at him. He screamed in fright, the sound high pitched and screeching. "Dear Lord!" Unease and profound fear flooded him, and he felt his bowel loosen on the saddle. "Run!" he screamed at the horse.

The woman vanished again, and Seth looked rapidly left and right for her. *There! To the left! Standing in the field!* Her head turned with him to follow his passage. *No shadow, she has no shadow!* Seth was losing control. The fear was consuming him. He felt the horse falter, and he regained his control. The heart of the horse was straining to pump blood and air to the demands of the legs and muscle. *Lord help me! Save me from this demon!*

With a sudden dawning, Seth recognised her. *It was the Target's mother. The bitch I killed ten years ago. She now haunts me.* Seth spewed scripture and kept the horse running for Lakeside.

Fear and shame fought within him. He reached inside himself for the calm and surety he normally enjoyed. It was hard when she would disappear and reappear alongside the road as he rode the horse hard. She kept with him and stared at him with that look. Panic threatened to overwhelm him. He knew the horse would die soon. He felt it shuddering between his legs. With an effort, he slowed the horse but kept it moving. He was finding it hard to concentrate on keeping the horse alive and focusing on escaping the demon.

He spotted the woman standing near a small copse of trees and with a will, he stopped the horse and returned the stare. Foam fell in big globules from the horse's mouth to the ground. He reached out with his senses to the demon and bit his tongue when he felt her presence everywhere. The woman in front of him was nothing but an image. *An apparition. A ghost*, he thought. Her eyes bore into him with such an intensity that he felt small and insignificant. He forced himself to sit upright and glared back at it. *God did not raise me to be afraid of the evil in this world. He taught me to fight it.*

"Begone!" he commanded with a wavering voice.

"What are you?" asked the apparition. The voice was familiar. An echo of years ago. It was the voice of the bitch from Munsten. The woman that spawned the Target. That same sultry and smoky voice that he hated. With a hint of a tease but nought else. Wanton. Evil. The voice of a demon.

Seth fought to control his voice and put strength behind it. "Begone! The power of the Lord compels you!"

"What are you?" demanded the voice more loudly.

"Begone demon!" Seth felt stronger, empowered.

"You are not what you once were. How have you corrupted my power so? What are you?"

"Begone!" screamed Seth and used his power to add force to the words. He felt the life energy around him react and fall back to the push in concentric circles around him. He yelled in triumph when the woman rocked back on her feet. *I killed her once*, he thought with satisfaction. *I will do so again if God allows me.*

She slowly raised her head to look up at him with an expression he didn't recognise. A mixture of hate and fear, perhaps. She continued to stare at him for a long moment and then she was gone. Seth waited for her to reappear and when she didn't he finally relaxed and took a hold of his final remnants of fear. He dismounted felt the horse try to lie down to die.

"Live," he commanded the horse and poured his power into the animal. *There is no way I am walking all the way to Lakeside.* The horse fought him, and Seth felt pain sear his nerves. Such lovely pain. He laughed and fought the will of the horse. It wished to die, and he wished it to live. It was a simple matter and Seth laughed at the futile efforts of the animal and then gave a casual push of God's power. The horse went perfectly still. Its heart and breathing stopped and Seth counted to thirty before the heart started to pump at his urging.

Seth was surprised. The horse was no longer a horse. It was something else. It lived and yet it did not. It breathed and its heart pumped blood. But everything else that was life was missing. The horse turned its head to stare at Seth. The blood vessels in the eyes had all burst. The teeth were tinged with blood and the foam was turning pink. Seth laughed out loud.

"Don't you look charming!"

The horse defecated and pissed all over the road. Seth stepped back away from the spray and splatter. In a matter of moments, the horse voided itself, all the while staring blankly at Seth.

Seth stood in stunned silence and watched the horse for a few minutes. It stared at him non-stop and without blinking. It disturbed him. "Blink, damn you!" he ordered but nothing happened. "Move to the side of the road."

The horse merely looked back at him. Seth thought about the horse blinking and *pushed* with his power and the horse blinked. He thought about the horse moving and Seth watched the horse walk over to the side of the road and stop.

"Excellent."

Seth felt a presence behind him and he turned expecting to see the bitch again. Instead, he found his Lord standing before him. With a cry, he averted his eyes and fell prone to the dirt and prostrated himself. "My Lord!"

"Rise, Seth, and look upon Me."

Seth scrambled to his feet and looked at his Lord's face. He was beautiful.

His face was aglow and his beard full and white. He looked like peace and serenity and love. Seth felt small and insignificant.

"You are doing well, my son. You must continue to Jaipers and seek the Reeve. He has answers you need. Find him. Kill him quickly. Then find the Target. The Reeve will tell you where he is."

Seth felt a moment's confusion. He was connected to his Lord. He could feel his presence in a way that was unique. He could see that his strength and power came from Him. He also felt the glee coming from the Lord. An emotion that surprised him.

"My Lord, it shall be as you command."

"You are changing the world, my son. It will be a better place when you are done. Kneel."

Seth fell to his knees with a crunch of gravel beneath his knees. The pain added to his pleasure of the moment. He knelt before his Lord looking up at His magnificence and felt such joy.

He watched his Lord reach out with a hand and lay it on top of his head. "Seth Farlow. You are my most beloved. I bless you in My name."

The power contained within Seth twisted painfully and Seth moaned. Something changed within him.

"I am yours, my Lord. I suffer for your good graces. I am your sword and shield."

"I am pleased," said the Lord and vanished.

Seth cried out in the sudden absence. He felt it almost as a physical blow. He fell to his knees in the vacant space the Lord had just occupied and reached out with his powers to search for Him. At first, he felt nothing, but slowly he started to sense the presence of the Lord everywhere he looked. He was in the shadows, the brown grass and in his horse.

Seth remained in the spot his Lord had stood for an hour until he recognised he was kneeling only a foot from a massive puddle of horse piss and a mound of shit. He chuckled and rose. He picked gravel out of his knees and used God's power to heal the wounds.

Seth walked to his horse and rummaged in his saddlebag until he found his whip. He pulled it free and walked over to the grass on the side of the road. He tore off his clothes and tossed his soiled underpants into the brush. He knelt on the ground and started his prayers. He whipped his back after every line as hard as he could, rocking back and forth. Stroke after stroke landed and split his skin and soon his back ran red with his blood.

Fourteen

Jergen Garrison Complex, 900 A.C.

MAJOR GILLESPIE STRUGGLED to remain standing at attention. It had been years since he had forced his body to position itself in such a rigid manner and already his lower back was starting to pain him. He stood in the middle of an office in the Garrison Officer's building with the sun just rising through the window to his right. He stood about four feet in front of a beautifully ornate desk surrounded by military memorabilia placed everywhere the eye chanced to look. It was the office for a flag officer and it was the one given to General Brent Bairstow during his stay in Jergen. Major Gillespie had presented himself to this office twice a day for the last ten days: once at dawn and once at dusk. He was inspected, questioned and dismissed. He learned on day one not to arrive smelling even remotely of alcohol. He had his hair cut to a stubble and was clean-shaven. Now, the General was behind him inspecting the crease of his trousers.

"You have a spot of mud on the back of your right boot heel, Major."

Gillespie kept his mouth shut. He had learned on the second day not to answer questions which were not questions. The General was offering an observation, and it was not up for discussion. It merely was.

"How did you get mud on the back of your boot heel when it is perfectly dry outside? It hasn't rained since we've been here."

Gillespie thought hard. *That is a question I have to answer. The problem is: I have no idea how it got there.* Gillespie mentally retraced his path to the office. He had left the stables and checked himself in the full-length mirror kept at the back entrance to the building. *I look pretty good*, he had thought. He tried to remember any signs of water or mud and drew a blank.

"Answer me, Major," said the General with a deceptively quiet voice. Gillespie knew the danger of that voice now. It was the voice he heard just before a shit storm came down on his head.

"Suh, I have no idea, suh," *Honesty. That was always the best policy when it came to the General.* The General could ferret through lies faster than Gillespie had thought possible for any man. He felt a bead of sweat form beside his ear and start to move down his sideburn. It tickled and itched and he wished he could reach up and wipe it away.

"A mystery then, eh Major?"

Gillespie stayed quiet. It didn't feel like a direct question to him and he decided to keep his mouth shut. Not for the first time, he wondered how he had managed to put himself into this position. All his plans were in disarray. Gately and David had been dealt with the first night in Jergen. When they didn't show up the next day, Gillespie had reported it dutifully to the General. It should have been a quick report, a promise of a search, and then down the road to Jaipers. Instead, when he had reported the men missing he received a drilling from the General. When his answers became vague and evasive the General had changed. He went from a calm inquiring officer to a tyrant in a heartbeat. Now Gillespie's life was a blur of reporting twice a day in an immaculate uniform, with the remainder of his time organising useless search parties and investigating the disappearance of the two men. He knew where the men were: they were long since devoured by the sea life. His men had killed both of them the first night in Jergen, then cut up their bodies, and disposed of them at sea. Nothing remained. They were gone. *It was supposed to be it, done and done. But now look at me. I'm trapped in this nightmare with no way out.*

Gillespie had tried to make up stories to cover where the men could have gone. He spun stories of desertion to muggings to drunken wanderings. Each time Bairstow tore the stories apart or tasked Gillespie to hunt down the so-called leads and bring witnesses forth.

Gillespie had learned on the third day he was not very good at making up stories to cover the actions of his men. He was struggling now, and he was almost certain the General knew he was involved. He could see it in his eyes— the blatant hatred for him that lay smouldering there. It was unnerving. He had tried to drink but Bairstow smelled it on him and made his life miserable for days. None of the men were allowed to drink until the missing men were found. General's orders. And the men chaffed at it. One had broken the rule and now lay in military cells and was inspected hourly until his trial. The trial was tomorrow and Gillespie worried the man would break and tell the truth of what had happened to Gately and David. More sweat formed and ran down into his collar and Gillespie shuddered. *This is a nightmare.*

"Cold, Major? Strange on such a hot day. Hopefully, you aren't coming down with anything," intoned Bairstow, and he rounded his desk and sat down and looked up at where Gillespie stood. "Are you? Coming down with something?"

"Suh, no, suh!" barked Gillespie.

"That would be terrible, no? To have this burden of finding our lost men and fighting a cold at the same time? Nasty business. And summer colds are so hard to shake."

Gillespie kept his mouth closed and waited for the first question.

"Your dress is better than yesterday, Major. You have lint on your collar and the spot of mud is unacceptable. Report at noon for inspection and see to it those areas are corrected, clear?"

"Suh, yes, suh!" answered the Major with a loud voice. A loud voice was expected for those kinds of answers. He was supposed to answer like some dog for a treat. It grated on him to no end.

"Report. What news do you have?"

"Suh," Gillespie saluted smartly and remained at attention. "Situation: Since reported the morning of Luain, 14 of Lunasa, 900 A.C., Gately and David are still absent without leave. Last seen in the Split Crow pub when it closed at 0200 on Lunasa 14 leaving together, apparently heavily intoxicated. The mission remains to locate the men and bring them in for questioning. Execution: Search parties continue to be organised with assistance from the garrison personnel. Me and Captain Dixon brief all parties and provide details, routes, and timings. We debrief all search parties on their return. Almost all of Jergen has been searched without evidence or signs of the men's disappearance. As reported yesterday morning, the city Reeve and his deputies have organised a door-to-door campaign to see if the men are hiding or being held hostage. Nil reports to date. Nil ransom demands. The navy in Jergen has commenced trolling the waterfront with nets and hooks looking for bodies. Nil reports to date. Last night the reports from the garrison men on duty the night of the disappearance were compiled with no mention of the two men.

Conclusion: men remain AWOL and no signs of their disappearance or reasons for their disappearance have been discovered. Search continues. End of report, suh." Gillespie saluted and remained at attention.

The General remained seated, looking pensive and deep in thought. The silence stretched out and Gillespie wondered what new horror would be visited upon him now. He could hear the long-case clock in the outside hallway ticking loudly and he focused on it to keep his mind from screaming in frustration. He hated the General more so now than ever. He hated how he humiliated him daily and in front of the men. He hated how he forced this military bullshit on him and forced him to continue to look for two worthless pieces of shit men. *This isn't fair*, he thought. When I kill him, it won't be soon enough. Each night he fell asleep thinking of ways he would slay him. His fingers twitched as he imagined himself wrapping them around the General's throat and slowly squeezing, watching the fear light up those soulless eyes before they dimmed to become dull and lifeless.

"Your recommendation?"

"Suh?" said a startled Gillespie, drawn out of his imaginings. He glanced to the General and saw a new look there. The man looked... tired. *Is that it, then? Is this over with? Dare I hope?* He thought with his mind racing.

"What recommendation do you have?" A flash of anger covered the General's face, and he slapped his desk with an open hand, the smack loud in the office. Gillespie blinked at the noise.

"Suh, I..." he started, not sure what he could say. The days of frustration and futility had exhausted him and he simply wanted it over. He would do anything to have this over with. He had already contemplated having one of his men killed and framed for the murder of the two other men but that option was soon abandoned. Gillespie didn't think he could pull off another murder while the General was so distrusting. It was too risky. *Perhaps now we can move on toward Jaipers and continue this damn mission*, he thought. *And then I can get back to Munsten and my promotion and my new wealth*. "Suh, I think we have done all we can. We have stretched the city resources thin and I am now trying to convince the garrison and magistrate to continue the search on our behalf. They are no longer willing. They say the men are gone and we should put them behind us. They said they would send word to us if they are found. Dead or alive. Plus, the men are tired of Jergen and want to return to the mission. Suh."

The General leaned back in his seat. The wood creaked under him and he placed the palm's of his hands down on the desk and extended his arms out straight. He remained like that looking down at the desk for a couple of minutes. Gillespie ran what he had said through his head a couple of times and could find no fault in it. Everything he had said was true. Under any other normal disappearance of men, the search would have ended after a couple of days and a bulletin issued to all the garrisons in the Realm to be on the lookout for them. What they had been forced to do here in Jergen went beyond the normal. No one looked for missing men this long. They simply weren't worth the expense. Plus, the General had overstayed his welcome in Jergen. The mayor now inquired daily as to his intended departure date. The garrison men were pissed at the extra work they were forced to do and were saying it was too disruptive and it was time for them to move on.

The General finally looked up at Gillespie and he seemed defeated. "Major, prepare the men to depart tomorrow. Full inspection on the garrison parade ground at sunrise. We will breakfast in the mess hall and be on the road before ten hundred hours. Dismissed."

He couldn't help it. A grin broke across Gillespie's face at the orders but faltered when fury replaced the defeated look on the General's face. The General leapt out of his seat and leaned across the table.

"You, Major, are a disgrace to the officer's uniform you wear. *You* are responsible for the loss of those two men. I know it. You know it. I have no doubt those men are dead and gone. Now get the fuck out of my sight. YOU DISGUST ME!"

The last words came out as a roar and spittle sprayed across Gillespie's face. He remained standing at attention and glared across the desk at the General. For a brief moment, he thought of drawing out his sword and running the bastard through, but as quickly as the thought appeared he suppressed it. The scenario would not end well for either of them. A major simply did not run generals through no matter how much they deserved it. *And if I'm honest with myself, I wouldn't win.* He clenched his jaw and forced himself to deliver a crisp salute before smartly turning ninety degrees to the left and moving toward the door. As his hand touched the doorknob, the General whispered to his back. "I still want you here at noon for inspection, Major. Do not be late."

Gillespie paused a moment and then twisted the knob hard and yanked the door open. "Aye, suh. Noon sharp."

Gillespie exited the office and slammed the door shut behind him. He lifted his boot and looked for the mud. There was nothing there. His boots were spotless. *Fuck*, he cursed to himself. He strode out of the building and went straight to the stables. Sergeant Henson waited there for him.

"Henson, we leave tomorrow. Inspection at first light on the parade square.

Make sure the men are ready to leave. We are finally getting the fuck out of here."

Henson nodded and wrung his hands. Gillespie raised an eyebrow. "What?"

"Sir, I've just heard from the captain. The men have been switched out."

"Switched out? What do you mean?"

"Men, from Munsten. Just arrived late last night. Replacements they said."

"Replacements for who?"

"Us, sir. They are replacements for us!"

Gillespie turned in place back toward the offices, a look of horror and anger fighting for dominance on his face. "Fuck!"

Captain Dixon knocked on the door to the General's office right after Major Gillespie left the building. He had waited around the corner and smiled when the door was banged shut by the clearly frustrated major. He heard a muffled "enter" and opened the door, strode in and saluted the general who sat behind his desk.

"Sir!"

"At ease, Captain Dixon. Close the door, pull up a chair and have a seat beside me."

"Sir, yes, sir!" Dixon closed the door and grabbed a spare chair and set it down near the General. He watched as the General pulled out a piece of parchment and laid it on the desk before leaning back and raising an eyebrow at him. "Sir, the new men are comfortable in the inn. They will be ready tomorrow morning. Good men. All handpicked by your brother, it seems."

"James, call me Brent, we're alone in here."

"Aye, sir, I mean Brent. Sorry. Habit."

"A good habit, don't apologise. I want the men kept apart. I don't want Gillespie to have any opportunities to screw this over. He'll be here at noon today. That should keep him on his toes at least for now. We will see him off tomorrow morning. We'll leave the day after. This evening I want guards posted."

"Yes, all arranged. They know to look out for Gillespie's men. They know them. Know their reputations. They'll stay clear."

"Great. They made good time getting here. Better than I had hoped. It was getting harder to keep ourselves planted here. This morning Gillespie thought about trying to run me through, I think. The man couldn't play cards to save his life. Everything he thinks is right there on his face to read. He's an idiot."

"Of the first order."

Brent nodded and chuckled and then grew quiet. "Now, James. Tell me. Have you any answers?"

"Yes, I'm afraid so. It appears Gillespie had the men killed and tossed to sea. I found a prostitute that worked down by the docks. She had just finished with a client and was heading back to her home by way of the alleys. She said she heard a strange noise from a shed down by where they gut the fish for market during the day. She saw a light through a window and snuck a look into the shed down there. Said she didn't see much, but she was certain it looked like a couple of our men were chopping up a body. Another body lay nearby, and she's pretty sure it was David."

Brent grimaced. "How was she sure?"

"She said she could see through the window that the man on the ground had his same hair and she described the rash he had from the poison oak. It's enough, Brent. It was them."

"Will she give witness?"

"Not a chance and even if she would she's a whore, Brent. No magistrate will take the testimony of a whore."

"I see. Did she recognise the men doing the deed? Could she pick them out?"

"No, sir. Said she could only see that they wore the Munsten uniform. It's enough that *we* know. It will be enough, later, when we return to Munsten. We can prosecute them in a military court. I hate them and want them dead, but justice must prevail."

"Hmm. I agree, but we need to make it back first to do that, don't we?"

"We will. The new men know what's up. Your brother briefed them personally. We can trust them. I know most of them myself. They're led by Captain Marcel Mayer. I know the man. He's trustworthy. Stalwart."

"Stalwart? Where'd you learn that big word, James?"

"Ha! You should talk!"

"Piss off, you cheeky bugger! I'm a General, show some respect!"

James laughed and clapped Brent on the shoulder. It was an act he could not have imagined doing mere weeks ago. The past month had proven to the two men they were alike in many ways. Once James got past the high rank he had relaxed and realised he had a good friend in the General. He was glad for both of them. Brent had been pretty stressed. He had been alone on a road with a group of the worst soldiers Belkin had to offer. At first, they had talked of horses, and then careers and then of truths. Friendship had just kind of followed.

James now knew the history of the brothers and the truth of Bill Redgrave and their mission. It was surreal. But he believed. All that seemed to matter now was getting to Jaipers and back in one piece. What came next would be anyone's guess, but, for now, James was content he had an honourable mission and with a man he would gladly give up his own life to protect. He had said as much to Brent's brother back in Munsten. He had said the words then but, now, he meant them.

"Brent, I have nothing but respect. Anything for me?"

"Yes, keep an eye on Gillespie. He will do something rash now. He has little to lose. Watch yourself, too. You're in danger, you see that I hope?"

"Aye, I do. I'll tell you this, the day that sorry excuse for an officer gets the better of me is the day I swim out to sea as far as I can go and then swim straight down."

"Pft. Do you know how to swim?"

"No, not a stroke. That's kind of the point."

"Ass."

"Wipe."

The men grinned at one another. James rose, saluted, and turned to leave the General to his letter to his brother. He moved to the door but stopped and looked back just as Brent pulled out the inkpot and quill. He looked up at James and arched an eyebrow.

"What?"

"The ladies have asked for our presence again this evening."

Brent smiled. "Of course, they have. Please extend an invitation to dine with us at my accommodations, say at six?"

"As you command, sir," replied James, and a grin came easily to his face. "Do you want food ordered?"

"No, last time it was just left untouched, wasn't it?"

James laughed and left Brent to his writing.

Fifteen

Jergen Cathedral, 900 A.C.

RENT ENTERED THE cathedral through the normally sized door inset within the massive double front doors. He closed the door behind him and the sounds of the streets of Jergen were shut off. The cool air inside the narthex was a balm, and he quickly pulled off the brown cloak he had used to cover himself. He moved over to the cloakroom and hung his garment on one of the wooden pegs on the wall. His was the only cloak, and he shook his head sadly.

Gone are the days when a man can follow his faith without fear of recrimination, he thought and he moved to the entrance to the nave. His eyes were already adjusted and looking around the inside of the cathedral. It was a marvel of modern architecture. The stonework and the lighting were spectacular. The eyes were drawn along exquisite lines of artwork carved into every exposed piece of stone until you took in the serene beauty of the transept and chancel. Sitting on the chancel was the altar: a massive stonework rising above the rows of wooden pews. Rising above the altar was the Icon of the Lord. There for all to behold and worship. Brent remained standing there until he felt worthy to enter this holy place of worship.

He knelt, quickly unfastened his boots and placed them in the bin near the entrance to the nave. The soft carpet on the floor felt wonderful to his sore feet as he started the long walk down the centre of the nave toward the altar. He could almost hear music in his ears as he approached the altar, and he smiled. He couldn't explain it, but the cathedral felt so right to him. He had spent many hours here over the past days and he loathed to depart its quiet serenity for the road and Jaipers and who knew what else beyond that. *I feel a pull here, a need to be here and witness*, he thought.

He stopped at the foot of the carpeted stairs leading up to the altar and fell to his knees and placed his hands together in front of him, lowered his head, closed his eyes, and prayed.

Lord, I'm in that place again, on my knees, laying my life out before You. I want to live forever in Your grace. So I ask now for Your forgiveness for the wrongs that I have done and the things that I have neglected. I ask for Your forgiveness for the people I have hurt along the way and for those who I have failed to love as You love. I ask for Your forgiveness and ask that you provide resolve in my heart and that with Your strength I determine not to make these errors again. Teach me how to walk away from everything I know to be wrong and embrace everything I know about You. For the kingdom, the power and the glory are always and forever Yours. So mote it be.

Brent remained kneeling and thought long and hard on his words. He meant every one of them. There was a time he searched for signs while searching for proof of God's existence. This was a realm where believing in God was ridiculed and worshippers were attacked in the open. There was a time when a sign from God would have gone a long way to making him feel stronger about his faith. One day, without warning, he stopped searching. He realised he didn't need or want proof. It was enough he had faith. It carried him through good times and bad. It was enough.

After a time, his knees began to complain despite the woven carpet. He rose with a groan and moved over to sit in the closest pew to the altar. This morning had been difficult. He had gathered Gillespie and the men and then dismissed them back to Munsten. The fury in Gillespie's eyes had been a sight to behold. Captain Dixon had stepped forward and drew his sword by an inch. The sound had stilled the square and Gillespie had looked from Dixon to his men and then to Brent. He had seen the thought there plain for all to see. He wanted nothing more than to strike them both down. It had been tense and Brent recalled actually hoping the idiot would follow through with it. *Then he rode off with his men trailing behind in a ragged band*, he thought. *But he isn't done with me. Gillespie and I will have a reckoning if God wills it.*

He leant back, dismissed his worry and closed his eyes and fell asleep almost at once. When he opened his eyes, he could tell by the slant of the sun through the stained-glass windows that perhaps an hour had passed. A sense of shame quickly came and went. He was tired, and the church gave him such incredible peace of mind. He felt safe here and closer to God. There was no shame.

He suddenly felt the presence of someone near him. Turning his head, he was surprised to see an older man reclining at the other end of his pew. He wore plain clothes over an ample stomach and carried a close-trimmed, white beard. He had his legs stretched straight out and crossed in front of him and Brent could see he wore plain, brown leather sandals. The man looked over at him and nodded once.

"Good day, sir," said Brent in greeting. "Well met." He smiled and tried not to look too intimidating. Most commoners were afraid of military men. *It is always best to be polite lest they panic and do something stupid*, thought Brent.

"Aye, well met," replied the man with an oddly resonant voice. Almost like two voices in one. *The acoustics in here are terrific*, thought Brent and he looked around at the vaulted ceiling towering tens of yards above him. The man looked up at the same ceiling and then back to Brent.

"It's not often I meet someone of faith," probed Brent a bit openly. *You couldn't be too careful*, he thought. *Any crazy could be in here. A follower of the Word looking for trouble*. It happened often enough in Munsten, he knew, although here the reverse seemed to be true. In Munsten, the Guard was always tracking down people for the Archbishop. It was almost a daily event. They would look for followers of the Word camping out near churches and they would find actual people of faith instead. Brent wasn't certain, but it seemed the Church was gaining favour in the land once again. *It paid to be prudent*, thought Brent. *One wrong word to the wrong person and your whole life could change and for the worse. But I sense something positive about this man.*

"True," replied the man. "I think faith is what carries those who believe when others would falter."

Brent nodded slowly at the words. "Often that has been my experience," he said cautiously and looked the man over a little more carefully. His clothes were clean and not dusted from the streets outside. His sandals were immaculate as well. *He must work here in the Cathedral and change his clothes here as well.* His feet were, oddly, in very good shape for the feet of an old man. He looked to the man's hands and was surprised to see hands unworn by age or hardship. He looked at the man's face and found him smiling back at him with perfect white teeth and deep blue eyes. Brent's eyes went wide.

"Hello, Brent. Welcome to My Church."

On hearing his name, Brent scrambled out of the pew, reaching for a sword he didn't wear. He stood a few feet away, looked to the exit, and stared at the man. A ghost of fear crossed his nerves.

"Relax, Brent. Relax. Calm down."

Brent calmed himself and settled back down in the front pew, twisted in the seat to keep his eye on the man and the exit. "Who are you? How do you know my name?"

"I am the Dean here at the Cathedral. I watched you ride in. It's not often the General of the Lord Protector's Guard rides into Jergen."

Brent stared dumbly at the man and waited for him to say something else. He merely sat there and smiled back at him.

"And you recognised me? Here in Jergen?"

The man laughed a rich hearty laugh and Brent found himself smiling. "No. Sorry. Although, the uniform is a dead giveaway. And the large number of military men travelling with you. No, my son, word came ahead of you from the church in Munsten you frequent. Reverend Taylor sent word you would be stopping by."

Brent relaxed. Reverend Taylor Martin was a good friend and trusted. He confided in him often. *I never had a chance to tell him I was heading this way. He was a smart man though—perhaps he figured it out.* The man had given him a fright. *For a moment, I thought...* but Brent refused to finish the thought. *I need to be careful. I'm still not sure I can trust this stranger.* "Reverend Taylor is a good man. His son is his spitting image."

The man looked back at him with the same smile. "And now you would test me? Fair enough. You should know, Reverend Taylor is my son. And I'm not aware I have grandchildren. He never married."

Brent blinked and then laughed with relief. "You're his father? Dean Martin, then. Your son spoke of you. My apologies, sir. I had to be sure. Men of faith are tested all the time and by the most unseemly people who later turn out to be spies for the Word." Brent paused when the Dean's smile grew a little wider. "Sorry," said Brent. "You'd know better than most."

"Don't apologise, young man. Men and women of faith are tested every day, just as you say. For some, they believe faith is faith, and that is everything to them. Others question it until the day they die, never quite sure if they were right or wrong—always looking for proof. And others find their faith and simply wear it like a favourite shirt. Comfortable and familiar. Those people don't want or need proof. They don't question why God has to remain hidden and only through faith can people believe. You, I can see, have a favourite shirt, am I wrong?"

Brent felt emotions tighten his throat. He nodded and swallowed against the lump.

"I thought so," said Dean Martin. "We understand one another. My son has written about you so much I feel I already know you. The world is in for a shit storm and I need to speak to you about it."

"You swore."

"I did?"

"You just said *shit*. In a church."

"Yes, I did. My church, I might point out."

Brent said nothing.

"Brent, you need to get moving and I don't want to hold you up. This is a great building with one of the best libraries in the Realm. But the people inside the church are not true followers of God. They're assholes, to be frank."

Brent nodded mentally adding *assholes* to the list of things he could now say at will. *Oh wait, I already do.*

"Very funny. I'll give you a complete list of swear words later—I have a list going back aeons. But never mind that. Pay attention." Brent blinked quickly sensing something was wrong but not able to put his finger on it. Dean Martin continued without pause. "The world is about to change. The Church is corrupted from within. The people who profess to understand what God is all about have it wrong. And a particularly bad sort are working out of this very church we sit in *and* they report directly to the Archbishop of Munsten, the very head of the Church of the New Order. They call themselves the Sect of the Church. They are self-serving and seek merely to hold power over man and woman. They kill with lust and claim to do so in God's name. They are lost and I'm tired of it quite frankly. Anyway, it all has to end and you, my friend, are already wrapped up in it."

"I am? Why?" *No shit, I'm wrapped up in it*, thought Brent. *Here I am on the road to oblivion. All alone.*

"Good questions. You're not alone, by the way. But I'll give you an honest answer. Because."

Brent felt uneasy. Something strange was happening here. "Wait, what? Because? That's the answer?"

The man stared at him for a moment and laughed. "No, just kidding. God has picked you for a reason. You believe, Brent. You are a true believer. One of the few actually. And you have a pure heart. You care about people. Before yourself. When you helped Bill Redgrave when he was close to death, you proved your worth. You did it selflessly. You did it because it was the right thing to do. That is the true test of faith. Belief and faith are not measured by how much you pray or how much you try to help others because you think you will be rewarded by God. Those are exactly the *wrong* reasons, you understand? The most unworthy people of faith are those who do good things only because of a fear of a horrible afterlife or because someone of faith told them to do that. You need to come to it on your own. The words help, I won't lie, but seriously, unless you are doing it because you know it is the right thing to do, you are wasting effort. Trust me in that."

Brent nodded. He felt a little light-headed.

"Breathe. Relax. This will be over soon. I have to warn you of something. What you do with the warning is up to you and I'm not making you do shit. You have to want to do something about it because it is the right thing to do and not because I'm warning you."

Brent nodded again. He was following all this. He really was. *It was just... just... so...?* "So what is this warning?"

"Something bad is going to happen. You were followed out of Munsten by Seth Farlow. Ah, I can see in your eyes you know this man. He is the dagger for the Archbishop. Heads up the Sect of the Church of the New Order. The same Sect that mothers tell stories of to scare their children to go to bed. But they're real. Too real. They base here in Jergen in the basement of this Cathedral. Right under our feet. They did terrible things over the years. Unspeakable things. It couldn't be stopped. Can't be stopped. I have no power over them. None." The Dean took a deep breath before continuing. "Seth was following you and where he goes death is sure to follow as well. He is now ahead of you. I fear for you, Brent. But I have hope for you. You are smart and you showed it when you got rid of those men that came with you. All of them Protector's men, but you knew that."

Brent nodded. Seth Farlow was forefront in his mind. He had the displeasure to encounter him on several occasions over the years. It was never pleasant and left him feeling sullied. There was nothing in the man's eyes. Like he had no life in him. Brent shuddered.

The Dean seemed to wait until Brent settled before speaking again. "You are heading to Jaipers. There is a man there you need to meet. He is the Reeve. Reeve Comlin. A good man. He will help you and you will need his help. A group of the Sect left a week ago for Jaipers. It's no coincidence. So head to Jaipers with your men and stop them. Stop Seth. Do what you need to do there and get out."

Brent raised his eyebrows. Taking orders from his brother and the Lord Protector was ingrained in him. Taking orders from a man he just met was something altogether different. He wasn't sure how to respond. "Meet with the Reeve and stop the Sect. How will I recognise them?"

"They wear black, soft-soled, boots. Very distinctive."

"I see. And why would they be heading to Jaipers?"

"I suspect you already have the answer to that. They answer directly to the Archbishop. Remember that. There was a time when the Archbishop answered only to the King. Now he is nothing but a figure. Crippled with age and humiliation. Head to Jaipers; meet with the Reeve."

"The Reeve," repeated Brent.

"Yes. Here, take this." The man handed Brent a wooden amulet tied to a leather thong.

"What is it?" Brent held the amulet up to his face and examined it. It was plain hardwood, polished and oiled. It had the symbol of the Church of the New Order on one side and a triskelion on the other. It was the same symbol he had seen on the coin he had sent down to Bill Redgrave all those many months ago.

"An amulet. You'll recognise the symbol of the Church of the New Order. On the reverse, however, what you've recognised is an old symbol of the Word. No one today would recall the ties of the Church to the Word. There was a time men and women of the cloth understood and worked with the men and women of the Word. Religion and Science, as they were called back then. They used to get along. Then they almost destroyed the world in their hatred for one another. Never mind. Wool-gathering on my part. Please wear it and do not remove it. Whoever recognises it on you are those whom you can trust."

Brent didn't respond but pulled the amulet over his head and tucked it inside his shirt. He stood up and walked over to the stairs leading up to the altar. The colours from the sun through the stained-glass were beautiful. *It is too bad all this beauty is tainted by the politics of the Realm*, thought Brent. *And I'm right in the middle of it now.* He trusted Reverend Taylor and remembered he had once spoken of his father the Dean of Jergen Cathedral—the memory was fleeting—spoken over too much wine.

Brent knew he had nothing to fear from a weasel like Seth, but this Sect... if they had the numbers they could pose a real threat. Jaipers and its garrison would need his help. *Faith and proof.* Brent snorted to himself. *I have faith, of that I am sure. Faith in God but not in people.* A glimmer of a memory returned to Brent. He recalled his conversation with Reverend Taylor. They were seated at his kitchen table in his house, three bottles of good wine gone. As always, they talked of the Church. In this memory, they had talked about faith and people. Taylor had been talking about his father: the Dean of Jergen Cathedral. He had said his father's favourite saying had been '*Have faith in God but less so in people*'. His father, he said, had been killed during the Revolution fighting an insurgency within the church.

Brent spun around to find himself alone in the Cathedral. The hairs on the back of his neck stood up and his eyes darted to all the corners looking for movement. Dean Martin was gone. Vanished into thin air. *A man dead these past ten years.* Fear rose up quick as a snake and grabbed hold of his reason. Brent couldn't help himself. He bolted for the narthex and the cloakroom and snatched his cloak. He could feel eyes on him and he shivered despite the heat. A panic filled him and he had to escape. He fumbled at the latch, finally engaged it, and pulled the door open forcefully lunging through the opening and down the steps of the Cathedral, his feet beating a staccato on the stone.

The summer heat beat down on him but he still felt cold. So cold he was shaking. He ran out across the street and bumped into a few people as he pushed his way to the far sidewalk. Some cursed him and declared him drunk. He kept moving down streets, keeping to the open and soon reached the far side of the district. He stopped, panting, with fear eating at the edges of his strength, and he felt weak. He forced himself to stand tall and turned to look back over the rooftops at the Cathedral. It stood silent and bright in the sun. The fear began to sweat itself out his pores, and he breathed a sigh of relief and pushed back the hood of his cloak.

After the shaking went away. Brent half convinced himself he had imagined it all. He hadn't eaten yet today. And he had drunk too much wine the night before. He had slept in the Church, perhaps it was only a waking dream. He was hallucinating, he was sure of it. He shook himself and started back toward his rooms. He walked a few feet and then stopped and snapped his hand to his neck and chest and felt the wooden amulet still around his neck.

James sat comfortably in his saddle and looked around at the men gathered in front of him on horseback and with the carts in line. They had just completed muster in the parade square of the garrison. These men were the replacements for Major Gillespie and the others. These men were handpicked by Brent's brother, Major General Frederick Bairstow. They looked eager and attentive. It was a good start. James glanced at Brent beside him but the other man looked deep in thought and so he adjusted his weight a little in the saddle and judged the horse's reactions.

His horse was well suited to his style of riding and he had to admit to a certain fondness for the animal. His father often scolded him for being too attached to the *beasts*, but James had ignored his advice and the use of the word. Horses were not beasts. Men were beasts. The truth was simple: his father simply couldn't suffer the loss of the animals and instead chose to distance himself from them. *His loss*, thought James. *Horses were in many ways better than people.* James reached forward and patted his horse's neck and the horse blew out air. James looked the men over again. *These men are not beasts. Quite the contrary.*

"They will be reliable and trustworthy," Brent had said before the muster. "But I still fear a spy in their midst. I think it safe to assume at least one is in the pockets of our Lord Protector."

"Hmm, yes," was James' reply. "I think that is a safe bet, sir. We'll know soon enough. What I fear most, however, is Major Gillespie not heading north as he should. How do we confirm that?"

Brent had drawn quiet for a time, contemplating before he spoke again. "We don't. There's no way to know. We will need to send scouts behind our travel. Gillespie will follow and watch for that. Despite how much of a scoundrel he is, I don't dare doubt his military mind. He'll find a way. He can't return to Munsten empty-handed. It would be his death and he knows it. He'll pick his most trustworthy men and follow us at a safe distance. All army men I should think."

James had merely nodded. Brent was probably correct. *Generals usually are*, he had thought.

As ordered, they were mustered. Captain Marcel Mayer and James had inspected it at dawn. Their kit had checked out clean and ready. Weapons and armour beyond reproach. These were good men. All army and all strong men and well-honed by years of experience. The men had arrived on horseback and they had no shortage of mounts now. Two of the men James knew for their horse skills. One was once a farrier, and the other had worked making saddles before joining the military. James liked men who understood horses. They were usually more reliable in the long run.

Brent was beside him and looking out towards the gate. He kept reaching up to grasp something under his chain shirt. His face looked troubled and James had tried to broach the subject but had been gently persuaded not to bother. James hoped whatever had happened to make him look that way would not be a sign of more trouble ahead. He would watch him and be prepared to help him if he could. Brent was more than a friend. He had become a mentor, a man James hoped to be like. He was professional and had a natural leadership style James could only envy. But he had a wild side to him as well. The two of them had managed to find a couple of fine ladies to spend their evenings with. All due to Brent's charm and wit. But it was his military bearing that made James want to be like him. Already the men were responding to Brent's leadership, and it had only been less than twelve hours.

The man doesn't even need to try. He exudes leadership like some men sweat. By the Word, I want to be more like this man.

James leant back in the saddle and his horse shifted slightly under the change in weight. James smiled, pleased with the horse. Brent had called the horse *Shitters* after it proved to want to shit at the most inopportune moments. James knew horses well enough to know the horse was doing it intentionally. It was one of the reasons he liked it so much.

Brent inclined his head and James leant slightly forward and to the left and his horse immediately moved to follow behind Brent's horse. Brent led his horse to the front and wheeled to face the men. Captain Mayer sat on horseback holding the Army Standard. It flapped lazily in the slight wind. James shifted in his saddle to steer his horse and then squeezed his legs to stop the horse beside Mayer.

"Gentlemen," began Brent in a slightly raised voice. A voice meant to be heard but not abrasive. *Brent has the knack of that down pat,* thought James. "First of all, I thank you for travelling at such speed to Jergen. Time was short, and you did not let me down. I apologise I cannot allow you time to recover here in Jergen. Trust me when I tell you: you are truly missing out on some fine sights here."

Two of the men chuckled and glanced at one another.

"Yes, you two made quite a name for yourselves with some of the wildlife here in Jergen. Well, done. I heard from some of the other wildlife you left quite the impression."

The men laughed easily, and the others joined in. James found himself smiling. Brent and he had found a couple of ladies who were worth returning to Jergen for. A rare form of wildlife. Women who spoke their mind and considered themselves equals, if not better than men. James had found it refreshing and satisfying. *I could love a woman like that,* he thought. *Isabelle is bold, outspoken, and intelligent—an equal in life, mind and body.*

"Sadly," continued Brent with a raised hand to quell the laughter. "We must be on our way. I know my brother briefed you personally before you left and I have no doubt the city has ears and eyes on us today. You understand the threat. You know the mission. That is enough for now. I don't imagine that this will be easy. This mission will be a challenge and you will be hard pressed to apply your military experience. This is political and petty and we have enemies. Enemies that look like us and talk like us. You know what I mean.

This will be a long journey. You will be placed in situations where your lives may be in danger. I trust you to use your judgement. I have explained how I want force used and when. I may not be there when you will need to make a snap decision on whether to strike or not. Know this: I trust you to make the right choice. We are brothers first on this journey. Officers and enlisted second. Are you with me?"

The men barked loudly in unison. "Sir, yes, sir!"

The echo of the shout returned in the large, walled, parade square. James smiled. *This is a completely different sort of adventure now*, he thought.

Brent looked over to Captain Marcel Mayer when he rode his horse up along the right side of his horse Shitters. The Captain touched his forehead in respect and then looked ahead. James rode up beside him on the other side and nodded to Brent. They rode in silence for a few minutes.

Behind them, Jergen disappeared around the bend in the road. It was a fine day for riding: warm, overcast, but with little chance of rain. The men were spread out behind them, staggered, using both sides of the road. The carts and spare horses were placed in the middle of their train. Every single one of the men was regular Army and knew how to ride and remain vigilant.

"Sir, this is Captain Marcel Mayer," said James by way of introduction.

"Pleasure, Captain. Glad you made it as soon as you did. Tell me, how have you managed to get so spectacularly lost? Shouldn't you be conducting manoeuvres in the vicinity of Curachan?"

Captain Mayer laughed a bright peal of laughter. "Sir, yes. Those were my orders. Not sure what happened exactly. We went straight at the crossroads when we should have gone left. Next thing we knew we were in Jergen. Imagine our surprise. I blame my corporal, sir. He's not very smart with maps and the like."

Brent heard an exclamation from behind him and smiled. "So it seems." He nodded to Marcel. "Thanks for making such good timing, captain. It was getting harder to remain in Jergen. James tells me you knew each other back in

Munsten?"

"Yes, sir. We go back a few years. We attended the same advanced tactics class in ninety-six. Got along well enough, didn't we James?"

"Well, enough, I suppose, Marcel. Except for the incident with the same girl that time."

Brent listened to the two banter and smiled to himself. It felt good to have trusted men at his back. The strain seemed less. The road more open and inviting. James and Marcel quieted and the only sounds were the occasional bird call over the hooves of their horses.

"Tell me," asked Brent. "How's my brother?"

"The Knight-General is doing well, sir. He told me to tell you that he hasn't discovered anything new. That mean anything to you, sir?"

Brent said nothing. The message meant that Frederick was still investigating the Lord Protector and hadn't discovered anything of substance. "Anything else?"

"Yes, sir. He said to hurry back."

"That we will, Captain."

"Captain Marcel and I have worked together many times over the years, sir. I trust him with my life," injected James.

"Do you now?" Brent lowered his voice. "So tell me Captain Marcel, how many of your men can you trust."

Marcel grew quiet. The sound of the horses' hooves was loud in the morning air. Brent thought he felt a drop of rain and looked up to try to spot another. *Overcast, but it shouldn't rain,* he thought. Brent stole a glance at Marcel. He was seriously thinking about the question.

"Sir, I think so. But hard to say. I can vouch for every one of them but that doesn't mean I will always be right. The Protector may have got to them. Best I can say. I will add that I would be surprised if they were against your brother, sir. Knight General Frederick Bairstow is highly admired by the Army. Much like yourself. We'll see you safe to Jaipers and then back to Munsten. My men are highly trained and motivated, sir. I can promise you if any turn out not to be working for the Army I'll see to them myself."

"I appreciate the candidacy."

"Sir."

"How are things in Munsten? What's happening back home?"

"The General is being called before the Assembly almost every day now. There's some talk in the Officer's Mess that he's being investigated. Most don't believe it."

"What do you believe?"

"Sir?"

"I asked you whether you believe my brother is being investigated."

"I'm not one for gossip, sir."

"I'll take that as a yes, then. Anything else?"

Marcel thought for a moment in silence, snorted once, and then said no.

"What was the laugh?"

"Just a passing memory, sir. The Archbishop has been acting strangely. He's been seen all over the castle. Sleeping."

"Sleeping?"

"Yes, sir," Marcel barked another laugh. "He's been found sleeping all over the castle. In corners, on benches, in the garden amongst the flowers. When he isn't sleeping he is talking to himself. The Lord Protector has placed guards on him to watch for his safety."

"And Church services? Have they stopped?"

Marcel looked surprised. "Church? Well, yes. They have stopped. But no one ever goes, anyway."

Brent clenched his jaw. "No, I suppose not."

"General, sir. Are you of the Church?" asked James quietly.

Brent sighed and reached up and grasped the medallion beneath his shirt. *God, I'm tired of hiding my Faith. Give me strength*. A raindrop landed on his forehead. He looked up and saw that the skies had darkened a little. *Maybe it will rain, after all*, he thought.

Brent looked at James. "Yes, James. I most certainly am."

Craobh

Sixteen

Jergen Waterfront, 900 A.C.

I T WAS ALMOST three weeks before we left for the farm. I had told Nadine all I remembered from the conversation in Reeve Comlin's house all those months ago. How he had a friend who ran a farm with his wife and daughter, a daughter Nadine and I could now sense through our bond. And with Dog, too. Dog was now spending more time with Nadine than I. She had a way with him I lacked. She smiled and simply said animals had always been kind to her.

Nadine instructed me to ask her friend to move into the house and to care for it. Nadine's new younger look could never be explained, and she hid from her neighbours. She would be a stranger to them. So, I had met with her friend and, after my tense explanation of why Nadine had decided to let her move in, her friend wept and agreed. We left the house to her and her three children, two cats and a large dog. Her husband had passed away a few years before and she had been living hand to mouth. For her, the house was a huge boon. The garden would keep her family fed and with coin in their pocket.

I spent a week showing her how to tend the garden and prune the fruit trees. Initially, she was affronted with a young man such as I teaching her but she soon relaxed and listened to what I had to say. Nadine stayed clear through all this. I passed the woman some papers Nadine had drawn up and read and explained them to her. It was notarized and gave her permission to use the home.

With the money from the sale of herbs, we purchased a small but strong donkey and a small, two-wheeled cart. Nadine assured me the donkey was up to the task and said the donkey knew it was heading to a farm and would have open fields to enjoy. I learned how to hitch a donkey to a cart and how to balance a load in the bed. I loaded Nadine's cherished possessions into the cart and then she happily perched up on the double seat and patted the spot next to her. When I told her, I preferred to walk to the farm, Nadine looked put out.

"Why won't you sit up here with me?" she asked, her green eyes flashing.

"I feel lazy. I need to stretch my legs. Feel the soil beneath my feet."

"You're wearing boots, young man."

I looked down at my new boots. They were simple, and I liked them. Nadine and I had stored the black boots in our baggage. After I had shown them to her, she had spent many nights examining them and the two red gems. She wouldn't tell me what she was looking for and would swat at me if I got too close. I left them with her. Hopefully, she would figure them out.

"I am."

"Well?"

"Well, what?"

"Why won't you sit up here? Do I scare you?"

"Yes, Nadine. You do."

"What?" she all but screeched at me.

I chuckled. Since Gaea had exposed our love we had laid out two bedrolls on the floor. At first, Nadine had been very reserved and shared the same fears I had. More so for her. She was still the old woman in her mind. I didn't see her as an old woman anymore. I saw the woman I loved and the woman she would be once again. I sent my love down our bond, and she shuddered and melted into my arms. We were the age when most people get married and start a family. We talked about that. Nadine told me draoi marry as everyone else does. She said she didn't need marriage with the bond we shared, and I agreed. That was the first night we slept together, and it was wonderful. Nadine was patient with me. Once the nervousness fled, we became lost in each other through our bond and, after a fearful time, we finally separated ourselves. Afterwards, we learned how to remain within ourselves. But for a time, we had become one person. It had been frightening, to say the least, but it had also been powerful. The fear of being lost panicked us more than a little so we practised all the time to make sure it didn't happen again.

We found, through trial and error, just how close we could become without merging again. As such as I loved it, Nadine was wearing me out. It turns out women can keep going long after a man is ready to collapse. Which is one reason why I wanted to walk on the road. I had to get in better shape and sitting so close to her in the cart would prove too much for me. Plus she was punching me in the arm more and more now. I asked her about it once.

"It means I love you," she had said.

"Love punching me," I had replied. Then she smiled at me and I forgave her.

For now, I was looking up at her and could sense her ire. I could *see* her ire. See it looking down at me.

"Do I scare you?"

"No, you don't scare me, love. I just want my arm to heal for once. Plus, I wouldn't be able to keep my hands off you."

Nadine blushed and then leered at me. "And would that be a bad thing? The donkey knows the way. We have a whole cart here. Lots of room."

I laughed and shook my head. "Nope, walking. Gaea said to make haste, and we have lost nearly a month already. Time to get going."

Nadine laughed and with a finger combed her long hair back over her ears. Her hair was such a bright red it flashed like fire in the sun. Freckles were popping out all over her new young face and she hated them. I thought them gorgeous and traced images with them when I had the chance. She loved when I did that and would lie still and smile her delicious smile and name what I drew. Those were the times I cherished. We spoke in those quiet times of her being the new Cill Darae, like my mother before her. Last night she admitted her reservations while lying back in bed.

Nadine lay back with her eyes closed and murmured an appreciation. "In a way, I am the Cill Darae after your mother. It makes me sad, to be honest. She was the best of the draoi. The strongest of us all. Now I have power and I can appreciate her all the more."

"Hmm," I said simply and traced a constellation with the freckles on her upper arm.

"I want to be like her. As good as her. As strong as her. I don't want to fail Gaea."

"You won't," I said and ran my finger from her upper arm over to her sun-reddened cheekbones and gently traced pictures with the dots. She smiled.

"And how do you know, young man?"

"Because you are the Cill Darae that has never been before. You come with the experiences of a lifetime. And with the wisdom that comes from that. Years from now you will be a legend. Mark my words."

Nadine opened her eyes, and I stared into those deep green depths.

"I love you, Will Arbor. You're awfully fine to me, do you know that?"

"Yes, I do, old woman."

With a growl, she flipped me over and took charge of yet another expression of our love.

I stood on the road looking over at Nadine sitting on the front edge of the cart. I could see the strength within her. She seemed so confident and so strong. Beneath it, and only because of the bond we shared, I knew she was worried about disappointing Gaea. I was worried about disappointing her, too. But warring within me was an anger. I wasn't convinced I could trust Gaea. She seemed to be a god of sorts but I doubted she was able to see the future. Plants and animals looked only to today. Few planned for the future and I wondered if Gaea was able to. She had put things in motion and we were all paying the price.

Nadine looked over at me, smiled and patted the place beside her. I reached over and slapped the donkey on the ass. It brayed and started trotting, snapping the cart along in the harness. Nadine squealed and nearly fell back into the cart bed from the seat.

"You son-of-a-bitch!" she yelled as she grasped for the reins. With a gasp, I could see she realised what she had just said, and she covered her mouth with eyes open wide. I heard a muffled "Sorry!" followed by a giggle as she trundled off down the road.

"Dog, let's go!"

We reached the farm in eight glorious days. After so much time on the road alone and even with Dog, nothing can compare to being on the road with the woman you love. We talked and laughed and kissed and lost each other in our love. When we rode up over the last hill before the farm we stopped the cart and looked at each other across the cart bench. Without words we knew our fleeting days together alone would not return anytime soon. And would be replaced with work and potential hardship. We hugged and kissed and looked out over the vast farm.

It was nestled in a wide valley with a small river cutting through it. It looked like a patchwork quilt undulating and meandering alongside the river.

Buildings were erected at various points and Nadine explained they were silos for holding grain. She pointed out the fields to me as wheat, barley, potatoes, corn, and a few fields for grazing cattle, sheep and dairy cows. In the centre of the valley was an expansive building. You could easily make out the home. It towered over the outlying buildings. It was more than a house—it was a mansion. Beside the house were three large barns and four large paddocks. I could see a horse being trained by a person holding a rope and a long thin pole in one of those paddocks. The horse was circling around and around. Farm hands were everywhere. A dozen women were in the potato fields bent over with large baskets tied to their backs. Everywhere I looked there were people working the land and animals. It looked idyllic and busy all at the same time.

I followed the bonds Gaea had given Nadine and I. The person with the horse was the girl. I focused on her for a moment and sensed a sharp surprise. The girl stopped turning with the horse and despite the distance, we could see her staring directly at us. I watched as she raised a hand no higher than her shoulder and gave a little wave. She dropped the rope and pole and ran inside the house.

"That would be her," said Nadine.

I looked up at her in the cart. "You think?"

She smiled. "Pretty sure."

"Okay then. Let's be about this."

"Wait. You think we should just drive down there and say 'Hi, we're draoi and we've come to train you?'—do you?"

"Love, we talked about this. Reeve Comlin bade me come stay with these folk. He knows them. We'll be welcome. We just need to get them to trust us first. We'll know when to bring it up."

Nadine chewed her lip. We had had this discussion a couple of times in the past week. Now that we were on the doorstep we felt some trepidation. I had come to know Nadine a bit better lately. She poured her heart out to me. She had been alone for so long and so scared all the time. Finding me, her equal, and falling in love had burst the wall she had built to keep everyone outside her thoughts. She cried a lot. Both in happiness and sorrow. She was getting stronger every day.

"It will be fine, Nadine. If this fellow is anything like Reeve Comlin, we will be warmly welcomed. I have no fear. None. This is where Gaea bade us come. We can't question her."

Nadine nodded and looked down at me. "This is where it all changes, you know that right?"

"Yes. This is the place where we rebuild the draoi. We rebuild it into something good for the world. You and I. Together."

Dog bounded up with a grouse in his jaws and dropped it beside the cart. He had been hunting aggressively all that day, and we had a dozen grouse, a few braces of rabbits, and one large turkey in the cart. Dog knew we were coming to the farm and made sure we had food to offer. He was a smart dog. I got down and rubbed his head and picked up the grouse and tossed it into the cart with the others. Nadine kept her eyes on the farm.

"She's excited and scared."

I knew Nadine was talking about Katherine down below on the farm. I could sense her emotions as well as Nadine. I was a little better at sorting emotions out than her. Katherine wasn't exactly scared. She was apprehensive. I wasn't sure about what yet but suspected it had to do with her father. Our powers were limited in many ways. We could sense her as a draoi and get a feel for her emotions but that was all. It was the same between Nadine and I. What I had with Dog seemed to be the exception and Nadine and I had tried to make sense of it but failed. The Manuscript said nothing of it.

"Excited, yes. Her father hasn't accepted it yet. She is worried about him."

"You know that, do you?"

"Um, yes. Pretty sure. I think."

Nadine smiled at me and then jiggled her reins and Bill the Donkey leant forward and pulled the cart down the dirt road to the farm. "Love you, Will Arbor!" yelled my wise-ass girl.

"You better!" I yelled back. I looked down to see Dog looking up at me. I crouched down and removed a grouse feather caught between his front teeth. "I love her almost as much as you, Dog."

Dog licked my face and bounded after the cart nipping at the hooves of Bill. Bill kicked out a couple of times causing Nadine to cry out and curse Dog. "Dog, you stop that, you little shit! Right now, mister or I'll kick your arse all the way to the farm, do you hear me?" yelled Nadine. She had a voice that made you stop and obey. Dog was no exception, and he bounded off into the fields beside the road. I ran to catch up with the cart and climbed up beside Nadine. She slipped an arm around my back and pinched my butt.

The road leading up to the farmhouse was overly wide and led us in a circle past all the buildings and paddocks before sweeping past the large double doors at the front of the house. As we trundled down the road, the farm hands in the fields stopped and lifted their hats or waved kindly at us. Everyone seemed happy and content and Nadine and I waved back and called out greetings. As we approached the house, we could see a small family standing on the porch: a middle-aged man and woman, and Katherine. The girl stood in front of them in work clothes and leant back into their protective embrace. She was smiling a crooked smile like she shared some truth and was about to be proven right. The man, who I assumed was the father, glared out past the floppy, wide-brimmed hat he wore. His sleeves were rolled up past the elbows and he wore dusty overalls and work boots. The hand he had placed on his daughter's shoulder was strong, dirty and worn: the hand of a man who worked the land. The woman beside him was the wife, I assumed. She was thin and frail and I knew by looking at her that she was ill. My senses flashed out, and I knew at once she was dying. Consumed from within by a disease. It took all her strength to stand there. She leant on her daughter for support. Her face was dark, the skin tight like a mask, but I could still see the beauty there. Whatever had a hold of her was tearing her life away. I looked at Nadine with concern and she returned the look.

Nadine stopped the cart by the porch and no one said a word. We looked back at one another and Katherine scrunched up her nose. She had a lot of freckles on her face framed by unruly long brown hair.

"Hi," she said.

"Hi," I said in return. "The Word is the path."

"The Truth will set us free," replied the man automatically and he and his wife made the sign towards us.

We sat in more silence and then, to our surprise, Nadine started laughing out loud. We all stared at her in shock and then, one by one, we all started laughing with her. The father was the last to join the laughter, but he finally did. I jumped down from the cart and walked around to the porch and stopped at the three stairs, each the width of the front house, leading up to the front door.

The father pulled himself away from the others and, smiling, came down the stairs with hand outstretched to shake my hand. "Will Arbor, I presume?" he said by way of introduction and grasped my hand in a strong grip. I was not expecting to hear my name, especially from such a rough and deep voice, and I looked from him to his daughter, thinking somehow she had figured out my name through the bond. The man laughed at my confusion. "Stephen Comlin sent me a note. It arrived about a month ago. Was wondering if you would ever show up and here you are."

"Reeve Comlin warned you about me?"

"Warned? No, informed, yes. Said you could be trusted. To treat you right. Reeve, huh? That will take a bit to get used to hearing. Comlin was never one for the law. Things change." The man turned to Nadine and looked up to her. "Who might you be young miss?"

Nadine looked down at the man and then to the wife on the porch as if expecting something. The woman frowned in confusion at first and then scowled at her husband. "Ben Rigby. Mind your manners. You've gone wild here on the farm!"

Ben had the good sense to look ashamed and removed his hat and cleared his throat. "Sorry, miss. I'm Ben Rigby. This is my wife Agnes and our daughter Katherine."

"Well met, sir," sniffed Nadine. "I'm Nadine Opal. You've met Will." She held out a hand, and I moved over to take it and help her down from the cart bench. *Not that she needs it*, I thought, *she's more limber than I.* I looked at her and mouthed *Opal?*. She grinned and nodded. With her feet on the ground, she stretched a moment before beaming a smile up at Agnes. "Your house is magnificent, miss. The farm is a place of wonder. Such vitality and growth. So many happy people in the fields."

Agnes looked a little confused at the words but beamed at the praise. "Thank you, young miss, um, Nadine? It's all right if I call you Nadine?"

Nadine tutted and smiled. "Yes, yes, of course. You call me what you like, I'm too old for all this politeness." Agnes looked startled. "Will has been a dear getting us here but we've so much to discuss."

Ben looked back at his wife for a moment before turning to Will. "Well, you have us at a disadvantage. The ways of the young folk today are a mystery to me. I suppose the city changes people. We're simple folk here. I was expecting only Will, not a young miss, a donkey and a cart..."

Ben was interrupted by Dog running up to the house barking his fool head off. Katherine squealed in delight, tore herself away from her mother's arms, and jumped straight off the steps to the ground to wrap her arms around Dog's neck. Dog twisted his face around to get in as many licks as he could around Katherine's high-pitched squeals of delight.

"This is Dog," I said smiling.

"I see," replied the low growl of a voice from Ben. "Dog. Interesting name. And the donkey?"

"Bill."

"Of course. Why not just Donkey?"

"Because he says his name is Bill," replied Nadine matter-of-factly.

"Right," said Ben. He stood for a moment as if deciding something. "Well, let's get you settled. I had a guest room put aside for Will. Will you need *two* rooms?" Ben left the question hanging and shuffled his weight from one foot to the other.

Nadine laughed and came up behind me and wrapped her arms around me. "Nope." She kissed my neck with a loud smack.

"Ah, okay. One room it is. Stephen never said there'd be two people. No matter. Katherine will see you to your room. I'll have the farm hands move your gear to your room later. There's fresh water in the basin. Chamber pot is emptied in the morning, but there are jacks out back. The bed is a double, I imagine you'll be comfortable. Supper is at six. Lunch around noon—you'll hear the bell. We eat lunch in the big barn over there..." Ben pointed to the barn behind us. "It's a farm affair, we're all family, and all join in who can make it in from the fields. Earth's bounty to those who tend it. That's our motto." Ben ran out of words all of a sudden and stood there uncertain.

Nadine came around me and I stepped to the side. She took one of Ben's hands. "That sounds delightful. We can talk at supper. We have much to talk about." Nadine turned to Katherine and laid a hand on her shoulder. Katherine looked up from Dog and smiled at her. "And you, young lady. We have even more to talk about."

Agnes made a sound and Nadine turned to her and frowned. I could see Agnes was struggling.

"My wife, Agnes, she's not well. It's not contagious. She's just not well."

"I can sense that," said Nadine in a soft voice.

Katherine rose and looked at her mum. "Mum, you need to get back to bed. You look so tired."

Nadine turned to me, "Will, can you...?"

I nodded and walked up to her. "Ma'am, can I examine you?"

"Ex-examine me? What?"

"I'm a healer, ma'am. It might be I can help."

Ben moved forward between Agnes and I and wrung his hat. "We've tried that, young man. We had healers from Jergen come and examine her. They bled her, gave her mercurial pills, everything. We sent them away. They caused more harm than good. Rest does her the best good. We're done with so-called healers."

"Da," said Katherine, looking from me to her mum. "This is different. I've tried to tell you. These two, they're special. Like me. Except more. Let them try.

Let him try, please. Mum? Please?"

Agnes nodded and turned and started inside her home. "Come with me."

Agnes led us into a large sitting room with a large window looking out over the front entrance. It was in the corner of the house and a second large window opened up on the side to look out over an orchard next to the home. Apples weighed down the branches and workers were erecting large wooden pens to store the bounty they were soon to be picking. Agnes went over to a large couch, covered in pillows and blankets. It was clear she rested here with a view to the outside and the feeling of the breeze blowing through the open windows. It was a beautiful room. Expensive furniture and rugs filled the space. Paintings hung from the walls and a large portrait of the family hung over an overly large fireplace. *You could fit an entire cow in that fireplace for roasting.* My eyes were drawn to a portrait hanging on the wall behind us in a place of honour. It was a portrait of Reeve Comlin, dressed in leathers and with swords strapped to his waist. A black cloth was wrapped around his head. The face was unmistakable, it was Reeve Comlin, but the clothing was not. The clothing was all wrong. He looked like a raider.

Agnes settled back on the couch and pulled a blanket up over her legs and sighed. The tension on her face eased, and she laid back fully and closed her eyes for a long moment. When she opened them, she focused on me.

"Okay, what are you going to do?" she asked curtly. "I've been through so much. Unless you have a bag full of miracles, I doubt you can do much for me. Excuse the blankets, even in the summer heat I can't seem to stay warm."

Nadine came in behind me and pushed me gently toward the woman. "Go on. See what you can do."

I knelt beside the couch and closed my eyes. I heard Katherine whisper something to Nadine but I couldn't make it out. Nadine shushed her, and I opened my senses to the woman.

The disease was all over her body. It wasn't motes or a poison or anything I expected to see. Her body was damaged by some source deep inside her blood and bones. It was like her body was forgetting what it was supposed to be. Her own body was fighting itself. As a result, her skin had thickened and darkened and was sensitive to touch and the cold. Her joints pained her, and not just one or two, it was all of them. Everywhere her muscles were thinning out and hardening and pulling. It was horrible. I looked to see what I could do, but all I saw was damage with no source to target. I had no idea how to heal a person whose own body was fighting itself. I felt grief consume me. I wanted to help her but could not. I felt useless. *What use was there in having this power from*

Gaea if I could not use it to heal people who desperately needed it?

I searched for solutions within the woman but found none. I felt Nadine's power merge with mine and felt her try to ease my grief. With the joining, I sensed a moment of her own life. She had been trapped in a body aged beyond repair. She had felt and feared the death she was sure to follow, but she had met it with a strength she had drawn from her own life and experiences. This poor woman, Agnes, this woman I now grieved for, she was stronger than all of us. Stronger than Nadine had to be. Agnes suffered by the minute, but gave no voice to the pain and I admired her all the more for it. She feared death— but not for herself—she feared what her death would do to those around her. I felt humbled and tears streamed down my face.

Before I withdrew, I looked to see how I could at least ease her pain. The pain was an unwelcome side effect of injury and one I could deal with. I could mask it. I remembered Daukyns and how I helped him but this time, armed with a better understanding of the human body, I blocked specific nerves, eased the acid in her stomach so she could eat better, and loosened the tightness in her muscles so she could move better. It was temporary and I would have to repeat it every couple of days or so, but it should help. Satisfied I opened my eyes and found Agnes staring at me with eyes swimming with tears. She reached out a trembling hand to mine, and she took it with her new strength and squeezed. Her hand was cold and strangely smooth to the touch.

"Thank you," she whispered through a throat tight with crying. "By the Word, thank you." She let my hand go and reached up to her husband who rushed to kneel by her side and they embraced each other and cried. I stood with Nadine's help and stepped back to give them room. Nadine embraced me and then I felt Katherine embrace the both of us.

"I saw what you did," whispered Katherine. "I don't know how, but I saw. That was… that was amazing. So gentle. So. So…"

"Shh," whispered Nadine. "We will talk. For now, let's leave your mum and dad to each other. Show us to our room, please."

We felt Katherine's nod against us and she broke off and took one look at her mum and dad and led the way upstairs to our room.

Craobh

Seventeen

Rigby Farm north of Jergen, 900 A.C.

NADINE AND I cleaned up and helped the farm hands place our belongings in the guest room. Nadine unpacked all our bags and then spent a few minutes examining my clothes. She announced they would all likely have to be burned and said she was going to get the farm hands to go to town to buy me something more appropriate.

"More appropriate?" I asked.

"Yes, you can't be leading the new draoi wearing clothes you patched together from who knows what."

"From other clothes, thank you very much. I made all these clothes. Well, I mostly made them. They did well enough for me."

"On the road, yes. The love of my life will not be seen walking around looking like a poor peasant."

"Why not? I don't care. I know many 'poor peasants' as you call them and they are terrific people! I have met more *rich assholes* in my life to prefer the peasants."

"That's not the point. You need to look the part. Your mum would have told you. She understood. She was a princess in the castle. Beautifully dressed all the time."

"Not as beautiful as you."

"Huh, what? Not as beautiful? What are you blathering about?"

I turned her around from the bed where she was laying out my clothes. She tried to keep her head turned to what she was doing and, finally, turned her face to look at me. She scowled. "Beautiful as you," I repeated.

"Who, me?"

"Yes, you. You are more beautiful than my mother." I leant in to kiss her but she twisted her face away.

"Are you comparing me to your mother?"

"Yes," And then sensed I answered wrong.

Nadine scowled at me. "I keep forgetting you are fifty years younger than me. Never. And I mean never, compare your love to your mother to me. Not smart." Nadine pulled out of my arms and moved over to open another bag.

I stood there feeling sorry for myself. I had just tried to compliment her and failed somehow. I was about to open my mouth to explain myself when a soft knock came to the door. I walked over and opened it and found a farm hand standing there. She wore the same blue thick cloth for pants everyone here at the farm seemed to favour and a thin blouse. Her hair was tied back with a red bandana and she looked a little flushed. She was unmistakably pregnant. At least seven months along.

"Hi, the kitchen sent me up to remind you supper will be in fifteen minutes."

"Oh, thanks…" I raised an eyebrow questioningly at her.

"Anne. Call me Anne. I work the kitchen these days," she patted her belly to emphasise the reason. "Stairs can be a bit much in the heat."

"Thanks, Anne. Call me Will. This is Nadine."

Anne leant forward to look in the door a bit better and spied Nadine and said hello. Nadine answered back but kept to her unpacking. Anne smiled and turned to go before stopping and hesitating for a moment. She opened her mouth once, closed it and then set her lips in determination before speaking again. "The kitchen staff, they said you helped Mrs Rigby. Is that true?"

"A little, yes."

"So it's true, you're a healer?"

"Yes. I am. So is Nadine."

Anne moved closer and her chin trembled a little. "Could you? Can you check my baby?"

"Your baby? Why?"

"He hasn't moved in a long time. And I'm worried. The midwife—we have one on the farm—she looked at me and said nothing was wrong. But I'm worried. It's silly, I know, it's just…"

I interrupted her. "Shh. Of course." I reached out and sensed the life within her. It was a girl, healthy and content. She was asleep and already head down. She had ten fingers and ten toes and I couldn't see anything wrong with either her or her mum. "She's fine."

Anne's face lit up and she searched my face for lies. "Truly? You never even touched me."

"Yes, right as rain. She's asleep right now. Head down already. You and she are as healthy as can be. I don't need to touch you."

Anne looked searchingly in my eyes for falsehood and then darted forward and kissed my cheek. "Thank you!" And she turned to leave before stopping and whirling back. "She?"

"Yup. A girl."

Her face lit up, and she danced away.

I closed the door and turned to find Nadine standing there before me with both hands on her hips. She looked up at me with an expression I couldn't fathom. She reached up with one hand toward my face and I flinched. With her thumb, she wiped away the wet spot where the woman had kissed me. "No more kisses from strange women, you hear?"

I nodded.

Nadine stepped back and with one motion pulled off her top. "I'm yours, right?"

I nodded.

"We have fifteen minutes."

I smiled.

Nadine and I were downstairs in thirty minutes and apologised for being late. Agnes and Ben exchanged a knowing look, and I blushed clear down to my toes. They led us on a quick tour of the first floor of their house. I couldn't get over just how large and clean the home was. From a Jaipers scale, it was massive. From a Jergen scale, it was a mansion. The Rigby's were very well off. Farm hands whisked in and out of the rooms and greeted each other fondly and by name. I felt such a sense of peace here. I felt just as at home here as I did in Jergen with Nadine in her home. A glance at Nadine and a check through our bond confirmed she felt the same. I sensed Gaea had spent some time and effort here getting the farm ready for what was about to come. It was a bit of a load off my mind. Nadine and I had spoken over the past few days and we had both been concerned about what would happen once we got here. We couldn't imagine walking in and declaring Gaea wanted us to set up a school for the draoi.

Ben and Agnes talked as we moved through the rooms. Each room was furnished with decadent furniture, expertly carved and stained. They gleamed with the late afternoon sun. Each room had large glass windows allowing the natural light to brighten the deepest corners. Always there was a rug filling the centre of the rooms. There was seating for many people and you could hold Jaipers town meetings in most of them. I felt dwarfed and awed. Nadine held my hand and Katherine skipped ahead of us.

Katherine seemed about ten years my junior despite knowing she was the same age as I. I watched her with some amusement. Dog trailed after her and it seemed he had all but forgotten Nadine and I. Agnes moved with a grace she must have missed. I could see the woman she must have been before her disease stole her strength. A steel had returned to her gaze and the ease in her pain had brought a smile to the corner of her eyes. I was pleased to have helped her. Nadine squeezed my hand, and I sent love through our bond.

I was so fortunate to have her love. She gave me strength when I didn't know I needed it. Already the days of solitude and loneliness were fading from my memory and I couldn't remember how I had tolerated it. She and I were one. More so than I could have thought imaginable. Our lives were forever linked. I was timid in so many ways and she loved it. She taught me every time we slept together, and I marvelled at all her intricacies. When I spoke of having children, she laughed at me and reminded me we were draoi and I stopped bringing it up. I was naïve in so many ways. She was my teacher in life. Many times I wanted to just run away with her and hide from the world and just revel in her presence. I sensed the same desire from her and we fought the constant battle of just dropping everything and running for the woods.

The only bad thing about the house was the wooden floors. We felt cut off from Gaea. I missed the dirt floor of Nadine's home. It was comforting. Lying in bed I could just lay a hand on the earth and feel nature. I dreaded sleeping in the huge bed upstairs. I would be like the Inn in Jaipers all over again. Over the last eight days since Jergen, Nadine and I had slept naked against the earth, covering ourselves with a thin blanket for modesty. I had the best sleep of my life with her in my arms on the dirt and moss. Waking next to her was Gaea's blessing to me. Now I felt tired and a bit disoriented.

"Will?"

The question interrupted my thoughts, and I realised it was not the first time my name had been spoken. Ben and Agnes stood hand in hand looking at me with a smile on their faces. "Sorry, yes?"

Ben laughed. He seemed more at ease now. "Day-dreaming, Will? Sorry to interrupt. I had merely asked what you thought about all the rooms."

"Oh, sorry. It is all a bit much for me. I grew up in the wild, you see. The largest homes were in Jaipers and until this summer I had never stepped inside one. This is massive. Huge beyond belief. I feel like a little wee mouse who steps outside into the world for the first time. So much sky and so much room."

"I know what you mean," said Ben and looked to Agnes who smiled back at him, sharing some secret look. "It wasn't always this way. Did Stephen talk about us at all?"

"No, not until just before I left Jaipers."

"I see. Well, we'll fill you in over supper I suppose. We weren't always wealthy. It was *earned* you might say."

"Earned?"

"In a manner of speaking. Dinner will be getting cold. We should head to the dining table. Follow."

Ben and Agnes led us to a dining hall with a massive, soaring, thick-beamed, ceiling. It was more of a banquet hall with a series of tables forming the shape of a pitchfork. Three rows of tables with one across the top. Torches and serving tables lined the walls. Tapestries covered the walls and seemed to tell a tale of some kind. It looked like armies fighting on horseback. Swords were raised and carts were overturned. It was beautiful and oddly out of place with the peace of the farm.

It's more than a farm, isn't it? I questioned myself. *This is so much more. Who builds something this epic?*

We moved through the dining hall into a smaller room. Here was a more familiar setting for eating. A table for ten people. Enclosed and more intimate. A fireplace centred the far wall and I could smell through the adjoining door the kitchen lay not far beyond it. The table was set for five with two place settings at one end. Agnes and Ben moved to those places and gestured for Katherine, Nadine and me to sit at the other set places. We all sat at once and as soon as we settled the door swung open and Anne came through with a large earthen crock and plunked it down in the middle of the table. The door swung back out the other way and when it swung back to our side another woman came pushing through, smiling, with hot, steaming bread and a small crock full of fresh butter. She placed those beside the large crock and rushed back out the door.

"Hey folks," chirped Anne. "Enjoy! The chef says you better like it or else." She disappeared through the door and was gone. I watched the door swing back and forth a couple of times before it stilled.

Ben stood up and lifted the lid to the large pot. Steam billowed out and with it the scent of meat stew. I smelled rabbit and game bird and my mouth watered.

"So, we found all the game in your cart. The chef claimed it all, I'm afraid, and divided it amongst everyone. This is our share. Katherine said your dog said it was okay. Does that make sense to you?" Ben hesitated with a ladle in his hand over the stew.

I laughed. "Yes, that sounds perfectly reasonable. Dog hunted them. They were his kills and if he wants to share them, then he wants to share."

Ben stared at me for a moment.

"And you know this how?"

I leant back in my seat. There was a lot to be explained and I figure I may as well start coming clean now. I had Reeve Comlin's word about these people, Gaea told me to come here, and I felt nothing but amusement through my bond with Katherine. Nadine was thinking only about food at the moment. I looked at the bonds between us and saw the draoi bond between Katherine and Dog. It was also there between Nadine and Dog. That was interesting but not unexpected.

"Well, Dog and I communicate. It is part of my powers from Gaea. The same powers your daughter has. We all have bonds to each other and to Dog. Dog is one of us—somehow. It's why we are here, sir. Gaea sent us here. Nadine and I are druids. The first in a very long time. And so is your daughter, Katherine. We are druids. Or draoi as they used to be called."

Ben sat and put down the ladle. The food was forgotten, for now.

"You should have waited until after he served the stew," muttered Nadine under her breath. Dog whined under the table and I glanced under to see him staring up at Katherine, tracking her every move.

"Oh. Well," breathed Ben. "So. What does that mean?"

"I'm not sure, sir. We've only just arrived. It's not what we expected, to be honest with you. I thought this would be a small farm. Just you and your wife and Katherine. This..." I waved my arms about. "This is much more than just a farm."

Ben smiled weakly and his wife laid a hand on his. "Yes. It is. This is a transformation. This is what people can do when they find the right motivation. Tell me, do you plan on stealing our daughter?"

I blinked in surprise. "What? No, Word forbid! Why would you think that?"

Agnes responded and her eyes flashed with a flint that matched her steel. "Katherine did. She said, 'Mum, people are coming. Really good people. I need to be with them. Gaea told me.' Then she skipped off to tend the horses."

"Ah," I said. "Well, true I suppose in a way. Except we aren't taking her anywhere. It's here we are meant to be."

"On our farm?"

"Yes, ma'am."

"Stop calling me ma'am. You make me feel old."

Nadine nodded, and I scowled at her. She stuck her tongue out at me. "You aren't old, Agnes," said Nadine. "Try being sixty-five. You're only, what? Forty?"

Agnes pursed her lips at Nadine. "You keep talking like an old woman and yet you are only eighteen. It's not right that a young woman should talk like that."

"That's only because I actually am sixty-five."

I smirked at her and pointed a finger up in the air.

"Okay, sixty-seven. But only just. My birthday was only about two months ago."

"You're sixty-seven?" sputtered Agnes.

"Yes."

"And we're supposed to believe that?"

"Yes."

"I don't see how, mum," added Katherine.

Agnes held a hand up to quiet her daughter. She looked at Ben who looked liked he was about to get very angry. *This could be going better*, I thought. *So much for honesty.*

"Not now. We entertained your notion of some mysterious woman telling you about druids and powers and other such nonsense but not now."

"Agnes," I said quietly. "It's all true. You felt me heal you, didn't you? Do you not believe that?"

"I don't know what to believe, to be truthful. I feel so much better that's true. You came into my room, stood before me, closed your eyes and I felt better. You never touched me. You hadn't done anything that I can see."

"And seeing is believing?" I asked quietly.

"I haven't lived this long without demanding proof. My husband and I built this society you see here. We are surrounded by the people we swore to protect. Our brave men and women. I won't have just anyone come riding in and change all that. The only reason you are being treated the way you are is that one, Stephen Comlin vouched for you—and for that man, my husband and I would lay down our lives—and two, our daughter vouched for you, but that was before she had even met you. All this mumbo-jumbo, it's unbelievable. I feel like we are being conned. And we know cons, believe me. So. Prove it. Prove you are what you say you are. Prove it or you will be leaving our commune sooner than you think."

I sighed. Their tone was civil at least. Nadine and I had discussed this. Nadine had hoped until now we wouldn't have to use our powers to prove who we were. It went back to the days when draoi powers were kept strictly secret. I didn't see the need for keeping secrets. Either the powers existed or did not. Hiding them changed nothing. Showing people what they could do would only benefit Gaea and the Earth. Gaea trusted me in this and my instinct was telling me to show them what we could do.

"Hasn't Katherine showed you anything?"

Agnes and Ben looked at one another and then to Katherine. "Yes, she showed us how she could get the horses to do what she wanted. She tells us our crops, trees, bees and animals all do better because of her. We see that they do, but nothing proves it was her. We try to believe her but without seeing it with our eyes it is hard to really believe."

Nadine answered. "I understand. A lot of what the draoi do is not visible. We affect the growth of plants. We encourage animals to consider doing certain things. We can see into the life of others and see things others cannot."

"Okay. Prove it."

I closed my eyes and sensed Ben. His aura was brown, earthy, but shot with orange. He was a good man, loved the farm, but under a great deal of stress. I examined his body and tried to find anything unique about it to prove what I was saying. What I found startled me. I looked him over and then opened my eyes and stared at him.

"Does Katherine know?"

Ben jerked in his seat, gasped, and looked to Agnes. Her eyes grew wide, and she shook her head quickly. She moved to open her mouth, and I felt a flash of irritation from her. They were in denial or something. They knew their daughter had magic and yet they refused to believe it when I took the pain from Agnes. They were demanding proof and now I would give it to them. I felt Nadine's concern but felt my instincts urging me on.

"Do I know, what, mum?" asked Katherine. She looked to her father. "Da?"

Ben shook his head at her and silenced her with a look. Ben turned back to me and I couldn't fathom his expression. I sensed disquiet but pushed on, determined to prove we were draoi.

"I can sense from your body, Ben, that you have been injured at least a dozen times over the years. Almost all from sword and arrows. You have a piercing wound in your upper left shoulder from an arrow strike twenty years ago. It was the last of those kinds of injuries, so I would imagine that whatever life you led back then stopped. It severed an artery and someone with great skill patched you up before you bled to death. Before that, you had four other arrow strikes, two in the upper left leg, one in the lower back that just missed your kidney and one in the upper right bicep. One leg, the back and bicep all occurred at the same time. The other leg the year before that.

Your sword injuries are too numerous to recount. You were impaled through the stomach twenty-two years ago and it very nearly killed you. I think the same person healed you as before. Someone with power and I would guess another draoi. His powers or knowledge were not completely up to the task, but he saved you. You probably didn't know he was draoi. We hid our powers back then, according to Nadine at least.

Before that, you took a strike to the left lower arm that shattered the bone. It was set professionally. You took a strike to the head that caused a massive concussion. That should have killed you but didn't. More importantly, twenty years ago you took a sword strike to the groyne. One testicle was completely severed and removed. The other damaged so badly that your sperm production was stopped. A draoi, probably the same one as before, healed you, made sure that you would continue to be a man with desires and strength. But you could not have children. Your daughter Katherine cannot be yours. She's too young. Is that proof enough for you?"

Ben stared at me in fury. Agnes had her head lowered and wept. A part of me was shamed by what I had just done. Another part of me knew it was exactly what had to be said. I looked over to Katherine and saw her sitting calmly at the table. *She knew already.*

Agnes looked at Ben and took his hand and pulled it toward her. "Look at me, Ben."

When he refused, she shook his hand and spoke a little louder. "Ben. Look at me!" Slowly he turned his eyes from me and looked to his wife. "It's okay. Think for a second. Look to your daughter. *Your* daughter. The one you raised with me from birth through all these years. You knew one day we had to tell her. But look at her, Ben. She already knows. She has for a few years now. She came to me one day and said she knew about your injury. She had sensed it and explained it to me. By the Word, I refused to believe. I'm daft. But there you have it! It's all right. She never stopped thinking of you as her da. Look at her! You're her da, not Steve."

My heart missed a beat for a moment. *Did she just say Steve? Reeve Stephen Comlin was the father?*

Ben looked at his daughter then and found her grinning at him. "Da, it's no bother to me, you're my da, right? Always have been. Been the one to teach me to ride and build fences and plant the seed and how to harvest. You picked me up when I fell. *You're* my da. I've known for years. No man can jump on a horse like you do without wincing. Thought you were tough but not that tough!"

Ben stared at his daughter in surprise and then his face softened. Then he cracked a smile and then, finally, he laughed and we all joined in. Tension fled the room and Ben's aura lost a little of the orange.

When things quieted, he picked up the ladle and started to serve the stew, starting with Agnes. We passed our bowls down to him. "Okay," he said, filling the first bowl. "So explain all this druid stuff. What do you need my farm for?"

Nadine and I told our tales during our meal and well into the early evening. I would have thought so much history would take considerable time to tell. It turned out it only took a couple of hours. To be fair, the Rigby's didn't ask many questions. They listened like they were used to briefings and, I suspected, based on the injuries Ben had, his life had been one involving the military and listening to people.

Nadine started the tale and explained the history of the draoi and what they did. It took a lot of prodding. She didn't want to speak of the draoi to non-draoi. It went against everything she had ever been taught. I held her hand and helped her start and then it came out in a flood. She explained the Purge and how she had remained hidden for all those years. She cried a little, and I held her until she calmed; the others looking away in respect. When she finished, she sat back with her cup of wine and pulled her knees up to her chest and lost herself in thought. She looked so young and fragile at that moment.

I told my story. I kept it simple. I condensed all those years alone in the wild to a few sentences and jumped right to the attack outside Jaipers, my capture on the road to Jergen, and finding Nadine and our journey here. We ended up holding hands and looking into each other's eyes, our joining in love still fresh and vibrant.

Agnes reached across the table and took Nadine's free hand in hers to examine it. "You really were an old woman?"

"Yes, until a month ago."

"And the first thing you do is fall in bed with a young man?"

Nadine laughed. "Yes, apparently, that's exactly what I did. If it helps, Gaea herself blessed us. Said it was unexpected, but she was in favour. Believe me, it was hard for me to accept."

"Uh-huh," replied Agnes sounding unconvinced.

"Seriously," laughed Nadine and pulled her hand free from Agnes to place it over her heart. "You have to understand: draoi can see our bonds with one another. Before I had my powers, Will would tell me of the white band between us. I am a draoi lore master. A white band can only be love. A love of the strongest kind. When I first laid eyes on Will, I felt it but dismissed it. He was eighteen, and I was an old woman. I fought it. I truly did."

"You still are an old woman," I muttered trying to be helpful. Nadine let go my hand only to smack me with it.

"Hush, your elders are speaking."

Agnes smiled but still looked troubled.

"But you understand love, Agnes. I see it between you and Ben. Not the bond. But I see it in your eyes. How'd you meet? How did you find each other?"

Ben looked at Agnes for a moment and nodded. Agnes sighed once. "Okay. Ours is not a story of peace and nurturing. A little like your Purge. Violent. Full of death. But love is at the end of it and so is this farm." Agnes looked at me. "Your Reeve Comlin was not always on the right side of the law. This tale may change your opinion of him. Are you sure you want to hear this?"

I nodded. Regardless of his past, I knew the Reeve's aura shined the brightest blue. "Yes, I'm sure. He's a very good man. Trust me in that. He was like a father to me growing up. I need to hear it. Please."

Agnes nodded and rang the little bell sitting on the small table next to ours. A woman we hadn't met stuck her head in the door. "What?" she snarled. She wore a black leather eye patch over her right eye. She was beautiful despite the disfigurement. I fought an urge to examine it with my senses.

"Be a dear and bring us more wine, lots."

"I'm busy. I'm making bread for tomorrow."

"You can spare two minutes, Franky."

Franky glared at us with her one eye for a couple of heartbeats before disappearing back through the door.

"Franky has been with us since the start. She was one of our captains. Now she's a cook in the kitchen. Says she loves it. Hard to argue with a woman who can skewer you with surprising ease with a simple kitchen knife."

I thought back to Dempster and wondered how he was doing. Nadine let go of my hand under the table and then shook it to air it out. We were both sweaty and nobody likes a sweaty grip no matter how much you loved the person. Dog was snoring under the table and seemed at peace with the world. Ben and Agnes were admiring her new mobility, and she was shrugging her shoulders and twisting her arm around.

"I could probably draw a bow again, dear," she said and smiled.

"Wouldn't that be a treat to see? Maybe tomorrow?"

Agnes nodded. Just then the door banged open startling Dog awake with a growl. Franky burst into the room and dropped a tray loaded with wine and large goblets. She stormed out of the room just as quickly as she had appeared and we all just smiled at one another. I was about to speak when Franky returned and dropped a tray of cheeses and sliced apples beside the wine.

"Enjoy. No more damn interruptions."

Ben grabbed one of the wine bottles and started to fill the goblets. The door banged open and Dog gave a confused bark, then a whine and combined growl, and looked around. Franky stomped back in and slammed a thick, lit candle on the table. "Light." Franky disappeared once more, and we watched the door swing to a stop.

"Okay. Grab a goblet. This will take a while. Let's see..."

Eighteen

Highwayman Camp somewhere between Lakeside and Jergen, 880 A.C.

STEVE COMLIN WHISTLED exactly like the dark-grey jackdaw common to the region. He remained under cover behind the rock outcrop and waited. The whistle meant 'proceed with the plan'. All was set. The plan was rehearsed. All contingencies discussed and planned for. This is what set his crew apart from any other. This is what allowed him free rein in these parts while others were hanged from any nearby tree. *And scruples,* thought Comlin. *I have scruples. I only take from those who can afford the loss.* He wasn't worried. He only feared one of his crew would lose their lives under his leadership. It took a little part of his heart with it, each and every time. What also set him apart was his attention to detail and the rehearsals. He had all his ambush sites picked out along this road but more importantly he had similar places in discrete locations where he could practice the entire attack until the operation was smooth and practised. Precision and attention to detail—that was his secret.

He had twenty of his men and women gathered here on this mission. He grinned to himself. He loved calling them missions. It pissed the crap out of Ben and Agnes. They liked the word *heists. Pft,* thought Comlin, *it sounded far too criminal. And this wasn't criminal. My crew worked for the Baron of the county of Turgany.*

This should be straightforward, he hoped to himself. A small convoy with twenty guards escorting three covered armoured carts was expected to be heading for Jergen carrying a king's ransom in salts from Finnow Mines. The attack would begin with targeted bow shots at the front of the convoy to take out the lead guards and then bow shots at the back to take out the rear guards. This would force the others to concentrate in the middle. It was human nature. Comlin's crew would then pour down continuous bow fire from both flanks angled in to reduce accidental crossfire. Twenty guards should be dead or disabled within thirty-seconds of the first arrow. The crew could then walk in, disarm the rest of them, and take the carts whole.

The Baron of Turgany would welcome the added influence. He would pay well for the goods and by ensuring the mission was successful he would gain significant leverage over the Lord Protector. Comlin didn't know enough to form an opinion, but the Baron allowed him to take what he wanted on this road provided it directly impacted the Lord Protector. Comlin knew the firms and companies who transported the trade that fed the coffers of Healy. Finnow Mines was one such company. They had heavily reinforced convoys. They avoided the river like the plague. Who knew salt and water didn't mix?

This would be the fourth convoy this year and the second in as many months. The Finnow Mines were desperate to get a shipment through. Comlin smiled. The intelligence provided by the Baron's men was always the best. Comlin knew better than to get overconfident. *I try to keep my ego in check but, by the Word, it's hard. And this is going to be sweet.*

Comlin heard the second jackdaw from the other side of the road. The convoy was sighted. He cautiously raised his head to look through the open crack in the outcrop. It gave him a direct view of where the convoy would first be seen when it rounded the bend. The road on the other side of the bend rose to a hill, not a large hill, but one that slowed down any retreat. This stretch of road straightened for two hundred yards and had towering trees on either side, trees his crew had built camouflaged blinds in. His best archers were positioned there now, waiting to hear the first cries and sound of bow shots. Further down, the road turned hard to the right to avoid the cliffs beside the river. It was an ideal location. Prime for an ambush. Lucky for him, the convoys knew and tended to tighten their order of advance. It made the ambush that much easier for him.

Comlin started counting. In two hundred seconds the convoy would be ideally placed and the attack would begin. He counted calmly and when he reached two hundred, he heard the first bowstring snap. It was quickly followed by five more and then screams from dying men obscured the remaining shots. He moved quickly around the rock with his sword in hand and advanced on the convoy. He could see at least ten of the guards down, still or thrashing. The carts were still and the horses calm. The drivers slumped in their seats sprouting arrow shafts. One hung over the side with his foot caught in the cart frame. The air was filled only with the sound of pain from the struck men. There were no other noises and Comlin grinned. A few yells and orders sprang from the remaining guards and Comlin watched them concentrate to the centre of the convoy. *Perfect.*

Comlin reached his observation post just as the second volley from the flanks drove down into the ranks of the guards. It was a slaughter. Comlin checked his internal clock. *Maybe twenty-five seconds. Not bad.* He strode forward and his ground crew rose up out of covered trenches to move with him. No words were spoken. None were needed. Comlin and his crew moved quickly through the fallen men and gave them mercy.

Comlin cleaned his sword with a rag and tossed it aside. He watched his drivers climb up into the cart benches and push the dead drivers to the ground. Others kept the horses calm. Still others cleared bodies off the road ahead of the carts. *Good.* Agnes Butrill appeared next to him with her bow in hand and he smiled at her. She smiled back and Comlin watched it widen toward someone else behind him. Comlin turned to see Ben Rigby striding up with his sword in hand, flashing his own charming smile. *How I wish she loved me as much as she loves Ben. My two best friends, but I can't have her. I envy the bastard but I can't find anger in it. He is the best man—at least to her.* Comlin sighed and, on a nod from Ben and Agnes, he gave the third jackdaw whistle. His crew dropped on ropes from the nearby tree blinds and formed up on either side of the carts. The drivers gave the reins a shake, and the horses took the strain and the carts moved down the road, resuming their ride as if nothing had happened. *Perfect.*

The team started around the sharp bend ahead. Comlin lingered toward the back of the carts and heard the first cry of alarm. He was about to react when a second alarm was sounded from behind. Comlin wheeled to see men on horseback thundering down the road behind him. The horses were destriers, and Comlin instantly recognised the mounted men were trained in their use. *This is a trap.*

He heard the raised cry from the front. The pounding of hooves was loud in the afternoon quiet. His team was caught between two teams of chargers and the cliffs by the river. Comlin reacted.

"Retreat! Execute Plan Foxtrot Uniform!" he screamed. His team reacted immediately. Drivers pulled the reins hard to the left and his crew beside the horses slashed their rumps. The horses bolted, and the drivers leapt from the benches. The horses, insane with pain, ran off the cliff. The screams of the horses and the snapping of bones were excruciatingly loud as they tumbled down the cliff. Comlin swallowed the bile rising in his throat and forced his mind to concentrate on getting his team out alive. Plan Foxtrot Uniform was simple: destroy the cargo and bug out by the fastest means. Swords to protect archers. Straightforward and necessary. His swords understood. It took years to train an archer. Months to train a sword. Comlin grimaced and turned to see Agnes kiss Ben before she sprinted into the trees. Ben saw him staring after her and looked apologetic. Ben knew he loved her. Agnes had no idea.

"Plan Foxtrot Uniform. A great name now that we are finally executing it. Let's do it," smiled Ben and turned toward the rear to draw in the attack. Comlin watched his swords turn grimly to their task. He couldn't be prouder of them.

"For the Realm!" screamed Comlin and moved in beside his best friend as his crew repeated the rallying cry. He and Ben had fought together for years. They were a team and could fend off almost any attack. They stood side by side and watched the destriers descend on them like something out of the Church teachings. *Four horses of the something or other*, he thought. *Bullshit, all of it.*

In the garrison years ago, he and Ben had practised against men on horseback. It was a tricky thing and their chances were not good. They had taught their crew what worked best, and they hoped the training would stick. You had to trust to the tactic and stand firm until it was time to move. The terrain was your best defence. Then it was nice to have a long pike to plant in the ground and drive into the forequarters of the horse. Neither was an option at this point and never would be for their line of work. Comlin's men wore no armour other than a supple leather chosen more for camouflage than for any other reason. They had to be able to move quickly and light and they trained to those strengths. There was a moment with any horse attack where the rider became committed to the attack. The best riders would use the horse to attack. If the horse missed the follow-on attack was typically a short halberd. These men were using halberds and Comlin smiled. *They could do this, they could.*

And then suddenly the horses were on them. Instinct and training kicked in and overrode thought. There was a blur of dirt, hooves, and screams. He dove through the air, sword slashing, and then tightened into a controlled roll across the ground. In a moment Comlin picked himself up from the ground, unhurt and sword glistening red. The charger he had struck lay screaming a few feet past him. One leg completely sheared off and gleaming wet on the ground near him. The rider had been thrown and was slowly picking himself up off the ground. His armour was bulky and cumbersome and Comlin grinned. He glanced left to see Ben advancing on his own rider, sword dripping blood to the ground.

In a moment he clashed with the armed man. He carried a sword, not unlike his own. Simple and efficient. Comlin wasted no time. He couldn't wear the man down—his men depended on him finishing these opponents off and coming to their aid. He looked for a weakness and sensed it almost at once. The man favoured his left side. He must've landed on it from the fall. Comlin feinted, the man moved too slow and opened his defence and Comlin slid the sword in through the gap in the armour joint and felt the slight resistance the ribs provided before his sword burst through and deflated both lungs. Blood sprayed from the mouth of the full helm and the man collapsed in on himself. The fight was over for him, death his only reward.

Comlin looked up and saw the chargers had made it through their turn and were starting their second charge. "Riders! Second attack, brace!" he screamed to his men, trusting they would hear and react. He felt Ben position near him and waited.

The second charge was on them in a blink of an eye. More dust, more hooves and more screams. He dove through the air and slashed with his sword. He felt the shock of his sword striking a halberd and he cursed. He rolled and picked himself up and watched the charger thunder off down the road, the rider still intact. He looked over at Ben and watched him close his fallen rider. Ben feinted, and the knight struck low. With an impossible slowness, the rider's sword struck Ben in the groyne. Blood blossomed and Ben arched his back in agony. Comlin was moving before he had thought. He closed on the rider and drove his sword point between helm and neck guard. His sword bit down and Comlin twisted it in anger and then ripped it free. He reached Ben and knelt beside him. Ben's eyes were rolled back white in agony and held his hand tight to his groyne. *By the Word*, thought Comlin, *please no*.

The vibration in the ground warned Comlin. He turned to see the charger coming back toward him. He moved to the side to put distance between Ben and him. In an instant, the horse closed and Comlin repeated the tactic, but this time throwing himself across the horse's path. The rider had moved to the expected side and Comlin slashed his sword and severed the horse's leg. The rider flew through the air and landed on his head with an audible snap of his neck. Comlin took in the area. His men were mopping up the riders. Only one remained on horseback. At least half his swords were dead, trampled, or run through. Those who stood had stuck to the tactics. Comlin watched his men take down the last two riders. "Full retreat. Mercy for those who ask for it!" Comlin turned to give his friend mercy and rocked back on his heels. Ben was on his feet. His pants bulged in the front and were covered in blood. He had stuffed something down the front to staunch the blood. He looked white and in pain but, by the Word, he was walking.

"Good man. Keep up, my friend."

Ben nodded once and limped off after the others. Comlin knelt by the guard who had broken his neck and looked him over. *Finnow Mines men for sure.* The minnow symbol was etched into the armour. A leather thong at the man's neck caught his attention, and he snapped it free. The thong was attached to a symbol of the Church. The crescent moon with the star in the centre. The reverse was smooth and blank. *Strange. Not many believers in the Church these days.* Comlin wanted to search the others but had no time. He had to stay with his men and help Ben make it out.

He had been betrayed here. His ambush, the location, and timing had been known. It could only be someone from within his crew. No one else knew the details. *I have a traitor in my midst.*

Two weeks later, Comlin finished with his meeting with representatives of the Baron of Turgany. They had no news other than the traitor was most certainly within his own crew. Both he and the Baron had conducted an investigation into their men. All he had confirmed was that the traitor was not within the Baron's men. No others had known of the ambush location except for his own crew. Comlin took a closely guarded route out of the meeting place in Jergen and stayed hidden for two hours until he was certain he had not been followed back to the safe house. He gave the knock at the door in the alley and, when the door opened, he slipped inside and murmured the password to the woman guarding the door. They clasped hands and Comlin went down the stairs to the room where Ben was laid out.

Agnes sat beside the bed next to Ben. Ben was hallucinating and moaning in his sleep. The other figure next to the bed was examining the wound. It had not turned septic thanks to the herbs the man had administered. The man was on loan from the Baron. He worked miracles that was for sure. Ben should be dead. Any lesser man would have succumbed. The man looked up at Comlin when he entered and rose to greet him.

"Any change?" asked Comlin.

"No. But that is good. He is recovering, but it will simply take time. Agnes is assisting. She does good work. Her touch is gentle, and she seems to sense what he needs."

"My thanks, Peter."

"None are required. The Word teaches that all who are injured deserve our care. Your man is strong of will and body. He will recover. But not completely."

"Not completely? Then there is no hope?"

"Not entirely. He has lost most of his manhood. One bollock was removed completely. The other damaged beyond full recovery."

"Then how? Why not completely?"

"I have managed to save the basic functioning of his remaining bollock. He will not have children. But bollocks also make the man. They provide what a man needs to be strong and grow muscle. That ability remains and it will make sure he can still function as a man."

"But no children?"

"No. That is beyond him now. His seed cannot flow."

Agnes looked up at these words and a small sob escaped her. She turned back to Ben and laid a cold cloth on his forehead and stroked Ben's chest. Ben seemed to relax to her touch.

"She has the touch. That and her love for him will see him through the worst."

"The worst? What could be worse than losing your balls?"

Peter looked at Comlin for a moment. "You are a man of action. You've seen how these kinds of events can change a man. Steal his resolve. Give him night sweats and fear that loosens the bowels."

"Yes, many times. Those men have other uses. I never abandon them."

"That is because you are a good man in here," and Peter tapped Comlin over his heart. "He will need strength to overcome what will happen up here." And Peter tapped Comlin on the forehead.

"I see."

"Do you? Yes, I think you do. Tell me, what plans have you now?"

"What do you mean?"

"Is this the life you would continue to live? The Baron feels that your role is no longer necessary. You've done your part, but he fears that you can do no more. You've been compromised, my friend."

Comlin sighed. He knew it for truth. "How is it that you have the ear of the

Baron to know such things?"

Peter smiled. "The Baron trusts me and others like me."

"Like you how?"

"So many questions! Relax, there is much I can't tell you. I return to the Baron tonight and then to the capital. Something is happening. Something beyond the ken of the Baron. I join the others in my profession to try to determine how to best stop it. I fear bad times are fast approaching. You should take your crew and find a safe haven. There will come a time when the Baron will have need of your particular expertise. You are unequalled in the county, Steve Comlin."

"Nice to know. I still have not located the traitor in my midst. I cannot rest until he or she is exposed."

"I understand. Here take this." Peter moved back to the bed and rummaged through his belongings. He placed herbs and ointments on the nightstand and then pulled out a piece of parchment, rolled and sealed with wax bearing the impression of the seal of the Baron of Turgany. He handed the parchment to Comlin.

Comlin broke the seal, unrolled the parchment, and scanned the contents. "He can't be serious."

"Yes, he is. I recommended this to him. You will see the name of the owner is left blank. The Baron felt you would best decide who should own it. Fill in the name and I will return it to the Baron as soon as I can."

"This is too much. I cannot accept."

"You will and you must. Think of your people. They deserve this after so much sacrifice. I only caution you to discover who your traitor—or traitors— is. Deal with him, take what you are offered, and rest. Does land scare you that much?"

"Scare me? No. It is just not my calling." Comlin thought for a moment, then asked for quill and ink. Peter indicated the side table and Comlin walked over, dipped the quill and wrote two names in the blank at the top of the parchment. He sprinkled sand from the small pot on the wet ink and then blew it away. He fanned the paper and handed it back to Peter.

Peter scanned the name and then looked at Ben on the bed. "A good choice. The Baron has picked a good man in you, Steve Comlin."

Comlin nodded and looked at Agnes who looked questioningly back to him. Comlin shook his head and Agnes went back to her ministrations. "And I've picked better people in turn. Do you head out now?"

"Yes, I'm afraid. Time is precious now. I've done all I can here. Time will cure this man and the love of this woman will see him the rest of the way. And your friendship. Funds have already been transferred to the account. All is taken care of."

Comlin nodded and hugged the man. Peter stiffened and then relaxed and patted Comlin on the back. "Rest easy, my friend. Trust that there is a purpose in all this. Have faith."

Comlin choked back a laugh and let go of Peter. "Faith? You sound like the clergy."

"The clergy?" laughed Peter. "No, never that. The Truth will set us free."

Comlin nodded and watched Peter gather his things and place a jar of ointment in Agnes' hands. He whispered to her, and she hugged him briefly and murmured her thanks. With a rustle of cloth, Peter left the three of them alone in the small dark room.

Comlin looked at his friend, Ben Rigby and Agnes Butrill, now landowners in Turgany County. A massive piece of land in a beautiful valley. It was the only gift he could give his two best friends. It would need to be enough. He didn't know what else to offer them. His crew would join them and learn to toil the land instead of raising weapons against what remained of the Lord Protector's oppression. But they would live to fight another day. That would have to be enough.

Ben and Agnes completed their tale and refilled our goblets with the last of the wine. The cheese and apples were long gone and the four or five candles in the room were burnt down to the last couple of inches. Nadine and I leant against one another. The wine had gone to our heads, but we felt alert and awake.

"That was an amazing tale," I said at last. "Reeve Comlin had quite the history. I would never have imagined the life he led before Jaipers. Never. I can see why you admire him so much."

Agnes nodded and sipped her wine. She looked long at her goblet and then to me. "Used to be I couldn't drink wine anymore. It burned me terribly on the inside."

"Yes. I corrected for that. But it won't last, I'm afraid. I'll need to correct it every few days."

"And you can't cure it can you?"

"No, Agnes. I can't. Not now anyway. Maybe with more time. But, I doubt I ever will. It's… difficult. I won't give you false hope. It's pretty bad right now. It's progressing. You know that already."

Craobh

"Yes. Ben and I don't talk about it, but there it is. Out in the open. How long do you figure?"

"I honestly have no idea. I'm very new to this. That is something that takes experience to answer. I can judge by the damage I see. With my continued assistance, you could probably have another year of this kind of mobility and comfort. It will get worse quickly. I would say two years, tops. The last year won't be pleasant, but I can keep the pain away."

"I appreciate your honesty, Will. You are a good man. I can see why Steve likes you so much. You were the son he always wanted but could never have, I think. You remind me of Peter, you know."

"I do?"

"Yes, I see now he must have been a druid. It explains much. He healed so many of us back in those days. He was killed ten years ago. Horribly. He didn't deserve that. But we founded a home here and we healed, found a peace Peter and Steve deserved just as much. Steve gave us that peace. He handed it over and walked away." Agnes grew quiet. "I'm glad you know Steve so well. We haven't seen him in over ten years. I am jealous of you. He came to visit his daughter Katherine twice. Once after she was born and the last right after the start of all the trouble that poured out of Munsten." Agnes turned her head to smile at her daughter. "She was eight then. Then he left for Jaipers and fell out of touch. When the letter arrived from him telling us of you, we weren't sure we could believe it, to be honest. You should know: we trust you now."

"Thanks. That means a lot to me."

"My pleasure," she said. She took a deep breath and forced herself to stand. She leant in to kiss her husband. He looked at her with such love I couldn't help but stare and wonder if Nadine and I looked at each other that way. I hoped we did. It was beautiful. I looked at Nadine and found her looking at me strangely.

Agnes started to make her way around the table. "Night, love. Don't stay up too late. The sheep are yours tomorrow. Don't forget."

"I won't. I'll be but a moment. Night, love."

"Night, everyone."

We all bid her a good night and watched as she made her way out of the small dining room to her bedroom. Ben took a final sip of wine and emptied the goblet.

"So," he said. "We talk tomorrow about how to share this farm with these draoi you say are coming. It was likely meant to be. Katherine. To your bed, hon."

"Yes, da." Katherine rose and gave both Nadine and me a quick hug. She went over to her father and hugged him hard and whispered something in his ear. He nodded and held her tighter before letting her go. "Come on, Dog. Bedtime for you too."

Dog rose and gave one guilty look to me and disappeared after her.

"How about that?" I asked Nadine.

She grabbed my head with both hands and kissed me soundly on the lips. "Yes, how about that? Come. Bedtime for you too, young man."

"Yes, old woman. Need help up the stairs?"

"Are you sure you want to piss me off before we get to sleep together in a large, soft bed for the first time?"

"No, I'm not sure."

Nadine looked from me to Ben and then kissed me again and left for our bedroom leaving Ben and me alone in the room.

"It was Agnes' idea."

I nodded knowing what he referred to.

"She said we needed a child to ground us to the farm. I spoke too much of revenge. About returning to the life of a highwayman. She wanted nothing of it anymore. Said we had a better life to follow. That we should provide our people with stability and we could not abandon them. Steve came to visit once shortly after we settled and we talked. Agnes was very convincing. Said he and I were brothers in more than friendship. In the end, Steve agreed. I convinced him in the end. It took a lot of doing."

Ben grew silent. "It took weeks to take hold. When the time was right, they would come together. Afterwards, I would find Steve drunk beyond belief, crying in his room. It was harder on him than Agnes and me. He loved her, you see. What we asked him to do was cruel. I see that now. When she took with Katherine, he left right after and never came back except once when Agnes demanded he see his daughter at least once. He came, met with her and left. We knew he took the job of Reeve in Jaipers. He borrowed some of the crew one day. They came back one short, the traitor finally dealt with. I'm glad to hear he found a calling as a magistrate. It let him put his skills to good use. I've never met his equal, Will. He could track a mouse across a wet field at night. It was supernatural."

We grew quiet and thought our own thoughts. I thought Ben was asleep and moved to leave when he spoke again.

"When I see my daughter, I see him in her eyes. The way she moves. She's his daughter by blood but mine by heart. Do you see?"

"I do. She is your daughter, Ben. She admits it freely and with love in her heart. I can sense it through our bond. It is Truth, Ben. You should be proud. She means it when she says you are her dad. With all her heart."

Ben sobbed, and I moved over to hold him. "I do. I truly do. That man, Stephen Comlin. He is the best of us. I live to honour him and his sacrifice to us. I have never forgotten. He is alone in a small town out West and his crew, the love of his life and his best friend and daughter live in ignorance of all that he is. That's cruel too, don't you think?"

I had no answer. In time, he got control of himself and I returned to my seat.

"I have something you should read, Will. Steve asked us to keep it from you but you deserve to read it." Ben reached into his tunic and pulled out a slip of paper. He slid it across the table to me and I held it against the table with my fingers. Ben rose unsteadily, stopped behind me and patted my shoulder and slowly exited the room, closing the door behind him.

After a time, I dragged the paper across to me and lifted it and unfolded the paper. I held it up to the candlelight and read the contents.

Dearest Ben and Agnes,

Somebody may come to visit you. He is a young man who goes by the name of Will Arbor. If he hides his name, you will know him by his blond hair, blue eyes and the unwavering look he will return to your eyes. You will see the truth behind those eyes and recognise a young man who I assure you carries such conviction and strength that he weakens me in comparison.

He is the son I would have had should fate have allowed me such fortune. I ask that you take him in and care for him like you would your own. Love him as I do and help him when he asks. He is alone in this world and needs friends such as you. Find a place for him, I beseech you. He is followed. Hunted, I believe. Our past returns to haunt us.

He is of the same ilk as Peter, but much more so. He will need allies to protect him. The world is about to change and Will stands at the centre.

Your friend,

Stephen Comlin

I folded the paper and placed it in the pocket of my tunic. I finished my wine and blew out the remaining candles. I staggered to my feet and realised I was very, very drunk. I thought of the note and what it meant to me. I realised I had three father figures in my life. My father who I had thought abandoned me and then was killed. Daukyns who taught me how to love nature and life and then died. And now another who lived alone in another town and hurt with the fact that all he loved he had to abandon.

For better or worse, I was home. I blew out the candle and stumbled through the dark to find the stairs and my bed. I needed to hold Nadine and never let go.

Craobh

N i n e t e e n

Jaipers, 900 A.C.

B RENT BAIRSTOW CLUCKED to Shitters and urged the horse to keep its pace. The horse was tired, and it hadn't yet caught the scent of the town of Jaipers. Brent could make out the sprawling buildings by the river and the walled main part of the town. It had been a long journey, and he was glad to see the town.

"Doesn't look like much," said James, riding beside him.

"No, it doesn't"

They rode in silence for a moment.

James looked over at Brent. "Captain Mayer reported back. The scouts found nothing. No sign of the Major."

"Okay."

"I don't know what his game is. He has to be back there somewhere."

"You increased the range?"

"Yes, sir, as ordered. And we deviated from normal procedure. Doubled the back sweep range of the scouts and still, nothing found. Maybe he isn't following us. Maybe he went back to Munsten."

Brent snorted. "Unlikely. Healy would have him put down like a rabid dog. There is no reward for failure."

"Where do you think he is? He must be back there somewhere."

"I've no idea. He might be waiting for us to finish our business here and wait in ambush for us to return."

"That seems likely. Or he circled around and is in town waiting for us."

"I thought of that, too, but think it unlikely. He would attract too much attention in town."

James scowled. "I do, too. I'm grasping at straws. Thinking out loud. I know. I'm being repetitive. We've been over this." Brent glanced once at him and smirked. "Sir, if he isn't following us then he's lying in wait. Somewhere on the road back to Munsten. He must be."

"I agree with you. He doesn't need to follow us to Jaipers. He knows our return route. He'll be north of Jergen on the road. The scout reports confirm that."

"What if we take a ship from Jergen to Munsten?"

Brent's horse caught a whiff of smoke from Jaipers and tossed his head. Brent reached out and patted the neck and shushed the animal. "There, there, Shitters. Hush. We'll be there soon." The horse settled and Brent looked back to the column of men behind him. They were looking ahead at Jaipers and not watching the fields and woods. Captain Mayer behind him turned to see what his General was looking at and started yelling at the men to resume their vigil. Brent smiled, *Mayer's is a good officer.* "The horses will want to run soon. They can sense stables up ahead. Clean water and oats."

"True. I'll send a runner ahead shortly. Have him confirm with the garrison captain when we arrive and what we need."

Brent said nothing. He didn't have to. James was a thorough officer and didn't need small words of encouragement to know his worth. "Not by ship, James. I won't risk the cargo."

"Aye, sir."

Brent looked over at James expecting to see an insubordinate smirk on his face. James was looking serious. "That's it?"

James laughed. "Yes, sir. I only presented options. I didn't think using a ship was the solution but had to voice it all the same."

"Pft. Sure you did." Brent clucked at his horse and squeezed his knees a little. The horse slowed a little but threw its head forward. It wanted the town ahead. *Oats and brushing and all the other good horsey things*, thought Brent. "Let's see what happens in town and discuss this later."

A short time later, Brent and his men rode up to the open south gate of Jaipers. The runner had returned with a member of the garrison who requested they use the southern gate. He had also warned Brent that he should expect a formal welcome. Brent had grimaced at that. It had meant stopping to change into ceremonial armour and swords. Before the gate, the garrison man rode ahead of them to give warning.

As they rode into the open area, Brent was pleased to see the garrison out in full colours. The people of Jaipers had come to watch the event and Brent counted a couple of hundred people standing in the area surrounding the barracks and garrison office. The area was largely open, almost like a parade ground. Brent focused on the men of the garrison who were out in front of the barracks in a parade state and lined in three even rows. Brent wheeled his men past the garrison captain standing out front of his men with a sword in his hand. Brent called out orders and his men formed up in lines still on horseback. James and Marcel stopped just behind him and Brent could hear the colours of Belkin and the Lord Protector's Guard flapping on the standards they carried braced on their saddles. The carts halted behind them. A silence and their raised dust descended on the area.

Brent dismounted and drew his ceremonial sword. He held it straight out before him with a bent elbow and then marched up to the garrison captain. He heard Captain Mayer take his place behind him. Brent halted three paces in front of the garrison captain and waited. The runner had informed him his name was Gendred. He looked fit enough. He vibrated with anticipation. *He probably saw this as a way to boost his career*, thought Brent. The captain raised his sword before his face then swiftly lowered it to a position angled slightly out and away from his body. It was the salute of a junior officer to a senior and the captain had executed it flawlessly. Brent raised his sword to his face and lowered it back to the bent arm position. His sword held to the vertical, all the weight balanced on top of his closed fist.

"Captain Gendred reporting the Jaipers Army Garrison. One officer and twenty non-commissioned members ready for your inspection. Ten other men on patrol and guard duty, sir."

"Very good, Captain. It will be my pleasure to inspect."

"Very good, sir." Captain Gendred swung his sword up to the front of his face and lowered it to the vertical. He did an about-face, drew in a deep breath, and yelled at his men in his parade voice. "Jaipers Army Garrison will be inspected by General Bairstow, Head of the Lord Protector's Guard. Front rank, one pace forward—march!"

The front rank took one practised step forward in unison. Captain Gendred did an about face and nodded to Brent. Sighing inwardly, Brent stepped forward to inspect the garrison.

* * *

"The men were very well turned out, Captain. You should be proud. The uniforms were excellently maintained. It's a credit to your leadership." Brent completed the circuit of the small office, stopping now and then to pick up a small memento to examine before putting it back down. The Captain's office was immaculate, and he turned to smile at its owner. Captain Gendred sat at his desk looking a little uncomfortable but beaming at the praise. Brent had ordered him to sit and the good captain, feeling it to be too inappropriate, only sat at his insistence. *The man loves his sense of duty*, thought Brent. *I can't fault him for that. I, on the other hand, need to stand after a half day of riding.*

"Thank you, sir. If I may say, never has an officer of your rank or station come by our small town."

"No, I don't suspect anyone has."

"No, sir, never. It is quite an honour. It pleases me to receive you. Your runner came as a bit of a surprise. I didn't believe him at first."

Brent laughed. "Yes, he told me."

"Begging your pardon, sir. The runner also said that Jaipers is the end of your journey."

Brent stopped and turned his full attention to the captain. "Yes, our destination is here."

Captain Gendred seemed uncomfortable and looked away. Brent saw his jaw clench and then look back at him. Brent approved. *The man has character*, thought Brent. *How'd he end up in the middle of nowhere?* "Well, sir. If I can be so bold, what business do you have here? I've a lot of good people here in Jaipers and if something is amiss, I would like to be the first to know."

"Captain Gendred. I can only tell you so much. I do apologise. I have some questions first." Brent stopped by the window and looked out over the area outside the barracks. James and Marcel were taking charge of the men and getting their equipment moved into the barracks and stores. He watched a man emerge from the small building across the way. He was sure of step and he stopped to watch the men for a moment before walking unerringly over to James and Marcel. *He recognises rank*, thought Brent.

James and the man talked for a moment. James looked surprised and then turned toward the garrison building and pointed. The man thanked James and then walked toward the building. Brent watched him approach and was sure he knew who it was.

"Captain, a man just emerged from the small building across the way. He's coming over here. Who is he?"

"That would be the Reeve, sir. Reeve Comlin. The small building is the gaol and his office. Excellent man. Very disciplined. Looks out for the town and the region."

With the name confirmed, Brent flashed back to the Cathedral in Jergen and his conversation with the Dean. He had mentioned Reeve Comlin and said he was a good man. "Trustworthy?"

"Oh, aye, sir. Completely."

"He's the one that killed the assassin?" The captain didn't answer. He turned to see the captain looking thoughtfully at him. "Well?"

"Yes, sir. He's the one." The captain paused a moment. "He's not in any trouble, is he? He did a good thing there. I sent my report. It was all in there. The assassin had killed one of our town members. Bill Burstone. Murdered him in his own home. The Reeve hunted him down and killed him. All within his authority."

"Yes. It's why I'm here. And no, the man is not in trouble. Quite the contrary. I was told about him. Told he was a good man. On that, have you seen anyone with black boots around town?"

The captain opened his mouth to speak when a rap on the door interrupted whatever he was about to say. Brent raised an eyebrow at him and the captain flushed a little. It was his office.

"Enter," he called out.

The door swung open and Reeve Comlin stood in the opening. He looked directly at Brent and looked him over quickly. Brent recognised the look: he was being professionally appraised. Already Brent could see the man carried himself with an air of authority and military bearing. His clothes made for easy movement and concealed knives. They also offered some protection. He carried his weight equally on both feet. A trained fighter. Skilled. Experienced. *Not your typical small town Reeve*, thought Brent and decided he liked the man.

Brent smiled and held out a hand. "Afternoon, Reeve Comlin. Good job killing the assassin. It's why I'm here. Thanks for joining us. You, me and Captain Gendred have much to discuss."

Comlin looked pointedly at the hand for a moment and then shook it firmly. "Pleasure's mine. How can I help?"

"I'm here to gather up the belongings of Bill Burstone—the chest more specifically—and return it to Munsten."

"Right to the point," replied Comlin.

"I've come a long way, sir."

Comlin looked him over and seemed to make a decision before replying.

"Fair enough. The chest is in my gaol."

"In your gaol?"

"Yes, behind bars. Only safe place in town."

"Fair enough," he said, intentionally repeating the Reeve. "Let's go."

"Right now?"

"No time like the present. No offence, but I want to get started back to Munsten as soon as I can."

Comlin looked a little offended but, surprisingly, it was the captain that spoke next. "Jaipers too small for you already, sir?"

"No, Captain. The size of your town means little to me. I have my duty back in Munsten. I must return swiftly."

The captain and the Reeve exchanged a long look before Comlin took a step to the door and swung it open. "After you then, sir. Let's get this over with and have you on your way."

Comlin led the way out of the small garrison building and out into the late summer sun. James saw them emerge and joined them as they crossed over to the gaol. James matched Brent's stride and looked at him for instructions. "Stay with me, James. The chest is in the gaol."

"Aye, sir."

"Captain James Dixon meet Captain Gendred and Reeve Comlin."

"Gentlemen," said James.

"Captain," said Comlin and Gendred at the same time.

They marched over to the gaol and entered behind the Reeve and closed the door. Comlin took a key from around his neck and opened the small gaol cell. Brent was pleased to see the gaol was made of a solid steel cage that had been built as a free-standing structure in the building. *So often bars were built into the wood structure. This, on the other hand, was a very secure gaol cell,* thought Brent.

Comlin stepped aside and Brent could see the ornate chest resting in the middle of the cell. Brent looked at James and walked forward and opened the chest. Gold crowns gleamed up at him. Brent could barely believe the wealth contained in the large chest. *Bill really did it,* he thought. *He took all that gold out of Munsten. I didn't believe it. I really didn't, but here it is.*

"Has it been counted?" he asked.

Comlin jerked. "Actually, no."

Brent stood and turned to Comlin. "No?"

"Well, I wouldn't let anyone see it. Gendred had his men carry it over here. Bloody heavy thing. I didn't see the need to count it."

"How would you know if any went missing?"

"Missing?" scoffed the Reeve. "I am the only one with access to it, General. I would only have myself to blame, wouldn't I?"

Brent had no answer to that. Internally he wondered how a man could not want to count all that gold. The temptation must have been huge. Brent looked into the man's eyes and saw no deception. A solid man. Sure of himself. *Interesting.* Brent turned to James.

"We need to count it, James."

"Thought we might, sir. I'm eager."

"We'll divide the pile into four. Let's carry it out into the room and empty it."

Comlin grunted but nodded and together all four lifted the chest and hauled it out into the open area of the room. Brent swung the lid up and looked inside.

Comlin coughed into his hand and Brent looked at him. "If I can suggest?" Brent nodded. "Just dump it out."

Brent thought a moment and nodded. The two captains grabbed the chest on either side and tilted it over. Coins poured out in a steady metallic stream. The gold poured over the edge and then suddenly went from gold coins to copper.

"Woah!" yelled out Brent. "Stop!"

They righted the chest and Brent strode over and dug his hand deep into the coins and pulled out a handful. Dull copper pence filled his hand. Brent stared at the men and could see the surprise on their faces. He dug deeper and pulled out more copper coins. Brent thought back to his conversation with Bill Redgrave all those years ago.

"Aye, I took his gold. All of it," said Bill Redgrave as he finished his goblet of wine at Brent's kitchen table. He slammed the goblet down on the table and reached for the wine carafe over the selection of cheeses. Bill had just returned from his infiltration of the castle.

"How is that possible, Bill? He had a massive treasury of gold stored in the castle vault," said Brent.

"Emptied."

"Emptied. You took it all…" said a disbelieving Brent.

"You might say that," replied a smug Bill as he refilled his goblet.

Brent stared at the copper coins. "You might say that," he whispered and the beginnings of a laugh started deep within him.

Comlin stared at him. "Pardon?"

Brent chuckled.

"Something funny, General?" asked Comlin. Brent could hear the disdain in his voice and the need to laugh increased.

"Yes," was all he managed to say and laughter escaped him. James looked at him with something akin to horror. He was embarrassed for his General. Brent threw his head back and laughed out loud.

James, Gendred and Comlin stared at each other in disbelief and then turned as one to watch Brent laughing. Brent couldn't help himself. All those years thinking one thing and now finding out another. *Ah, Bill*, he thought. *You were always a crafty bastard.* The laughter took hold of him and he found himself sitting next to the pile of pence running his hands through the coins. Of the total, perhaps a hundred coins were gold crowns. Somewhere in Munsten castle thousands of crowns were hidden. Enough to run the Realm for a year. Sitting right under the Lord Protector's ass. Fresh laughter stole Brent's breath, and he pounded the chest lid in glee.

After a little while, Brent recovered and looked at the others. James was smirking and waiting to hear the joke. The Reeve and the garrison captain were looking a little more than apprehensive. Brent wiped at his face and calmed himself. *Not proper for a full General to be sitting on his ass in a town gaol,* he thought and fought to keep more laughter away.

"Okay, sorry," he said and stood up and dusted himself off. "A lot of history there. All of it funny as hell. An inside joke." Comlin forced a smile. "I'll explain later. For now, let's just get this coin back in the chest."

The four of them put all the coins back into the chest. They separated the gold crowns, counted ninety-three of them, and Comlin placed them in an empty burlap sack. They placed the sack on top of the other coins and closed the lid. The chest went back to the gaol and Comlin locked the door and returned the key around his neck. He paused for a moment and then took the key off and handed it wordlessly to Brent.

By now they were sweating profusely in the stifling small room. Comlin suggested they head to the Woven Bail Inn and Brent agreed. James ran over to tell Captain Mayer where they were going and joined them as they walked over.

This is a dry and dusty town, thought Brent. Children ran about carefree and barefoot. The common building looked vacant and out of use. The open area by the barracks could fit maybe a hundred men in formation but not much else.

This is your typical frontier town in Belkin, he thought but kept his face neutral. *Barebones and unforgiving*. They arrived at the two-story inn and Brent looked back over the south entrance of the town. His men were unloading the carts, and the garrison seemed to be helping. Children ran laughing around them and asking for coin. A few townsfolk had gathered to watch. *Peaceful and quiet*, he thought and followed the others into the inn.

Comlin spoke to the owner, and they were given one empty side of the Inn to themselves. The other guests were openly staring at Brent and James like they were on display. The proprietor shooed them away and soon they found themselves more or less alone. The owner called out to the back for food and then poured them beers and dropped the drinks on the table along with a pitcher of water and goblets.

The men took swigs of the beer and smacked their lips in appreciation. They sat in silence for a moment when, suddenly, an overly large and sweating man appeared, towering next to their table. He dropped a large platter covered in cheeses and prepared meats. Brent immediately sensed the man was deathly afraid of him. The man's eyes darted to the rank and insignia that marked him as being of the Lord Protector's Guard and to his face and back again. The whites of his eyes showed and Brent could sense the man was only moments from flight.

"Easy, sir," said Brent softly. He saw Comlin lean forward slightly and knew he would defend this obese man should he have to choose. "I have no quarrel with you. Whatever you fear it is not me."

The man took his apron in his hands and wrung them. He took a step backwards. "Sir, yes, sir. I-I..."

"You have nothing to fear. I have no idea who you are or what you are doing here in Jaipers. If Reeve Comlin trusts you—and I can see that he does since he has moved his hand to the knife at his waist—then I do, too. Fair?"

The man nodded and looked to Comlin. Comlin nodded and leant back in his seat and released his hold on his knife. "Go, Dempster," said Comlin. "Back to the kitchen. It's all right. They're here for Bill Burstone and the murder. Nothing else."

Dempster nodded furiously and backed away and disappeared into the back.

Brent watched Comlin carefully. This was a dangerous man. Skilled, quick, and loyal. A man you wanted to be your friend and not your enemy. Brent looked at James and smiled and James sat back and relaxed a little. Captain Gendred didn't know where to look or what had just happened. *Perhaps that is why he is way out here*, thought Brent. *True to duty but oblivious to the obvious.* Brent took a sip of beer and then picked a piece of dried meat from the selection in front of him. He chewed it and smiled around the burst of flavour that exploded across his tongue. Hot spices and herbs and something else. Something that made him feel alive. *Life salt?* he thought. *Impossible, but it must be. This is an expensive sampling of food.*

Comlin seemed to relax and took a long pull from his drink to prove it. "Dempster owns the Inn. You wouldn't know it. Most people think it's John who owns it—the fellow who just served us beer. It's an arrangement. Problem is, Dempster, he forgets he owns it and defers to John all the time. Dempster just wants to cook. Used to be he cooked up in Munsten. I don't know the details, but he's here now and whatever happened back in Munsten... well, it doesn't matter out here."

Brent just smiled. "Tell him he's safe. I really don't care. Obviously you two..." Brent indicated Comlin and Gendred with his beer mug. "... don't care, so why should I?" Brent snagged another piece of the meat and chewed it. "He's brilliant. This food is remarkable. Bursting with flavour."

Comlin and Gendred shared a smile. "Dempster had a good source for his herbs and spices."

"Had?"

"Yes, well. An inside story—or joke if you will." Comlin smirked.

"Uh-huh. Okay. Enough. Business."

Comlin grabbed some cheese from the platter and sat back and gestured for Brent to continue.

"I'm here for Bill's chest. But I want to hear what happened that night. I read Gendred's report. What's missing from it?"

Gendred choked on his beer and James pounded his back. "Drink your beer! Don't breathe it!"

John, the innkeeper, came over and hovered until Gendred recovered, red-faced. Comlin noticed him and beckoned him over. John leaned in and whispered in Comlin's ear but Brent heard what he said: "A letter was delivered by one of the barge captains, Steve. Says it's for you." Comlin seemed startled and took the note with a broken wax seal into his hands.

The innkeeper bobbed his head. "Reeve Comlin, the seal was broken when Dempster took it. So he swears. He's a good man, honest he is. I believe him."

Comlin looked at the note then tucked it unread into his tunic. He looked up to the innkeeper. "I'll talk to Dempster later. Tell him to relax." The innkeeper retreated to the back of the bar and Comlin turned back to Brent.

"The report?" Brent reminded him.

"Nothing missing from the report, General," said Comlin. "The man broke into Bill's house. Bill caught him and had his throat slit from ear to ear. A patrol happened to come across the man leaving the house and chased him. He climbed the wall and was gone into the night. I tracked him and killed him."

Brent felt that the Reeve was holding something back. "Anything else?"

"No, not really."

"The report mentioned a young man being held hostage?"

Comlin gave Gendred a look before answering. "Yes, that's true. Not important though."

"I'll be the judge. What happened?"

Comlin scowled before answering. "A young man who used to hang out around these parts. Gathered herbs and traded them in the market. The assassin stumbled across him that night, probably drawn by the fire. Used him as a shield."

Brent waited for him to say more and when he didn't he leaned forward. "Yes, and then what? Did the young man die? Reeve, I suspect you are much more used to giving detailed reports than this. You seem overly hesitant to be forthcoming on this matter. You are starting to piss me off. Bill Red... Burstone... was a friend of mine. This is more than duty for me. This is personal."

Comlin looked startled. "He was a friend of yours?" Comlin glanced at the insignia on Brent and James' uniforms. He looked thoughtful for a moment. "You served together?"

"You might say that," replied Brent.

"Bill had an interesting past. Not one he shared with anyone around here."

"He also had a chest full of coin."

"Yes, that he did."

"And the scars of burns all over his body," said Brent.

"That he did, too," replied Comlin, so quietly Brent strained to hear him. "He was constantly in pain. Drank here every day. Drank till the pain went away. People thought him the town drunk."

"But you didn't, did you?" asked Brent.

"No," he replied, and he looked to Gendred for a moment. "No, he was an honourable man, but with a past that haunted him." Comlin looked at Brent's uniform. "He has a uniform that looks remarkably like the one you are wearing. General, is it?"

Brent nodded. "Yes, General. Did I tell you my brother is the Knight General of the Realm, Reeve? His uniform is similar to mine except right here..." Brent pointed to his shoulders where his ailettes stood proudly showing his rank. "Right here you will find a five-pointed star with rays between the points. Ever see that?"

Comlin nodded. "Might have. Let's finish these beers and head over to Bill's house. There's something you are going to want to see."

Brent, James, Theo Gendred and Steve Comlin climbed the stairs up to the second floor of Bill Redgrave's house. Gendred had carried a key to the house and explained that the house was contested in town. Too many people wanted to move in.

"I won't let them," explained Comlin. "It's too soon, and I expected to see someone from the capital show up."

"Why?" asked James.

"You'll see," said Comlin, and he opened the door to what Brent could see was a study of some kind. Comlin held the door for him and he pushed past him into the room.

The floor and walls were stained with old blood, brown and flaking. The desk was huge and filled most of the space. All around were bookcases filled with books and scrolls. Military memorabilia-filled niches and special places. Brent turned and saw the suit of gleaming field plate armour on an armour stand in the corner. Also hanging from the tree was a hand-and-a-half sword in its sheath.

It was the sword and armour of Knight General Bill Redgrave. On the shoulder, ailettes were the distinctive gold stars of the Realm. They looked similar to the symbol of the Church of the New Order but were the insignia for the rank of Knight General. Brent looked to Comlin.

"May I present the armour of Knight General Bill Redgrave, a traitor to the Realm," Comlin whispered. He looked from Brent to James and, seeing the two of them standing silently, he knew he had guessed the truth correctly.

"Bill Redgrave!" sputtered Gendred. "Bill Burstone was Bill Redgrave! Here in my town all those years!"

"Calm yourself, captain," ordered Brent and placed a firm hand on his shoulder to emphasise the order. "At once, and lower your voice."

Gendred sputtered and looked to Comlin who said nothing. "It can't be true, can it? You aren't serious! Redgrave was killed all those years ago. Burned to death in his mansion! Burned...." Brent watched a light flicker in Gendred's eyes. *Ah, he is putting it together now*, he thought. "The fire. His burns... he couldn't have survived."

"Oh, I assure you he did," said Brent.

"How can you know?" asked Gendred, disbelief still evident on his face.

"Because I was the one that saved him."

Comlin started. "You saved him? *You* did? How?"

"I was only a young officer then. I was there and watched as his children and wife had their throats slit in front of him. The Lord Protector ordered the bodies tossed into the fire and then they threw Redgrave, alive, in after them. He escaped through the root cellar. I found him there and nursed him back to health."

"And the chest?" asked Comlin.

"He recovered in my house in Munsten. Once he was well, he snuck in and raided the treasury. Said it was the best way to hurt the Protector. That is what I expected to find here. Thousands of gold crowns."

"And you didn't, did you? You found copper pence. Not even one groat."

"Correct."

"Which means the gold is still in Munsten," replied Comlin. Brent was impressed with the speed at which the Reeve was putting this all together.

"Yes, somewhere. I need to find it."

Comlin went over and fingered the rank on the armour. "How'd the assassin find out?"

"Find out what?"

"How'd he find out Bill Redgrave was hiding out here?"

"He didn't. The Church did. They followed the coin."

"The gold?"

"No. The coin I sent Bill. A particular coin. It had a three-armed symbol on it." Brent pulled his wooden amulet out and held up the side with the triskelion on it. "Like this. Bill asked me about it and I just happened to come across one. I sent it down here to him. They tracked it here to Jaipers to try to recover it. They killed him for it."

Comlin came over and held the amulet and looked at the symbol. He turned it over and saw the symbol of the Church. He looked up at Brent and raised an eyebrow. "Who are they?" He released the amulet. Brent tucked it back into his shirt where it lay against his chest.

"The Church of the New Order. Now the coin is gone and Bill is dead. They have a Sect. Led by a fellow called Seth Farlow. They wear black boots."

"Black boots. The man who killed Bill wore black boots. Hold on a second."

Comlin reached into his tunic and pulled out the note he had received earlier. He examined the broken wax seal and uncurled the short note. His eyes scanned the page quickly, and he looked up to Brent. "Well, the coin isn't here anymore."

"Where is it?"

"In Jergen. Turns out the Church is still looking for that coin and the owner."

"The owner?"

"Yes, the young man I spoke of earlier? He has it and what's more, he can use it."

"Use it?"

They were interrupted by a bang on the front door and a hoarse cry for Captain Gendred. Gendred looked up, and they rushed down the stairs. In the doorway was one of the garrison soldiers, he was covered in blood and holding his midsection with both arms held tight.

"Sir, we've been attacked!" Blood was pouring between his arms.

"Attacked? By whom!" ordered Gendred.

"From within, sir! The garrison is killing the newcomers and we're fighting ourselves! The barracks are on fire! Sir, I..." The man slumped to the floor and let go of his midsection. His insides poured out onto the floor. He had been eviscerated, the smell ghastly in the front hall of the house. James rushed to his side and checked his pulse and shook his head.

"He's dead."

Twenty

Rigby Farm, 900 A.C.

ADINE AND I walked back to the main farmhouse with Katherine and
Dog. We finished a tour of the main outbuildings and the fields
surrounding the central area. It was a beautiful day, and the farm had
been remarkable to see.

"Your dad came up with the hub and spoke concept for fields?" I asked
Katherine.

"Yes. He told everyone it came to him in a dream one night. He said he
floated above the ground and looked down and saw a wagon wheel design. The
main farmhouse in the middle and radiating out fields of different plants and
rotation. The river running through helps and we managed to irrigate the fields
with hand and wind pumps. We grow just about everything here. Lots of grass
for livestock, but wheat, barley, and oats, too. Vegetable fields, as well.
Potatoes, carrots, and turnips. Everything to get you through winter. We
provide most of the produce this side of Lakeside. Jergen ships it to Munsten
and who knows where else."

I could hear the pride in her voice and I stole a glance at her. Through the
bond, I could sense she was hiding something. "What else, Katherine?"

Katherine looked shyly over at me. "I. Ahem. I was involved, too. The farm
wasn't always this way. Before it was just fields that they planted in. No order

to it. They were militia pretending to be farmers. They knew nothing. When I was old enough to be able to convince my ma and da, I told them what they should be doing. Da said later he had the vision, but I think it was me that gave it to him."

Nadine laughed at that. "Men," she said. "All alike. Always claiming ideas for their own."

"That's not true, love," I answered automatically. "I've never laid claim to something that wasn't mine first."

"Hmm. Well, perhaps there are exceptions. I'll allow that."

"Allow that? Who gave you the power to allow anything, old woman!"

Nadine growled and tried to punch me again. I twirled away and avoided it. "Ha!"

"Ha, yourself, young man!"

"Why do you say that?" asked Katherine.

Nadine looked over at her. "Say what, dear?"

"Old woman and young man. You're my age, Nadine. And yet you talk to me like my mother does."

Nadine pursed her lips. "Do you not sense me through the bond, girl?"

"Yes, I do."

"And what does it tell you?"

Katherine scrunched her eyes closed. Nadine gave a withering look to me and I smiled and shrugged. "You don't need to close your eyes, girl," she admonished her. I frowned a little at the tone.

"I know, it's just easier for me. I can concentrate better." Katherine stopped walking and Nadine sighed and waited.

In a moment, Katherine opened her eyes and made a petulant sound. "I can't tell," she complained. "It's too complicated. Not at all like the horses and sheep and stuff."

"Nothing in life is easy. People are just more complicated than animals," answered Nadine with a hint of patronising. "Come along, we have a long walk back."

Katherine caught up and gave Nadine a scowl. "See what I mean? You talk to me like you're so much older than I. You aren't. You and Will are the same age as me."

Nadine blew air out her mouth. "Actually, no, I'm not. I was sixty-two..."

"Seven," I interrupted.

"Two," said Nadine glaring at me. "Gaea gave me my youth back. And my health."

"Mum said that, but I didn't believe her," gasped Katherine. "It's true? Will? Is it true?"

"Yes, Katherine. It is. I fell in love with an old woman and she robbed the cradle of a young man. Terribly inappropriate."

"Hmm, yes," purred Nadine and stole a kiss from me and ran off a ways, looking back to see if I would chase her. Dog ran after her barking and I laughed and followed.

"Why can't I get a straight answer from those two?" asked Katherine to the air.

An hour or so later, supper was eaten, and the plates washed and stacked. Nadine and I were sitting on a swing set out by the farm windmill. The windmill was a miracle of the Word and pumped water from the well to the livestock barns nearby. Ben had tried to explain it to me but apparently, I wasn't *mechanically inclined*, whatever that was. I found it peaceful here, and I was reminded of Nadine's home in Jergen. The sun would be setting soon and I hoped that when I was finished speaking to her she would be willing to see another with me.

She knew something was wrong, and I struggled to find a way to broach the subject. Truth was, I wasn't too sure myself what the problem was. I needed to talk to her openly about it. She and I needed to agree on the next steps and why they were important. Daukyns always told me to simply take small bites when faced with a large problem, and I meant to do that, I just didn't know where to start.

"Nadine, I..."

"You're upset with me."

I grew quiet. I wasn't upset. I was, something else. Not sure. "I don't think so. Not upset exactly. I need to say something to you and I don't know how to and I'm afraid I will mess this up."

"Will, you're afraid to lose me. You won't. I'm too old for mincing words. Something is bothering you. I can sense it through the bond. Tell me, love. You won't lose me. We'll figure it out. I haven't spent a lifetime looking for someone like you to lose you only after a couple of months."

I felt her love through the bond. I was still afraid. I took a deep breath and started. "Well, the way you talk to Katherine. It's a little harsh."

"Harsh?"

"Yes, you speak to her like she's a child. You roll your eyes and sigh all the time. That's not helpful."

"Not helpful?" Her voice rose a little in pitch.

"Yes, love. Just... just hear me out. I don't have the answers. I can only follow what I think is right. Daukyns used to teach me all the time. Despite his love of his own voice, he always made me feel like I was worth teaching. Made me want to do better—for him to be proud of me. He inspired me."

"And I don't. Is that what you are trying to say? I don't inspire Katherine?"

"No. Wait. Yes. I guess?"

"Will Arbor, you better explain yourself better than that!"

"Nadine, how were the young draoi—the duilleogs and craobhs—how were they taught before?"

Nadine grew quiet trying to remember the past. We continued to swing for a time and I heard Dog barking in the house before being told to 'shush' by Katherine. They were a pair, Dog and Katherine. She had a way with animals that was a marvel to see. It was her strength, I realised and felt a piece of the puzzle click in place.

I thought perhaps Nadine had forgotten the question when she finally responded, making me jump a little. The sun had maybe twenty minutes left before it disappeared over the horizon. "It was a long time ago but I remember it well. Sorry, I was remembering all the tricks and ways of teaching the draoi. It was a simple set-up to tell you the truth. Traditional and as old as the draoi themselves. We divided the draoi by sex. Girls in one class and boys in another. They learned differently, you see. Boys couldn't stay focused for long.

"First, they were taught traditions and lore. I taught the girls and sometimes the boys. We taught history, plant lore, rules of the powers. All academic topics. It was important to understand what the draoi were meant to be. How they were supposed to interact with the world."

"How did you do that without powers of your own?"

Nadine shot me a look. Surprise and anger mixed together.

"Nadine, no offence, you know that. I am trying to understand something. First, I need to understand how you taught the draoi before."

Nadine nodded and smiled an apology at me. "Sorry. Still sensitive, I suppose. To answer you, I had no practical method of teaching. I had the manuscript and the knowledge. I passed it on to the new draoi."

"That must have been hard for you. And for them."

"Well, yes. It was hard for me. It was hard to stay motivated to the subject when I knew I would never be able to use the power. Why do you think it was hard for them?"

"Did you resent them?"

"Who the students? No, never."

I turned and took her hands in mine. "Are you sure? It sounds like you were jealous of their power and yet you had to teach them. Perhaps?" I pushed love down our bond to lessen the hurt of the question.

"Perhaps. I don't know. I never thought so and never questioned myself about that."

"So the draoi were separated, taught by someone with no powers, no understanding of the challenges they faced in controlling those powers, and then felt jealousy from their teacher."

Nadine threw down my hands. "Will Arbor!" I sensed and saw the flare of her anger. I had hurt her, deeply. But I couldn't stop. I had to get this out in the open.

"When I was with Daukyns, he taught me that only those who truly had gained knowledge could teach that knowledge to others. It wasn't fair to you that they made you teach those draoi all those years ago. You were not in a position to help them. We can't do that again. We need skilled draoi teaching the others. Surely you can see that. It can never be a competition. This is important, Nadine. You and I are about to set the standard for future generations of draoi. We need to develop practical methods of teaching and standardise how we assess our students.

"I believe that Gaea provides powers unique to each individual she touches. You and I need to investigate that more. If it's true, and I think it is, then our teaching methods will need to be varied to the individual and like individuals. There can't be girl classes and boy classes. There need to be teachers unique to each skill set. Take Katherine for example."

"Katherine? What about her?"

"What is her speciality do you think?"

"Speciality? There are no specialities. All draoi have the same abilities. Some stronger than others, but the same. It is all part of the balance."

"No, Nadine. I don't... I can't believe that. It is about harmony. Harmony!"

"Harmony? Balance is harmony. We use our magic to affect the balance of the world. To keep it stable."

I took a deep breath. "Nadine, Katherine can work magic with animals. She understands them so deeply, so intimately. She knows intuitively what is wrong with them, what they need, how to provide their harmony. Watch her with Dog and the horses. Sense her through the bond. It's wonderful. Then watch her try to make sense of human interactions. She has no idea how to make sense of it. It is the blind spot of her power. We need to be able to recognise those strengths in the draoi and nurture them and *trust* them to apply their skills in the world. We aren't going to be teachers, we are going to be guides."

Nadine looked at me in wonder. "You can't mean that. Will, you've only just come into your power. How can you be sure of all that? The draoi have been teaching draoi for hundreds of years. Will, surely you see that the old ways were the best ways? Our magic is a miracle from Gaea. It has the power to change the world. We need to teach control of that power."

I shook my head. "Druid powers are nothing more than the application of the Word and its principals. Just because we don't understand how it works doesn't make it magic! The draoi need to move out into the world and be part of it. No more hiding in the shadows. We teach the draoi to gain confidence in their powers and strengths. We have to show people those powers and gain their trust."

"You want the draoi to expose themselves to the world? Oh, Will, that's what destroyed us! The Church hunted us down."

"No, it was your secrecy that destroyed you. If you had been part of the world—accepted by the world—the Church could never have wiped you out. Not again. When we come to strength, we will need to show the people of the Realm not to be afraid of magic and our powers. We must use it to bring harmony to the Realm. To restore order but by accepting all that is nature."

"You would willingly expose the draoi to the world?"

"Yes, Nadine I would and I will. I think that is exactly what Gaea wants. That and harmony."

"I don't understand. I heard Gaea speak to you about harmony. You pleased her. But how? For generations, the draoi have pursued balance. Why now? Why suddenly start speaking of harmony? Why abandon balance?"

"I have an idea about that." I truly did have an idea but, honestly, it frightened me more than a little. "First, I have an opinion about harmony and balance. They are different. Let me explain.

"Draoi have, for years, been willing to destroy one thing to provide balance to the whole. That is actually contrary to nature. Nature finds a way to let everything co-exist for the greater harmony. You have to accept those parts you don't like. The rabbits would love to see the foxes all disappear. But without the foxes, they would breed too much and eat all their food sources. They would die. They need to accept the harmony."

"I would call that balance, Will."

"You're missing the point. When people think of balance, they think of two objects of equal weight on a scale. This is the desired state. Symmetry. Balance. Equality. Harmony is something more. Harmony is how all parts of a system work together as a whole or as parts of a whole. If someone were to place a small weight on a scale, you would need to remove an equal weight from the other side in order to maintain that balance. You would need to be willing to give something up to maintain the balance. In the end, you are not likely to arrive at a system that brings any balance to your life or to nature.

"Imagine if in order to maintain balance you had to give up one of your children. The loss of the child brings balance but destroys the balance of your life. There is no harmony in that. Balance requires sacrifice. Harmony requires acceptance and adjustment.

"Nature is full of strife and challenges. Nature has learned to work through these challenges and accept them. With harmony, you must accept the good with the bad. Sometimes there is a sacrifice, but more often you merely adjust. It's okay that there may be more weight on one side of the scale than the other. Who says it has to be in balance perfectly? We should find a way to work around it. We pursue harmony instead and life should become that much more enjoyable."

The sun touched the horizon, and the shadows stretched before it.

"Nadine, I think Gaea started off thinking balance was the right path. After a time, she was sacrificing too much of herself and far too often. She seeks harmony now. She is willing to accept the bad with the good and find a way to co-exist. The draoi, for years, have been willing to destroy one thing to provide balance to a whole. This is contrary to nature. Nature finds a way to let everything co-exist for the greater harmony. You have to accept those parts you don't like. Gaea is learning that."

I stopped talking. I looked out over the fields and the setting sun.

"You speak of her like she is only just figuring out who she is."

"Yes, I am saying exactly that. I think Gaea is only as old as the draoi."

"You can't be serious!"

"I should clarify. I think the conscious Gaea is only as old as the draoi. That's what the humans did. Before she worked in silence. Unaware. Perfecting the harmony of the world. Then we woke her up. We did something. Something bad and we have been working to fix it ever since."

"Oh, Will. How can you possibly know that?"

"I just do, Nadine. I'm certain of it. We are all Gaea, Nadine. You, me, the draoi, the non-draoi. All Gaea. What she knows, we know. We just don't know it."

"Will Arbor, you are speaking nonsense now." Nadine moved closer to me. The part of her that remembered being an old woman feared the cold of the night and she automatically came to me for warmth. I thought the evening pleasantly cool. The Fall was fast approaching. With the Fall came change. Something was coming this way. Something terrible. I shivered and Nadine hugged me tighter.

Nadine waited until Will's breathing slowed and a soft snore escaped his mouth. She stared at the man she loved and wondered how she had arrived here. Her life had been full and almost complete. Death had not been that far away, and she had almost come to terms with it. She had expected it any day in Jergen when she had felt her heart first falter and knew it was weakened. The simplest of activities had her heart thumping painfully in her chest. It had been only a matter of time.

Now, Gaea had returned her to a youthful body, and she preened with the joy it gave her to simply be able to move around freely without pain. With her youth came a fierce appetite to love and be loved. And now she lay in bed with an eighteen-year-old man who was her husband. A man she loved so strongly that the fear of losing him froze the blood in her veins. She would do anything for him to make him look at her just once more with that look of love in his eyes in return. Her heart swelled at the site of it. *I've become a moonstruck girl*, she thought with amusement. *My life of hardship has almost been worth it to arrive here at this moment.*

She gave Will a long look and stopped herself from reaching over to pull his hair back from his face. *He needs a haircut*, she thought. She sighed and slipped out of the bed and crept to the door. She loved her new mobility. One day, she knew with certainty, the arthritis would return. She dreaded that day but was determined to enjoy this stolen new life of hers. She reached the stairs and slipped quietly down them. Her new mobility was a constant wonder. Sometimes she wanted to jump and spin and throw her head and arms back and laugh. *Truth be told*, she admitted to herself, *I love more how my hormones rage inside me again and make me emotional and craving the touch of my man.* She wanted to scream for joy and never stop screaming.

As always the negative followed the positive. The guilt she felt for those before her that fell to the Purge tore at her. *Who was I to have escaped their fate? What made me so special? Why should I have a second life of youth while the others rot in shallow graves across the Realm?* She shuddered and stopped in the kitchen. She pushed the thoughts aside. The guilt was too much to bear at times. She had to push it away.

Nadine found her shawl on the back of a chair in the kitchen. She wrapped it around her shoulders and stopped by the front room. Agnes was awake. It was why Nadine was sneaking through the dark of the house. Nadine could sense she was awake from upstairs in the bedroom and decided she needed to speak to her. *There's no one else*, she thought. *No one else that can understand a woman of my age. Someone who faces death.*

She stopped at the entranceway and called out quietly. "Agnes, it's me, Nadine." She stepped into the front room and saw the dim form of Agnes sitting up in her makeshift bed.

"Oh dear, you frightened me," said Agnes with a hand held to her chest.

"No, I did not. You heard me thump down the stairs and followed me through the house with your ears. You forget I am a druid with powers now."

Agnes held the pose for a moment and then dropped her hand and chuckled. "Guilty. Come over and sit with me."

Nadine walked over to the chair by the couch and sank into it, wrapping her shawl more tightly around her. She reached out with her senses and felt the ravages of Agnes' disease. As Will had done, Nadine eased the pain and wished she could do more, but her disease was far too advanced. She and Will couldn't see the exact problem and couldn't fix it. It lay too deep within her and beyond their ken. Unaware, Agnes fumbled at something between her and the couch and pulled out a metal flask. She unscrewed the cap and took a swig and offered it to Nadine. Nadine took it, sniffed the opening and took a swallow. "Hmm. Cala whisky. Lovely. I haven't had that in years." Nadine passed it back.

Agnes frowned. "It is so strange to hear you speak like that with a face as young as yours. I keep forgetting."

"Hmm. Well, I'm actually older than you. I've lived an entire lifetime before Gaea saw fit to restart it. I need you to see me as that old woman. It would help if you could tonight."

"How's that? What's wrong?"

"I'm torn. Will spoke to me tonight about the future. I thought we would march together hand in hand and equally minded. Now I am not so sure. I don't understand where he is going and why. I am a sixty-year-old woman in here," Nadine tapped her head. "But a child in my heart. It would help to hear your thoughts. The thoughts of a woman who's lived a lifetime, too."

"I'm only forty-five and I thought you were sixty-seven."

"Hmm, well who counts the years?"

Agnes chuckled. "When I close my eyes, I can hear the older woman inside you. So don't mind me, I'm keeping my eyes closed. Tell me, get it out."

"I love him."

"Yes, we can all see that. It's a little cloy, to be honest. Like too much honey in your tea."

"It's more than that, Agnes. It frightens me. Gaea said that what we have is a rarity. I'm so scared to lose it. To ruin it. To lose him. To not be able to follow where he is running so very quickly. I am the Cill Darae. Gaea named me. But I feel like the child next to the parent. Unqualified. Uncertain. Will, he is so sure of himself. So confident."

Agnes said nothing.

"You know what he said to me the other day? He said 'I wish I was more like you. You are so sure of yourself. So strong.' I almost broke down right in front of him. He didn't know what he did wrong and just made things worse. I had to push him out of the room and find a new centre to myself. I'm lost, Agnes."

"You were never married, were you? In all those sixty-odd years."

"No."

"Or had a boyfriend. You kept to yourself in that house in Jergen. Hiding from the world."

"Yes, I suppose that's true."

"You have no idea what it is to have a relationship, my dear. It isn't you and him. You aren't two people anymore. You are a team. You will each have your strengths and your weaknesses. Learn them. Support each other. Accept that Will will be stronger at some things and that you are stronger in others. It will come in time. Trust me in this."

Nadine grew quiet for a time. Her emotions pulled at her until, to her shame, she started to softly cry.

"Oh hush, girl. You'd think a woman of your advanced years wouldn't cry."

Nadine sniffed, and wiped at her tears, and forced a laugh. "Yes, well I also didn't have all these hormones either. Dear Gaea, I forgot all about these damn things. Getting back my moon flow was a disappointment as well. I didn't miss that. And the cramps."

Agnes shared the laugh and then passed the flask back to Nadine. Nadine took a swig and handed it back. "So, what's really on your mind, Nadine?"

"Ah, see? This is why I wanted to speak with you. We women, we understand these things. Men, boys and girls are just stupid when it comes to social graces and awareness."

"Hmm. Some women stay oblivious too."

"I suppose. Were you a very good archer?"

If Agnes wondered at the subject change she didn't show it. "Yes, I was. One of the best. It's what captured Ben's attention. And Steve's, unfortunately. But, I loved archery. I rarely missed. I had a knack for it."

"That must've been hard. Sleeping with Steve to bear a child that would not be Ben's."

Agnes stirred for a moment. "You have no idea. I liked Steve. But, it was all work with that one. Ben was a hard, hard man, like Steve, but Ben had a soft side that Steve didn't. I needed both in a man. Ben was always my favourite. I loved how silly he could be. He made me laugh so hard I peed myself more than once. Nothing says 'marry that one' than having pee run down your leg. But I guess I had a thing for Steve, too. I loved his unwavering determination. He knew what was right and drove the crew toward it. You couldn't help but follow a man like that. I swear if I could have merged the two into one it would have been perfect." Agnes sighed.

"I think Ben and I were one of those rarities that Gaea spoke to you of. We joined to make a team Ben and I. Steve was a trophy of sorts for me. Something to conquer but not hold on to. He oozed confidence. I wanted that. If only for a moment. Ben and I talked about children after the accident. Ben wanted children with me so desperately. Now that he was unable, well, it consumed him. You always want what you can't have, I suppose. He came up with the idea of asking Steve. Proposed it. It didn't happen right away. It was bloody awkward. Taboo. Whatever. In the end, Steve and I accepted and then we were fucking every day I was ovulating. I hated it. I cried and cried. I wish it had taken at once. But it took a couple of months of trying. It was so hard on Ben." Agnes plucked at her blanket.

"It was worse for Steve. He left as soon as I quickened. Bolted actually. He couldn't look at Ben anymore. It destroyed him. Ben endured. It strained us but then we heard those cries! The cries of Katherine when she was born. It was a panacea! Ben and I never looked back. I insisted Steve come and see his daughter. He did. He looked at her. Held her once and left.

"So I made the right choice, didn't I? I ask myself every day whether Steve would be here by my side while this disease eats me away. I hear the answer in my heart as loud as my own voice. I know Ben will be. Steve... I'm not so sure. He would have resented it. Hated that he couldn't fight it. I made the right choice, my heart did. No regrets except it pains me that I must leave Ben one day. He doesn't deserve that. I'm thankful that you and your husband will give me a few more months with Ben and our daughter."

Nadine held out her hand and Agnes gave her the flask. She took a deep swallow and handed it back. Agnes took a drink and slowly screwed the cap back on.

"For men it's easy, isn't it," said Nadine. "They come, they leave. It's women who bear the weight of the world. Gaea is a woman. Not surprising, really."

Agnes turned a sharp look to Nadine. "Nonsense. Men have it just as hard as women. Never think they have it easy. Men and women have their own challenges. What's important is that we work together for a common future. Sometimes giving up something for the other. That's marriage. There has to be a sacrifice, at times, I won't deny that. But no marriage can remain in harmony if you are always looking for balance. It is what it is. Life is life. It finds a way."

Somewhere in the house, a clock rang three bells. Nadine turned her ears to the sound. She hadn't heard the clock before. "Thank you, Agnes."

"You're welcome Nadine. Now go to bed and back to that man of yours. Maybe wake him up, eh? Put those hormones to use."

Twenty-One

Jaipers, 900 A.C.

BRENT RUSHED TO the barracks with his ceremonial sword in hand. *The wrong weapon at the wrong time*, he thought and cursed it. Matching his sprint were James, Gendred and Comlin. The cries from up ahead were loud in the afternoon. Villagers were standing on the street and staring over the tops of buildings to the black smoke rising thick in the air in the distance. Shops and houses opened and people ran out into the street looking scared and crying the alarm.

Gendred yelled at them as they ran past. "Back into your homes! Off the streets!"

The people ignored him and some ran after them. Comlin joined the garrison captain's cries. "People! Hide in your homes! Off the street!" This stopped a few of them.

James drew alongside Brent and pulled his sword free. It, too, was ceremonial. "Our weapons, sir. They're with our equipment. These swords are almost useless!"

Brent spared a glance at James and grimaced. "I know. It will have to do. Whatever we find up ahead we need to rally our men. If they are being attacked, they need our leadership." Brent ran out of breath and focused on sprinting.

They rounded the Woven Bail Inn and Brent saw mayhem before him. The barracks and garrison buildings were fully engulfed with the flames that reached at least twenty feet into the air. Thick black smoke poured into the sky and obscured the field. The gaol door was smashed open and two figures were pushing inside. The chest held little concern for Brent. His immediate concern was the fighting in the square. His men, fighting alongside garrison men, clashed openly with other garrison men. Grimly, he could see that, of his men, only those that were armed were still standing and fighting. Everywhere lay bodies, unarmed and bleeding out on the ground. Captain Mayer was down and holding his upper thigh; heart blood spraying through his fingers. Horses lay bleeding or dead on the ground, hacked and butchered; their cries more horrendous than anything else. Amongst the fighters were men he did not recognise. They wore black boots and moved with an exceptional fighting skill; weaving in and out of the fighting and slashing at will with long sharp and pointed daggers gleaming red with blood. There was no order. The square was a full out melee and mayhem.

"To me!" screamed Brent and brandished his sword. His men looked to his cry and moved to disengage and join their General. James positioned himself to Brent's left and together they hit the attacking garrison men from behind.

Brent thrust low with his sabre. His sword was useless as a striking weapon. It barely carried an edge, but the point worked just fine. He took the man on the right side and drove the point through his kidney. The man threw his arms up in pain and Brent watched Corporal Ian finish him with a slash across the throat. Heart blood sprayed across him and Brent withdrew his sword. The man fell to the ground grasping at his throat. Brent watched the man's sword clatter to the ground but had no time to grab for it.

James drove his sword into the back of the man in front of him. The man spasmed and twisted. The snap of James' sword was loud despite the screaming that filled the square. James dropped the half of the sword in his hands and reached over his opponent and plucked his longsword from his hand. Brent was impressed; it was smoothly done.

Brent's men were backing up toward him, parrying and stepping carefully. They were exhausted and most carried wounds. A rallying cry came from Gendred and his men looked quickly to find the source. Brent spared a glance to his right and saw Comlin with a long dagger standing next to Gendred. They worked as a team and kept Brent's right flank protected.

Brent looked around the square. He had six men remaining, armed and still fighting. The garrison men still fighting for Jaipers numbered only eight. Opposing them were fifteen garrison men and ten of the men in black boots.

Two more men in black boots emerged from the gaol and moved to join the others. On the ground, men cried in agony holding wounds, but they were outnumbered by men who would move and cry no more. It was a slaughter. The barrack's roof collapsed and flames and sparks erupted into the air with a roar. Many ducked reflexively and looked over at the flames shooting in the air. The fire bathed the square in heat and made the figures on the ground writhe. Brent's men used the distraction to form a loose line.

This makes no sense, thought Brent. *What is happening? Why now? Dear Lord, I beg you, help us!*

Brent yelled in his best parade voice. "To me! Defensive positions!"

His cry was followed by a voice carrying an unearthly power. "Form up!" A man emerged from the gaol. His image was blurred, hidden from sight. Brent tried to focus on it and failed. The order from this strange figure caused the traitors to disengage from his men. An uneasy break in the action occurred.

Brent felt a pinch on his chest where the medallion from the Cathedral of Jergen lay against his breast. His vision blurred for a second and suddenly the man who had emerged from the gaol came into sharp focus. It was Seth Farlow, grinning and walking with confidence. Brent watched him fall in behind his men and then stand watching his men separate and form an opposing line. He carried a small crossbow in his right hand. Brent recalled the conversation in the Cathedral in Jergen. *He warned me about Seth. Warned me and I failed to heed it.*

The men split into two factions. His men and those of the garrison fighting for the town formed up in a single rank to his left and right. Across the square, with the burning barracks and garrison building behind them, the garrison traitors and men in black boots formed up against them. Brent looked at his men. They breathed with labour and many held hands to open wounds. Eighteen men against their twenty-seven. All the men trained in delivering violence, but only half his men carried swords, the others mere daggers. The opponents were all well-armed with swords. It had been an ambush. His men caught transitioning into the barracks. Storing equipment. Relaxing their guard.

"Seth Farlow! I see you!" yelled Brent across the twenty feet separating the lines. Seth looked surprised and scowled.

"General Brent Bairstow, you are siding with demons. Join me. Join the Lord."

"Demons? Have you lost your mind? You killed my men!" Brent reached up to his neck and pulled free the medallion and held it before him. "I am a man of

God. Acting on his behalf to secure this Realm from evil and men like you."
Brent saw the men in black boots look surprised and glance back at Seth.

"Demons can carry any symbol to deceive and sway the Lord's children
from His ways. You have been deceived. Your oath to the Realm demands you
punish those who work against it. Those men with you, they knowingly sided
with demons and aided them. I ask you one last time: join the Church of the
New Order or die. The Lord's punishment is swift and just."

Brent could not believe what he was hearing. The man was insane.
Demons? What was he talking about? He looked over to Comlin and saw him
thinking. He hissed over to him. "What is he talking about?"

Comlin shook his head. "He's insane. The black boots. The man who killed
Bill wore a pair. They're assassins."

Brent snapped back to Seth. "Seth Farlow, you have no jurisdiction here. I
am the General of the Lord Protector's Guard on a mission here in Jaipers.
Standing before you is the Captain of the Jaipers Garrison and the Reeve of
Jaipers. We are the only authority here in Jaipers. We represent the Realm. You
represent treason. Treason by the Church of the New Order. You have killed
men sworn to defend this nation. You have raised weapons against the laws
and order of the Realm. Stand down and surrender. Your trials will be swift and
just, I promise you that. You have my word."

Seth smiled. "There is only one law in the Realm. The Law of the Lord.
Suffer no demon to live." Seth whipped his crossbow up and fired the bolt. It
hissed through the air and took Captain Gendred in the throat. Gendred
dropped his sword and collapsed to his knees and grasped the bolt shaft. He
sucked in a wet breath and blood bubbled around the shaft. Comlin cried out
and knelt to his side.

"Attack!" screeched Seth. "For the Lord!" His men growled and raced
across the square.

"Hold the line!" yelled James, and the men clashed.

Brent met the man in front of him. He wore black boots and black leathers.
His eyes were wild, but whether lost in bliss or anger, Brent couldn't tell. He
carried a long thin dagger that glinted in the afternoon sun. Brent watched the
feet and the dagger arm. He cleared his mind and relaxed into his training. A
sword, even a ceremonial one, had a longer reach than a man with a dagger. It
gave him an advantage. Brent feinted. The man ignored it and moved to close.
Brent reached to the small of his back and pulled his dagger free. The man
moved inside his sword and then looked down and blinked. Brent had buried
his dagger up under his rib cage and into the man's heart. Brent twisted the

dagger and pulled it free. He twisted left and moved a step past the dying man and parried a sword strike from another garrison traitor.

For a time, there was nothing except his opponents and staying alive. *Sword fights are always quick*, thought Brent. There is a feint, maybe a parry, but almost always a quick strike. The idea was to be the first to strike. The man in front of Brent fought to bring his sword back in position and grunted once as Brent slashed his throat with his dagger. It wasn't a perfect slash, but it was enough to open one side of his throat. Brent ducked the heart blood spray and stepped back to maintain the line.

He looked right and saw Comlin fighting a black boot. Beyond the line, men moved to flank them. He looked left and saw James strike down a garrison traitor and step back to the line. Beyond the line and to the left, men moved to flank them.

"Circle formation! Move!" cried Brent. His men reacted and pulled the garrison men with them. They were too slow, too much confusion, and two of his men went down. The ringing of swords and the gasping of breath were the only sounds. Men struck down had not yet had a chance to scream in pain.

"Left side move quickly we're being flanked!" yelled James.

"For the Realm!" cried Comlin with a voice that spoke from experience. *He is a fighting man*, thought Brent. *Much more than a simple Reeve. Perhaps there is hope for us.*

Brent caught a swift movement in the corner of his eye. It was Seth, moving at an inhuman speed. He moved beyond his field of view and Brent lost him. He swivelled his head to find him and his head exploded with pain and light. *He got behind me somehow. No helmet, that was stupid of me...*

Brent awoke with a massive headache. He was sitting up with his upper arms tied to something behind him. His hands were tied together and on his lap. His legs were extended straight out and tied at the knees and feet. He was naked and sitting on the ground. He moved his head and nausea flooded him and he threw up in his lap. The pain in his head doubled, and he blacked out again.

He woke under a deluge of water. Water had been thrown in his face and he gasped to breathe. He blinked his eyes open and saw a man in black boots standing in front of him holding an empty bucket.

"Wha-what?" he croaked, his headache bounced around inside his skull and he groaned.

The man stepped back, and another stepped in his place. Seth Farlow looked down at Brent without expression. Brent looked around and saw he was tied up sitting on the ground. At his back, he could just make out James and Comlin. They were awake and tied together, James on his left and Comlin to his right. They were all naked sitting trussed together inside a large rectangular building. It was night beyond the windows. Benches were piled up on one side. Near them was a long table, with whatever on it hidden from their view, except for the large lantern that was providing the light. Two other men were in the room. Both wearing black boots. The one with the bucket set it down and joined his companion on the other side of the table.

"Good evening, General. I was worried you wouldn't wake."

Brent tried to focus on Seth but his face swam. *Concussion,* thought Brent. *Bad.* "Fuck off, traitor."

Seth calmly slapped Brent with surprising speed. It rocked his head back, and he clunked the back of James' and Comlin's heads.

"Ow," complained James.

"Silence," said Seth in a monotone. "General, you are going to answer some questions for me. How you answer those question will determine what happens next."

"Sorry, I don't think you heard me the first time. Fuck off."

Seth merely looked back at Brent for a moment and then rose and moved silently to the table. He stood before it with his left side to Brent. Brent watched as he reached out to the table and lifted a steel tool of some kind. It looked like a pair of scissors but with a small blade to it. *Exactly like a pruner for flowers,* thought Brent and its purpose dawned on him.

Seth stepped back to Brent and squatted before him and held up the pruner and twisted it. "See this?" he said. "With this, I can remove parts of your body. Fingers, toes, your nose. Understand?"

Brent nodded and swallowed.

"I can also remove your manhood. That usually works the best for quick results. The bad news is that I am not in a hurry. I have time to enjoy this. Draw it out. With the three of you. The night is young and quite frankly I am more than a little bit excited. It's been a long time since I got to enjoy my profession. I may be a little rusty, but I'm sure you'll forgive me. My brethren behind me need to practice. I'm going to start but they will have a chance to work on you before we are done. Education is important, don't you think?"

Brent kept his eye on the pruner as it twisted in front of him.

"I asked you a question, General. I expect a response when I ask a question."

"Yes."

"Yes, what?"

"Yes... sir?"

Seth cracked Brent's forehead with the pruner and light burst behind his eyes. The strike had been too quick to follow. He wasn't human. Nobody can move that quickly. "No, idiot. I asked you about education. It's important, no?"

"Yes, it's important." Brent closed his eyes against the pain of his forehead. A gentle slap on his cheek had him open his eyes to see Seth glaring into them.

"Keep your eyes open. You need to pay attention. I have some simple questions for you."

Brent kept quiet.

"Why are you here?"

Brent shook his head and pressed his lips closed.

Seth slowly shook his head. Disappointment marked his features. "Interesting choice. Let me describe to you a series of events. First, I am going to grab the little finger of your left hand. You are going to think '*he won't do it—he's only pretending*'. But then I will place the cold steel of the jaws of this marvellous device around the upper knuckle of that little finger and I will apply pressure. A pressure you will feel as pain. It won't be a real pain. Not yet. But you will imagine it as pain. And then I will slowly increase that pressure. The real pain will start. You will watch as the blades start to separate the flesh. You will feel the blades reach the bone. Blood will well around the blades. A lot of blood. You will think '*he's really doing it*'. The pressure will continue to build until you hear a sharp little *snick* sound and the tip of your pinkie will separate from your finger. It may fly through the air. Sometimes they do. I like it when they do that. We measure the distance. We keep accurate records of our efforts. It helps future generations. We're back to that education question, you see?

"At this point, you will scream. The pain will be very real but it is the horror of what just happened to your body that will make you scream the most. A piece of you will be gone. Gone forever. Never to be replaced. That will cause you no end of distress. Through that pain and distress, I will ask you the same question. The same question that you refused to answer that resulted in the loss of a part of you. You will wonder why you didn't answer it the first time and you will answer this time. Because it is a simple question and not worth losing a part of yourself over. So, General. I will ask one more time. This is the last time I will repeat a question without first removing a piece of you—or from one of your friends. So I want you to think for a little about that before I ask you again. You can talk to your friends. See what they have to say."

Seth stood up and moved over to his men. They spoke in whispers and Brent strained to hear them but couldn't. He was very afraid. He saw no way out of this. He was trapped like an animal and with a man who was clearly mad and possessing powers beyond his understanding. He had been cloaked from sight during the fight and had moved faster than was possible. Brent didn't understand what was happening. The movements of James and the Reeve focused his thoughts.

"James, are you okay?"

"Yes, sir. I was knocked out and woke up here."

"Same," said Comlin.

"He moves faster than anyone I've ever seen before."

"Yes," said Comlin. "He's using magic. I accused him of it and he reacted poorly. Said it was God's power and not magic. He's insane. Completely."

"What did he do to you?" asked Brent.

"Nothing. He just shouted at me. Then he calmed down. He just went quiet. You woke up then—the first time. It distracted him from me."

"Our men?"

"Gone, sir," said James. "We were slaughtered. Too many of them. All dead. I was the last to fall. I didn't expect to wake."

"It's the Church of the New Order and the Archbishop behind this," said Brent.

"Yes, so it appears," asked James.

"I was warned. In Jergen."

"Warned by who?"

"A dead man," said Brent.

"A what?"

"Long story, I'll tell you when we get out of here."

"Always stay positive," said Comlin. "Works for me."

Brent's opinion of the Reeve went up a notch.

Seth returned and crouched down in front of Brent. "Okay. Let's start again. Why are you here?"

Brent hesitated only for a moment. He would tell this man anything he wanted to hear. There was no point in trying to hide anything. Torture always works. He had to stay alive to escape this and bring this man to justice. Until then he would tell them anything they wanted to hear. His brother and he had debated this concept one day over too much wine. Frederick felt a man should die with his secrets. "Resist for the Realm," he had said. *It was all bullshit,* thought Brent. The only thing that would still his tongue was if it would result in the death of others. That was worth dying for. *Not secrets. Secrets are crap,* he thought.

"We are here to retrieve the belongings of Bill Burstone."

Seth smiled. "That wasn't so hard, was it?"

Brent glared at him.

"Next question. Who sent you?"

"The Lord Protector."

"Why you?"

Brent opened his mouth to speak and then closed it and thought for a moment. "He sent me to fail."

"Fail? Why?"

"He wants me removed. Killed on the road."

"Why does he dislike you so?"

"Because I do my job."

"You don't like the Lord Protector? The man you are sworn to protect?"

"No. But I will protect him. That is my duty."

"Explain the chest. Where did it come from?"

Brent looked at Seth appraisingly. "You know that already. Munsten. From the treasury."

Seth slowly nodded. His nose flared slightly but that was all. He kept his emotions in check. *Much like the Archbishop*, he thought. *They are a pair.*

"Bill Redgrave. He stole it from the Lord Protector."

"Is that a question?" said Brent and regretted it. Seth grabbed his left hand and pried the pinkie away from the other fingers and held it. "Sorry!" cried Brent. Seth placed the blades of the pruner just behind the first knuckle of his pinkie. He smiled and applied pressure to the pruner handles. Brent watched the blade start to cut the skin and pain shot up his arm and he screamed. "No! Don't!" Slowly the blade cut through the skin and blood poured out of the wound. The pressure continued until Seth paused at the bone. Seth looked into Brent's face and with a sharp *snick* the end of his pinkie flew off and landed a few feet away. Brent stared and screamed in horror at the damaged finger. Heart blood pumped in a long stream from the finger. *Dear Lord, help me*, he prayed.

One of the men behind Seth came forward and pressed a red-hot tool against the stump. Steam and smoke billowed from the stump and burning pain cut off Brent's voice. His head and vision spun. He caught a glimpse of a gleaming black figure standing quietly behind the two Sect members and he blacked out.

He woke to another deluge of water from the bucket. He gasped and looked around. Pain rose in waves from his finger in time to his heartbeat. *So much pain.* He looked at his disfigured hand and the remains of his pinkie finger. They had cauterised the wound to stop the bleeding, and it was now blackened and bright red. His blood lay soaking into the dirt floor and he followed it to see the tip of his pinkie lying on the ground. *This can't be happening.* Seth moved into his vision and smiled at him.

"Three feet, two inches. Not a record, I'm sorry to report, but a respectable result. You should be proud."

"You're a monster!"

"No. I am a man of God. I do God's work. He has blessed me and told me personally I do his bidding. There can be nothing finer in this life than serving the Lord. You should know that. You were a man of God until you joined with the demons. You wore his mark around your neck. The amulet is over on the table. It is desecrated on the reverse with the demon mark. The same mark that was on the coin you sent to Bill Redgrave. Do you admit to sending the coin?"

"The coin?" Brent struggled to keep track of the conversation. He was afraid to lose more fingers. "Yes. It came across my desk the same time as Bill asked for it. I sent it to him. I saw no harm. It was a worthless coin and misshapen. It wasn't even gold."

"No harm? The coin is used by the demons to awaken their power. It is the catalyst that allows them to reach into Hell and pull power from the fire. They twist nature to their whims. They conduct unholy rituals and fornicate with animals! That coin was the last of them. We had been searching for it for years. And you sent the coin here. To a traitor of the Realm that you harboured."

"I didn't harbour him."

"Do not lie. I won't warn you again. You harboured him. You knew he was here. Why else would he reach out to you in Munsten?"

"He... I... It wasn't like that. You weren't there. You didn't see the horror of how he was singled out and abused by the Lord Protector. He was an innocent man. Innocent!" Brent felt the futility of trying to reason with Seth. The man's eyes were lit by feverish religious zealotry. He was beyond reason. "How did you know about the coin?"

Seth cracked him in the head with the pruner again. It was a solid hit and Brent cried out. "I ask the questions!" Seth moved to the table and moved some objects around on it. Brent watched in fear waiting to see what new tool was selected. But Seth kept the pruner in his hand and returned to crouch down in front of Brent. "I will humour you. Your man. The one who delivered the coin to you. He is a true believer. After he delivered the coin to you he came to us—the Church—and he told us about the find. He had discovered it lodged between the stones in his chambers." Seth smiled. "God works in mysterious ways. Did you know we have people everywhere in the Realm now? In every town and every city? Coast to coast. There is nothing that we do not see or hear."

"I don't believe you. The Church is almost gone and has no power in the Realm. We hide ourselves and our faith."

Seth raised a single eyebrow. "Not so. But no matter. We tried to get the coin before it left Munsten but we were too late. We missed the courier but discovered the destination. We tried to retrieve it. We sent our best men. One of them our top assassin."

Seth rose and walked in front of the Reeve. Brent twisted his head to keep an eye on Seth. Seth grasped Comlin by the jaw and forced his head back. An excited gleam came to Seth's eyes. "And he was killed by this man. Your death will not be painless, Reeve Comlin, I promise you that." Seth jerked the Reeve's head out of his grasp and came back to crouch in front of Brent. "The evil of the demons was at play and the coin ended up in the hands of the last of the demons. The Target. The coin sought him out and woke his power. So you see, it all comes back to you, General. You unleashed evil back into the Realm. You are a traitor to the Realm. More importantly, you are a traitor to God. You will burn in Hell for this."

Brent had no reply to that. He didn't believe in demons. He believed in God and he believed men could be evil. But, not it demons, never that. It sounded like children's tales to him. Brent looked for the black figure he had seen but it was gone. He looked at Seth's face. Twisted within by an evil he couldn't see. *This insane man thought he knew God. He was a fool, lost in his insanity. God is about mercy, love and forgiveness.* "I was warned about you," said Brent.

"Warned? By who?"

"By God. In the Cathedral of Jergen. He gave me that amulet," Brent recalled the peace in the cathedral and found an inner strength. "Tell me, Seth Farlow, do you have Faith?"

"You lie! God does not speak to the likes of you. The Cathedral in Jergen is our most sacred location. God would not speak to someone who associates with demons! Demons have corrupted your soul!" Seth grabbed the damaged pinkie and forced it back to almost the breaking point. Brent cried out. Fear bubbled inside of him and he reached out to God and prayed for strength.

He fought to keep control of his thoughts. Reason would see him through this. Brent could see and hear that Seth was getting worked up. He had to push him beyond rational thought. He had to gain the upper hand. He spoke quickly. "I have Faith, Seth Farlow. I am a true believer in God," His voice was clenched with pain but he forced the words out. "I believe His words and heed them. The Seven Tenets of God rule my life. I sit here naked on the dirt and trust in God. I am defenceless and unarmed and yet I trust that He will protect me and deliver me from evil. Do you follow the Tenets?"

"Who are you to tell me what is faith and what is not? I am the head of the Sect of the Church of the New Order. God speaks to me directly. I commune with the Archbishop!"

Brent swallowed and forced himself to talk calmly and directly to Seth. "The first tenant is 'strive to act with compassion and empathy toward all creatures in accordance with reason'. I see no reason here. Do you recall the fourth tenant?"

Seth's face grew red.

"The fourth tenant is 'the freedoms of others should be respected, including the freedom to offend. To wilfully and unjustly encroach upon the freedoms of another is to forego your own'. You are not respecting my freedom or my friends."

Seth growled and lowered the pruner to his pinkie and closed the blades on the second knuckle. Brent shuddered and decided then to completely trust his Faith in God. He surrendered his life to God.

"The seventh tenant is my favourite. God tells us 'every tenant is a guiding principle designed to inspire nobility in action and thought. The spirit of compassion, wisdom, and justice should always prevail over the written or the spoken word'. You have no compassion. You work without wisdom." Brent was speaking calmly and clearly to Seth now. The words were right, and they needed to be said. *I trust in you Lord. My life is yours.* "Your justice is a twisted corrupt perversion of what you desire. Your own carnal delights. It is *you* that is the demon! Can you not see that?"

A *snick* sound was loud in the room and Seth leered in Brent's face. Brent looked calmly back at Seth. Seth looked from Brent to the pinkie and cried out. Brent looked over and saw the second segment of his pinkie lying next to the first. Fresh blood soaked the ground. He looked at his finger and saw that it was whole. His pinkie stood pristine. He could feel Seth's grip on it.

Seth screamed in a rage and brought the pruner back to the second knuckle and snipped the end of the pinkie off. It flew through the air falling short of the other two pieces. Blood spurted through the air and Seth made a noise of joy that quickly turned to a cry of dismay. Brent looked down and saw his pinkie remained whole. Seth scrambled on his hands and knees to the pieces of finger lying in the dirt and cradled them.

"How?"

Brent felt removed from the room. He felt as if he was floating. He felt no pain. His headache cleared and with it gone, clarity returned. He felt reborn with unlimited energy and potential. He smiled. *God watches over me.* The room seemed brighter, and he looked around, bewildered. The two men on the other side of the table were staring at him in fear. The strange light lit them up, and they blinked and shielded their eyes with their hands. Behind them, a lone black figure turned and ran. *It's me, I'm the one making that light*, realised Brent. *Like a beacon.*

He heard a high-pitched cry and the ropes binding him writhed and fell free of him and burst into flame before being consumed in a flash of heat and smoke. The cry cut off. He lifted his arms and examined them. Seth looked up in horror, still holding the remains of Brent's finger. The room grew brighter and Seth's men cried out and fled, leaving Seth behind. Seth scrambled away from him, dropped the finger pieces, and pointed at him.

"Your forehead! It can't be!" Seth cried out and jerked to his feet and ran from the building crying for help.

Brent turned to see Comlin and James standing and staring at him with open mouths. The light coming from him lit them up, and they blinked. Their ropes were gone, and they rubbed their wrists. "What?" he asked.

"Do you know you have the symbol of the Church of the New Order on your forehead?" said Comlin.

Brent reached up and touched his forehead and felt nothing. The light in the room flickered. "I do?"

"Yes," added James. "And, it's kind of glowing. A lot."

Brent swivelled his head, and the light tracked with it. He reached up to touch his forehead again. He felt nothing. No heat and no flame. The light flickered once and then was gone. The room seemed dark with just the one lantern lighting it. Cries were heard outside, and the men turned to look at each other.

"We need to leave. Now," ordered Brent.

"Follow me," said Comlin and started toward the door.

Brent grabbed his arm and stopped him. "Take me to Bill's house first. I want his armour and sword."

Comlin looked at him for a moment and then nodded. "Good idea and worth the risk. We'll need armour and weapons if we are to survive this. Plus, we're naked."

Comlin started toward a back door but Brent stopped at the table and looked down. Lying next to the lantern was his amulet. He reclaimed it and put it around his neck. *Thank you, Lord*, he prayed. He looked for the black figure but it was gone. He shuddered.

Brent nodded to Comlin, and they followed him out the back door and into the dark streets of Jaipers. Over to the left men were pouring out of the Woven Bail Inn. They wore armour and carried swords. They were Seth's men. Comlin kept them to the shadows.

"Follow me closely," said Comlin. "They won't see us. Not in my town."

Twenty-Two

Jaipers, 900 A.C.

OMLIN LED THEM quickly through the deserted town and Brent was impressed with his skills. Armed men were running down the streets and looking into alleyways searching for them. Somehow Comlin kept them from sight until they reached the small but pristine home of Bill Redgrave and entered through the back door. They stood in the dark kitchen. James kept an eye on the backyard by the door.

Comlin pulled Brent in close and whispered in his ear. "I'll leave you here and take James to my house for gear."

"What?" said Brent. "That's too risky. We stay together."

"If you think I am leaving this town without my own gear, you are mistaken. It will take you time to get suited up. During that time, James and I can be to my house and back again."

James interrupted before an argument broke out. "Sir, we will survive better with armour and weapons. He's right. We'll be fine. Where do we meet?"

Comlin answered. "We'll come back here. Then head to the docks. I have a friend who runs a barge down the river. We can escape with him. He's planning on leaving tomorrow morning. Hopefully, he will agree to hide us."

"Hopefully? That doesn't sound reassuring," snapped Brent.

"You have a better plan? Trust me. I've spent my whole life planning for contingencies. This is just one more. I'm not worried. The captain of the barge owes me. We'll be back in no time. I'll make this noise when I return." Comlin made a strange bird noise and then disappeared out the back with James following close behind.

Brent cursed but waited and listened for cries that they were discovered. When it remained quiet, he crept up the stairs to the study. He closed the door in the dark and found a thick candle on the desk. He struck a spark with the lighter and lit the candle. He placed the candle back on the desk and turned to the armour tree in the corner. The field plate gleamed in the candlelight and he could see his reflection in it. The sword hung almost as if it had just been placed there.

He reached up and touched his forehead but felt nothing. His reflection looked normal. He held out his hand and looked at his pinkie. Right away he could see that it was a new pinkie. His hard-earned calluses were missing from it. It was pink and lacked the tan of his other fingers. *Strange, it's as if it had suddenly grown back. Thank you, Lord,* he thought reverently.

Brent crouched down in front of the small chest in front of the armour tree. He opened it and coughed against the fumes of mothballs. Inside were a neatly folded gambeson, leather gauntlets with metal plates at the back of the hands, a surcoat, armour oil, wire brushes and rags. "Thank you, Bill," he whispered to his friend's memory and pulled the gambeson out of the chest and threw it on with practised ease. It felt good to not be naked. He felt less exposed and vulnerable.

He examined the field plate. It was a mix of a waist-hauberk, thin-hammered steel plates, and boiled leather. Plates covered the chest, shoulders and back, chain across the abdomen, and leather for the remaining areas. Plates also adorned the forearms and the area of the lower back covering the kidneys. It was beautifully crafted. All the plates were engraved with ornate scrollwork. The rank insignia for Knight General was engraved on small steel ailettes at the shoulders and worked with gold leaf. Brent could see that it was well oiled and cared for. The leather was hard but not cracked or dried. Like most field plate, nothing covered his legs. This armour was for field work and allowed maximum movement with maximum shielding. It weighed half what a full hauberk would. Brent could wear it and move easily enough. It was a useful artisan blend and Brent was pleased. *I don't know how you managed to get your old armour out of Munsten and down here to Jaipers, but I am glad you did, old friend. Thank you.*

He dressed quickly using tricks he had learned over the year. Tricks to attach pieces to the gambeson he normally would need a squire's help with. He took out the surcoat and shook off the mothball fragments. It was a formal surcoat and not one that Brent could wear in public without drawing everyone's attention. He was about to lay it aside when he noticed the inside was brown drab. He turned it inside out and smiled. *Reversible, how smart*, he thought and threw it over the armour. Finally, he stood in the study fully fitted out in armour and he felt calmer and more in control. He rolled his shoulders and flexed his arms and it felt right. The surcoat hid the quality of the armour nicely.

He took the hand-and-a-half sword—often referred to as a bastard sword by his men—down from the armour tree and pulled it partially free of the scabbard. It was honed and oiled. Small chips in the blade marked it as being a working sword. *And one Bill trusted with his life*, thought Brent. *I'll trust it with mine*. He slammed it home in the sheath and wrapped the sling around it.

He moved behind the desk and laid the sword on it and started opening drawers. Inside he found only papers and knick-knacks. He reached under the front of the desk and felt something there. He put the candle on the floor and knelt down under the desk.

"I should have bloody well done this before I put this armour on," he grunted. He looked up and grinned. Two daggers were sheathed under the wood. He ripped them free and strapped them to his legs. *Field plate is a wonderful thing*, he thought.

He looked thoughtfully at the desk again and re-opened the drawers and studied the depth. One looked slightly off and he rapped the back panel and it sounded a little hollow. *Like there is a space behind it*, he thought. He pulled on one of the gauntlets and punched the panel. His fist broke through with ease. He felt around inside the space and latched onto something. When he pulled back his hand, he saw what looked like a book wrapped in oilskin and small leather coin pouch. He laid the items on the desk and examined the contents of the bag. Several silver groats and a dozen or so gold crowns gleamed back at him. *A small ransom and more than enough to pay our way back to Munsten*, he thought. He unwrapped the oilskin and inside found a small diary. He opened it and started scanning the pages.

"Oh, you cheeky bugger!" he laughed as he flipped the pages. Inside was a complete account of the crimes of the Lord Protector with dates and names. Brent looked up to the heavens. "Well done, Bill Redgrave! Well done!"

Reeve Comlin led a quick route behind the buildings of Jaipers and paused in view of his home. He scanned the area but could see no one guarding or watching the place. They watched as a patrol of three guards marched down the street and away into the night. James touched his shoulder and Comlin looked back at him.

James was looking past him out to the street. "Clear?" he asked.

"I think so, do you know which home is mine?"

"Well, no."

"So how about I check it out first? I'll signal you if it's clear."

"And if it's not?"

Comlin just looked at him.

"Right, I'll know. Sorry, I'm a bit shaken. Thought we were dead."

"It will pass. Trust me. I've been held captive before."

"You have?"

Comlin didn't answer. Instead, he sprinted to the back door of his house and slipped inside. He paused, held his breath, and listened. After a count of thirty, he heard nothing and breathed again. He quickly searched his house and looked out onto the front porch. All was clear. He ducked out the back door and gave his bird call to James. He watched a shadowy figure separate from the fence near his home and join him at the back door.

"Follow," he whispered and led James into his house. He went over to the couch in the living room and indicated for James to take the other end. They lifted the couch and moved it to the other side of the room and set it gently down on the wooden floor. Comlin went back to the floor where the couch had been and lifted up a small ring handle. He pulled, and a trapdoor swung open silently.

"Oiled hinges," he whispered to James. James nodded appreciatively. "Come here, help me with this."

Inside the trapdoor was a small compartment dug into the earth and lined with oilskin. A flat wooden crate filled the space, and they reached in and pulled it free and set it aside. Comlin closed the trapdoor and together they moved the crate over to the back window and the moonlight. Comlin pulled out his familiar brown and green leathers, a beautiful longbow devoid of a bowstring, a matching quiver, and a plain sword in a black and green leather sheath. He laid them aside and pulled out another full leather armour suit, and a sword with a little ornate work around the pommel. These he pushed over to James.

He watched James stand up and start pulling on the armour and he did the same, saying nothing. The leathers were brown and green, offering perfect camouflage in late Spring through the Fall. The armour was remarkably tough but allowed movement at the joints and shoulders. *Expertly made, as I should know, they cost a small fortune.* He was certain the second suit would fit James and was pleased to see it did. *He's the same size as Ben*, he thought. James finished suiting up and looked over to Comlin. They could be twins except Comlin knew he looked like he belonged in the armour. Putting it back on again changed his whole outlook on life.

The Reeve is gone now, he thought and felt a deep pang of regret. He looked around the living room and felt nothing. *It was never truly my home. Just a place to hang my hat. But the job—that was important work.*

Comlin knelt down and started pulling out throwing daggers from the bottom of the crate. He handed six to James and took eight for himself.

"Watch," he said to James and took one dagger and inserted into a sheath built into the armour. James raised his eyebrows and did the same with his own armour and smiled. Comlin repeated this until James' daggers were gone and hidden in the suit. The last two daggers Comlin placed in the sheaths at his lower back. He finished by slinging the sword and picking up the longbow.

"Pretty slick," said James. "Almost as if you were not a nice Reeve in a small town. More like a highwayman."

Comlin didn't move. He merely looked back at James. A quiet descended on the room and Comlin could see James starting to look uncomfortable. Finally, Comlin laughed and James joined him a moment later. "Highwayman? What made you think that? Come, couple more things to grab."

Together they bundled up arrows, a fletching kit, bowstrings, maps and a large bag of coin. Comlin emptied the coin bag and James saw a red ruby in the mix. Comlin split the coin in two and put them in two smaller bags. He handed one to James. "For the road."

Last he went to his closet and brought out a second bow. He handed it to James. "Know how to use this?"

"Of course," replied James and accepted the bow. He looked it over and whistled softly. "Beautiful."

"Thanks, made it myself," he said and felt a little pride creep into his voice. "String up and let's go."

They each took a bowstring and strung their bows. Comlin finished his in a matter of seconds. James struggled a little but Comlin just watched until he had it done.

There was a small sound from the back of the house. Comlin whirled toward the sound, nocked an arrow, drew the bow, and released in one continuous motion. A grunt was heard and the sound of someone hitting the floor. Comlin nocked another arrow and drew. Two, then three heartbeats went by and a second sound was heard. Comlin released and something hit the floor with a loud moan. They moved forward quickly as a team into the kitchen and to the back door. Just inside the kitchen was a black boot dead on the floor with an arrow deep in his heart. Just inside the door and sprawled across the door jamb was a second black boot. He was still alive and moaning.

Comlin knelt and slipped a dagger up under the back of the skull and jiggled it. The man went silent and stilled. He withdrew the dagger and wiped it on the man's shirt before returning it to his leg sheath. He looked at James and was pleased to see grim determination there.

I was worried the man would be soft about this kind of stuff. Glad he isn't.

"Come. Let's go get the General and be off. I can feel the noose tightening."

Brent waited by the back door and listened. He could hear cries in the town and smelt smoke. They were searching for them. Brent kept wanting to think about what had happened in the large common room tonight, but his mind refused to want to dwell on it. *Later*, he thought. *Later I will need to find answers.* He thought again of the Cathedral in Jergen and knew he would have to return for those answers.

Brent had moved around the house in the armour, with the sword slung over his right shoulder, and was surprised by just how comfortable he felt in it. It had been years since he had worn field plate, but he didn't remember it fitting this well or being so light. The joints were well cared for and the chain components were silenced with very thin, but tough, leather placed between the metal parts. Overall, the armour was noisier than his cuirass but not much heavier. He liked it. *It suits me*, he thought and grinned. *Thanks, Bill. This time you are likely saving my life.*

A strange bird call sounded from the backyard and two shapes materialised on the back porch. Brent could barely see them. When they drew close enough Brent could see James and Comlin dressed in specialised leathers. Each carried a bow, quiver and sword. *Excellent, now to just get the fuck out of Jaipers.*

"You two are looking dapper. Nice leathers," said Brent and meant it.

Comlin and James looked over the surcoat and James pulled it back a little to peer at the armour underneath. "Looking good, sir. You'd think it was made for you."

"Bit of luck that. I won't jinx it," said Brent. "Let's be about this, gentlemen. Lead on Reeve Comlin."

"Steve. Call me Steve. Reeve Comlin is no more, I'm afraid."

"Steve? No, I don't think so. You'll always be Comlin to me, I'm afraid. But, pleased to meet you, Comlin. Call me Brent. You know James, I think? Now that we're introduced, please lead the way."

"Ass."

Brent chuckled. *This was going to be fun.*

Comlin pointed to the wooden fence behind his house and ducked low and ran over to it. Brent and James followed. Brent couldn't hear Comlin or James move. *I, on the other hand, sound a little louder than normal.* Neither of the other two seemed to mind. They reached the fence and Comlin lifted up a section of it and motioned for them to slip through underneath. This followed with a blur of backyards, fences and roads. Patrols would appear around bends and they would wait, hidden, hearts racing, for them to pass. At last, they reached an alleyway that opened up to look out over the closed North Gate. Torches lit the entire area and they could see the gate was manned by eight men. Four men in two groups patrolled the approaches and stayed within sight of each other and the gate guards.

Comlin ducked back down into the alley and stayed in the shadows at the back. Brent was very impressed with Comlin. He moved like no one he had ever met: completely silent and his armour hid him from view unless you knew where to look. His hair and eyes were the more telling and Brent said so.

Comlin looked surprised for a moment and then reached up to his collar and did something. He unrolled material sewn into the suit and pulled it over his head. It was a headpiece of some sort. Made of cloth but looking the same as the suit pattern. It pulled down over his eyes and nose and hid him almost completely. There were slits over the eyes.

"Right," said Brent.

Comlin motioned to James to come closer and twirled his finger. James turned his back to him and looked over his shoulder. Comlin reached into James collar and pulled out the same hood and helped him pull it over his head and tie it in place.

"I can't believe I forgot about these."

"Comlin, just what were you before you were the Reeve here?" asked Brent.

"Truth?"

"I prefer it."

"I was a highwayman. And, before you get all judgmental, I worked for the Baron of Turgany." Comlin looked at James and smiled.

James mouthed "I knew it."

"You worked for the Baron of Turgany. Robbing people on his roads." The doubt was clear in his voice.

"We didn't rob just anybody. We robbed the Lord Protector's people. And that money went straight to the Baron."

"Uh-huh."

"Don't judge, I said. We hate the Lord Protector down south. Not my fault you're sworn to protect him."

"Huh. We'll talk about this later. First, you two should know I carry a diary on me. Wrapped in oilskin. Tucked into my breeches. It was written by Redgrave. Outlines all the illegal things the Lord Protector did over the years. Well, at least back when Redgrave was the Knight General. Anything happens to me, see it gets to my brother in Munsten. He can add it to the case file we're building."

"Okay. Not judging either, then."

"Alright."

Comlin turned his attention back to the gate. "This way is fucked. No way to get past all these men."

"How about a diversion?" suggested James.

Comlin glanced over at James and snorted. "A diversion? So you're a romantic? Read all those fairy tales about knights confronting large numbers of adversaries and prevailing against the odds?"

James said nothing.

"Welcome to the real world, James. That way is death. This way..." and Comlin pointed down the alley to the village wall. "Is life. Choose quickly."

"Um, life?" said James.

"Good choice. Follow me."

Comlin led them directly over to the palisade. The thick wooden logs were buried deep into the ground and rose up over twenty-five feet. Here, near the gate, the wall was stronger and Comlin stopped for a second and took his bearings. Then he led them along the wall and away from the gate. After only thirty feet or so he stopped and looked around. They were standing on river stones. The whole area was thick with them. Comlin seemed to stop at random and then reached down and pulled up a section of stones. He grunted with the effort and James rushed over to help him. Brent couldn't believe his eyes. It was a trapdoor with river stones fixed to the top at least two layers deep. It was excellent workmanship. It must've taken a long time to manufacture and position. Brent looked down and saw a crawl tunnel leading down and under the wall. It was reinforced with wood to keep it from collapsing. It was a marvel and shouldn't exist.

"How?" he asked.

"I was here when the wall was built. I paid the crew to build this for me."

"Why?"

"I always have an escape route. Always."

"And this crew, why wouldn't they tell someone? Sell the information?"

"Because they were *my* crew, from my days as a highwayman. I had a problem to deal with and invited my crew down. Let me solve a nagging problem from my previous employment. Enough chatter. Let's go. We still need to make the docks."

They crept into the tunnel and lowered the trapdoor back down. It was completely dark, but they crawled on hands and knees by feel until they stopped some twenty feet or so on the other side of the wall. Brent couldn't tell exactly how far they had crawled, but it couldn't be much farther than that.

"Where does this emerge?"

"Inside an abandoned shack outside the wall."

"How do you know it's abandoned?"

"I pay for it to be abandoned, that's why. Enough questions—ask me all you want once we're safe and gone from here. James move up beside me and help me push."

Brent listened while James slid up next to Comlin and heard grunting. It seemed to get a little brighter and then Brent heard a dull thud. Brent moved forward and crawled out of the opening to stand up in a small wooden shack. The trapdoor was a pile of useless wood scraps on this side. They closed it and it disappeared into the clutter inside the shack.

Brent thought back to something the Reeve had said. "What did you mean about a nagging problem?"

Steve looked Brent straight in the eye. "I rooted out a traitor in my crew and dealt with him. We just crawled over his grave."

Brent looked down at the hidden trapdoor and thought back to the long, dark tunnel. *Surely the Reeve couldn't be serious about a body being buried under that? Surely, not.*

Steve interrupted his thoughts by clasping his shoulder. "The docks are only half a mile away. Normally it's pretty congested out here. Lots of people. I can't guarantee we make it unobserved. If we get separated where do you want to meet?"

Brent tore his eyes from the trapdoor and thought for a moment. "Jergen. In the Cathedral."

"Jergen? That's a long way off."

"Halfway to Munsten. Sounds like a good place to meet."

Comlin looked long and hard at Brent. "One day we will need to talk about what happened back in the community building."

"When I understand it, you will be one of the first to know."

"Okay, fair enough. Let's be about this."

Comlin led the way out of the shack and they blinked against the brightness of the moon. Comlin wound his way past the ramshackle buildings. Inside people were loudly snoring. Only occasionally did they see anyone awake and they stayed well clear and out of sight. Finally, after what seemed like hours to Brent, they reached the river. Ahead of them, the docks were lit up with torches and Comlin brought them as close as he could before stopping.

"All right. From here it will be tricky. See the barges? The one we want is on the farthest dock. It's called the *Seasonal Witch*. The owner is a friend of mine. He's the one that delivered the note to me earlier. Ah, shit!"

"What is it?"

"The note. That bastard took it."

"What was on it?"

"It was a note from the lad with the coin."

Brent raised his eyebrows.

"Yes, the very same coin. In the note, he tells me where he is. Places him in Jergen and he mentions the farm. Someone smart can put that together. Seth seems like that kind of smart—fanatical—but smart. The most dangerous kind."

"Why do I care about this lad and the coin?" asked Brent.

"Cause that young lad is a druid. Everything that has happened so far involves that young man and that damn coin. If you'd seen what he can do, you'd understand. That bastard Seth Farlow was hard after him. Ask yourself why the Church of the New Order would be so interested in him. Then ask yourself why you shouldn't want to keep him away from all that. I'm after Will to see he's safe. I need to join him and help him. The good news is that if he's at the farm, he is surrounded by some of the toughest sons-of-bitches there are in this world—my crew."

"Your crew?" asked James.

"Yes, *my* highwaymen. Baron Turgany gave us land when things started to get too hot. They work the land up there. Been years since I've been to visit but last time I was there it was a massive operation. I think you should head there and regroup. Figure out what to do next."

Brent grew silent and thought for a moment and sighed. "My mission is over and likely my career. I doubt I have a position in Munsten anymore." He looked at James and saw concern there. "Fine. We head east to this farm and meet this druid of yours. I'm curious to see if he's truly a demon like Seth says he is. If we are separated, we meet in Jergen at the Cathedral. Let's go."

Comlin studied Brent for a moment and then nodded. He looked about and then darted out onto the dock and started weaving his way around the crates and stores stacked by the barge gangways. Brent followed and then James. All the way down the dock Brent expected to hear shouts of alarm. His heart pounded in his ears. And then, suddenly, it was over. They reached the barge and crossed the gangway.

Comlin brought them across the open deck and directly into the large shack located centrally to the craft. Inside they found a sleeping barge captain. Brent shook his head in disbelief. *How could this man sleep through a crisis?* he thought. Comlin went over to him and covered his mouth and whispered in his ear. "Captain, it's me Comlin. I've a favour to ask you."

The man woke, startled, and then relaxed when he saw it was Comlin and the words sunk in. He rose with a grimace and glanced at Brent and James. He looked over their armour and then focused on Comlin.

"Reeve? What are you doing here? I thought you were killed!" The captain embraced him and then held him out at arm's reach. "Why are you dressed like this?"

Brent could hear the North-Western accent on the man. *He's a long way from home*, he thought. *From Cala or Central Port.*

"Sorry to disappoint and sorry to scare you, Captain Atwell. Yes, I'm still alive. We need passage east to Jergen. Can you take us?"

The captain looked at James and then Brent. "You," he said, pointing to Brent. "You are the General from Munsten?"

"Yes, sir. I am."

"Why should I take you to Jergen? What happens to me then?"

"I could tell you it's your duty to serve the Realm but I doubt that would sway you." Brent reached into his armour and pulled out a coin pouch. He opened it and pulled out four gold crowns. He held them out and dropped them in the open palm of the barge captain.

"I see. Very well. I can take you."

"Thank you, my friend."

Captain Atwell pointed to Comlin. "Him. He's my friend. You. You are paid passengers. I must tell you though. You are not alone here. There is one other on board."

"Who?" said Comlin.

"Dempster. He's in the secret hold. Says he must escape Jaipers. Says the Lord Protector has found him. Does that make sense to you?"

Comlin looked first to Brent and then back to the captain. He started to laugh. "Yes, sadly it does. Bring us to him. It's good he's here. We'll eat well at least."

Twenty-Three

Rigby Farm, 900 A.C.

I T WAS MID-fall and the Mabon Days were now fading. The farmhands had brought in the harvest and a great many were still living out on the outskirts of the farmland with their scythes and bailing wire. Carts and horses trundled in and out and disappeared for a few days to Jergen to sell their wares at the market.

The farm had changed over the past two months and Nadine and I had studied together and talked about how we would approach teaching at the farm. It was complicated in that we had no idea how many students we would have. Nadine and I practised our magic and together we were learning how to control what we did. I was getting used to life on the farm and went where I could to help with the crops and healing the occasional injury.

I watched as Katherine guided her horse around the paddock. The horse was running tirelessly and Katherine turned in place to keep herself facing it. She wasn't using her powers that I could sense. Instead, she was using her experience to teach the horse. She was in such control and I admired her skill.

The other day, Katherine had explained what she did with the horses when I had asked. I had thought it a simple exercise ring for the horses and when I had said that to her, she laughed and told me firmly "No, it's not that at all!" She explained—inordinately pleased to know something I didn't—that the paddock was used to get a horse to trust people. She said it was more mental than physical. I didn't get it. It looked like exercise but she just shook her head and tried again to explain it to me.

"The horse," she had said, "is focused on the human in the middle of the round corral. It barely registers that it is running. If you just keep running the horse, it will stop and stare at you. I hate it when they do that. They're smarter than dogs, you know. Anyway, you need to keep the horse focused on you. Make eye contact. Talk to the horse. I can't explain it better than that. The horse just kind of bonds with you. Learns to trust you."

Now, I leaned against the top of the fence with one foot up on the bottom rail watching her train the horse. I was wearing the same thick blue cotton pants the farmhands tended to favour. Ben had called it denim, and I liked wearing them. It wore well and offered good protection for farm work. Katherine glanced over at me more and more often until finally, she stopped the horse. She walked over to join me and squinted up at me.

The sun was high in the sky and the heat still reminded us of summer. I watched the horse. It seemed content to remain standing where Katherine had left it. Her control of animals was incredible. I used my *senses* but felt nothing between her and the horse. The horse simply followed her orders. I looked over to Dog who lay in a patch of grass near the paddock, panting in the unseasonably warm heat. He followed Katherine everywhere now—never left her side. I missed his constant presence, but I knew he loved me. Our bond was still strong. I could see that the bond between Dog and Katherine was tinged with white and I smiled.

"Hello, Katherine."

"Hello, Will."

"How long have you been working with this horse?"

Katherine turned her head sideways and glanced back at the horse. "Chester? Since this morning."

"You taught the horse all that in one morning?"

"Yeah, he was kind of ornery. Hard to get through to him. But we have an understanding now."

"An understanding?"

"Yeah. He'll listen so long as he gets the respect he wants."

"And you know this how?"

Katherine looked a little wary. "I dunno. I just do."

"Have you ever been wrong?"

"Wrong?"

"Yes, wrong about what you think an animal thinks or wants."

"Why would I be wrong?"

I chuckled and stood up straight and stretched. "Let's go for a walk. I think better when I walk."

Katherine nodded and whistled over to a farmhand working nearby. "Bill, can you brush down Chester and put him back in the stable?"

Bill nodded and started over.

"Bye Chester, see you in a bit!" called out Katherine and vaulted over the paddock fence. "Okay, where to?"

"The orchard I think. I like it there."

We walked in silence for a time. Dog trotted along beside Katherine. I looked at our bond and tried to get a sense of her. It was always a little strange with her. I felt slightly disconnected. I could get a sense of her emotions but not much else. I thought I understood it but had to find out for sure. I thought I knew what was happening. Gaea had changed the rules. Rules I was only just figuring out.

"You and Dog seem to be happy together."

"Oh, yes. He's a wonderful dog. He really likes the name Dog, by the way. He understands it and approves. His name before was something he didn't like. He won't tell me what it was."

"His name before?"

"Yeah, he lived on a sheep farm. Worked all the time. His owner wasn't very nice, so he left. That was hard for him. He's ashamed, I think."

"I see." The orchard was just up ahead, but I changed direction and started toward the sheep pen. "Follow me."

In a moment, we stood outside the pen and watched a couple of dozen sheep wander around. I could see no pattern in the movement of the animals. All I could sense were their desires and that they knew Dog was nearby. They weren't alarmed. They just felt that something about their life would change with Dog there. That was about it.

I looked at Katherine. She was looking the sheep over and I could see a frown on her face. "What's the matter, Katherine?"

"That one over there? The one with the little bit of black by the tail? She's not getting at the fresh grass as much as she would like."

"Why?"

"The others are being mean. That's why."

"Can you tell them to stop?"

"I already did. They will but I need to watch them. You can't trust sheep.

They forget too easily." Katherine laughed. "I told them Dog would get after them if they cheated. Now they can't keep their eyes off him. Dog thinks that is really funny. So do I."

I nodded. "What you do is remarkable."

"Huh?"

"The draoi could never do what you do. Did you know that? I asked Nadine about it. We searched the manuscript, too. There is no mention of draoi communicating with animals the way you do."

"Can you not hear Dog? He talks to you all the time."

"He does?" I looked at Dog and knelt down. He came up to me and licked my face. "I'm sorry, Dog. I can sense you. We've shared images but not words."

"Silly. They don't speak words! They send images. That's what I do. Images."

"Ah," I said. "I have done that with Dog. But not with horses and sheep."

"Really? Well, I suppose that makes sense. It's harder with sheep. They aren't very smart. They imagine all sorts of things all the time so it's hard to get them to pay attention. Cows are the same. Horses are super easy. And pigs. Really easy. Chickens—forget about it. Cats hear you but don't care. Very rude animals in my opinion. Sometimes I just have to push harder, you know?"

"Yes, I think I do. That's remarkable, Katherine. You have a gift that has never been seen before."

"What does that mean?"

"It means that how we teach the draoi needs to change."

A couple of hours later Nadine found me sitting alone in the kitchen. I had followed her moving through the house with our bond and let her know where I was. I had just finished with Agnes and removed some of her pain and symptoms. She was asleep now and resting. Her condition was not any better. I couldn't see any way to make it better for her and I was disheartened. I wanted to be the healer she needed but there was only so much I could do. Nadine felt my sorrow and came to find me. She sat across from me and poured tea from the pot I had made into a cup I had placed where she now sat. She took a sip and murmured appreciatively.

"That's good."

"Thanks," I replied.

"Franky and Anne?"

"I don't know. Somewhere. Not here. It's quiet. Reminds me of your house when it gets like this."

Nadine smiled. "Our house. How's Agnes?"

"Not much better, I'm afraid. I can only do so much for her. I think my estimate of her time left is wrong. She hasn't much time left."

Nadine nodded in agreement and reached out and snatched up a cookie from the tray in the middle of the table. She took a bite and grimaced. "Not yours?"

"No, Katherine's. They're for Dog."

"Oh," she said and placed the remains of her cookie on the table. "So, what's bothering you, love?"

"Everything."

"Care to explain?"

"I'm trying to figure it all out. Gaea says come here and train the new draoi that are soon to come here. It's been months and no one. And I worry that we can't do it. The manuscript is a good start, I'll admit. But there is more happening here."

"More? Why do you say that?"

"Take Katherine for example. Her powers are not the same as yours and mine."

"She just needs to learn how to use them better."

"No, that's not right, love. She already does. Better than you and I in some ways. I don't think she needs to be taught. I think she will be one of our teachers."

Nadine looked at me in alarm. "How can you believe that? She can't sense anything through her bond. It's as if she is weak, or stunted like I was. How can you expect her to teach others?"

"She has a different power, Nadine. I'm sure of that. We were just looking at her through our own abilities. Hers is different."

"Different? In what way?"

"She bonds with animals. All animals. Not equally but it appears to be connected with the animals' ability to reason. The smarter the animal the easier time she has of it."

"With animals? Not people? That's her power?"

"Yes. She does it like breathing. It's natural for her. She is an expert on animals."

"Are you sure? I admit she's great with the horses and Dog. But how can you think she can teach that?"

"I don't, actually. It's just my instinct telling me I'm right. Nadine, I don't think Gaea is giving her powers to the draoi the way she used to. The way you were used to. I don't expect you to believe me just yet, but I'll know for sure when the others show up. The manuscript talks about the three powers: *Vision*, *Sense* and *Influence*. But it talks about them in ways that the draoi use them to commune with nature and other draoi. It explains how we can reach into people and heal them. And understand what they are feeling. With Katherine, it is different. She has those same powers but they work for her with animals much more strongly than with people. You and I work with people, she works with animals."

Nadine pondered that for a moment. "Let's say you are right. How does that change things?"

I was very proud of her at that moment. I had expected an argument but instead, she was open to listening. I pressed on with more confidence. "Well, it changes how the draoi will need to be taught, Nadine. You and I can't help other draoi that don't share our same abilities. It would be like a farmer trying to explain how to seed to a blacksmith. A little would get through but their abilities are too different to make a significant difference. Like the blind leading the blind. That's not all, though. I think there will be many kinds of draoi. Draoi who work with plants in ways that have never been seen before. I told you about the oak tree when I was captured?" Nadine nodded. "It ignored me but I could sense it as a conscious being. There will be draoi that will be able to speak to plants as easy as you and I talk to one another—or like how Katherine talks to animals."

"You can, though. Talk to animals and plants. You admitted as much."

"True, but only a little bit. I'm a healer, Nadine. I can sense how a body works and functions. I can see the intricacies of bodily function and make improvements. Correct problems."

Nadine sipped her tea. "And me? What powers do I have that make me unique?" I could sense she wanted it to be something wonderful.

I looked at her. "You and I are alike, Nadine. We share the same power. Our bond makes it so. It is why our bond is the way it is. We strengthen one another. We..." I stopped talking as a thought came to me. "Follow me," I said, suddenly excited, and grabbed her hand and dragged her out of the kitchen.

"Will! What are you doing?" Nadine allowed herself to be pulled into the front room. We stopped in front of Agnes and watched her sleeping peacefully.

"Help me, Nadine," I whispered, careful not to wake Agnes. "Together we might be able to help her. Combine our strengths."

"Together?" she whispered back. "It doesn't work that way, Will."

"Yes, it does. I'm sure of it," I said. "Try it with me."

I led the way into Agnes with my senses. Nadine followed me travelling through our bond. We had done this before when we had slept together and made love. We had joined into something powerful and nearly lost ourselves. I felt her resistance. Her fear and longing competed and stopped her from joining with me. *Shh, hon*, I said to her through our bond. *Trust me in this. Look where I look and help me.* She resisted again but, at my urging, she allowed herself to join closer with me until we became one through the bond. We were lost for a moment as our hearts sang out to one another. The joining was full of such joy. Two souls joined for a single purpose. I nearly wept with the happiness that flooded me. To not be alone. To share your heart with someone who loves you so unconditionally back gave me such hope and strength. I could lose myself in her. So great was my joy that I released my resistance. This woman was the centre of my world. To lose myself in her would be such a great victory. I gave myself willingly to her and felt her do the same with me.

A great light filled my senses and a loud peal of pure sound overwhelmed all my remaining senses. I turned within myself and found myself holding both of Nadine's hands. I saw her then in all her beauty and flaws. My heart exploded with my love and a smile burst across my face. We spoke no words—we merely stared at one another—lost in the moment. We stayed that way for an eternity before I remembered, with an effort, why we had joined. It was easy once we remembered what we were doing. We were not lost in one another. We merely basked in the joy of the joining. I sensed a wicked delight from Nadine and knew our next lovemaking was going to be amazing. Our vision cleared and together we turned our attention outward to Agnes.

We examined Agnes and saw immediately where her disease lay rooted. It was deep within her cells. The damage was locked inside a strange twisted pattern that made her who she was. The pattern duplicated itself within all her cells: replicating and dividing, a great constant in her design. We examined it and saw the flaw that lay within. Her body fought a losing battle against the error. We sensed where the problem lay and struggled to find a way to reverse it. We saw what needed to be done and then we hesitated. We waited to feel the warning pain that came with the intent to cause harm to another. Gaea set those boundaries in our power and punished those who broke it. We were afraid that this would be considered harm. We were about to fundamentally change who Agnes was. We could change her hair colour, her skin colour, her height and even her sex if we wanted. We held within us the power to make great change. We felt a warning then from Gaea and instead returned our focus to the damage we had identified. The warning faded and bolstered, we reached out tentatively, joined in our power and focus, and made the small correction to one of her cells. It was like instructions that had been written wrong. We erased the error and rewrote what we felt it should be. It was beyond rational thought. It was instinct and we could no more fight it than we could fight falling out of a tree. Together we had a focus of intent that we lacked as one. We halted again and waited to feel our punishment. When nothing happened, we felt vindicated and the pressing need to heal this poor woman and we pressed on to other cells and fixed the problem there. Much like how I dealt with the motes in Jaipers, we pulled back and took in the error as a whole. Like holding hands, we merged our power and made the change in a single burst of will. A flash of light crossed our vision, and we opened our eyes and looked down on Agnes.

She slept, unaware of the change we had made. We examined her for a time and discovered nothing negative. We traced her disease and found it had been eradicated. We had healed her—together. We slowly pulled apart until we stood as two people again and looked at one another. A single tear slipped down Nadine's cheek and she pulled me close to hug me.

"Oh, Will," she cried against my chest. "That was beautiful. We healed her, didn't we?"

"Yes, my love," I whispered. "We did." Possibilities opened up in front of me and I felt hope for the first time.

Seth Farlow sat on horseback looking down at the farm and the little ants that were people who worked it. On top of the rise, he could overlook most of the farm, but it was his bloodstone in his hand that turned his focus to the farmhouse. He had watched the Target talking to a new demon and then disappearing inside the house. He had watched the house for an hour and saw no others. He could sense that three demons lived in the house. *Already they are spreading*, he thought. *From one small coin lay the seed to their growth. They will spread like a cancer across the Realm, devouring all that lay in their path until nothing remains.*

He twisted his back a little and felt the fresh scabs break and blood trickled down his spine. He was whipping himself at dawn and dusk now. Trying to purge his sins from his body. He had failed in Jaipers. He had allowed Bairstow and the Reeve to flee. His fear had taken hold of him and he had lost reason for a time. It was only when one of his Sect members had shown him the note hidden in the leathers of the Reeve that he had calmed. The note led him here to this large farm outside Jergen. He had arrived two days ago and watched and noted the movements of the farmhands and the demons. They would all have to die for knowingly harbouring demons. That was the law of the Purge. A law he was more than happy to enforce.

A smell of rot on the breeze turned his attention to his horse. It no longer breathed or had a need for feed or water. Flesh fell from its ribs exposing them. It was surprisingly maggot free. Seth had expected swarms of insects to follow him but, oddly enough, even the insects stayed clear. He wasn't certain how it still lived or moved. He was somehow giving it strength with his powers and he enjoyed the feeling. He leeched power from nature all around him and fed the horse that energy. His men recoiled from it and he felt their fear. He had been forced to show them what real fear looked like and now they obeyed without question.

Encouraged by his horse, he had raised one of the fallen men in the square in Jaipers. He had been with the men that had come with Brent Bairstow: one of his officers who had bled out on the ground. The man did what he commanded him to do with his mind. He fed him power as he did his horse. Seeing what he could do, Seth had raised all his fallen Sect members and he controlled them with very little thought. It was written in the bible that the dead would rise and now they did. It was Judgement Day. God willed it. A titter of excited laughter escaped his lips and Seth pressed them together to silence himself. His eyes danced with glee and he remembered how strong he felt when the men had risen from the blood-soaked ground.

He had wanted to raze Jaipers. His Sect brothers had convinced him to leave it. It had been a close thing. They said the townspeople had been ignorant of all that had happened within the walls and that none knew what had happened there. It had been a difficult choice but Seth was satisfied that coming here was the most urgent of his duties. So he left Jaipers untouched but now regretted that decision. *They harboured demons. Whether they knew or not, they should have known. That is death. I would see Jaipers burned to the ground. I will return to make that so.*

So much had happened. He felt out of control at times. The sight of Brent Bairstow with the symbol of the Church of the New Order blazing from his forehead into the dim light of the common house had frightened him beyond reason and a vision of that returned to him in his dreams. He doubted himself now and blamed Brent for it. He finally saw reason and saw the error of his doubt. The demons were good at deceiving people. They thrived on deception. They offered temptation and Seth now knew he was not immune to their power. He had been deceived by Brent. It shamed him and hence his increased self-flagellation.

He had gathered his people in Jaipers and rode hard for the farm. He called on the other Sect members in the area with his bloodstone and they responded. His stone drew them like moths to a flame. Down below in the farmstead lay the strongest of the remaining demons. He would rout them and burn them alive. They were the last. He would return to the Archbishop and declare the plight eradicated and seek absolution.

The Archbishop could then return the land to the Church and replace the Lord Protector with the bastard son of the late King he had hidden in Jergen. He would be a glorious King and reign with the law of the Church behind him. People needed to be returned to the way of the pious and religion gave them atonement for their many sins. The Word would be destroyed. Struck down and demolished. Burned from the histories and banished forever.

Behind him, he had over fifty men gathered in the nearby woods. Tonight he would anoint them all and ready them spiritually for battle. Tomorrow morning while it was still dark, he would strike and bring victory to the Church.

He turned his horse with a thought and returned to the woods.

Twenty-Four

Rigby Farm, 900 A.C.

HE SOUND OF horses whinnying outside in the stables woke me up from a deep slumber. A sense of dread descended on me and I quickly shook Nadine beside me. A faint cry from the farm outbuildings came to my ear, and I turned to my *vision*. I looked out through the walls of the house to the outside. All around the house figures crept. Most stood out with a red shimmering aura. Some had no auras, and they horrified me. They were more *not there* than there. My eyes slid off them and I fought to pierce through to what they were. Nadine sat upright, and I felt her *vision* join mine.

We scanned the entire farm area. About two dozen figures, both with red auras and missing auras closed in on the house and some were already inside the barn and stables. Their intent was clear. With a pulse, Nadine and I woke the others across the farm. We didn't know we could do that until we tried. The pulse woke the farmhands and Katherine's family in an instant. Cries filled the air, and I knew then that we were under attack. The Sect had found us and fear stabbed our hearts.

I felt Katherine reach out to the horses. There was a moment of silence from the stables and then screams of fear erupted from the attackers. I grimaced and tried not to think about horses intelligently fighting back against aggressors. *Hopefully, the horse will be okay*, I thought and rose from the bed.

"We are under attack," I whispered needlessly to Nadine. She nodded and grasped my hand. We crept to the top of the stairs and waited. We saw Franky appear at the bottom of the stairs and look up at us. She gripped a long dagger in each hand. Ben joined us and, in a moment, so did Agnes. Ben carried a well-used short sword in his right hand. A leather jerkin had been pulled over his head and offered protection to his chest, back, and abdomen. Agnes carried a beautiful longbow and a quiver bristling with long arrows. One arrow was held by two fingers and nocked to the bowstring. The arrowhead was steel and barbed and it glinted in the moonlight coming through the house windows. They glanced at Nadine and I and nodded with a grim look on their faces.

"You two should stay here," whispered Agnes. "This is our kind of fight."

Nadine and I nodded quickly. We fed off each other's fear and struggled to keep it down to a manageable level. I was scared and didn't know what to do. Nadine was no better. Staying inside while professionals dealt with what was happening outside seemed wise.

Agnes smiled and patted my arm. She was so much stronger now. She couldn't believe that her disease was gone when we told her and when she accepted it, she had cried and cried until her husband Ben had burst in and assumed the worst. After calming him down he had joined her, and I had sat back and enjoyed their happiness. Nadine and I had tried to help Ben with his problem but it seemed we couldn't grow back what was taken from him. Ben hadn't cared and thanked us for trying. Nadine seemed to think we could help with them getting pregnant, but Agnes wanted no part in it. The last few days had been wonderful here at the farm. The farmhands had joined in a great feast and celebrated Agnes' new vitality and future. Ben and Agnes were such strong leaders and their people had a fierce loyalty to them.

Looking at them together at the top of the stairs, I saw them in a new light. They looked fierce and capable. *They must've been something to see in their youth*, I thought. *I wonder what Reeve Comlin looked like?*

They moved to descend the stairs but Nadine stopped them with a word. "Wait. There is something strange about some of them. They aren't... normal. Be wary. Your people are all awake. Some of them are in the stables. Your daughter is working with the horses and fighting them. She's safe and in her bedroom with Dog and Anne."

Ben's eyes went a little rounder, and he glanced at Agnes and Franky. "Okay, good to know. Anything else?"

I nodded. "There are about twenty of them outside. Probably four in the stables that I can sense. I feel that there are more surrounding the outbuildings.

Your people are in trouble, but awake. Careful with the black ones. They... move... a little slower and something is unnatural about them."

Ben grasped my upper arm once and moved quickly and quietly down the stairs. Agnes moved in tandem but stopped mid-stairs and drew her bow. Ben moved to the front door on the opening side and Franky stood by the hinges. They listened briefly. He nodded up the stairs to Agnes and held up two fingers. Franky reached across the back of the door and grasped the doorknob and turned it hard and pulled it open into the front entrance. Beyond the door lay darkness lit a little by the half-moon.

Agnes released and pulled another arrow from her quiver, nocked it, drew the bow and released all in the time it took for three heartbeats. The first man through the door crumpled with an arrow through the heart. The man behind him took a similar arrow but kept walking. He held a sword in his hand and looked up the stairs to spot Agnes. Intent on her, he ignored Ben who stepped out from beside the door and took off the head with one blow of his short sword. Ben pulled the headless corpse through the doorway to clear the door and Franky swung it shut. Blood oozed from the neck but not with the fountain of blood you would expect. *Something is very wrong here*, I thought. *I felt the first man die, but not the second.*

Nadine and I rushed down the stairs to the men and examined them. They wore black boots marking them as members of the Sect. I heard Agnes bite back a scream and looked where she pointed.

"He's still alive!" she rasped in horror.

I looked down at the head of the second man. The eyes were moving, and the mouth opened and closed. My senses told me that this was not alive. It had no aura. Not anything to link it to life on Earth. A cold feeling ran down my spine and I shuddered. Without warning, Ben drove his sword into the head and its movements ceased. He placed a boot on the head and pulled his sword free.

"What the fuck was that?" Franky whispered.

Nadine had her hand over her mouth and she fought to keep from screaming. Agnes sat heavily on the stairs and placed her bow across her knees. She was shaking her head in disbelief. I looked at Ben and saw only determination there. This was a man used to fighting, but he was shaken. He looked a little white. Nadine turned quickly and threw up the contents of her stomach. The smell of bile mixed with the coppery smell of fresh blood. I swallowed back the bile that rose in my throat.

"I-I don't know," I said, and I didn't. "I can't see them with my powers. He's not of the earth. He's separate from Gaea. Even dead animals are still a part of her. Not this man. He is… *not*. Does that make any sense?"

"No, lad," said Ben gruffly. "This doesn't make any sense at all." He pointed his sword at the black boots worn by the first corpse. "Sect?"

I nodded. Ben grunted.

Cries could be heard all over the farm now. The sound of swords clashing became more and more frequent and urgent. Outside the house, a battle raged. I used my *vision* to scan the house and found two men at the back door just inside the kitchen. More surrounded the house and tightened their net.

"We're surrounded," I said. "Two in the kitchen. I can sense both. They're… normal?"

Nadine reached out and took Agnes' hand and pulled her to her feet. Agnes nocked an arrow and drew her bow and angled herself around the stairway and headed toward the kitchen. Franky followed behind her. Ben watched them go but kept his ear to the front door.

"Lad, keep the information coming. Don't stop."

"Al-alright," I said, my voice shaking. "Agnes and Franky are almost at the kitchen. The two men are still inside the back doorway. They're just standing there and listening. She shot one! Now the other. They're dead. Dear Gaea, she's fast."

"She's the best in the Realm she is. My Agnes is the best."

"She's staying in the kitchen covering the door. Franky is hovering near her. Three more are approaching the back. One normal, two… not normal. What do we call them? Um, two more coming up the front veranda. Normal."

Ben nodded and moved beside the door jamb keeping the door clear.

"Nadine, can you watch Agnes and the back? I'll watch the door here."

"Yes, I'll move closer to Agnes and tell her what's happening." Nadine didn't wait for an answer and disappeared around the stairway toward the kitchen. I sent *Careful!* down our bond and felt her respond with *Of course, stupid*.

I *sensed* the two outside the front door approach. "They're on the doorstep. One has his hand on the doorknob."

I watched the doorknob turn and the door swing wide open. On the other side stood a black boot. He saw me and cried out "The Target! Here!" He raced through the opening only to be sliced open across the stomach by Ben. The man screamed and collapsed over his ruptured mid-section. Ben hadn't moved and the second man burst through and was pierced through the side deep into his middle. The sword withdrew with a wet sucking sound and Ben lifted the blade up and drove it through the man's neck cutting his scream off. Ben stepped forward and drove the blade under the first man's skull and silenced the screams.

"Are there any more of them?" he asked, but I didn't have time to answer him.

Men were being killed in front of me and I felt their life fade from their bodies. Behind me, I saw Agnes drop the first man through the back door, an arrow straight through the heart. The second man without an aura stepped into the kitchen. An arrow blossomed in his heart but he kept moving. He didn't even flinch. A second arrow hit the forehead and punched through. The man fell forward without a sound. Behind him, a second non-aura stepped across the door jamb. Nadine whispered something to Agnes, and an arrow blossomed from the man's skull. He, too, dropped without a sound and lay still. I could see eight more men behind the house and six more in front. Half were the non-aura types. "Will! Where are they? Snap out of it!"

"S-six more in front, two are without auras. They aren't moving any closer. In the back eight more, four without auras. They're just standing there now."

"What else?"

"What do you mean, what else?"

"What else is happening on the farm? Can you sense it?"

"Y-yes, sorry. I see..." I looked out over the stable which was silent now. Eight men with auras stood outside the stable door and were lighting a torch. Over at the outbuildings, I could sense twenty more men. They were fighting the farmhands, the sound of steel on steel now loud in the night air. Ben's people fought with such skill it was a marvel to watch. They were outnumbered two to one and yet they held the enemy at bay. "Um. Men are over at the stable. They are lighting a torch. Fighting over at the outbuildings. Twenty to ten of your farmhands."

Ben winced. "Only ten? Any more of my people anywhere?"

I looked but found only the dead and wounded. I shook my head. "They are the only ones still standing." I reached farther out and picked up the other farmhands, twenty or more racing to close the main building. They were too far out and told him so.

"Who are they, Will? Black boots. The Sect, right?"

"I think so," I said. "I don't know who else they can be."

"My crew," he said and I could sense the crushing emotion that threatened to topple him. "After so long. We were safe here."

I said nothing. I watched the emotions play across him. He fought them down and one emerged and he looked sharply at me.

"You brought them here. To my door. You brought this upon my people."

I could say nothing to that. He was right and the guilt and horror of that descended on me. I fought to find a response. Something to deny the horrible truth. I felt the horror from Agnes and Franky. Nadine struggled to stay calm. She wanted to run and leave all this death behind her. The copper smell of blood filled the house.

Katherine and Dog appeared at the top of the stairs. Katherine had her hand twisted into Dog's neck fur. Her eyes looked wild and far away. Dog whined and pressed up against her leg.

"Da," she cried. "They killed three of the horses and the stable hands. They slaughtered them. Cut them down without anything but glee in their hearts. I fought them. The horses did. I k-killed them, da. They're setting fire to the stables but I got the horses out the back. Da, some of the men that attacked are dead already but they walk! They walk, da! It's not possible!"

I was startled and realised she spoke the truth. The men were dead but walked. *How do you fight something that is already dead?* I wanted to join Nadine and run and run from this farm. I had brought so much death here. I couldn't forgive myself. I had to leave so that these people could be left alone. I opened my mouth to say the words when a loud voice from outside stopped me.

"Will Arbor! I know you are in there. You and the other demons. The two women. Come out and face God's wrath. I command you in the name of the Father!"

I looked confused at Ben. He gritted his teeth and beckoned his daughter down the stairs to him. I reached out with my *vision* and saw a man on horseback standing outside the front door about thirty feet back. The man and the horse were not of the Earth. They were black holes in the life that surrounded them. The wrongness of him flooded me and stole my breath. I watched the enemy behind the house circle round to join the man at the front. Nadine spoke to Agnes and Franky and they joined us in the front hall.

"Who is that?" asked Nadine looking at me. "How does he know you?"

"I have no idea," I said. I saw the look of doubt from Ben and anger flared within me. "I swear! I've never met this man. I have no idea how he found me!"

Katherine touched her father's arm. "Da, it's true. He doesn't know. He's scared like all of us."

Ben glared at me and turned to Agnes. "Our crew is almost wiped out." He pointed at me. "He says there are only ten left standing by the out-buildings.

The others are coming but too far out to help."

Agnes wiped away a tear and embraced Ben. "I know, love. Nadine told me. What do we do now?"

"I don't know." Ben looked at me. "He says two women demons? He means Nadine and my daughter?"

"I think so. I think he thinks druids are demons. It's the name the Church gave the draoi during the Purge."

"How would he know my daughter is a druid?"

"He must sense it somehow, otherwise, I don't know. I'm sorry. I don't understand any of this."

The voice from outside yelled out again. "Will Arbor. Come face your final judgement. I killed your mother, boy. I will finish the job, by God's will. Come out! Bring the demons with you!"

At his words, shock, then rage, filled me. This was the man who killed my mother? This was the man that hunted my mother and I and then struck her down like an animal? My body shook. Before I could think I had opened the front door and strode out onto the veranda. All my grief from the past ten years flooded back to me. The years alone and afraid, hidden from people. Living off the land and harbouring with wolves. It all came back in a flood and I needed to strike this man down. Outside the flames from the stable lit up the night like day. Long shadows flickered across the entrance-way. Before me, sitting high on horseback, was a thin short man, narrow of face with a sharp beak of a nose. He sneered at me and raised a crossbow and pointed it at me.

With a flash of recognition, I returned to the night my mother was killed.

My mother and I stood near the edge of the woods. We had been running for what felt like hours. As we neared the edge, a figure rose from the bushes in front of us. My mother gasped and stopped me with an arm across my chest. She positioned herself between me and the man. I was strangely calm. I knew I should fear this man but I couldn't seem to feel anything.

Time seemed to slow. My mother tried to hide us. I knew how she did it. She bent the light around us and hid us from view. She did it now and then moved us sideways. I heard the snap of a string and the whine of something moving fast. My mother staggered.

I saw the man looking for us. My mother turned toward me and I saw the bolt in her chest. Blood poured out of her mouth and I knew that it was bad. She looked at me, fear across her face, I felt despair. The first emotion I had felt in days. It bubbled up inside me and I nearly cried out.

"Mom?" I asked. "Are you all right? Mom?"

"Run!" she gurgled around the blood. "Run and don't stop. Run and stay hidden. Hide who you are. Promise me!"

"Mom, what's wrong?" Despair grew stronger. My mother sank to her knees, and I knelt down beside her.

"Promise me!" she gripped my arms so hard they hurt.

"Mom?"

"Promise me!" she hissed. "Hurry!"

"I-I promise, mom," I sobbed once and swallowed. I felt tears flowing down my cheeks. I felt like I was underwater. No strong emotions but the one that threatened to overwhelm me. "I promise! Now get up. Let's go. Come. Hurry."

"Run! Run! Go now while I can still hide you. Hurry!" My mom fell to the ground on her side and her eyes rolled back. "Run," she whispered, and I felt a push of her power on my muscles, trying to get me to move.

I looked up and saw the man coming closer. A thin man, with a narrow face and a sharp beak of a nose. He was searching the ground and coming closer; his crossbow reloaded and the bolt tip glinting. I stood up and ran as fast as I could and kept running.

A little while later the cloud over my emotions snapped clear. My mother was dead. I collapsed to the ground and wailed. Blackness like no other descended on me.

The man across from me was the same man who had killed my mother in cold blood and left me an orphan in the world. The same man who had set in motion all the pain in my life. He sat there so smugly. So much evil fixated within one person.

I started to run toward him, screaming in a rage, when I saw him release the bolt from his crossbow. I heard Nadine scream in fear behind me and time, once again, seemed to slow. I felt a push from behind shoving me to the side. Ben Rigby crossed in front of me, pushing me out of the way of the bolt. I watched the bolt strike him in the chest. Blood exploded into the air and I heard Ben grunt once. I fell to the ground and watched Ben twist lifeless in front of me to lay across the stairs on his back staring sightlessly upwards. The bolt had punched through his heart. I felt his life flicker and then extinguish. I was powerless to help him. My magic could not replace his heart. Ben was dead. He died saving me.

I screamed in futility. "No!"

The man on the horse looked from Ben to me and started to laugh. His men formed a half-circle behind him and I could sense humour from those with auras. Over at the outbuildings, the battle still raged. Ben's crew now only numbered eight, but the enemy was down to fifteen. Agnes cried out her husband's name and rushed to his side and pulled him onto her lap. She kissed his face and cried his name and tried to wake him. I heard Franky and Anne stop Katherine on the porch and heard her cry of "Da!" ring out loud into the night. Rage and sorrow flooded me and I struggled to try to get to my feet. Nadine rushed to my side and kept me down. She held me tight and turned her head to Seth.

"What are you?" she yelled at the man. It seemed to startle him.

"I am Seth Farlow. The leader of the Sect of the Church of the New Order, demon."

"You are an abomination!" screamed Nadine. "You are not of this Earth. You should not exist!"

Seth blinked and looked lost for a moment before resolve hardened his features. "I have hunted demons for ten years. You seduce, twist reason, and offer nought but temptation. You are the abomination and a blight on this world. By God's grace, I am charged with striking you down where you stand. You three are the last of the demons. With your deaths, my life's task will be complete. Come forward and face your fate."

Nadine cried out and turned to hide in my arms. For her whole life, she had fled and hidden from the Purge and now here it was before her. I felt her anguish. Her fear. Her hatred.

Katherine ripped free of Franky and Anne and knelt by her mother and held her and her father. Dog sat beside her. All of us were on the veranda, exposed, helpless and at the mercy of this insane man and his unnatural men. I reached out with my senses and felt my powers slide off him as if he wasn't there. He was like his horse and men with no auras. Dead. Lifeless. But moving and talking. There was nothing I could do.

Seth was elated. He had finally tracked down the Target. He sat cowering on the veranda of the house, helpless and powerless before his might. His men stood behind him to bear witness. Soon he would purge the last of the demons from the world and free the Church to stake its rightful place in the hearts of man.

The fighting over by the other buildings did not concern him. Win or lose all that mattered was that the Target and his spawn died on the veranda. The

Archbishop would be so pleased. His service to God was his sole purpose in life.

He cocked back the crossbow string with practised ease and placed a new bolt in the flight groove. He took a moment to admire the bolt. This was the one that would kill the Target. He would need to retrieve it afterwards and keep it close. It would be his prized possession.

He lifted his crossbow and sighted down at the Target. The demon sat with his woman wrapped in his arms. *Perhaps I could strike them both down with one bolt*, he thought with a smile. *The men would talk of that for decades to come.*

A flicker of light caught his attention, and he turned his head to find God looking toward him a mere ten feet away. His men gasped and Seth preened that his men could now see how the Lord favoured him. Only he was worthy.

"My Lord, you come to bear witness to the completion of my Holy task. You honour me, my Lord."

God looked back at Seth and said nothing. Seth grew uncomfortable. Something was wrong. As he watched God transformed into the demon that had followed him down the road asking him over and over what he was. Seth started to shake with trepidation. *What is happening?* he thought. The demon stood in the form of a woman clothed in vines and dirt. The demon frowned at Seth and then shivered and looked about. Seth was about to cry out to banish the demon when it threw back its head and screamed long and loud into the night. The Target on the veranda and his bitch cried out in alarm and covered their ears. The dog barked and whined uncontrollably. As he watched, two black hands burst out of the middle of the demon's chest and slowly spread apart ripping the flesh in two. His men behind him screamed in terror and the living Sect members ran into the night. The newly risen remained standing bearing witness to the horror.

Beams of light burst from the figure and as the chest separated a solid black figure started to push out of the body. The scream of the demon cut off and the black figure emerged discarding the demon skin to the ground where it melted into the earth. The black figure seemed to absorb all light. It was so black that no features could be made out. It looked male with broad shoulders. It glistened wetly in the night.

The figure spoke with an oily, whispering voice. "I bear witness, Seth Farlow. Begin."

Seth sat on the horse in fear. *What have I just witnessed? Where is God? What is this demon in front of me?*

"You may call me Erebus."

I wasn't sure what I was looking at. A bright light had filled the area and then Gaea had appeared, and, for a moment, my heart had leapt in joy. I had thought us saved. Then she had screamed, and my powers came and went from within me. Sensations of heat and cold struck me repeatedly, and I felt Nadine shudder in my arms. I held my ears against the scream and watched in horror as a black figure had ripped itself out of Gaea's body. My powers recoiled from this new being. It was the exact opposite of Gaea. It represented death, pain and suffering driven with nothing more than the desire to perpetuate it. I knew all this in an instant. Now it stood staring at all of us. A smell filled the air that turned my blood to water. It was the smell of death, decay, and rancid oils: the smell of all that is wrong in the world. I wanted nothing more than to strike it down or run for as long as my heart could continue to beat.

Nadine twisted in my arms to stare at the horror. I felt her trembling uncontrollably in my arms. Dog was barking non-stop, a sound of panic and fear in the bark. Katherine was sobbing and backing away, abandoning her parents on the steps. Franky and Anne grabbed her and pulled her aside in a futile attempt to keep her safe. *Nothing was safe while this thing was here*, I thought. *Nothing.*

Seth Farlow sat on his horse and looked to be losing his mind. I heard a high-pitched sound escape his lips. The whites of his eyes were large and bright. The figure beckoned from Seth to me and seemed to urge him to shoot me with the crossbow.

Everything happened at once. Seth raised and fired the crossbow. I could see that it would hit Nadine and there was nothing I could do. I started to raise my hand in a futile attempt to intercept the bolt. Dog, moving impossibly fast, leapt across us and the bolt hit the animal high in the ribs. He yelped once and fell limp and flat to the porch. The heavy thud and subsequent silence seemed to go on forever. Katherine split the air screaming "Dog!" and started to move toward him but Franky stopped her and pulled her back. Agnes cried out, and I looked down to see Ben reaching up and wrapping his hands around her neck. Ben had risen from the dead.

Dear Gaea, I prayed. *Help us!*

I can't, she replied in my head, startling me. I hadn't expected an answer. *I am powerless against him. He blocks me.*

Blocks you? How? What is he?

He calls himself Erebus. You cannot fight him. You cannot win. I can only sense an absence where he stands. I am blind to him. Like the creature Seth and his minions. They are no longer part of the life of this earth. No longer part of me, voiced Gaea with a sadness in her voice.

What am I to do? How do I stop him?

You were never meant to. Help is on the way. Be ready.

I heard Seth scream in rage and looked up to see his eyes wide and wild. I looked up to see he was off his horse and loping toward me. A dagger was gripped in his hand and spittle flew from his mouth. In his other hand, he clutched something that emitted a bright red light that burst through his fingers and turned his hand the colour of blood. He was screaming as he ran toward me. Behind him, his men without auras remained standing where they stood, looking impassively on. The black figure remained immobile.

I heard a sharp, wet crack sound and looked to Agnes to see her head lying at an odd angle. Ben had killed her. A sound that stole my courage erupted from Katherine and across our bond I *sensed* something within her mind snap. I watched helplessly as Ben pushed his wife off him. Her body slumped down the stairs and lay still, her face pressed into the dirt, all who she was discarded and gone. Ben calmly reached up to the support post of the veranda to pull himself up. An arrow appeared out of nowhere to drive through Ben's hand and pin it to the support post. Ben continued to try to stand, ignoring the arrow. I turned my head to see Seth almost on Nadine and I. Three more steps and he would reach the stairs. I remembered how my mother had hidden me and I called the power up around me and rolled Nadine and I two feet to the left.

Seth screamed in frustration and slowed, he searched for me and the red light pulsed. I felt my power stutter and Seth locked eyes with me and a look of triumph filled his face, distorting it with bared teeth. Seth moved toward me with his dagger glinting. In a blur, a figure stepped forward from my left and intercepted Seth with the point of a long sword held in two hands. He was a stranger dressed in armour and with an impossibly bright light bursting from his forehead and from a wooden medallion hanging around his neck. Seth's momentum carried the sword through his chest until the hilt rammed home against his ribs. An expression of shock flitted across his face and he looked down at the sword impaling him. He looked to the face of the stranger in confusion. The light bathed Seth's face in pure light and then pushed through his head and burst out the other side. A look of understanding crossed his features for a moment and then he died. A high-pitched sound I hadn't heard until it stopped cut off and an eerie silence filled the air.

The last breath of Seth Farlow escaped from his slack lips and he slid off the sword to the ground. The still figures of the men standing behind him collapsed as one to the ground. The horse followed right after and collapsed with a wet sucking sound into a decomposed pile of meat and bones. Ben slumped to the ground and stilled. The stranger nodded once to me and I blinked against the blinding light. He turned to Erebus and took a step forward.

"Begone, creature of chaos. You hold no sway over these people. Begone!" He held forth the medallion and I could see the symbol of the Tree burning brightly on the reverse. A white light pulsed from the medallion and the man's forehead and they pierced the creature dead centre. It howled a deep low note that rattled my teeth, and it disappeared with the white light.

We stood immobile. The only sounds were now coming from Katherine who sobbed and tried to hold Dog, her mother, and father in her arms. Nadine sat heavily beside me, her strength gone. I watched in disbelief as Reeve Comlin walked out of the darkness to stand to look down at the remains of the dead horse. He looked up at me and forced a grim smile. Another man joined him, dressed in similar leathers, and I saw the surviving farmhands following behind him.

The stranger turned and smiled at me. The bright symbol on his forehead gone without a mark. "Well met, Will Arbor. I'm Brent Bairstow."

Craobh

Twenty-Five

Rigby Farm, 900 A.C.

WHAT FOLLOWED WAS confusion. At some point, I had grabbed onto the Reeve and not let go until Nadine pulled us apart. I introduced her to the Reeve and, when he realised who we were to one another, he grinned a huge smile and hugged her long and hard. After that, we were introduced to one another, and I shook hands with the former General of the Lord Protector's Guard, Brent Bairstow, and thanked him for my life. He introduced us to Captain James Dixon, and we then cleaned up the mess. Reeve Comlin freed Ben's pinned hand and then held him in his arms and cried a little, which surprised me. The surviving farmhands stood standing in disarray, holding bloodied swords and not sure what to do next.

Franky murmured something to Anne and together they carried Katherine inside the house and upstairs to her bed. Nadine and I took only a moment to heal Dog. We removed the bolt from his side and together we healed the brave animal. He licked our faces and then bounded into the house to be with Katherine. Reeve Comlin, now up and about, barked orders and the hurt farmhands came forward to Nadine and I and we healed them. They were awed by the act and some looked frightened. Brent watched it all, holding the medallion, and, I think, he prayed. Daukyns had told me religious men prayed, and I expected that was what I saw him do. I'm not sure I believed prayer would help. I knew my powers certainly did.

What seemed like hours later, Nadine and I tended to Katherine in her bed. Dog lay beside her on the bed with his head on her lap. Katherine pulled Dog into her face and cried. Dog whined and pressed closer to her. We combined our powers and tried to provide some healing to the poor girl. She had watched her father die in front of her and then watched the corpse of her father murder her mother. It had been too much for her. Her powers had made her feel those deaths, and she had lost her grip on her sanity. We tried to heal her mind, but it was beyond our ability and the best we could do was provide her with a sense of peace. We could heal the body but not the mind. A peace now warred within her thoughts and memories. Nadine and I felt nothing but grief and guilt. We left her sleeping with Dog and returned to the kitchen.

Once there, I was stunned to find Dempster cooking and arguing with Franky and Anne about who was doing what and how to do it. I ran to him and hugged him hard and introduced him to Nadine, my wife. He was overjoyed for me and held me tight. He told me he had travelled with Reeve Comlin and the others.

"It's good to see you, Dempster. I missed you."

"You too, Will"

"I'm sorry I left without telling you where I was really going."

"Nothing to forgive, Will," he said. "I'm no stranger to running. Come now, sit, and eat."

Dempster pushed Nadine and I to the table and told us to sit. I sat as close as I could to Nadine and drank the tea Dempster had steeped. Shortly after, Reeve Comlin, Brent Bairstow, and James Dixon joined us. I looked up to the Reeve and smiled. His presence gave me strength. They sat at the table and we looked at one another in silence. There was too much to talk about and no one knew where to start.

It was Reeve Comlin that spoke first. "Will, it's been awhile. Here you are. Safe and sound." His lips twisted into an ironic smile.

I looked at him in surprise and said nothing for a time. "I didn't expect to see you here, Reeve Comlin. You saved our lives. You, and Brent, and James."

"Will, it's just Comlin now. I'm no longer a Reeve." I sensed the pain behind his words. "We should have been here sooner. We ran into difficulties on the river." The men looked at each other. "But we made it. I only wish we could have saved Agnes and Ben. That will haunt me."

Nadine stirred. "Your daughter is upstairs. You should look in on her."

Comlin looked away. "She was Ben's daughter. Not mine."

"She has no one now, Steve Comlin. She only has you, her true father."

Comlin looked angry over at Nadine, he was with no doubt seeing her as a young woman and resentful of her words. Brent, beside him, laid a hand on Comlin's shoulder and squeezed. Comlin glanced quickly at Brent but then leaned forward toward Nadine. "Yes, I am her true father. But I didn't raise her. I am no one to her. Katherine's a grown woman now. She doesn't need a stranger pretending to be someone he isn't and never was."

"She is damaged," grated Nadine and tapped her own head. "Up here. She will need someone to watch over her and support her."

Reeve stood up, his face red. "Who are you, some young girl, to tell me what my responsibilities are?"

"Steve, easy," admonished Brent.

"I will not be *easy*! It is not my fault Agnes and Ben have died!"

"No one said it was," said Brent.

"Stop it!" shouted Nadine. "You are acting like a child, Steve Comlin. Sit down and shut up." The tone of her voice brooked no argument and Comlin slowly sat back down. "I am almost sixty years old. You see a young woman and don't heed my words. You are her father. You have a responsibility to her. You have a responsibility to her dead parents—your friends! Now shut up and think about that!"

I reached out and rubbed Nadine's back. She was right, I just wish she could be nicer about it. Dempster came around the table and set down a tray of sandwiches. I looked up at him and smiled.

"I missed your cooking, Dempster," I said and meant it. "How'd you end up with them? The Reeve, James and Brent?"

Dempster turned red in the face and looked to James for support. James laughed, and it sounded strained. James rose and patted Dempster on the back.

"This fine chef, who I might add gave us the most memorable meals on the barge, took one look at General Brent Bairstow, recognised the uniform of the Lord Protector's guard, and ran."

Dempster pulled a handkerchief from a pocket and wiped his brow. "Yes, well, it put such a fright into me. I was certain he had come for me."

Brent chuckled. "Yes. The Lord Protector so hated the chef that tried to poison him that he sent his General of the Lord Protector's Guard all the way to Jaipers to arrest him."

I looked from Dempster to Brent to see if that was a jest. Dempster looked embarrassed, and I knew it was true. *Dempster had tried to kill the Lord Protector?*

"It hadn't seemed so improbable when I saw you sitting in the Inn."

"What delayed you?" I asked. "You said you were delayed en route?"

Brent and James looked at each other and shook their heads. "That will need to stay a secret, I'm afraid."

Reeve Comlin interrupted with a laugh. "No secret there. They got us lost."

In unison, they turned to the Reeve and spoke. "Did not!"

"Yes, you did."

"If you had not managed to get hurt, we would have been fine."

"I wouldn't have gotten hurt if you hadn't..."

"Children!" barked Nadine and everyone turned to stare at her. "It's been a long night. The sun will rise soon. We need rest. Today will be a difficult day. We have many loved ones to bury. I'm going to bed. You should too."

I looked at Brent. He looked more than a little familiar to me. He nodded to me as if reading my mind.

When none of us moved, Nadine sighed and leaned in and gave me a quick kiss. "Goodnight, young man."

"Goodnight, old woman. I won't be long."

Nadine bid the others good night, and she left the kitchen for our bed. Franky, Anne and Dempster said their farewells right after and disappeared into the house and their beds.

Reeve Comlin, James, Brent and I sat around the table and looked at one another.

"Is she really sixty?" Comlin asked me.

I nodded. "Actually more like sixty-seven. Gaea made her young again."

Comlin looked doubtful.

"Trust me," I said. "She's older than she looks."

Suddenly Brent snapped his fingers. "Jergen!" he said and looked at me. "You were in the central park with that dog. I saw you there."

My eyes widened in recognition. "Yes, I remember! I saw you ride in."

Brent nodded his head in agreement. "Small world," he said.

We all smiled at one another and grew quiet. "The farmhands, what's left of them, they're taking care of the bodies?" I asked the question quietly to Comlin. They had embraced him. Consoling themselves in the loss of their friends and leaders by seeing their former leader appear from thin air. I watched as Comlin took charge and ordered them to tasks. That seemed to give them purpose, and they acted quickly. The stable was allowed to burn to the ground but in a controlled fashion. Small fires nearby were kept down and the surviving horses were rounded up. Graves were being dug and later today we would bury our friends. Seth and his ilk had been thrown into a mass grave.

"Yes, my crew will take care of that. It gives them focus." Comlin looked at his hands and then up to me. "Tell me, what happened to you once you left Jaipers?"

I sucked in a breath and then told the tale. All three men remained silent. When it was done Comlin looked to Brent. "I told you. He's a druid. A powerful one and now married to another. There is power here. You saw them heal my crew. The world is changing. Look what just happened outside."

"Hmm. I see the work of God. No offence, Will," said Brent and looked to me. I inclined my head to show I didn't take any. "I saw evil astride a dead horse, and we struck them down with Faith. Then the black demon was smitten. God empowered me."

"Can I see your medallion?" I asked. Brent nodded, pulling it over his neck to hand to me. I looked at both sides. One was the symbol of the Church of the New Order and, on the reverse, the symbol of the Tree. "Do you see this symbol?" I asked him pointing to the Tree. He nodded. "I recognise this. This is the symbol of the Tree, of the draoi."

Brent blinked at me. "You recognise this?"

"Yes, it is our symbol."

"Huh. The man in the Cathedral in Jergen told me that men of faith would recognise it. Does that mean you have faith?"

I had no answer to that. I knew nothing of faith. I knew of Gaea and said so. I tapped the symbol of the Tree. "This symbol. The triskelion. Nadine has taught me that it dates back centuries and was rooted in a religion similar to yours. The three arms represent three aspects of the faith. I believe in Gaea. She has appeared to me and spoke to me. She has guided me and led Nadine and me here to this farm. So do I have faith? I suppose I do. I have faith in Gaea."

Brent took the medallion back and pulled it over his head. He held it up and kissed the symbol of the Church. "My faith has been tested. My whole life I have hidden my belief in God from others. No more. I have seen such miracles, Will. James and Steve have too. Tonight God struck down the demon, Erebus. I was merely the vessel. His light shone through me and struck him down."

"True. I saw the medallion light up with both the Church symbol and the symbol of the draoi, together."

"Interesting," said Brent and looked doubtful.

"The man on the horse, he was the man who killed my mother. I thank you, Brent, for taking him down. He would have killed me and Nadine. He has hunted down every druid there was. He thought me the last. Now we are three.

You speak to me of faith. I speak to you of loss and the power that I possess given to me by the Earth Mother. Feel this."

I *reached* out to Brent with the power Gaea had provided me. I found where his muscles were torn and strained and corrected the problems. I cleared away that which would make him tired and energised him. I smoothed his scars and then pulled back. He sat gasping and staring at me.

"What did you just do?"

"I cleansed your aches and pains."

"That was incredible. I feel like I could run for days."

"Your scars are gone, too."

Brent looked at the back of his hands and his forearms. "They're gone. So it's true, you are a druid with powers."

"Yes, and not a demon. We commune with nature: plants and animals. We seek harmony with all life."

"Not so terrible then."

"No. Not so terrible."

Comlin finished a sandwich and looked to Brent and I. "What will you do, Will?"

"I stay here. This will be the place where the new druids learn to use their powers."

"And you, Brent, what now?"

"I head back to Munsten."

"As a General?"

"God, no. I intend to take back the Church. That is what God wants."

"And you know this how?"

"Faith, my friend. Through my Faith."

An hour or two before sunset, we gathered in the orchard. The remaining farmhands, forty-three strong, had cleared the enemy bodies, buried them in a mass grave, and shrouded our fallen. They lay in graves in a long row in the shade of the trees. It was a beautiful but chilly evening giving evidence that Fall was perhaps coming to a quick close.

Nadine, Katherine, Dog and I stood before the open graves of Ben and Agnes. Katherine had slept the morning through and woke late in the afternoon a little more together. The first thing she had done was to go to the horses and heal their hurts and calm them. We hadn't known she could heal until she had simply done the task and walked over to the orchard. Dog remained pressed up against her and had to be pried away to eat and relieve himself. Whatever was happening between her and Dog was having a healing effect on her. Nadine was hopeful that whatever was broken would be fixed. I didn't think anything but time would help her. I had lost my parents and still suffered for it. Katherine had witnessed horrors beyond imagining and I didn't know how she could recover. I watched her now as she stared, fixated on the graves of her parents, and paid no attention to those around her.

Comlin came up beside her and after a moment she turned to look at him. She looked confused for a moment and then turned to Dog. Something passed between them and she twisted back to Comlin and threw her arms around him. "Father?" she whispered. Comlin jerked a little and then wrapped his arms around her and held her tight. I saw a softening of his face and smiled to myself. Nadine took my hand, and I felt her happiness at the sight of a father and daughter reunited. They had too many years between them, but I trusted that Gaea would help them. Katherine had a future with the draoi.

Brent came up to us with James and bowed his head in respect. We stood in silence. No one knew what to do next.

A light filled the air, and we blinked against it. It dimmed and out from the cornfield stepped the glowing figure of Gaea. She strode up and looked down into the graves in front of us. There were so many. The farmhands were pointing at her and moving closer. Brent murmured a prayer of some kind. Dog barked once and bounded over to her and jumped up to try to lick her face. Gaea scowled.

"Dog, behave. Back to Katherine."

Dog didn't listen and kept jumping up.

"Will?" she asked.

"Dog, stop that," I ordered, and he finally stopped and returned to Katherine. Katherine reached down and touched him but her face remained shadowed in grief. She knelt down and embraced Dog and started crying.

"I cannot correct the damage," said Gaea looking at Katherine.

Brent stepped forward. "Who are you?"

"I am Gaea. The Earth Mother. Pleased to meet you."

"I don't understand," said Brent.

"You don't have to. You have a plan in your heart. A purpose. It is right for you. Follow your Faith."

Brent nodded but seemed shaken. He stepped back.

"What were they? What was Seth and what was Erebus?" I asked.

Gaea looked tired. "I don't know."

I looked at Nadine and she looked worried. "You don't know?"

"No. I knew that I would not be able to help in the end. It is why I sent Brent, Stephen and James to the farm here. They would make the difference. Allow this path to happen. Will Arbor, you have done well. I name you *Freamhaigh*. Find harmony in the world. I must go."

Without a sound, she disappeared and everyone started talking at once. I was shaken. Nadine and I shared a long look. Something was very wrong with Gaea. I felt a shudder through the earth and I squeezed Nadine's hand. The earth would need the druids soon. Time was running out, and I was only just realising it.

In time, everyone settled down and the burials resumed. Brent said words from his religion over the graves and then Nadine, Katherine and I stepped forward and caused the earth to fill the graves. Like I had done with Daukyns we sprinkled seeds and caused flowers to spring up and everyone said their goodbyes.

It was over so quickly. A part of me wanted the grieving to go on and on. Another part of me was glad it was over. I spoke to Brent about it and he had nodded.

"It is the guilt that all survivors face. It is our burden. Never forget, we say in the Guard. That is our most noble task: to remember the fallen. Never forget."

A few days later Brent and James left on horseback for Munsten. They said farewell and promised to stay in touch. We wished them well, and they departed. James said they would stop first in Jergen to reacquaint themselves with some friends and they left in good spirits. Brent had tried to speak to me about Gaea but, in the end, he had simply hugged Nadine and I and left. I was sure he needed to find his God and seek his answers. I had a sense of who his God was but said nothing. I could be wrong.

Comlin, who insisted that I now call him Steve, spoke with his daughter and then told me he was staying on the farm and running it with his crew. The men and women cheered and Franky stepped forward and embraced him. I sensed something between the two of them and so did everyone else. Franky looked cheerful for once but scowled at me when she caught me smiling at her.

Dempster was now running the kitchen and apparently the logistics of the farm. Franky had been upset at first and then declared that she was going to be second-in-command and glared at Steve until he nodded once. She came back having changed into work clothes and started ordering the farmhands to tasks. It seemed chaotic, but I sensed an order re-inserting itself. Life would go on.

Later that evening, as the sun was setting, Nadine, Katherine, Dog, and I stood over her parents' graves and held hands, Dog pressed up against Katherine. Katherine had a sadness in her eyes that I feared would never depart. I wasn't ready to speak to her yet of her loss. I was being a coward, I knew. I would soon and Nadine would be there to help.

We heard a rustling noise and looked up as one. Two people emerged from the cornfield, spied us and walked cautiously towards us.

I smiled and whispered to Katherine. "They're coming now."

"Who is, Freamhaigh?"

"Our students, the new druids. Now we start our school."

Craobh

Epilogue

On the Road to Belger, 900 A.C

ARCHBISHOP GREIGSEN STAGGERED into the displayed armour in the receiving hall outside the council chambers and it toppled to the ground. The sound of it hitting the stone corridor was loud and abrasive and drew the eyes of everyone in the corridor. He tried to right the damage, but soon gave up and moved past it, forgetting it in mere moments. Spittle was dried at the corners of his mouth and his hair was unkempt, oily, and ragged. His beard was knotted and foodstuff clung to it. He was completely naked. Dried urine clung to him and faeces spread down between his legs. He smelled atrocious.

People lined the walls and stared in shock at the sight. Some were now openly laughing and pointing at him. A few ran off to tell others. The Archbishop swiped a hand through the empty air at them and continued to stagger down the hallway toward the Church. This was the first time he had left his quarters in over a week. His use of the tears had increased rapidly and today he had used the last of it.

He wandered now, looking for more. He knew there had to be some somewhere. He just needed to find a chirurgeon. Or the Lord Protector. They were somewhere around here, he thought.

He recognised the hallway that led to the Church and started down it. The world spun, and he found himself with his back on the stone floor looking up bewildered. How odd, he thought. He struggled to his feet amid cries to stay down from those nearest him. Where did they come from? Perhaps the Lord Protector is nearby and can come with more of my medicine.

The Archbishop cried out in a voice cracking with lack of use. "Lord Protector! I'm coming for you! Come here!"

The people in the hallway erupted with more laughter. As word spread more people in the castle emerged to watch the display. The Archbishop reached the Church entrance and swerved away at the last moment to step into the corner to relieve himself. He hummed to himself.

Finished, he banged the doors open and staggered backwards but managed to stay upright. He pushed through the opening and slowly walked over to the altar steps, hesitating before them. This is a place of worship, he thought. I can't be seen staggering around. He was proud of himself for remembering that. He tried to lift his right foot to climb the stairs, but it was too high. He sat instead, staining the wool carpet with his soiled behind.

"Lord Protector, you ass! Get over here!" he cried out weakly. "You snivelling, conniving, son-of-a-bitch!"

He stayed there for an hour crying out and getting more inventive with his words. The crowd grew until the Church was filled and he was surrounded. Many laughed but most just shook their heads in shame for the Archbishop.

"Make way! Make way!" cried out a guard. The stamping of many feet could be heard coming down the corridor and people hurriedly moved out of the way. A contingent of ten Lord Protector's guard marched into the Church with the Lord Protector himself in the middle. They stopped in front of the Archbishop and Healy stepped forward and looked down in disgust at the Archbishop.

He was fondling himself and laughing oblivious to the audience he had around him. His eyes opened, and he looked right at the Lord Protector. A look of desperate need crossed his face. "More!" he cried and reached out his arms. "I need more!"

Healy backed away a step. "Guards," he said quietly.

The Archbishop rose to his feet, stretched his arms out toward the Lord Protector, and stepped forward. "More, God damnit! Give me more you bastard! Give me more or else!" The Archbishop surged forward and then stopped abruptly. He looked down at the length of steel impaled through his chest. He looked up to the guard who stood before him and opened his mouth in surprise.

Blood poured out of his mouth and down his naked chest. A sound escaped him and then his eyes rolled back. Archbishop Greigsen collapsed silently to the floor of the Church, vacated his bowels, and died.

No one moved and silence fell in the Church.

Frederick Bairstow ran into the Church and pushed past the people and the guard and looked down at the corpse. "What the fuck happened?"

The Lord Protector turned smoothly to Bairstow and smiled. "Nothing of significance."

End of Volume Two

Craobh

The New Druids Series continues with:

Stoc: A New Druids Novel (Volume Three)

By Donald D. Allan

Craobh

Acknowledgements

Writing this second volume was a pleasure. It was a pleasure because one, I wrote this book in my head months ago and putting it on paper was an exercise of simply telling a story I already knew, and two, I'd already written a novel and I had no pressure on me. I had fun getting it out into my MacBook Air and Scrivener.

I am an independent writer (aka an Indie author) and my writing is far from perfect. I do my best to hunt down and purge my writing of typos and the like. It's an ongoing and continuous process. I miss some. I hate typos because it pulls the reader out of the story. And my goal is having others who can share and enjoy my imagination. I've done my best work to date. You be the judge. Let me know what you think.

Thanks to my friends and family for their unwavering support of my writing. You have listened patiently while I waxed on about my writing. I must get boring after a bit...sorry. It's just a lifelong dream and I should have done this decades ago. To my game night buddies: you guys rock, thanks for the moral support and the maps.

Lastly: to my small but growing base of readers: Thank you so much for buying and reading my novels. I truly write them for you and no one else. This was yours. I hope you enjoyed it. If you did, or if you didn't, please provide a review on Amazon, and Goodreads. I appreciate any honest criticism. Indie authors live and die by their reviews. If you want more books from me, leave a review!

Ciao!

D o n
O t t a w a , C a n a d a , M a y 2 0 1 6

Craobh

World Details

Ranks and Hierarchies
Draoi (Druid) Ranks:
Freamhaigh (Root) – Head Druid
Cill Dara(e) – Druid Priest/Priestess (The Elevated Druid)
Stoc (Trunk) or informally just Draoi – Full Druid
Craobh (Branch) – Journeyman Druid
Duilleog (Leaf) – Apprentice Druid

The Church of the New Order Ranks:
King (in abeyance since Revolution)
Archbishop (acting head of the Church)
Bishop
Dean
Vicar

Army of the Realm Ranks:
Officers:
    Knight General (former rank from before the Revolution)
    General
    Brigadier
    Colonel
    Lieutenant Colonel
    Major
    Captain
    Lieutenant
    Second Lieutenant
Enlisted:
    Warrant Officer
    Staff Sergeant
    Sergeant
    Corporal
    Lance Corporal (appointment, not a rank)
    Private
    Recruit

Lord Protector's Guard Ranks:
The highest-ranking officer is General. Because the Lord Protector's Guard is a speciality occupation, the members come from the Army of the Realm, and occasionally from the Navy of the Realm. They share the same rank structure except that the lowest

Craobh

officer rank is Captain and the lowest enlisted rank is Corporal; those being the earliest rank you can be selected or request service in the Lord Protector's Guard.

Navy of the Realm Ranks:
Officers:
> Fleet Admiral
> Admiral
> Commodore
> Captain (Navy)
> Commander
> Lieutenant-Commander
> Lieutenant (Navy)
> Ensign
> Midshipman

Enlisted:
> Chief Petty Officer
> Petty Officer
> Master Seaman
> Leading Seaman
> Able Seaman
> Ordinary Seaman

It should be noted that the General of the Realm is the head of the Army, the Navy, and the Lord Protector's Guard. The Lord Protector's Guard recruits from the Army of the Realm, and rarely, from the Navy. The Navy's top rank, the Fleet Admiral, is not equal to the General. In this world, the Navy is not the senior service.

Calendar and Seasons
The calendar is in the background of the world and not specifically referenced except where it occurs accidentally. We don't dwell on the calendar and neither do the folks in Turgany. In this world, the Celtic names for things have slipped and are rarely used. The common language is English.

Seasons:
Winter (Geimhreadh) – December, January, February (Nollaig, Eanair, Feabhra)
Spring (Earrach) – March, April, May (Marta, Aibrean, Bealtaine)
Summer (Samhraidh) – June, July, August (Meitheamh, Luil, Lunasa)
Autumn (Fomhar) – September, October, November (Mean Fomhair, Deirreadh Fomhair, Samhain)

Time Frames:
Day – dia

Night – nocht
Week – 8 days and nights—deug
Fortnight – 15 days and nights – cola-deug
Month – mios

Days of the Week:
Sunday – Domhnaich
Monday—Luain
Tuesday—Mairt
Wednesday—Ciadain
Pluday (Extra)—Durdaoin
Thursday—Ardaoin
Friday—Aoine
Saturday—Sathurna

Breakdown of a Year:
365 days in a calendar year for which only 360 are provided actual dates. The extra five days per year (see Solstices/Equinoxes) are used as celebration days and are known by their title rather than as a calendar date. It works like this: there is a December 24th, followed by Christmas Day, which is then followed by December 25th.
24 fortnights (24x15 days) per year
45 weeks per year
3 weeks and 6 days per month (totalling 30 days per month)

Solstices (longest/shortest day of the year)/Equinoxes:
Vernal Equinox is the day after March 19th (or Marta 19) and is celebrated for 1 day as Ostara Day (non-calendar day).
Estival Solstice (summer) is the day after June 20th (or Meitheamh 20) and is celebrated for 1 day as Litha Day (non-calendar day)
Autumnal Equinox is the day after September 21st (or Mean Fomhair 21) and is celebrated for 2 days as First Mabon Day (harvest) and Last Mabon Day (feast) (non-calendar days).
Hibernal Solstice (winter) is the day after December 20 (or Nollaig 20) and is celebrated for 1 day as Yule (non-calendar day).

Holidays:
Samhain. Nov 7 (Samhain 7). The midpoint between Autumn Equinox and Winter Solstice. Celebrates the last harvest, the cycle of life and gifts for passing spirits. Preparation to survive winter, confront the possibility of death. Colours: black, brown, reds, oranges. Opposite to Bealtaine.
Yule is the day after December 20 (Nollaig 20) and is a non-calendar day. Shortest day and longest night of the year. Celebrates the end of darkness, the return of light to the

Craobh

earth. Herbs are at their least potent. Colours: green, red, white, silver, gold.

Imbolc. Feb 1 (Feabhra 1). The midpoint between Winter Solstice and Spring Equinox. Celebrates the quickening of spring, the end of winter, time of planning and hopes. Colours: red, orange, white.

Ostara Day is the day after March 19 (Marta 19) and is a non-calendar day. The first day of spring, the night and day stand equal. Celebrates the birth of spring, rebirth. Time of planting. Colours: red and yellow.

Bealtaine. May 6 (Bealtaine 6). The midpoint between Spring Equinox and Summer Solstice. Time of rebirth. Colours: blue, pink, yellow, green. Opposite to Samhain.

Litha Day is the day after June 20 (Meitheamh 20) and is a non-calendar day. Summer solstice, the first day of summer, longest day of the year. Celebrates the light and the sun without there would be no life. Time of strengths and accomplishments. Gather herbs as "herb night" is when they are at their most potent. Colours: blue, yellow, green.

Lammas. Aug 1 (Lunasa 1). The midpoint between Summer Solstice and the Autumn Equinox. First harvest festival. Celebrates the beginning of harvest season, the decline of summer to winter. Time to dismiss regrets, farewells, preparation for winter. Ceremonies involve bread, grains and corn dolls. Colours: oranges, greens, browns.

Mabon Days are the two days after September 21st (Mean Fomhair 21) and they are non-calendar days. Referred to as *First Mabon* and *Last Mabon*. Autumn Equinox, the first day of autumn. Celebrates harvest. First Mabon is harvesting time and Last Mabon is the feast. Time for thanks and learning, repairing all things. Colours: dark reds, yellows, browns.

Important Calendar Dates Summary:
February 1 (Feabhra 1)—Imbolc
March (Marta)—Ostara Day (Vernal Equinox) is the day after March 19th
May 6 (Bealtaine 6)—Bealtaine
June (Meitheamh)—Litha Day (Estival Solstice (summer)) is the day after June 20th
August 1 (Lunasa 1)—Lammas
September (Mean Fomhair)—First/Last Mabon Days (Autumnal Equinox) is the two days after September 21st
November 7 (Samhain 7)—Samhain
December (Nollaig)—Yule (Hibernal Solstice (winter)) is the day after December 20th

Currency
1 crown (large round gold coin) = 36 groats = 144 pence
1 half-crown (large round gold coin with a centre hole) = 18 groats = 72 pence
1 mark (small gold coin) = 9 groats = 36 pence
1 groat (silver rectangular coin) = 4 pence
1 tuppence (a small silver coin or large copper coin) = 2 pence
1 pence (copper coin) = 1 pence
1 half-pence (copper coin with a centre hole) = 1/2 pence

344

1 farthing (small rectangular copper coin) = 1/4 pence

Coins are measured by known weights under the Turgany Weights and Measures Act. For example, a full crown must weigh one royal ounce (28 gramme). A half-crown weighs a half ounce (14 gramme). And a mark weighs a quarter ounce (7 gramme) which means it is heavier than a Canadian quarter (25 cent piece) but sized about the same. A groat weighs the same as a mark (but is larger), and a tuppence weighs half that of a groat (hence if it is made of copper it will be larger). Typically, wealthy merchants will carry coin scales to verify that they are not being cheated with counterfeit coins. The habit of biting a gold coin was to prove that it was indeed gold—which is soft—and not some impostor.

Seven Tenets of Morality

1. Strive to act with compassion and empathy toward all creatures in accordance with reason.

2. The struggle for justice is an ongoing and necessary pursuit that should prevail over laws and institutions.

3. One's body is inviolable, subject to one's own will alone.

4. The freedoms of others should be respected, including the freedom to offend. To wilfully and unjustly encroach upon the freedoms of another is to forgo your own.

5. Beliefs should conform to our best scientific understanding of the world. We should take care never to distort scientific facts to fit our beliefs.

6. People are fallible. If we make a mistake, we should do our best to rectify it and resolve any harm that may have been caused.

7. Every tenet is a guiding principle designed to inspire nobility in action and thought. The spirit of compassion, wisdom, and justice should always prevail over the written or spoken word.

About the Author

DONALD D. ALLAN is a Canadian author of fantasy and science fiction and a retired senior Royal Canadian Navy officer.

He is the GOLD medal winner of the Dan Poynter's Global eBook Awards 2016 for the category Fantasy/Other Worlds for his debut novel Duilleog, the first novel in his New Druids series. The second novel, Craobh, won the BRONZE medal in the same category in 2017.

Donald lives with his wife Marilyn, son James, daughter Katherine, and dog Woody, in Ottawa, Canada.

Connect with Donald D. Allan:

BLOG: http://donalddallan.com
FACEBOOK: https://www.facebook.com/donalddallan
TWITTER: https://twitter.com/donalddallan/
EMAIL: donalddallan@gmail.com